CHET WILLIAMSON

SOULSTORM

TOR
HORROR

A TOM DOHERTY ASSOCIATES BOOK

To Laurie

SOULSTORM

Copyright © 1986 by Chet Williamson

First printing: September 1986

A TOR Book

Published by Tom Doherty Associates, Inc.
49 West 24 Street
New York, N.Y. 10010

ISBN: 0-812-52718-6
CAN. ED.: 0-812-52719-4

Printed in the United States

0   9   8   7   6   5   4   3   2   1

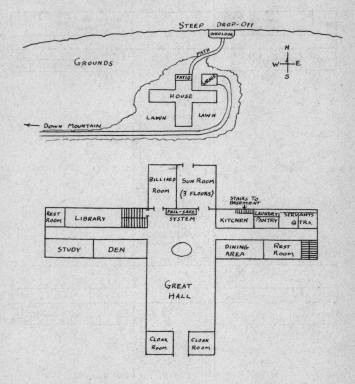

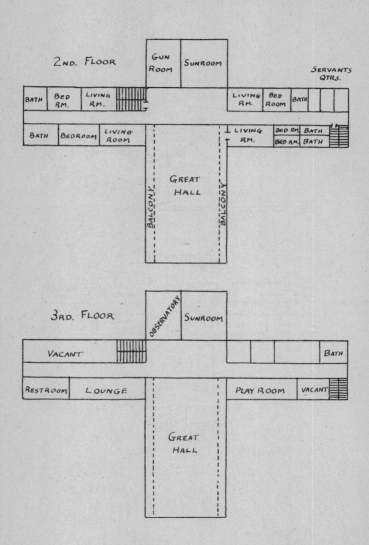

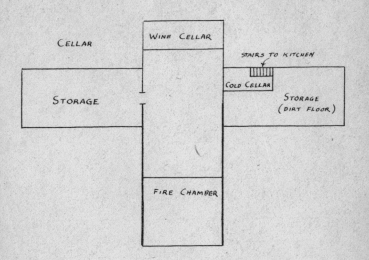

CELLAR

WINE CELLAR

STAIRS TO KITCHEN

STORAGE

COLD CELLAR

STORAGE
(DIRT FLOOR)

FIRE CHAMBER

Prologue

These were the swift to harry;
These were the keen-scented;
These were the souls of blood.
—Ezra Pound, "The Return"

Within The Pines it waited, not with the patience of men, but of stone. And as it waited, it dreamed, not knowing if its dreams would ever live as it did.

It dreamed of men, of the time when men had come, and of the time men would come again, though it could not say if such a time would ever be.

As it dreamed, it ached with need—the need for dream to become reality. But this time would be different. This time need would be tempered with wisdom. This time the dream would live. All it needed was for men to come again.

Men and the needs of men.

And at last men came, moving through its dwelling like beetles crawling through an empty skull; and in the presence of men the dreams screamed for release and were let slip once, twice, and then held in check. For the time was not right. These men had not come to stay. But from their words it learned that other men would come soon, others who *would* stay, who would have no choice but to remain and dream the dreams, do the deeds.

It waited now, not with the patience of stone, but of the damp gray moss that clings to it.

Manhattan 12/14

"Did you hit him or didn't you?"

The captain was angrier than Wickstrom had ever seen him. He was standing, leaning forward over his shabby

1

gray desk like a school principal confronting a rest-room smoker.

"Well?"

"Yeah," Wickstrom said. "Yeah, Cap. I hit him."

The captain sighed, and most of the redness left his face as he let his fat body fall back into the worn leather chair. "What's the matter with you, Kelly? You're a goddamn good cop, but you'd be a helluva lot better if you weren't so hot under the collar."

"I'm sorry, Cap . . ."

"Sorry, yeah. Great."

"I read him his rights . . ."

"I know you read him his lousy . . ."

"But then he took a punch at me."

"Then *subdue* him, for crissake, don't break his nose!" The captain shook his head in frustration as Wickstrom looked down at his hands in his lap. They were big hands, fleshy but sharp-knuckled.

"I didn't mean to hit him so hard."

"You didn't mean to hit your wife so hard either, did you?"

As soon as Wickstrom looked up, hurt and angry, the captain was sorry he'd said it. "My ex-wife," Wickstrom corrected him.

"Yeah." The captain nodded. "Yeah." They glared at each other until the captain spoke again. "You know what this means?"

"I'm out. Right?"

"You don't seem too upset about it."

"It was gonna happen sooner or later."

"I tried, Kelly. I mean I really tried."

"I know."

"You haven't made it easy. First that pimp, then that foreign kid, now this spic . . ."

"Cap, the pimp pulled a knife on me, this Garcia guy tried to tap me out, and that French kid, who you damn well know was packing enough snow to make the whole city fly, was so stoned himself that he put up a *hell* of a fight!"

"You didn't have to blind him."

"I didn't try!" Wickstrom roared. "It was a lucky punch!"

"You don't mean that," the captain said after a moment of silence.

"No."

"Because if I thought you did, I'd have your ass in a sling so deep, you'd be bumping bedrock." He pushed back his chair and put his polished black shoes on the desktop. "There's going to be a hearing next week."

"What if I just resign now?"

"It'd be better," the captain said, nodding. "For everybody."

Wickstrom gave a twisted smile. "Will that satisfy the spic? Or will he want to press charges too?"

"He won't. I'll see he doesn't."

Wickstrom stood up, took off his badge, and set it and his ID on the captain's desk. "Thanks for that much."

"I'm sorry, Kelly. I really am." He stood and shook Wickstrom's hand. "Good luck, huh?"

Wickstrom smiled. "I sure as hell could use a little."

Rio de Janeiro 3/11

George McNeely sat in the waiting lounge at the airport. A tall thin young man in his early twenties sat beside him, flipping through a Portuguese edition of *Playboy*. When the young man came to the centerfold, he surreptitiously unfolded it.

"Great interview this month, eh?" McNeely asked.

The young man laughed. "Been a long time, George. Be nice to get some States pussy again. Jesus, I'm sick of south."

McNeely inhaled deeply, wishing he hadn't quit smoking. "Hamilton's recruiting for the Mideast."

"No shit? Which?"

"I forget the name. Another emirate that needs a show of force."

The young man shook his head. "Christ. Show of force. That's all we were supposed to do for Fernandez."

"Yes. Well, sometimes mercs have to do what they're paid for. Thank God those times are few and far between. A man could get killed."

"Like Welsh," the young man said. "Or Tony or Skip."

"Or Fernandez," McNeely said with a small smile.

They sat in silence for a while, and then the young man spoke. "Was it true, George?"

McNeely raised an eyebrow.

"You know what I mean. Did you start it because you knew he'd take the first shot?"

"I suspected we were advancing into an ambush, fired, and killed, you'll recall, a sniper. There were more. It was simply Fernandez's misfortune to be walking point."

"The other guys said that the rebels wouldn't have bothered us, that they'd've let us pass without firing."

McNeely turned his eyes directly on the young man, who shuddered at their cold grayness. "Do you believe that?"

The young man steeled himself and nodded.

"You're smart," said McNeely. "So did I." He kept looking at the young man, who stared back like a bird fascinated by a snake. "We were there to kill rebels, right? Well, those little bastards in the trees were rebels. And we killed every single one."

"But Fernandez . . ."

"Yes. Fernandez and Tony and Welsh and Mecklin and Skip. I remember. They were soldiers. Sometimes soldiers get killed." He looked away from the young man, out to where the plane was taking on baggage. "It was stupid, though. You're young. Don't ever make a mistake like that. Don't ever hate any son of a bitch that much. And if you do, slit his throat in the middle of the night." He gave a short laugh, the self-consciousness of which surprised the young man. "It's finished me."

"What? What do you mean?"

"Hamilton wouldn't take me for the Mideast. Heard I wasn't safe anymore. Heard I got people killed."

Instructions to board the flight to New York came on the P.A. system, and McNeely stood up. "Take care. Stay away from people like me, huh?" He held out his hand and the young man took it.

"That's bullshit, George. You're still the best."

"Not bad with an AK-47, maybe. I don't know about the rest."

The young man grinned. ''Jesus, I'm gonna miss that gun.''

''Sell it?''

''Yeah. Got eighteen hundred. How about you?''

''It's in my luggage.''

''In your luggage? You're taking it to the States?''

McNeely shrugged. ''An unemployed merc's got to find something to do in his fatherland. And something to do it with.''

''How you gonna get it through customs?''

''They never check me at customs.''

''But what if they do?''

''Then I suppose I'll have to kill most of them, save a few for hostages, and steal a plane. Good hunting.'' George McNeely picked up his flight bag and started for the gate.

Manhattan 3/27

Seth Cummings looked at the picture of his wife for a long time before he took it down from the wall. But finally he lifted it off the hanger and placed it gently in the suitcase beside his pipe rack, desk set, and other memorabilia of his ten years at Stahr, Incorporated. Then he closed it and snapped the latches shut. He sat down behind the oak desk one final time and looked across the wide office out the window to the harbor beyond, where Stahr freighters sat side by side like a gleaming row of cities.

God damn Vern Warren, he thought bitterly. *God damn that son of a bitch to burning hell forever*. Ten years. Ten years of his life wiped out in a day. In a way, Seth Cummings was disappointed in himself. He'd never thought to find anyone more ruthless than he was.

But was Warren really ruthless, Cummings thought, or wasn't it more a stupid antagonism combined with dumb luck? Cummings hadn't been ready for such a blunt frontal attack. He'd been looking for something more Machiavellian, more . . . civilized. A dagger in the ribs, poison in the glass. But instead, he'd received a conk from a shillelagh.

Dirty photos. Jesus, but what he wouldn't have given for those negatives. All Warren had had to do was ask.

He'd have given him money, all his influence in the company . . .

And I'd have ruined the bastard first chance I got. Of course it was stupid to pound old man Stahr's daughter, but she'd asked for it, hadn't she? So he'd drilled her right on the floor of the conservatory, never suspecting that Vern Warren or his hireling—he'd never learned who—was behind the nearest arras with a brand new Nikon. A few glossies in the right hands, and Cummings was out of his vice-presidency, out of the business world, and out of his marriage, which made Cummings angriest of all. What's more, Warren had impounded Cummings's files as company property, and no doubt had tidily squirreled away for himself all the deep dark secrets Cummings had accumulated during his cometary decade at Stahr.

Maybe he deserved it, he told himself. He'd been a nasty son of a bitch for a long time, ruined several careers—maybe his sins were finding him out. . . .

And that was bullshit. He'd been stupid, he'd been weak, he'd thought with his cock instead of his brain, and he'd gotten what he deserved.

His office door opened, and Vern Warren walked in. There was a broad smile on his broad jock's face. "Taking off, huh?" he said.

"Yep." Cummings smiled back even more broadly. He was damned if he was going to give Warren the satisfaction of seeing him miserable. "Time to move on to greener pastures."

"Well, we'll sure miss you, old buddy. Got any hot prospects for the future?"

Cummings stood up and walked over to Warren. "Just one prospect," he said quietly. "Revenge. You know what *that* is, don't you, Vern?"

Warren's smile faded. "You threatening me, Seth?"

"No. I'm telling you." At five foot eight Cummings had to look up several inches at Warren's face, but it was the taller man who paled. Cummings kept smiling his soft smile. "I'm not going to hurt you, Vern. I'm going to *ruin* you. I'm going to take everything you have, everything you ever loved. I'm going to make you so poor that shit'll taste like caviar."

He picked up his suitcase and walked to the door, the gentle smile still in place.

"Be seeing you, Vern."

Manhattan 9/12

David Neville did not stop chinning when Simon Renault entered the exercise room. He merely grunted, and continued to count until he reached thirty. Then he dropped from the bar, stretched, and sat in one of several canvas chairs.

"You're in very good shape," Renault observed.

"Outward appearances can be deceiving. Have you gotten the information then?"

"I have." Renault hefted his briefcase and looked about for a table on which to place it. There was none.

"Not here," Neville said, springing to his feet. "The solarium, I think. It should be lovely today."

Renault followed the younger man out of the room, down a short hall, and into the sunroom. Lush plants were everywhere except for a twenty-foot circular area against the far windows, which they reached by a wide aisle. Shorter paths broke off through the greenery for the convenience of Neville's gardener. The morning was sunny and Renault was dazzled, as always, by the wonders of the room. The wide variety of blooms, the blueness of the sky all around, and the rich humidity never failed to make him feel as though he were in some exotic jungle rather than the middle of New York City. He noticed with pleasure that the solarium was further graced by the presence of Neville's wife, sitting in a white kimono and reading the *Times*, a silver service of coffee on a tray by her side.

"Good morning, Madame," Renault said heartily.

She looked up in surprise. "Simon! How nice to see you." Renault thought her smile made the room even warmer.

"I'm sorry, Gabrielle," said Neville. "I forgot to tell you Simon was coming over this morning."

"Simon is always welcome," she said, standing and taking her husband's arm. They looked so perfect together, Renault thought, almost as though they were brother and sister rather than husband and wife. They shared the same classic Gallic features, the same midnight black hair, olive complexion, the same aura of health and vitality. . . . *Outward appearances can be deceiving*, Neville had said. It was, Renault thought sadly, so very true.

"So," said Neville, "let's see what you've got." He took the newspaper and the cups from off the serving table, making room for Simon Renault's briefcase. From the case Renault took three dossiers, which he handed to Neville.

"Shall I leave, David?" asked Gabrielle.

"No. Please stay. It's about The Pines. About the men who will meet us there."

"Who *may* meet you there," Renault corrected him. "We cannot kidnap them, you know."

Neville flipped through the dossiers. They were quite thick. "Can you tell me briefly? I'll read these later."

"Of course," Renault said. "I believe they are all ready for a contact. Mr. Wickstrom has been trying to get a P.I. license for months now. Unsuccessfully, need I add. It appears his savings are nearly depleted, as he's pawned several items from his apartment. Mr. Cummings is also living on savings, but it seems that alimony payments may lower his standard of living in the near future. He has not been able to find employment commensurate with his abilities. As for Mr. McNeely, he can find no mercenary contracts whatsoever. He has let it be known that he is available for 'solo jobs,' by which it is meant he would accept assassination assignments. However, it appears that his reputation has sunk considerably and as yet he has no customers for his services."

"How is he financially?" Neville asked.

"Quite sound. He has substantial accounts in several foreign as well as American banks. His net worth is somewhere north of half a million."

"But you think he'll accept our offer anyway?" Neville poured coffee for Renault and himself, and refilled Gabrielle's cup.

Renault nodded. "Mr. McNeely lives for adventure. He is one of a dying breed. I think our main problem with him will be to make The Pines sound . . . challenging enough.

No, for him the payment will be secondary, though nothing to scoff at.''

"If Mr. McNeely is such a man as you describe, Simon," said Gabrielle, "I can't imagine how we could keep him away from The Pines." She started to butter a croissant. "When are you planning to contact them?"

"As soon as possible," Neville said. "We'll offer them retainers to remain at liberty until the house is fitted. How long will it be, Simon?"

"Monckton reports that it should be ready in another few weeks. Say, the beginning of October. That is, if there are no more delays."

Gabrielle raised an eyebrow. "Delays?"

"Last week," said Renault, "one of the workmen fell off the balcony."

"Oh, dear God . . ."

"The damned fool went off alone," said Neville. "How can you warn them enough? They may not even be safe in numbers."

Renault shook his massive head. "He didn't make a sound when he fell. They knew it had happened only when some of them entered the Great Hall and found him lying there."

"Did any of them resign?" asked Gabrielle.

"No," said Renault. "They know nothing about the house. Except, of course, that they should never leave the sight of their work partner. An eccentric whim of the owner, they were told. They don't complain, particularly not at the salaries they're being paid."

Neville took a bite of croissant, then asked, "Where does the work stand?"

"The house has been refurbished to your specifications, and the fire chamber is completed. The work on the shutters has begun. After that, only the ventilation and the release system remain."

"Tell Monckton," said Neville, "that it must be finished and stocked by the first of October. That is when we will arrive."

Renault gave a nervous laugh. "But if there are unexpected delays . . . would it not be better to arrive mid-October? A few weeks contingency?"

"Simon, I have no time for unexpected delays. You know that. Tell Monckton October first, no later. And prepare the letters to our three . . . colleagues today. I leave the wording to you. You know what is necessary."

Renault nodded. "Very good."

"Would you stay for breakfast, Simon?" Gabrielle offered.

"Thank you, Madame, but it's going to be a full day."

Neville rose. "We understand, Simon. You'll send me copies of the letters."

"I'll drop them by this evening."

"We'll be out. Leave them with Peter."

"I shall." Renault snapped his briefcase shut and turned to go. At the solarium door he looked back at the young couple surrounded by plants, looking like primal gods. "M. Neville, do you . . . are you certain you wish for me to proceed? Once the letters are written you can hardly turn back." His tone was apologetic, and he slouched as if expecting a reprimand.

But instead, Neville's words were calm, and there was the trace of a smile on his face. "I have no intention of turning back, Simon. I intend to keep walking forward, right up to the point where the locked windows and doors of The Pines make it impossible for me to retreat."

Renault looked desperately at Gabrielle for support. "Madame, I—"

"Please, Simon," she said. "My husband's fate is of his own choosing, and I have chosen to be with him."

"I don't want to speak of this again, Simon," Neville said. "Do you understand?" There was no weakness in his voice, no chink in which Renault could wedge an objection.

"I am sorry," the older man said. "I apologize." Neville's upraised hand signified both forgiveness and dismissal. Renault left the room.

Gabrielle sighed. Her muscles relaxed as if exhausted from a display of strength she did not truly feel. "We shouldn't have been so short with him," she said, her eyes on the floor. "He's concerned only about us."

Neville sat beside her, taking her hand. "I know. I think perhaps that if I *act* firm and unafraid in front of him, that I'll actually begin to feel that way." He cupped her chin in his free hand and turned her face toward his. "I still don't want you to come."

"If you go, I go."

He shook his head, a sad smile on his face. "I love you so. I simply don't want anything to happen to you."

"Nor I you."

"It's too late for that."

They sat in silence for a moment. "I have . . . so much fear," Gabrielle said, "that The Pines will destroy you."

"It may destroy me," Neville whispered, "but at the same time, it may make me immortal."

Part I

Midway upon the journey of our life
I found that I was in a dusky wood;
For the right path, whence I had strayed,
was lost.

—Dante Alighieri
(Lawrence Grant White, translator)

Chapter One

What a crazy world, thought Kelly Wickstrom as he drove through the cool fall air in the rental Fairmont. A month ago he'd been ready to declare bankruptcy, and today, here he was about to start out on what could be a completely new career. Jesus, but didn't God take care of fools though?

As he pulled around a curve in the road, something brown merged with the trees in front of him, leaving a flicker of white that sparkled for a second in the head-light's beams. He recognized it gleefully as a deer. God, he hadn't seen a deer outside of a zoo since he was a kid, when he and his mom had visited his Uncle Harry in Connecticut for a week. Wickstrom slowed the car and rolled down the window, listening. But there was no sound of it moving through the dry brush, only the night noises of crickets and frogs singing their loudest before winter finally quieted them.

He drove on, wondering if there would be any deer at The Pines. There would have to be, he decided. If there weren't any deer on the top of a mountain in northern Pennsylvania, where the hell *would* they be? He turned on the radio, but got only static. Too hilly, he supposed. After a while he found himself wishing that there was something he could listen to beside the hum of the radials on the asphalt. Even that twenty-four-hour religious station he'd had before but lost was better than nothing. Funny that he should be getting spooked driving at night through the woods.

Or maybe it wasn't so funny at that. All his life he'd lived in cities. If he hadn't been surrounded by steel and neon, at least he'd been surrounded by brick and streetlamps. Out here you could drive for twenty miles and never see another car, let alone a town of any size. He wondered what it was like in the daytime, if the road was filled with cars and semis hauling ass up the steep grades, if in the light he could see hundreds of houses set back from the road, invisible in the thick forest dark.

No. Probably not. There was nothing here but trees, never was anything and never would be anything but trees.

As he thought about trees, he noticed the black land-scape ahead was shifting again. The broadleaves were thinning out and giving way to evergreens. It was almost as if the two couldn't get along, couldn't live in peace except in clumps of their own kind. A lot like people, Wickstrom thought, except maybe trees were a little harder to talk to.

He rolled up the window all the way. The wind was blowing more briskly, making the Fairmont shimmy the few times the road passed over open ground, mostly cleared strips where the big power lines crossed the highway. Wickstrom wondered where the hell the electricity was going to since he hadn't seen a house for over an hour. It got stuffy with the window closed, so he opened the dash vent. Damned if he was going to listen to that wind in those branches. He laughed at himself for the thought. *Tough up, Kelly*. But there was no denying the discomfort he felt. There was a difference between the wind's voice in the broadleaves and its manifestation in the evergreens. The maples and the oaks just rustled like *trees*, like he'd heard on quiet nights when he had the Central Park beat. But the pines were another story. In them the wind was weepy and whispery like some sad girl (or her *ghost*, he thought) crying for her lost lover. Would it be like that in The Pines, he wondered, and suddenly he remembered a song that his mother used to sing at night to put him to sleep. He couldn't recall all the words. Something about a black girl . . .

Tell me where did you sleep last night?
In the pines, in the pines,
Where the sun never shines . . .

He couldn't remember how it ended.

It was too cool now with the vent open, so he closed it, wondering what kind of people he was going to find at The Pines. It had all been so damned secretive, like one of those spy novels he used to borrow from Daniels, his partner. The letter had been properly enigmatic:

Mr. Wickstrom:

Enclosed find a cashier's check for ten thousand dollars payable to your account. It is yours to do with as you wish, provided you follow the instructions in this letter, which will also serve as a letter of agreement between the parties involved. Your cashing of the check constitutes your acceptance of the following terms:

1. You hereby agree neither to seek nor accept any employment between September 14, 1986, and October 1, 1986.

2. You hereby agree to attend a meeting to be held at a private home called The Pines in Potter County, Pennsylvania, at 6:00 A.M. October 1, 1986. A car will be supplied for your transportation.

3. You hereby agree to carefully listen to and consider the proposal of employment to be presented to you and two other applicants at that time. The proposal will be completely legal. If, after due consideration, you do not wish to accept it, you may leave immediately, and the ten thousand dollars is yours to keep.

4. You hereby agree, in the possibility that you should accept the proposal, to bring with you enough personal items for a period of thirty-one days. Food, toiletries, and linens will be provided.

5. You hereby agree to tell no one of the contents of this letter or of your destination.

6. Any deviation from the above items of agreement will result in confiscation of the ten thousand dollars.

(signed) Simon Renault

Also attached were maps and directions showing how to reach The Pines, as well as a rental car receipt for September twenty-eighth pickup. And, of course, the check.

At first Wickstrom had thought it was a come-on, a lure intended to get him to buy a lakeside lot in some Pocono village development. But the check made it very different. He had read the letter over and over again, looking for the catch, for the small print that said, "Ten thousand dollars negotiable only as down payment on a Pocono Pines lot of $100,000 or more," but there was no small print, no catch at all. It was a check made out to his name, with no strings attached. Wickstrom had never seen a cashier's check before, and was astonished at how easily it slipped into his terribly depleted account. Once he had assured himself of the check's legitimacy, he had every intention of doing exactly what the letter said, especially the part about the money being "yours to do with as you wish." He paid his overdue bills, his back rent, two months advance on the alimony to Cynthia (just in case he decided to accept whatever offer would be made), and enough new clothes so that he'd look at least presentable when he arrived at The Pines. All that, and he still had seven thousand dollars left in his checking account, enough to see him through for a few months if the offer was unacceptable.

Jesus, but what could it be, he wondered for the hundredth time in the past few weeks. Nothing illegal, the letter had said. Then why all the secrecy?

He looked at the glowing numbers on the dashboard clock. Four forty-five. Flipping on the map light, he skimmed over the directions once again. Good. He'd be there in plenty of time. He glanced in the rearview mirror and thought he saw the black sky turning dark gray with the approach of dawn, but decided it was just his imagination.

And then out of the blue he remembered the last line of that song his mother had sung—

> In the pines, in the pines,
> Where the sun never shines,
> And I shivered the whole night through.

He couldn't hear the wind in the evergreen needles, but he saw the branches dance and sway as he drove under them.

George McNeely drove his BMW up the dirt road. It was rough, but he'd been over worse. At least there were no limbs in his path. The tracks in the road ahead told him that others had been on the road that morning before him. His prospective employers perhaps, or maybe the other applicants the letter had mentioned. He'd smiled when he'd read the part about there being nothing illegal, for he suspected that something *highly* illegal was about to be proposed to him. In a way, he hoped it might be a kill. He'd never performed an assassination, and wondered if he'd be able to accept it as easily as he thought he might. A man's got to do something, he told himself, and if all a man knows how to do is fight and kill, then that's what he does.

There was another switchback in the road, and he pulled the wheel to the right. The mountains were higher than he'd expected to find in a state he'd associated mostly with steel mills and the Liberty Bell, and he swallowed to relieve the pressure on his eardrums that the change in altitude had caused. The darkness was less oppressive now as he drove upward toward the east, and he felt sure that once he was free of the encroaching trees, the morning sky would be seen in its full brightnesss.

Suddenly there was a flashing red light ahead of him. As he drove closer, he saw that it was attached to a large iron gate across the road. A small single-story cabin squatted several yards away, and on its rustic porch stood a tall burly man holding a .12-gauge shotgun loosely in his arms. He was not uniformed, but wore a pair of worn denims and a gray checked wool shirt with a red hunting cap. McNeely rolled down his window and stopped his car several feet in front of the gate. The man walked toward the car and mumbled something McNeely couldn't make out.

"Sorry?"

"What's your name? Sir." The "sir" was an afterthought, as if he'd been coached.

"McNeely."

"You got a letter? Sir?"

McNeely handed it to the man. He glanced at it, then pulled some photographs out of his shirt pocket. He looked at McNeely, then at one of the photos, and back at McNeely again, then nodded. "Okay. You can go in."

"Wait a minute," McNeely said. "You have my photograph there?"

The man looked at him hostilely. "Yep."

"Where did you get it?"

The man didn't answer.

"May I see it please?" This didn't feel good, not at all.

The man shook his head. "Sorry."

"I'm afraid I'll have to insist."

"I said no."

"Then I turn around and drive right back to New York."

The man's hand went farther up the stock of the shotgun in an unmistakable warning. "I don't think you'd better."

"*I* think," said McNeely calmly, "that you'd be a fool to try and stop me . . ."

"You . . ."

". . . because I can have the Colt in my armpit down your throat a whole lot faster than you can step back and bring up that twelve gauge."

Though he had no pistol, McNeely felt perfectly safe. He could tell that the shotgun was for show by the way the yokel held it. The man was no bodyguard, probably just a local hired to take tickets. "Now let me see the photograph."

The man hesitated for a moment, then handed it slowly over. McNeely focused his full attention on it, knowing that the effort expended to get him this far precluded his being blown away by the man. It was a recent photo, which surprised him. That it had been taken surreptitiously he was certain. It was a black and white three-quarter profile. Only the upper portion of his body was visible, and he was wearing a T-shirt. There were trees in the background, and he knew it had to be the park during one of his morning workouts. These people were good despite the pitiable guard they'd chosen. He should have known it when they took his picture, but he hadn't. It was a good shot, slightly grainy, but he was easily recognizable. Tele-

photo, he thought, or a Minox in the bushes. Either way, it
showed him that these people knew what they were doing,
and convinced him more than ever that the proposition
would not be on the up and up.

McNeely handed the picture back to the man, who
scowled at him and walked to the gate, which he wrenched
open violently, gesturing for McNeely to drive through.
He did so, tipping an imaginary hat at the man, who only
scowled all the more.

The road went a mile higher, winding back and forth
and hugging the side of the mountain with just enough
room for two cars to pass. Then on his left the trees were
gone, and a large lawn stretched up to the house.

It was much lighter there at the mountain's top, without
the covering shadows of the thick evergreens, and his
breath caught in his throat at the sight of the building in
the sudden morning glow. It was shaped like a huge stone
T, the arms serving as two long wings off the thick upright
which jutted out to the road. The stones of which it was
built were massive, irregularly cut gray granite blocks,
which gave it the solidity of a medieval castle. But it had
none of a castle's architectural fillips. No turrets pierced
the crisp fall air, no cupolas curved skyward. Indeed, the
lack of ornamentation gave the impression of a great stone
block, a monolithic slab forgotten by a race of titans. Even
the roof allowed no relief from the stiff horizontals and
verticals. From McNeely's viewpoint it seemed perfectly
flat, so that he could not see its surface. The only evidence
of the roof's existence were foot-wide eaves that surrounded the house, jutting sharply outward as if embarrassed to cause a line that did not meet another.

As McNeely drove nearer, he could see that many of the
windows were stained glass, and here and there dim gleam-
ings of color shone from rooms inside, where lamps were
lit. He pulled up to the front door at the base of the T and
stopped. A short stocky man in a black windbreaker opened
the car door for him. "You can leave your car here, Mr.
McNeely. I'll take it around the back."

McNeely nodded and got out. "Feel free to go in,"
said the stocky man, climbing into the driver's seat and
wheeling the BMW to the left behind the house. McNeely

stood alone for a minute, looking up at the house that towered three stories above him, then at the wings that stretched away from the rear of the house to either side. Large lawns lay within the two areas between the wings and the trunk of the T, but trees were everywhere else, pines mostly, though McNeely noticed a good many broadleaves as well—mostly oak, maple, and a few poplars. From the front of the house across the road to where the trees began was less than thirty feet. It was disquieting, thought McNeely, oppressive. He looked across the lawn at the righthand wing and grunted appreciatively at the size of the place. Each wing had to be at least sixty feet long, and it looked to be sixty feet from the front back to the wings. He wondered if there was another extension lost to his view that would make the T a cross.

Then he noticed, high in a third-floor window near the end of the righthand wing, a dim glow. At first he thought that it was the reflection of sunlight in the windowpane, but realized immediately that the sun was still far behind the eastern trees. Within a few seconds it became too bright to be an electric light, and the whiteness of it made him think of burning magnesium. When it flared even higher, dazzling his eyes with its white fury, he started to cross quickly to the front door to alert the occupants.

Then, even faster than it had burst into being, the light faded until the eye of the window was dark once again.

McNeely stood there, confused. He wondered if it had been an illusion, or if something had reflected the sun's low rays off several surfaces until it touched the glass of the window. Or perhaps an acetylene torch . . . a workshop.

The man who had parked his car appeared around the end of the wing, walking across the yellow lawn. When he noticed McNeely, he called to him. "You can go in, Mr. McNeely."

McNeely nodded, but waited for the man to draw nearer. "I thought I saw a fire," he said, "in that window up there."

The man looked up at the window and nodded. "Real bright light?" he asked. "Almost white?"

"Yes."

"I've seen that already," said the stocky man. "Some

sort of illusion from the clouds or somewhere. That room's empty. Not a thing in it."

"I thought it might be a workshop," McNeely said. "Acetylene torch, maybe."

The man shook his head. "No such thing. Pretty peculiar though." He gestured to the door. "Like to go in?"

McNeely nodded thanks and pushed the massive double door inward into a short antechamber with a red velvet curtain at the other end. To his left and right were two dark rooms—cloakrooms, he thought. Drawing the curtain aside, he stepped into a room so large that at first he thought himself in a chapel. The ceiling lofted up for all three stories, ending in an arched roof of dark timbers. The walls were a dark brown stone in sharp contrast to the lighter gray of the outer walls, and the heavy stone floor underfoot did nothing to alleviate the gloom of the place. Two men stood talking in low tones at the other end of the room. The older of the pair, who was facing McNeely, noticed him entering.

"Hello there!" he cried out. He squinted to make out McNeely's face, and came closer, the younger man following. "Mr. McNeely, is it?"

"That's right." He held out his hand, which the older man took in his large paw like a bear snaring a fish.

"A pleasure. My name is Renault. Simon Renault." Renault smiled as he pumped McNeely's hand. A bear, McNeely thought again. Renault *was* a bear, tall, layered with fat, a huge moustache, gray-white hair, and brownish tweeds, which completed the picture. He probably loved honey. "And this," said Renault, "is Mr. Kelly Wickstrom. Mr. Wickstrom, George McNeely."

As he shook Wickstrom's hand, McNeely regarded him admiringly. He was as tall as Renault, well over six feet, but there the resemblance stopped. Whereas Renault undoubtedly tortured the scales, Wickstrom was, McNeely estimated, not over two hundred pounds, most of it muscle. His blond hair and faint moustache would have made him look like a slightly over-the-hill beach boy if it hadn't been for the lumpy-looking face that was brutally accented by a broken nose.

"Glad to meet you," Wickstrom said in an unmistakable Brooklyn accent. He looked uncomfortable, like a secretary about to be interviewed fresh out of business school.

McNeely turned back to Renault. "You're the gentleman who sent the letter, then."

"That's correct," Renault nodded. "I trust there was no trouble with the check?"

"None at all. I must admit I felt somewhat guilty taking it"—Renault looked puzzled—"for such a little service as driving up here, I mean. When will we talk about the further proposition?"

"Just what I've been asking him," said Wickstrom.

Renault smiled and looked at his watch. "It's six o'clock now. Mr. Cummings has not yet arrived. . . ."

"Cummings?" McNeely asked.

"The third applicant," said Renault. "I hope he hasn't gotten lost. At any rate, why don't we begin breakfast, and you can meet the owners of The Pines. We'll wait to outline the proposition, of course, until Mr. Cummings arrives. Just step this way." He spoke, thought McNeely, like a man used to being obeyed.

The three of them walked past the huge round fireplace near the center of the room. Four feet above it was a chimney opening like the bell of a giant trumpet. The copper chimney pipe shot upward between the balconies on either side of the room until it pierced the ceiling high above. "Quite a chimney," observed McNeely.

"Isn't it," said Renault, never breaking stride. *He may be friendly*, McNeely thought, *but he's certainly not talkative.*

They entered the first door on the right. It was a dining room, complete with china closet, buffet, and a long rustic oak table surrounded by two dozen hand-hewn chairs. A man and a woman were seated, drinking coffee at the far end. They rose when the others entered. They were, thought McNeely, quite handsome, and he stole a sidelong glance at Wickstrom to catch his reaction upon seeing the woman.

He was not disappointed. Wickstrom's mouth opened slightly and his eyes grew dreamy for a second before he smiled and nodded politely. There was little guile in this

Kelly Wickstrom, McNeely thought. He would be easy to read.

The man at the end of the room, however, was a different story. McNeely disliked him instantly, though he did not know precisely why. There was an aura about him of something wrong. He was a bit too good-looking, a bit too tall, a bit too controlled and confident and overwhelmingly at ease in the way he gazed condescendingly at them and rested his thin tapered fingers on the woman's shoulder. It was clear to George McNeely that this man was a fool, albeit a rich and dangerous one.

But there was something else, something that made the hair on McNeely's neck stir, the longer he looked at the man. McNeely had lived too long with the scent of death not to recognize it now.

"May I present Gabrielle and David Neville," intoned Renault. "And this is Kelly Wickstrom and George McNeely." The couple crossed to them, the woman first, the man following, and Kelly Wickstrom struggled to keep the grin of wonder off his face. He'd seen pretty women before—hell, his wife had been pretty as anything—but he couldn't remember ever before standing in the presence of beauty, its violet eyes shining into his.

He managed well enough so that the grin just felt dopey as she shook his hand, and he realized that she'd said something he'd missed.

"Pardon?" he asked. He could feel his cheeks getting hot and hoped she wouldn't notice.

There was amusement in her eyes. "I asked how was your drive up here?"

"Fine. Fine, thank you. It's beautiful country."

"A bit untamed for the East, eh?" said Neville, turning from McNeely to grasp Wickstrom's hand. Wickstrom thought the grip was a little too strong to be friendly, but resisted the urge to squeeze back. He needed the job too badly to antagonize his prospective employer.

"Untamed is right," said McNeely. "Desolate is more like it."

"Very true." Neville smiled. "The nearest towns are twenty miles on either side of our mountain. Wilmer is north—on a clear day you can see it from the overlook out back. South is Ticono."

Wickstrom chuckled. "Sounds like an oil company."

"Doesn't it?" Neville said politely, but beneath it Wickstrom sensed an undercurrent of impatience, and decided not to joke again.

"Shall we sit down?" Gabrielle Neville asked. Wickstrom could barely keep his eyes off her as the party moved tableward. She was utterly elegant, feminine without being in the least pneumatic. Her figure was slim, almost boyish, and Wickstrom wondered what it would be like, not to bed her, but just to hold her. At that moment he envied Neville his wife far more than his wealth.

While the others sat, Renault and Gabrielle disappeared into the hall and returned within a minute with plates of eggs, toast, and bacon. Behind them, pushing a tray with a coffee service for eight, was a man wearing a denim jacket and chinos. He was tall and gaunt, and his hair was pure white, belying his age, which Wickstrom judged to be not over fifty. Renault introduced him as Whitey Monckton, a New York architect and contractor who had just finished some work on the house. Monckton seemed friendly enough, but ill at ease, and Wickstrom caught him jumping at small noises in the hall and overhead that seemed to be only the sounds that any old house makes.

The five of them were halfway through breakfast when the man who had parked Wickstrom's car came in from the hall, followed by another man in a Burberry topcoat with a briefcase.

"Cummings," barked the stranger in a crisp tenor. "Seth Cummings. Jesus, I'm sorry I'm late, but I must have taken a wrong turn back along the line. Then, of course, when I got here, I wanted to drive straight through, but the . . . gentleman at the gate seemed rather security-conscious, so I had to spend some time with him." Cummings looked around the table, smiling at each in turn.

"Quite all right," Renault boomed. "You've not missed a thing of import." Introductions were made, and Wickstrom noticed an odd reaction from Cummings when the Nevilles were introduced, as though he recognized the name. But he said nothing, and soon was eating along with the rest.

When the meal was finished, Monckton and Gabrielle cleared away the dishes, and Neville rose to his feet. "The time has come, the walrus said, to speak." Wickstrom smiled at the allusion without being able to place it. "I think that we may adjourn to the den for the proposition we have to make to you gentlemen. If you'll follow me . . . ."

They walked down the hall, past the mammoth room through which they'd entered the house, and across to the other wing into a large den whose windows looked out on the front lawn. Once they were comfortably seated in thick leather chairs, Neville nodded to Renault.

"Mr. Wickstrom, Mr. McNeely, Mr. Cummings," said Renault. "First of all, we wish to thank you for being here today. The offer that we are about to make is one that you need not feel required to accept. The retainers you have been paid are yours to keep regardless of what you decide today. Of course, we hope that you *will* accept, but the choice is entirely yours.

"What we are asking for are your services for one month, thirty-one days starting today through the end of October. Does that pose a scheduling problem for any of you? . . . Good. All we ask is that you live here, inside The Pines, for that period of time."

Renault looked around as if expecting a question. Wickstrom gave him one. "Doing what?"

"Whatever you wish. There will be the three of you and Mr. and Mrs. Neville. There are restrictions, of course. And certain things that may seem eccentric to you. Nevertheless, there are good reasons for all of them.

"I can see the questions on all of your faces. What *is* this really about, I suppose you're asking yourselves. Well, to be honest, there is more to this than just a one-month vacation. The Pines is an odd house. Things have happened here, and things have been heard and seen here that are difficult to explain. Mr. Neville will go into greater detail in a moment. It is primarily from curiosity on his part that this project was conceived. The house has stood empty for a number of years, and when Mr. Neville was made aware of its curious history, his interest in it grew until he came up with the idea of spending a long period of

time here to see if the rumors and legends had any truth in
them.''

Rumors? Legends? What the hell, Wickstrom wondered,
was this all about? And what was next? Vincent Price
popping out of a closet to tell them ghost stories? The
whole thing was crazy.

George McNeely was doubtful, too, not of Renault's
sanity, but rather his honesty. Curiosity? *Bullshit*, McNeely
thought, biting back a smile as he looked at David Neville.
The man was practically ravening. Not outwardly, but
McNeely could see it in the eyes. There was more than
curiosity there, even the curiosity of an out and out occult-
ist. McNeely had worked a long time on reading men's
eyes, and even longer on keeping his own blank and
emotionless. The skill had saved his life several times.
Words lie, acts lie, but eyes? Never.

"Of course," Renault went on, "it would be necessary
to have companions, so you gentlemen were—"

"Why?" asked McNeely.

"Why . . . what?"

"Why are companions necessary? Surely a few servants
would do as well." He knew his comment might be
interpreted as rude, but he wanted to break Renault's
irksome air of preparedness, to see how he handled a
protest, and mainly to see how Neville reacted to the
question.

"Let me, Simon," said Neville with a cold smile. "Mr.
McNeely, disposing of servants was my little idiosyn-
cracy. I wanted a certain type of person around my wife
and myself . . . people very much like you and Mr. Cummings and Mr. Wickstrom. *Tough* people. People who
wouldn't be scared by a few ghost stories, whose imaginations wouldn't run away with them. For that same reason I
didn't want any so-called psychics. They feel *obligated* to
see ghosts, and if there aren't any to see, they'll make
them up."

Wickstrom cleared his throat. "Why, uh, why us specifically? I mean—"

Neville held up a hand. "Please, Mr. Wickstrom, all in
good time. I've already jumped about more than I like,"

he said, glancing at McNeely. "I'd like to tell you about the house now, and then Simon can fill you in on the details of your acceptance . . . if, of course, you all accept.

"The Pines was built by my grandfather, Robert D'Neuville, who later took the name Neville. He'd been in this country since 1880 and decided to finally Americanize it. The family was, and still is, in the import-export business. Trade was particularly good in the first decade of this century, and my grandfather found himself a multimillionaire. He'd worked nonstop for many years, but was now secure enough to want to take things easy for a change.

"So he built The Pines. He scouted for a location for a number of years, looking for someplace no more than a day or two's journey from New York, yet a place that was isolated, many miles away from the nearest town or even the nearest house. He found it here.

"He chose this mountain because of its spectacular northern view. One can see nearly a hundred miles on a very clear day, and on a clear night the lights of Wilmer are easily visible. That was, however, as close as my grandfather wanted anyone to come. So in 1907 he bought hundreds of thousands of acres all around—it was the property of the National Forest Service, but already by that time the Neville family had done the Roosevelt administration a great many favors, so the transaction was easily made, particularly since Grandfather wanted to leave it in its pure state. The forest service had named this mountain, predictably enough, Pine Mountain, because of the pines that blanket it, so Grandfather decided to call the house The Pines."

"Imaginative, wasn't he?" McNeely said dryly.

Neville bristled. "He was a businessman, Mr. McNeely, and as such had little time for imagination." Then he smiled in discomfort, as if angry at himself for being baited. "I think you can see that from the design of the house, which he did himself. He wanted it simple and functional, which it is, except for the Great Hall, the large room through which you first entered. There he wanted the feeling of an old royal hunting lodge. The house was to be an escape, a retreat to which he and his family could come in the summer to hunt and relax. It was, however, many years before he could occupy it.

"The construction started in 1909, and was plagued with accidents. Three men were killed during the first year, when a scaffold collapsed, and in 1910 a fire broke out when there was no one on the site, completely gutting the structure. Only the stone remained. Grandfather had it rebuilt, and in late 1913 The Pines was completed. But the war was coming, the shipping lanes were endangered, and Grandfather was busier than ever. He spent none of the summer of 1914 here, nor any summers of the war years that followed.

"At last, in 1919, he had the place furnished and brought his family here, along with several servants, intending to stay through July and August. Unfortunately, his youngest son, my father's younger brother, became ill one night and died before morning. It's still not known what caused his death, though the examining doctor called it a 'brain fever.' The boy's death crushed my grandfather. He took his family back to New York at once, and refused to bring them here again. The next summer he returned with a few business associates and some other acquaintances, though he would not take either of his surviving sons. He also brought friends here to hunt deer in the fall. Then, a few years later, strange things started to happen.

"There was a rumor, never substantiated, that a poet friend of my grandfather's had something to do with the death of a woman here. Supposedly she was the mistress of one of the guests, and her death was hushed up for fear of scandal. Whether the poet purposely killed her or drove her to her death in some other way is not known, but he himself committed suicide not a year after the supposed event."

"I don't understand," said Wickstrom. "There must have been a body. . . ."

"Always the policeman, eh, Mr. Wickstrom?" Neville said patronizingly. "Now, if *you* were wealthy and a death of an unknown and uncared for person occurred in your house—miles from civilization—and it threatened to destroy the reputations of two of your friends, don't you

think you could somehow see to it that that unknown
person *stayed* unknown?"

"No," said Wickstrom simply. "I don't think I could."

Neville looked at him for a long moment. "No, I suppose you couldn't. Maybe my grandfather didn't either.
Maybe it never happened. It's a moot point anyway, as it
was only a rumor. The next event, however, really did
occur.

"An industrialist, of a family whose name you would
all recognize if I mentioned it, went mad in this house in
the fall of 1928. No one knows why nor how. His manservant
simply found him in bed one morning babbling incoher-
ently. It was assumed that something he'd seen or heard
during the night had stolen his wits, as the novelists put it.
At any rate, he never regained his sanity."

"Excuse me," Cummings interrupted, "but was he at
all unbalanced to begin with?"

"Evidently not, Mr. Cummings. He was a shrewd businessman with little time for trifling or believing in the
supernatural. Not unlike yourself, eh?" Cummings chuckled politely while Neville went on. "After that, the shit,
you'll pardon the expression, hit the fan. Guests started
seeing visions both night and day around the house and
grounds, people who looked real and substantial one moment and would vanish in the next. There was no rhyme or
reason to the appearances, and it seems that these ghosts,
if you will, were all very different from one another. In
fact, it seems that no two guests ever saw the same apparition, so there is no 'Lady in Gray,' or 'Headless Nun'
of long tradition.

"Nightmares became plentiful, and the guests were also
filled with highly realistic premonitions. It's said that one
young and healthy financier felt so strongly that his own
death was imminent that he made his will and settled all
his accounts. A month later the crash of '29 sent him and
dozens of others out of their office windows to the pave-
ment below.

"My grandfather, oddly enough, was never victimized
by any of these phenomena, but after a time he grew to
believe in them. In 1930 he shut up The Pines, placing a
permanent guard at the cabin you passed below. Between

then and the forties there was not one attempt made at burglary or vandalism.''

"That's more incredible than the ghosts," Wickstrom said, "especially during the Depression. Didn't people know about this place or what?"

"Oh, they knew about it," Neville answered. "Everyone in the county did. They just stayed away. The rumors spread, and, after all, they were mountain people with mountain superstitions."

"Were there any superstitions locally," asked McNeely, "about Pine Mountain itself?"

Neville shook his head. "Not a one. Not even any Indian legends as far as my researchers could tell. Indians, settlers—everyone just seemed to stay away from the place."

"That's surprising," said McNeely, "considering the terrain and the water table. The stream at the bottom would flow into the river a few miles away, wouldn't it?"

"I'm afraid I don't know my Pennsylvania rivers, Mr. McNeely. Perhaps if you decide to stay, you can investigate that in the library."

That's two, McNeely thought.

"My grandfather died in the forties," Neville went on. "Since my surviving uncle was killed in the war, my father, John Neville, took over the company and family holdings. He knew the stories about The Pines, even though he barely remembered the house, as he was only six when they stayed here in 1919. Not having any real firsthand knowledge of it, he decided to open it once more, and brought two of his friends here, intending to stay overnight and see how the place had held up.

"It had done so admirably. In fact, he swore there was not the slightest sign of decay. The stone was barely weathered, the windows were all clean, there was little dust to be seen anywhere. Not even spider webs were found."

Cummings chuckled bravely. "Not a very popular place— even for bugs."

Neville did not return a smile. "You're right, Mr. Cummings. Not popular for anything. Do you recall what you heard when you drove up the mountain this morning?"

Cummings shrugged. "Nothing, I guess."

"That's right," said McNeely, remembering. "Those woods should have been filled with bird cries at six A.M. I didn't hear a one. Nor insects."

"Very observant, Mr. McNeely," said Neville, and for once there was sincerity in his tone. "Birds and animals shun this place. My grandfather and his hunting cronies never took a deer within five miles of here. It's as if they know something is not quite right." Neville's head went up slowly, as if listening for something overhead. He seemed to have forgotten the others for a moment.

"You were speaking," McNeely interrupted softly, "of your father."

Neville turned abruptly toward the group once more. "Yes, I'm sorry. He and his friends didn't last the night. One of them claimed to see a terrifying apparition—a man strangling a young woman at the foot of his bed. He ran screaming down the hall into my father's room, and within a few seconds all three were there together. All of them had felt highly uncomfortable and unable to sleep, which might have had its origin in the stories Father told them on the drive up. They packed their few things and drove away, and they never laughed about it later.

"Father had the house locked and guarded again, and forgot about it. But in the fifties when the Bridey Murphy thing hit the papers and interest in the occult was revitalized, he hired a psychic medium to investigate the house. The man stayed for three days, but despite some slight 'psychic discomfort,' as he put it, he found nothing." Neville laughed scornfully. "His crystal ball and ouija board were empty. Nevertheless, Father would neither reopen it nor sell it—if indeed he could have. He actually believed that there was something . . . I hesitate to use the word *evil*—it's so melodramatic . . . something *unpleasant* here, and that it would be best to simply guard it, like a house in quarantine, I suppose. So guard it he did, and forgot about it."

Neville's eyes softened, and he gazed down at the Turkoman carpet at his feet. "He died last spring. I knew nothing about the house until then. When I was going over the holdings I'd inherited, I came upon a file concerning The Pines. Along with the deeds and legal papers was an

informal history of the place written by my father after the
fifties investigation. It contained much of what I've just
told you. Simon, who was a close friend of my father's,
filled in the rest for me.'' He sighed heavily, and looked at
each of the three men in turn. ''I knew that I would have
to come here, to find out whatever the truth was about this
place, and perhaps to find out what things can survive after
death. You may not fully understand my motives, gentlemen, but you won't be asked to do that. You will be asked
only to stay here with me while I play with''—he gestured at the house around them—''with my giant toy for a
while.''

Renault stood up. ''Well, gentlemen, how does the
prospect of spending a month here strike you?''

Wickstrom, McNeely, and Cummings looked from Renault to one another. There was no fear on any of their
faces, but there was hesitation nonetheless. McNeely was
the first to speak. ''A month, you said.''

''That's correct,'' Neville answered.

McNeely sat back in his chair and interlaced his fingers. ''The ten thousand dollars we've each received was
only to get us this far. Might I ask with what you're
tempting us to stay the full time?''

''Simon,'' Neville said, the order implicit. From his
inner jacket pocket Renault withdrew three slips of paper
and handed them to Neville. ''These are cashier's checks,''
said Neville, ''made out to each of you for the sum of one
million dollars.''

''A million dollars?'' Wickstrom was halfway to his feet
in an instant. Cummings's jaw dropped. Only McNeely
showed no outward reaction.

''That's correct, Mr. Wickstrom. As soon as you agree
to the conditions, these checks are yours. You may keep
them on your person or have Simon hold them for safe-
keeping. Or even have him deposit them in your accounts,
for that matter.''

Wickstrom laughed unsteadily. ''The Chemical Bank
would shit!'' Gabrielle laughed, too, and Wickstrom blushed.

''I'm sure,'' said Neville dryly.

''What's to insure,'' said McNeely, ''that we won't take
the checks and leave before the thirty days are up?''

"Thirty-*one* days," Neville corrected him. "And you won't leave, Mr. McNeely. None of us will, because we won't be able to."

"What do you mean?" said Cummings.

"We'll be prisoners here," Neville answered. "We will be shut in. The windows and doors will be not only locked, but sealed and covered, so that we won't even know whether it's day or night."

McNeely's stomach tightened. He'd hated to feel that he was confined ever since he'd spent two weeks in the sweatbox in 'Nam. The Pines was a lot bigger than that four by four bamboo cage, and if what Neville said was true, there wouldn't be a leech or a rat within miles, but still, the idea of being sealed up, no matter where, was anathema to him. "What's the purpose of that?" he asked, hoping that his voice showed no sign of the unease he felt.

"Would you accept 'my whim,' Mr. McNeely? No, I didn't think so. Then let me say that I want to abolish time. I want our minds only on our surroundings, not thinking about how long it's going to be before we're out. It's simple—no day, no night, no time, no countdown to worry about." Neville walked to the window and pointed to the top of the frame. "You'll see a slot here. When we are ready, a half-inch steel plate will descend over this window and every other window and door in the house, sliding four inches deep into the bottom slots. No daylight will be able to come in. We will in essence be trapped, so that whatever things reside here in The Pines will be able to show themselves to us at their leisure. And we won't be able to deny them by running away . . . not to suggest that the supernatural holds any fears for you three men."

"Which reminds me," said Cummings. "You said you'd tell us later why us three? Why us specifically?" Wickstrom nodded in tacit agreement and leaned forward for Neville's answer. But it was Renault who responded.

"This undertaking was not begun lightly. We wished to utilize men who were tough, hardheaded realists—even ruthless, if the truth be known. But to have them all from the same line of work—all bodyguards, for instance—might pose problems. The men might know each other, for one thing. Too, there is a streak of romanticism in many private investigators. The white knight syndrome, one might call it. But here we have a policeman, a soldier, and a businessman. Men too busy with the realities of survival to permit their imaginations free rein.''

"As for how we learned about you three as individuals,'' Neville added, ''we simply used our contacts. You, Mr. Wickstrom, were on a list of names supplied by the assistant district attorney of New York County; we heard of you, Mr. Cummings, through business associates, and Mr. McNeely . . . we heard of you through a friend.''

McNeely returned the smile. ''Friend?''

"Yes. With the initials C.I.A.''

"One more thing,'' Wickstrom said. ''Why so much?''

Neville looked puzzled. ''So much . . . ?''

"So much money? I mean, you could get me for a month's work for a helluva lot less than a million dollars.''

"First of all,'' said Neville, ''three million dollars means very little to me, though I don't want to seem boastful. Secondly, we really have no idea of what we'll confront here. There may be risks of which we know nothing—perhaps our lives may be in danger. So I felt the reward should be commensurate with . . .''

While Neville smoothly spoke on, Whitey Monckton, nearly forgotten by the others, sat at the back of the room and shuddered inside. Risks, he thought. Risking your life was one thing, but risking your sanity was something else. He didn't envy the three men their million one bit. He knew there was something here in the house that over the period of a month might be enough to shrivel them until that million would be so much worthless paper. All of Neville's fortune wouldn't be enough to keep Monckton in the house for a week, let alone a month. Not after what he'd seen.

It had been three days ago, when the work was almost finished. He'd ignored his own orders to stay with a buddy, and had gone up to the third floor to examine the observatory dome. He'd felt a little funny about going off alone, especially after Cole's death a few weeks earlier, but it was noon on a sunny day, and the glass doors to the sun room brightly lit the third floor hall. Keller, his assistant, was in the basement for a final look at the fire chamber, and Monckton hadn't felt like trotting down three flights to fetch him. So he went into the observatory alone.

He turned on the light and walked over to the seventy-year-old eight-inch reflector that looked as though it had been installed yesterday. Next to the mounting was an iron crank that he grasped and tried to turn. It moved a fraction of an inch and stopped. Good. The pie-shaped wedge of steel overhead through which the telescope had once peered remained firmly in place. He moved directly underneath it to determine if there was any way to circumvent the locks. Then the light went out.

Heart pounding, he swung around toward the open door, cursing himself for being such a fool. But instead of the upright rectangle of light he'd expected to see, there was only darkness. The door was shut.

Easy! he told himself. *Relax—a draft, nothing more.* And then the light began to form.

At first it was no bigger than a pinpoint, but its hot glow was so intense that he noticed it immediately. It was white. Not the dull whiteness of paper or even the pure whiteness of new snow, but a hot burning whiteness that nearly blinded him. It widened slowly, like an eye's pupil dilating in the dark, until it seemed to be yards across.

The intensity of it was so stunning that he didn't notice the faces at first. There were hundreds of them, swimming on the white surface like gray petals in a pool that mirrors sunlight, and he felt his bowels twist in terror as he slowly discerned the lineaments of their expressions. Madness, anger, evil shone from each pair of eyes, white on white. Though colors had surrendered to the light, he was able to make out the features of Orientals and blacks as well as Caucasians, and others so bestial in appearance as to fit none of the races of man. They whirled in the brightness, a storm of leering faces that seemed to drift ever closer to his own. And then among the faces were some he recognized, and he knew he had to be going mad.

Eyes of searing fire stared with silent lunacy into his own, and with a shock of horror he recalled the blurry news photograph of Dean Corll, the homosexual killer of teenage runaways. The wizened face of Albert Fish, the child murderer, was the next he recognized. The papers had been full of his pictures when Monckton was a boy, and now the old man's face writhed before him, bony jaw clattering up and down like a castanet, the pale tongue sending dark unfelt spittle flying toward him.

There were others before, between, and after, coming with such speed and in such profusion that Monckton barely had time to notice and gauge each face. But Corll and Fish had been visual archetypes for Monckton, embedded forever in his subconscious, and the glimpse alone was enough to lock the memory in as on radar.

The next familiar face, however, was the one whose look of mindless fanaticism, whose all-encompassing hatred was so great that it drove Monckton to his knees. His stomach gave up then, and he vomited, spewing his terror onto the polished wood of the floor. He lay there, sanity wrenched away, lungs heaving, eyes at last tightly shut. But the whiteness seemed to slice through his lids as though they were thin as paper, and he pressed his hands over them and curled fetally, as if wanting to crawl into himself.

He didn't know how long he lay that way, but gradually he became aware that the light was not piercing as strongly through his fingers and his eyelids as it had been. Slowly he took his hands away and opened his eyes.

The light was on. The door was open. There was no trace of the preternatural white flame in which he had seen those lunatic faces, no sign of the twisted and contorted features of Adolf Hitler, whose rolling eyes and look of ultimate malevolence had driven Whitey Monckton temporarily but undeniably insane.

Chapter Two

He *had* been crazy, Monckton thought. Whether what he had seen had been real or not, it had cracked the veneer of what he regarded as sanity. At first he'd told himself over and over again that it had been merely a hallucination—that the atmosphere of The Pines combined with his knowledge of its past history had caused him to create his own phantasmagoria of horror. What other explanation could there be for seeing such absurdities? Corll, Fish, Hitler, and all those others as well—on the top of a mountain in northern Pennsylvania? There was no sense to it at all, and that was exactly why he finally thought that he *had* truly seen it.

If, he reasoned, he'd imagined it all, it would have been more coherent, had more personal meaning to *him*. He'd only recognized a few faces, and all the others he *knew* he'd never seen before. There had not even been that odd, dislocated feeling of déjà vu in their presence, only a feeling of terrifying unreality, of shock at the *unfamiliarity* of the apparitions.

Monckton hadn't mentioned it to anyone, but he was certain that Keller had noticed something wrong. Since that time he did not allow himself to be alone in the house. Perhaps the next time he wouldn't be so lucky. Perhaps the next time he'd be found like Barney Cole, crushed on the hard stone floor of the Great Hall.

He looked around the room and frowned. If these fools had any brains, he thought, they'd leave right now. He was tempted to warn them, to tell them what he'd seen in the observatory. But he'd made an agreement with Neville, and he intended to stick by it, even though he felt that after this day, he would not see Neville alive again. Monckton shivered, and listened.

"In short," Neville was saying, "we have no idea what we'll experience. I want to make sure you understand that, and if what *I* suspect about this place is true, believe me, you'll earn every penny of the payment."

"What *do* you suspect?" said McNeely.

"That there *are* ghosts here, and that possibly they are capable of harm."

"Then why stay?"

"Mr. McNeely, I told you you did not need to know my motives and I am standing by that. I wish to know the truth about this place, and that's all I'll say on the subject."

Cummings took a deep breath. "I don't know about the rest of you, but—"

"Please!" Neville barked. "No decisions yet. You agreed to consider the proposition carefully before answering either yes or no, and I want you to know everything first. For that reason I asked Mr. Monckton to be here. As was mentioned, Mr. Monckton is the man who prepared the house for our stay, and I'd like him to take you through it and point out some special features."

Monckton stood up. "Follow me," he muttered, and led the way into the hall. "The house is laid out like a cross, with its head pointing north, so the wing we're in is the west wing, and the other is naturally the east. As you saw when you came in, the entire southern arm is taken up by the Great Hall. The balconies are accessible from the second and third floors. The west wing on this floor contains the den we were just in, a large library across the hall, and a smaller study."

He walked toward the center of the house, stopping as they came out of the hall. "The short head of the cross," he said, "holds only the sun room, which goes up for three floors, and the billiard room down here, a gun room on the second, and an observatory on the third."

"Unfortunately," said Neville, "the sun room door is already sealed by a plate, as you can see. Since the walls are glass, we would have had to put steel shutters over the entire room. Much more practical to use just one.''

As Monckton led them down the east wing hall, pointing out the kitchen, pantry, and servants' quarters, Kelly Wickstrom smiled admiringly at each new disclosure, but his thoughts were grim. Maybe if Cynthia had been able to live like this, maybe then they'd still be together. The five years since their divorce had not lessened the hurt. He still missed her and ached for her, as if it were a hand or a leg and not a wife he'd lost. What did she expect? he asked himself again. What *could* she expect on a policeman's salary? And hell, he hadn't even been a cop when they'd gotten married—he was still in the factory then.

Jesus, how she'd have loved this place. She always liked nice things. That's why she went to work, became a gofer for that son of . . .

And then he was walking up the stairs with the others, and Neville was talking again. ''Sorry it's so dark on the steps. The west wing stairs were used much more. These were mainly for the servants.''

When they reached the top, Monckton turned and faced them. ''Except for the gun room between the wings, this floor is occupied only by bedroom suites and servants' quarters, these three small rooms on your right. The suites on the north side have balconies, but the doors to them will be shut off too.''

''There are four suites,'' Neville said, ''Whitetail, Bear, Eagle, and Dove, which is set for double occupancy. That is where my wife and I will stay, with the other three intended for you courageous gentlemen.''

Smartass, thought Wickstrom. *How smartass would you be without your money?*

''We'll go to the third floor now,'' said Monckton, ignoring his employer's jibe. He didn't walk down the hall to the central staircase, but passed between the others and started up the dark servants' stairway again. ''You probably won't spend too much time up here,'' said Monckton. ''Most of the rooms are vacant, though we've put in a small gym at the end of this wing so you can exercise, and there's a large lounge with a stocked bar in the west wing.

The rest of the rooms consist of unused bedrooms and a children's playroom, and of course''—he hesitated—''the observatory in the north annex—''

"With closed dome, naturally," interrupted Neville, "but there are books on astronomy there if you're interested, and observational journals my grandfather kept. The nights are quite clear here. I suppose they were even clearer in the twenties." Neville cocked his head. "Are *you* a stargazer, Mr. McNeely?"

But McNeely wasn't listening. He was looking at Monckton, intrigued by his pause before mentioning the observatory. For McNeely, that hesitation, along with Monckton's involuntary glances upward during breakfast, had pinpointed Monckton's fear. The observatory.

"I'm sorry?" McNeely murmured.

"I just thought you'd be interested in my grandfather's astronomical journals," Neville said smoothly.

McNeely nodded. "Yes, I'll get to those right after my research on the rivers. But tell me," he went on, smiling inwardly at his remark, "are these vacant rooms accessible?"

"Yes," said Monckton. "All unlocked."

McNeely moved to the door on his left. "May I?"

"Feel free," replied Neville.

McNeely opened the door. He had easily deduced that this was the room out of which he had seen that intense white light beaming, and he was surprised now to find it empty. It was a small room, only fifteen feet square, and, by the looks of it, had never been occupied. There were no darker spaces where pictures had once hung, no thin scrapes on the bright wood floor where furniture had heavily passed. McNeely wondered anew exactly what he had seen through that innocent-looking window.

"Satisfied?" Neville said. McNeely nodded in response.

"I hate to bring this up," said Cummings, "but are there any contingencies for emergencies of any sort? I mean, what if one of us would get sick, or there were a fire, or . . . or we run out of gin," he added with a laugh.

"Mr. Cummings, you anticipate me brilliantly." Neville smiled. "I'll let Mr. Monckton demonstrate what would happen in that event."

Monckton led them back downstairs to the first floor once again. They stopped where the two wings met, between the billiard room and the sealed sunroom. There was a twenty-foot-wide horizontal wooden panel against the wall. Monckton turned a small knob in its center and it dropped down revealing four keyholes spaced six feet apart, and a telephone.

"This is your escape route," Monckton said in his cold, dispassionate voice. "If one of the party should be injured, the remaining four can open the doors and summon help by simultaneously turning keys in these locks. Another man and I will be at the cabin below, and we'll call you on this phone. The phone will be inoperable until that time."

"If, however," said Neville, "the keys are turned *before* the month is up, the three million dollars is forfeit, so we must all take very good care of one another."

"What's to insure," Wickstrom said, "that one of us wouldn't steal the others' keys and set the thing off by himself?"

"You'd need four very long arms for that, Mr. Wickstrom. Besides, the keys will be soldered on a chain around each of our necks before we start. The only way to get them all would be with a hacksaw."

"Or to remove the heads," McNeely said with a straight face. Wickstrom snorted a quiet laugh. The rest remained silent, though Cummings and Gabrielle smiled slightly.

"That hadn't occurred to me," replied Neville blandly, "but I suppose it would work." He turned toward the kitchen. "We'll examine our fire protection system now."

Crossing the wide white kitchen, he opened what looked like a closet door and started down a narrow flight of stairs. "Watch your step," he called up to them as they followed. They found themselves in a small cellar room with a concrete floor. Cans and jars of food lined the walls, and there was a large freezer in the corner purring steadily. "Part of our provisions," Neville said. "There are more in the pantry upstairs. This room, by the way, is called a cold cellar. Nothing to do with its temperature, really, just a local name." He passed through a door at the end of the room, leading them into a larger area. "We're under the Great Hall now. There are other cellars on the other side of those partitions under the wings. Back there"—he pointed toward the north end—"is the wine cellar. There are actually a few vintages left from my grandfather's time, most of them rare vinegar now, no doubt. But this is what I really want to show you."

At the southern end of the cellar was a thick steel door which Neville opened ponderously. "This is a fireproof ventilated chamber that we can use in the event of a fire. There's a month's worth of freeze-dried food and water for five, a chemical toilet, and cots. Mr. Monckton has assured me that the house above could be a roaring inferno, and the hottest we would feel would be ninety degrees."

"Reassuring," said Cummings. "Would we have to spend the entire time in here then?"

"If the fire were such that Mr. Monckton didn't notice it from the base of the mountain, yes."

"Jesus . . ." Wickstrom whispered.

"Mr. Wickstrom?"

"This is . . . this is just a little weird. I mean, are you serious about all this?"

Neville looked offended. "I'm dead serious, Mr. Wickstrom. But no one is forcing you into it."

"A million dollars packs an awful lot of force," Wickstrom answered.

"Please, gentlemen," said Renault, "why don't we return upstairs, where you three may decide among yourselves whether or not you wish to accept?"

The Nevilles, Monckton, and Renault led the three men back into the dining room. "Have another cup of coffee," Renault said kindly, "and when you've made your decision, simply come to the den. One more thing. It must be unanimous. You all stay, or no one stays."

"Well," said Cummings once the three were alone, "nothing like a final blockbuster. So what do you guys think? Go or stay?"

"I'd like to stay," answered McNeely.

"*I'd* like the million dollars," Wickstrom said, "but like I said, this is a really strange scene."

"He's eccentric, that's all," Cummings said comfortingly.

"No, Mr. Cummings, he's insane." McNeely sipped his coffee. The others looked at him questioningly.

"You don't mean that," said Cummings.

"I do. I've seen insane men in my profession. And David Neville is one. He's obsessed with this house. And with us."

Wickstrom started. "With us?"

"Haven't you noticed the sidelong glances he's been throwing each of us when he thinks we're not looking? It's like he's hungry."

"Oh, come on, McNeely!" Cummings rose and walked down the table toward the bigger man. "This place is goofy enough without your imagining things!" He paused. "Wait a minute—you'd stay anyway?"

"I intend to. Neville doesn't frighten me. I think I can handle him. If not me, then certainly the three of us together."

"Good. Then it's settled."

Wickstrom cleared his throat. "I haven't said I'll stay yet."

"Jesus Christ!" exploded Cummings. "What do you mean? There's no work here, no danger—the million's a gift along with a month's vacation!"

"I don't know," Wickstrom said, shaking his head. "There's something not right here."

"Mr. Wickstrom," McNeely said, "you're right. There *is* something strange about this house. I don't claim to either believe or disbelieve in the supernatural, but when I drove up this morning I saw an odd . . . manifestation." And he told them about the intense white light in the third floor room.

"Aw, the guy who parked the cars was right," scoffed Cummings. "It must have been the sun reflecting off something."

"It wasn't the sun," said McNeely. "But even if it *was* something paranormal, so what? Lights can't harm us. I don't know much about the supernatural, but I'm fairly sure that there's no history of a spirit ever physically harming anyone."

"And how about going crazy?" said Wickstrom. "What about that poet? And the banker?"

"*Stories*, Wickstrom! Ghost stories!" Cummings threw up his hands in disgust. "Don't tell me you're gonna piss away a million dollars apiece for us because you believe in spooks?''

Wickstrom's cheeks reddened. "I didn't say that," he growled. "I just wanted a chance to think, that's all."

"Okay, you've had your chance. Now what do you say?''

Wickstrom looked full into Cummings's eyes, hating him. "I'll stay."

Cummings nodded brusquely. "Good. That's settled then."

"One thing," McNeely said. "I think we ought to stay very closely in touch with each other through the stay here. If we see anything peculiar—from Neville or his wife or anything else—we share it with the others. No surprises. Agreed?''

The other two nodded. Then they joined the Nevilles, Monckton, and Renault in the den. Monckton and the girl turned sharply when they entered, Renault casually, Neville, thought McNeely, like a snake eyeing its prey.

"We're staying," Cummings said, appointing himself spokesman.

"How nice." Neville chuckled.

McNeely made himself smile. "You seem to have expected that, Mr. Neville."

"I think I read men fairly well," he said, a challenge in his tone. "But I'm glad you're all staying," he went on more heartily, rising to his feet. "Simon?''

Renault handed a document to each of the men. "Please read them and sign, gentlemen. I think you'll find nothing to disapprove of.''

The document spelled out all the conditions of which the three had been told, plus several more, one of which gave McNeely pause. "Could you be any more explicit," he asked, "about this fourteenth item, the part about performing any reasonable request that does not endanger us or others?''

"Not to be blunt, Mr. McNeely," said Neville, "but for the next month you three are servants, albeit highly paid ones. I don't intend to treat you like kitchen help, but my wife and I *do* intend to treat you as bodyguards. I think in that context the clause is clear enough, don't you? Are there any other questions? From any of you?"

There were not; the papers were quickly signed and went into Renault's briefcase. "Now the checks," Renault said. Wickstrom chose to keep his, while McNeely and Cummings both instructed Renault to deposit the sum in bank accounts.

"Your luggage has been taken to your rooms," said Neville. "Mr. McNeely, Mr. Wickstrom, you will be in the Bear and Whitetail Suites in the west wing. Mr. Cummings will be in the east wing in the Eagle Suite. I'm sure you'll find the accommodations satisfactory. Now, if you'll just give your wristwatches to M. Renault . . ." They took off the watches and saw them disappear into Renault's briefcase. "Say good-bye to time, gentlemen," Neville said, "to the sun and moon and all that, and say hello to the long night of The Pines, and whoever dwells within."

"For your sake, Mr. Neville," said McNeely, "I hope no one's oiled the doors. A little creaking would complement your dialogue."

A short time later Monckton and Renault said their farewells to the rest and left through the front door. Then the four men went to the locking unit at the end of the Great Hall and took out the keys that Monckton had just soldered around their necks. At Neville's instructions, they each placed a key in the proper hole and turned it.

The house shook as dozens of steel shutters simultaneously crashed down across windows and doors, closing the occupants off from the morning sun. All five stood rooted for a minute in the half-light, listening to the silence of the house. Wickstrom was the first to speak.

"You hear it?" he whispered.

"Yes." Gabrielle knew what he meant. "The wind. I hear the wind in the pines."

They all listened. Somehow through the thick steel, through the stone walls, they could hear the soft sighing of the needles as the cool fall wind danced among them.

"This is wrong," said Neville slowly, and McNeely heard more than ordinary concern in his voice. "It was supposed to be soundproof."

"Then listen," McNeely said. "If it's not, we should be able to hear the cars leaving."

They couldn't. Although they stood listening for a long time, all they heard was the rush of the wind.

Cummings laughed hollowly. "What are we all so up-tight for? It's just a . . . a natural phenomenon, that's all. Probably coming from above—the trees are higher than the roof. That's why we can hear the wind but not the cars. Right?"

Just then a new sound began. At first it was so low that no one was sure they really heard it, and they looked at one another for confirmation. Then it began to increase in volume and frequency, until the might of it made the stone floor shiver beneath their feet. It came in waves of low and high, evenly spaced at first, but finally the high pitch won out, shrieking about them with just an occasional dip to a lower timbre.

It sounded like the laughter of a god.

They pressed their hands over their ears, but the sound cut through their palms like a scythe through a tissue and they began to scream as one in an involuntary attempt to drown out with their own cries the laughter that tore through The Pines, shook their sanity, and rattled halfway down the mountain to where Whitey Monckton looked up from the road and stopped the car. Simon Renault stiffened in the seat beside him.

"Did you . . . ?" Renault began. "I thought I heard something just now. You heard it too?"

"Thunder," Monckton said, unable to keep the thrill out of his voice. "Thunder, Simon."

Renault leaned forward to where he could look up at the sky through the windshield and the screen of pines. "There are no clouds," he said. "The sky is blue."

"Distant thunder then," Monckton replied, thinking that the sky would not be blue in The Pines. He put the car in gear and continued down the road, faster now, as if to get beyond the range of the huge voice he had heard booming from above, and the small voice within him that perversely whispered a siren song to turn the car around and drive back up to the mountaintop, where the laughter was just beginning.

Part II

I readily believe that there are more invisible beings in the universe than visible. But who will declare to us the nature of all these, the rank, relationships, distinguishing characteristics, and qualities of each? What is it they do? Where is it they dwell?
—Thomas Burnet,
Archaeologiae Philosophicae

Chapter Three

"Someone is happy we're here." McNeely's voice sounded harsh against the sudden silence. The huge laughter had died away and the five of them were coming out of their individual protective postures, all sense of unity lost in the unexpected shock of the situation. Gabrielle Neville was expressionless, and McNeely wondered if she had gone into shock. Wickstrom and Cummings were both looking about fearfully, near-panic etched in the lines around their eyes and mouths.

David Neville was smiling. It was not the snide demeaning smile he'd worn before, but rather an expression of jubilation mixed with a religious wonder. "It's true," he said, and the echo of the words made McNeely realize how akin the Great Hall was to a temple. "Dear God in heaven, it's true. There *is* something here. . . ."

"Jesus," said Cummings, "I don't know how you did that, Mr. Neville, but it certainly scared the hell out of me."

"I didn't do anything."

"Come on now, it was a sound system or something, wasn't it? Big speakers, like that Sensurround thing, right?"

"There weren't any speakers," Neville replied, his face still enraptured as he looked up at the dark vaulted ceiling high above.

McNeely frowned. "Maybe not. But I'm sure you won't mind if we look for them just the same."

Finally Neville looked at them. He seemed slightly irritated at the way his attention was being drawn away from what he sought. "Suit yourself. Look all you want. You'll find no speakers, no radios, TVs, stereos—nothing to amplify sound. What we just heard was something that no man—no *living* man—produced."

"Why . . ." said Wickstrom, swallowing heavily, "why was it laughing?"

Gabrielle finally spoke, and McNeely realized that what he had taken to be dulled shock had simply been intense concentration. "Perhaps Mr. McNeely was right. Perhaps it *is* happy that we're here. *Why* it should be happy, that I can't say."

Cummings laughed nonchalantly. "Probably hasn't had a bite to eat in decades—and here are five tasty morsels locked in for the duration."

"That may be more true than you realize, Mr. Cummings," said Neville with no trace of humor.

"Speaking of a bite to eat," McNeely said, "I hate to bring us back to the harsh realities, but are there any set times when we should eat together?"

"You are a pragmatist, Mr. McNeely."

"My stomach will calm down in a few hours, Mr. Neville."

"Since there is no time here, you may eat whenever you feel hungry," said Neville. "The kitchen is loaded with prepared foods and, of course, a dishwasher. If you want to keep track of the days by the number of meals you eat, go ahead and try. I don't think you'll succeed. In fact, at six A.M. on October thirty-first, when those plates shoot up, I expect we'll all be greatly taken by surprise."

There was a silence, then Gabrielle spoke. "Well, it's been a . . . long morning. I suppose we'll all want to get settled in our rooms and make ourselves comfortable."

"I think I could stand a nap." Cummings smiled. "It was a long night's drive up here." The others murmured agreement.

"If there's anything you need—linens or towels—let me know. I'll show you where to find them."

"I'll be in the den, Gabrielle," Neville said as he disappeared down the hall.

Gabrielle showed the three men to their suites, then

returned downstairs. Neville was sitting in front of the cold fireplace in the den. "David?" Gabrielle called softly from the door. "Are you all right?"

He turned and smiled at her, all traces of cynicism gone. He looked, she thought, like the boy she had met in Paris. "I'm fine," he said, "better than ever now."

"It was real? The manifestation?"

"No doubt of it." He held out a hand to her. "Life after death, Gabrielle. It must be."

She ran to where he sat and embraced him. He held her and began to cry. "I never want to leave you," he said, his throat thick. "But if I can wait here, wait for you . . ."

Then she was crying, too, and they each became lost in the other's tears.

Neville's physician had directed him to the Sloan-Kettering clinic when the symptoms began. At first they had thought it was localized, could be contained. But further tests showed that metastasis had begun, and that David Neville's body was a breeding ground for carcinoma cells. That had been in January, and they'd predicted it would be a year before the pain would necessitate hospitalization.

Neville, naturally enough, hadn't wanted to die. It wasn't so much the fear of death itself that bothered him as the separation from that which he loved most—his wife. So he began to seek immortality. He found most religions vexing because of their inability to prove any existence after death, and considered cryogenics too undeveloped and hap-hazard to be relied on. It was not until May that he became interested in hauntings, and the more he read, the more he became convinced that there was some substantiality be-hind the legends, that there were places on the earth where consciousness could survive after the body that housed it had died. Shortly after that he came across the papers concerning The Pines and, always a gambler, decided to place his stake there.

"If other things live on there," he had told Gabrielle, "then why not me? If I can die there, perhaps I can live there as well, waiting for you, until we can be together forever."

It had not been unexpected. She had seen it coming

slowly, seen the idea take root and grow in his imagination long before he seriously made the suggestion. When he had, she'd been ready for it, and had agreed only on the condition that she could accompany him to the house and stay with him until he gained the knowledge he sought.

And now that knowledge was within reach, and they cried both in relief and in sorrow, and what heard them remained silent.

The suite was nice, very nice. It was like what they called railroad car apartments when Cummings was a kid—a long living room, bedroom, and bath joined end to end. The living room had a couch, three comfortable chairs, a desk, and a fireplace, as well as a tall shelf of books, mostly new hardcover best sellers of the past few years as well as some reference works and a few coffee table volumes. The bedroom was comfortable without being lavish, and the bathroom was the largest Cummings had ever seen—about ten by fifteen with a large clawfooted tub and a separate shower stall that he put to immediate use after he'd finished unpacking.

The warm water felt good, and he was happy to find that the shower head was a modern jet-spray job. As he luxuriated in its needle-sharpness, letting the steam wrap around him like a hot fluffy towel, he looked beyond the thirty-one days to the time when he would leave this place with a million dollars. It would be more than enough to pay back some old debts he owed. But beyond even that was the thought of David Neville. And David Neville's billions.

With a man like Neville behind him, there would be no limits to what he could do. And here he was, locked up with him for an entire month. He'd have to be careful, though—couldn't afford to be too pushy. Neville would spot that right away. Maybe he'd been born into his wealth, but it would still make him jaded, distrustful. Hell, he'd been enough of a smartass so far.

But a month was a long time, and Neville would probably be looking for someone to talk to, relate to, and Cummings as a businessman would certainly have more in common with him than McNeely or that jerk Wickstrom.

As long as he played it cool, maybe let Neville come to him . . . but the wife could be a problem. Neville seemed to be pretty tight with her, and Cummings hoped the month wouldn't turn into a haunted house honeymoon for the pair to the exclusion of himself. Maybe there was a way to slide the two of them apart.

Like Iago. The day Dan Percy had been let go, he'd come into Cummings's office and called him Iago. Far from insulting Cummings, he'd been flattered by it, and that night he'd read *Othello* for the first time since college. He especially liked the line, "And what's he then that says I play the villain . . ." It was true, he thought. It all depends on where you stand.

He turned off the spray and stepped onto the bathmat, drying his hair vigorously. The towel was over his face when he heard the voices, and he froze, suddenly afraid to pull it away and look at what was grunting and moaning in the next room.

The fear remained, but the curiosity made him slowly draw the towel away from his face until he could see into the bedroom through the bathroom door he was certain had been closed. A man and a woman lay naked on the bed. The man was kneeling over the woman, his hands locked around her throat. Though the man's back was to Cummings so that he could not see the face, he could see the woman's. It was horribly distorted, the eyes and tongue bulging like a dead animal's he had once seen on the highway. The skin of her face was a bluish-purple, and her hands swayed crazily in the air as if trying to beat the man away. The man's large penis was fully erect, towering over the woman's breasts and glistening wetly, stiffening with each pulse of the man's fingers on the woman's neck.

"No!" shouted Cummings, involuntarily rushing forward, ready to push the man off the whimpering victim. But instead, he found himself lying sprawled across the empty bed. Panicked, he threw himself onto the floor and backed away into the corner as though the bed held a rabid grizzly.

What happened? he thought over and over again. They could not have been ghosts—they had been too real. He hadn't been able to see through them, they hadn't been wispy and insubstantial—they had been two living *people* on his bed who had simply vanished, turned off like a light bulb.

What happened?

When he stopped trembling, he stood up and looked at the bed. Except for the rumpling of the bedclothes he himself had caused, there were no other marks. No sweat, no semen, no blood. It was as though the man and the woman had never been.

Chapter Four

"Hello?" Wickstrom called softly. "Anyone there?"

He'd showered and tried to take a nap, but had been unsuccessful. Every time he'd drift off to sleep, the memory of that huge voice that had filled the house would come surging back into his mind. So he'd gotten up, dressed, and started to explore. The gym on the third floor was his first stop, and he'd been happy to find a Nautilus system as well as free weights, two benches, and a stationary bike. Maybe later today he'd have a little workout.

Later today. He smiled and shook his head, wondering what the hell later today meant. The lack of a clock was going to be harder to get used to than the ghosts, if ghosts there were. He was damned if he could come up with any logical explanation for what had happened in the Great Hall. At first he'd thought, like Cummings, that it had been a trick with hidden speakers. But after he'd seen Neville's face, he'd known that if it were a trick, even Neville wasn't in on it.

Wickstrom stepped into the hall again and walked toward the center of the building, planning to visit the third floor lounge next. He stopped, though, at the railing overlooking the Great Hall three floors below. The room was impressive, even with the steel shutters covering the exquisite stained glass. He noticed the balconies then, running the length of both sides of the room. There were a pair on the second floor, too, and he wondered about their pur-

pose. They were narrow, two feet wide, and they led
nowhere, only down the sides of the hall.

Ornamentation perhaps, he thought, remembering the
nearly hidden clerestory walks at St. Patrick's Cathedral,
where his mother had taken him for mass once a year
instead of St. Anthony's, their usual parish church. He
remembered wanting to find some hidden stairs to lead
him out on those stones in the shadows under the arches,
where he could look down and see everyone praying and
singing, never suspecting that he watched them from above.
It would be, he'd thought, like God felt.

The memory took him then, and he walked slowly and
carefully out upon the left walkway. The railing was low
and insubstantial, and he feared to put his weight on it. At
the center of the walk he paused and looked down. All the
illumination was from below, and he wondered how he
must look. Like a ghost, he thought, a ghost like the one
he imagined stalking the clerestory walkway of the
cathedral—a cowled monk, holding a guttering candle,
extending a clutching hand . . .

"Exploring?"

The nearness of the voice surprised him, and as he spun
toward it, he lost his balance, tottering on the narrow
walkway. He lurched back from the rail and struck the
wall with an impact that sent him to the floor of the
balcony. McNeely was by his side in an instant.

"My God, are you all right? I'm sorry—I thought you
saw me!"

"Saw you?" Wickstrom muttered, rubbing his head
where it had hit the wall. "I didn't see you at all. Just
heard your voice like you were right next to me . . ."

"I thought I saw you nod at me. At any rate, I
apologize. Stupid thing to do to startle someone out on this
. . . precipice. Are you okay?"

Wickstrom nodded. "Yeah. Just too jumpy, I guess.
But honest to Pete, I thought somebody was right beside
me."

McNeely frowned for a moment. "Let's try something.
You stay here." He edged past Wickstrom and walked all
the way to the southern end of the building. Then he
turned and spoke. "Can you hear me?"

It was only a whisper, but Wickstrom heard it as clearly as if McNeely were a foot away. "Yes," Wickstrom whispered back. "Perfectly."

McNeely nodded, and Wickstrom could see that he was smiling as he rejoined him. "A whispering gallery. I can see this place is going to be full of surprises."

"How does it work?"

McNeely shrugged. "Beats me. But with this kind of acoustics it's no wonder that whatever it was was so loud this morning."

"Is it still morning?" Wickstrom asked.

"You've got me. I've heard of those internal clocks some people have, but it's something I've envied rather than possessed. I *suspect* it's around eleven or so, though I wouldn't wager any money on it."

"Why not? We're millionaires."

"We're millionaires the day we get out of here and not before." He gestured toward the third floor wings. "Let's get back on terra firma, eh?" The suggestion suited Wickstrom, and together they left the balcony. "As I said before," said McNeely, "exploring a bit?"

Wickstrom nodded. "The gym looks good. I was just going to check the lounge."

"Want some company?"

"Love some. This place gives me the creeps."

"I know what you mean," McNeely said. "When I was putting my things away, I had the craziest notion that I was being watched."

"You probably were. I'd expect Neville to have hidden cameras in each room."

"He doesn't."

"He . . ."

"I looked. In my room at least."

"Oh." Wickstrom nodded admiringly.

"You were a policeman. Ever get into electronic surveillance?"

"Had a class in it, but I was never involved firsthand."

"Here we are," said McNeely, opening the door of the lounge. "At least the lights work. Now, just give me a second." Wickstrom watched while McNeely circled the room, lifting, peering, tapping in a series of fluid motions.

After two minutes he stopped and smiled. "If there's a bug in here, it's a damned small one. Well, what'll you have? The bar's well stocked, as promised."

"Any beer?"

"Let's see." McNeely opened the small refrigerator. "Bass ale?"

"Fine."

"Me too." He opened the bottles and passed one to Wickstrom. "Here's to an interesting month . . . what's your first name?"

"Kelly."

"Kelly. Mine's George. To you, Kelly." He took a large sip while Wickstrom drained half his bottle.

"What, uh, what line of work are you in, George?"

"I *was* a soldier. Now I'm in the line of work you're in." They both grinned.

"Army?" Wickstrom asked. "Marines?"

McNeely held up a hand. "Stop right there. Marines," he nodded.

"In 'Nam?"

"Yes. You there?"

Wickstrom nodded. "Just a grunt. Sixty-six to eight, right out of school."

"See much action?"

"Some."

Wickstrom's face told McNeely he didn't want to elaborate, so he let it go. "It was a hell of a war," he said. "I was there on and off the whole time. Saw a lot of good people die."

They were both silent for a moment, and McNeely wondered if he should tell Wickstrom what he did for a living after the war had ended. He was surprised to discover that he liked the younger man a great deal. Wickstrom reminded him of Jeff in a way, and as McNeely realized that, he drew back emotionally. Things were going to be hairy enough without something like that to complicate matters. He wondered how Jeff was going to deal with this absence. After south, he'd promised that it would be the last. No more long trips, no four- and five-month sojourns to countries Jeff had never heard of. But he knew he couldn't have kept the promise. He loved Jeff, but he loved war more.

Or was love the proper word? At times he thought the motives for war were absurd, insane. But placing that aside, forgetting that there was (and was there ever?) a right side and a wrong side, war was the only thing that made him feel alive and useful. That gut-grabbing tension of not knowing if you were going to finish the day alive was like a drug to McNeely. He needed it, and needed it enough to go after it over and over and over again, long after "noble" wars only existed in veterans' feeble minds.

"So what did you do afterward?"

McNeely looked into the open honest face and told the truth. "I became a merc. A mercenary soldier."

"Jesus. I bet you have stories."

McNeely smiled. "Hardly. There's a lot more bullshit to wade through is about the only difference."

"Where've you been?"

"Pardon? Oh, I get you. Mostly south. South America, Central America. Africa, of course. Another beer?"

Wickstrom drained the bottle and nodded.

"You shoot pool?" McNeely asked.

"As long as it's not for money."

"Let's have our next beers in the billiard room. Maybe we'll put a couple of bottle rings on Neville's table, eh?"

Wickstrom laughed. "Sounds good, George." And together they walked downstairs.

Wickstrom felt better, a hell of a lot better. He'd been afraid that the month in The Pines was going to be unpleasant at best. The Nevilles certainly weren't his type, though he thought that perhaps the wife had smiled at him a bit too warmly; Cummings was a shit—he'd found that out almost immediately; and at first McNeely had seemed very cold and distant, so he'd had little hope of forming a friendship to see him through the stay.

But now it seemed he'd found, if not a friend, at least a very congenial acquaintance who, as it turned out, could teach him a considerable amount about pool.

"Do you play much?" asked McNeely after winning the third straight game of eight ball.

Wickstrom shook his head. "I did when I was a kid. Being a cop didn't give me much time for it. Pretty rusty, I'm afraid."

"A month of practice should pick you up." McNeely swung his head back and forth as if trying to get his bearings. "Do you remember which way the rest rooms were on this floor? The ale seems to have gotten to me."

"Either end, I think."

"I'll find it. You can rack them for another game if you want."

"Okay, I'd like that." Left alone, Wickstrom racked the balls and took his cue to the cue rack, thinking that a shorter one might help his aim. Finding one, he sat in a Morris chair in a corner away from the lamp over the pool table and relaxed for a moment. He wondered idly what time it was and closed his eyes.

He hadn't realized he was so tired. Hovering between wakefulness and sleep, the silence seemed to embrace him, drawing him into a vast warmth that caressed his body luxuriously, until he surrendered to it and let himself drift into the comforting restful darkness.

Suddenly he was poleaxed by whiteness.

It came upon his consciousness with the force of a thousand photo-floodlights jabbing into his eyes, and his whole body lurched with the impact. He blinked wildly, trying to make his fire-bleached pupils create form out of the landscape of white that held him in thrall, but the effort was useless. There was only whiteness.

Then the cold came. It was as though the heavy sweater and wool slacks he wore had vanished, as though a chill beyond imagining ate through his flesh and muscle to freeze the bones beneath. Any second they would splinter like icicles. He was lost in a frozen waste, he who had lived surrounded by people all his life in the honeycomb of New York. There was no one around him now, nothing but coldness and whiteness stretching away forever and ever and . . .

He screamed. And a buffeting wind hit his face with breathtaking fury. It seemed to be calling something that sounded like his name. Through the rush and blast of terror that battered his mind, he could hear it, far away and faint.

Tekeli-li . . . Tekeli-li . . .

Clearer now . . .

Tekeli-li! TEKELI-LI!

KELLY! KELLY!

Wickstrom's eyes jerked open.

"Kelly!" McNeely called again, driving short sharp slaps onto his pale cheeks. Wickstrom's hand sprang up and grabbed McNeely's wrist. McNeely tensed as if about to pull away, but instead, he smiled and ignored the pressure of Wickstrom's iron grip. "You've been dreaming."

Wickstrom looked at him, not recognizing McNeely at first. When he did, he let his grip relax and wiped beads of sweat from his forehead and beneath his eyes.

"It must have been a beauty," said McNeely.

Wickstrom shook his head dully. "It . . ." The words locked in his throat and he cleared it roughly. "It was horrible."

"I didn't know if you were going to come out of it or not. I called your name a couple of times but couldn't wake you."

"Yeah. Yeah. I heard you, but it sounded like something else in the dream," and he told McNeely all he could remember.

"Tekeli-li," McNeely repeated thoughtfully. "That's from Poe. *Arthur Gordon Pym.*"

"About . . . about the cannibals?" Wickstrom's face was strained, reaching for a memory.

"Yes," McNeely nodded. "A sea voyage. There's cannibalism among the survivors of a wreck. You've read *Pym*?"

"Long ago. Oh, Christ, it must have been high school. *Junior* high. I remember though. I haven't thought about that in years. That last part . . . they're in the Arctic . . ."

"Antarctic, I think."

"Yeah, okay. Anyway, it's all white . . . and those *birds*—yeah, the *birds* are saying that Tekeli-li thing, and I remember it scared the shit out of me because I thought—" He paused.

"You thought they were calling your name."

Wickstrom looked up and nodded. The fear was still in his eyes. "And that thing," he said softly.

"Thing?"

"The big thing that they saw at the very end. The big white thing that stood up in front of them."

"Yes?"

"You never knew what it was. Because the story stopped there. With that white thing in front of them." Wickstrom shuddered and hugged himself. "I dreamed about that thing for weeks. If you hadn't woken me up, I think I would've dreamed about it again." He looked at McNeely. "And I think I would have known what it was this time."

"Forget it," McNeely said more heartily than he felt. "Frosty the Snowman, probably. It's only natural that this place'll work on our heads a little. Give us some frights we'd forgotten about. But even if it can do that, that's *all* it can do." He paused, thinking. "Do open spaces bother you?"

"Hah. Damn right they do. I guess that's a city boy for you. 'Nam really got to me. If I wasn't hunkered down in a hole, I was miserable. I just felt so fucking vulnerable all the time."

"I know what you mean. I feel the same way about enclosed spaces."

As soon as he said it, McNeely wondered what the hell he was doing. That was one of the things he never told anyone, not even Jeff. Reveal your weaknesses and people can use them against you. Yet he'd blurted it out like a California executive dripping all over an analyst's couch. Why?

"You're kidding," said Wickstrom. "How in hell can you stand being locked up in this place?"

"I'm not locked up," said McNeely with a smile, hoping that Wickstrom would think he *had* been kidding. "Like I told our host, all I have to do to get out is to cut off everyone else's heads." He laughed, and Wickstrom laughed with him.

"Jesus, I hope it doesn't come to that," Wickstrom said, rising and chalking his cue.

Jesus, thought McNeely, *I hope it doesn't either.*

*   *   *

Gabrielle was sleeping. Neville watched her small breasts rise and fall beneath the thin coverlet. Her breathing was slow and easy, and he knew she would sleep for a long time if she was not disturbed. He let his hand rest for a moment on the soft flatness of her stomach, and then he rose quietly from her side. At another time he might have caressed her until she stirred from her sleep, and then made love to her, but that was before a great many things had occurred, and he wondered if before the month was up he might make love to her once again.

As he stood watching her, his hand went down to touch himself. There was no response. He bit back tears and walked through the living room of their suite into the hall.

It seemed alive.

And life was what he needed. For so long now his thoughts had been on death. Every waking moment it walked with him, a dark shadow at his side. Only in dreams could he escape its companionship. His dreams, ever since he had known of his illness and its final and fatal denouement, had been clear and clean and happy, and so he slept more and more, changing his schedule from seven hours a night to ten or more, with frequent naps in the afternoons. It was the only way to relax his churning mind, give ease to his sympathetic body. He hoped he would die in the middle of a dream so that it would never end, and he would never have to face the parting.

But now, standing in the hall of The Pines, he could forget death. For whatever was there had transcended it, beaten it down, shown it in its reality as a miserable faker. *Death be not proud,* he thought, and for the first time he meant it. It became more than Donne's sacred rationalization—now it was a battle cry that his mind and body, crazed and sane cells alike, shrieked in silent triumph through The Pines.

"I will beat you," he said to the gray thing at his shoulder. "They will show me how."

He could see the shadow now, and he laughed at the look of wary concern in its dull eyes, the unaccustomed frown that banished its usual death's-head grin. It seemed to shrink away from him, as if *it* were at last afraid, scorned by his mockery.

"Oh, no," he whispered to it. "Stay with me. You've frightened *me* long enough. *Death, thou shalt die!*" he quoted, beckoning to it to follow him, follow and learn.

He passed down the hall to the central stairway and walked downstairs, listening all the while. Slowly it dawned on him that it was not the whispering of the trees outside they had heard when the doors and windows had been sealed, but instead, the house itself and its residents whispering to them. He could hear it now, and could even make out, if not words, at least individual syllables. Were they trying to talk to him? Trying to tell him how to join them in immortality?

There would be time enough. Time to listen and learn to understand.

The fireplace in the Great Hall had gone cold, and Neville felt a sudden hunger gnaw at him. He'd lost his appetite in the past few weeks, whether from the disease or his fear or the excitement of coming to The Pines he could not say, so the insistent growling of his stomach came as a surprise. He walked into the kitchen, intrigued with the idea of fixing himself a meal for the first time in years, and found Seth Cummings sitting at the table, eating a chicken sandwich and a small green salad.

"Well, Mr. Neville." He smiled, leaping to his feet. "Felt a little hungry. I guess we have to go by our own clocks now, right?"

"I suppose so." Neville was far from happy to find Cummings there, but his hunger drove away his distaste for the man's company.

"Can I get you anything?" Cummings asked.

"No thanks. I'll manage." Neville opened one of the tall cupboards. Shelves full of brightly colored cans towered to the ceiling. Soups, spaghetti, stews, tinned meats, smoked oysters were all plentiful.

"There's a lot in the freezer if you don't feel like canned. And fresh meat for sandwiches in the fridge. The chicken's great. Fresh fruit and vegetables too." Cummings indicated his salad. "Might as well eat them up before they go bad on us, huh?"

Neville made himself a chicken sandwich and selected a piece of fruit from the refrigerator bin.

"Do you want any milk?" Cummings asked, holding up the bottle.

"No thank you. I don't like milk."

"Me neither, but with my stomach, what can you do?"

Cummings's sandwich was gone, his glass nearly empty. Neville wondered why he didn't finish and leave. He didn't *want* to mingle with these men, and the sooner they knew that, the better. They were here for a purpose beyond their knowing, and he would deal with them when he was ready. But until that time he didn't want to know them any better than he knew them now. "Are you finished?" he said dryly, hoping Cummings would take the hint.

"Oh. Yeah. I am. It's just that . . . well, it's nice to be able to talk to someone. This place is pretty lonely."

"Really," Neville said, taking a bite of sandwich and looking away from Cummings.

"There's . . . another thing." Something in Cummings's voice made Neville look up. "I'm fairly sure—I think I saw a ghost." He sounded embarrassed.

"A ghost?"

"*Two* ghosts really."

"Where was this?"

The intensity with which Neville asked the question startled Cummings. "Why, my room. My bedroom." Cummings told exactly what he had seen. The effect on Neville was amazing. His half-smiling mouth hung open, and his eyes widened like a child entranced by a new bedtime tale.

"And you really *saw* it? No dream, no hallucination?"

"It was no dream. And I've never had a hallucination in my life. I saw it all right, whatever it was. Do you want to go up there with me?"

Neville started to say yes, but stopped. Cummings seemed almost too eager. How did he know he was telling the truth? And even if he was, did he want to meet these ghosts Cummings had described, who rutted and strangled and vanished?

No. This house was *full* of ghosts. He knew it. And he would wait until they sensed his need and showed themselves to him. There was time enough for that.

"No, Mr. Cummings. Thank you for the invitation."

It was obvious from Neville's tone that he didn't wish to go *anywhere* with Cummings, and the affront did not go unnoticed. *You prick,* Cummings swore inside. *Okay, prick, play your game. I'll find you out yet. Find what makes you tick.* But he said only, "I don't blame you. It wasn't a pleasant sight."

Neville rose and left the room without saying a word. Cummings watched him go. "Nice talking to you too," he said quietly to the empty kitchen. "Better be nice to me, Mr. Neville. I'm going to be the only friend you've got."

He started to finish his milk, but paused. There was something about the color of it that made him ill at ease.

He poured it down the drain.

Time passed, though none of them could say how much. McNeely tried to keep track of it by counting both his sleeps and his meals. So far the sleeps numbered four, the meals seven. But he suspected that he'd been sleeping to pass the time, and that only three, maybe even two calendar days had gone by. During that time he'd played countless games of pool with Kelly Wickstrom, had had two good workouts in the gym, and had explored the library, which he happily found stocked with old and new fiction and nonfiction alike. He had seen nothing out of the ordinary. On the contrary, his surroundings seemed almost pleasant, a reaction which came as a surprise, considering his usually claustrophobic response to being confined. He'd run into Cummings twice, once in the kitchen, where they cooked a steak together, and once in the gym.

Cummings, McNeely learned, was a fitness freak, having a workout shortly after every second meal, regardless of his sleep pattern. He had a gymnasium body, functional, good-looking, confident in its motions. But McNeely wondered if it would bear up to any real exertion. He'd always trusted muscles shaped by working rather than those sculpted twenty minutes a day in a gym. On his own body he could count on his legs because he used them most in his work. Then his back and stomach, and finally his arms and wrists. McNeely wasn't musclebound by any means, but the muscles were there like thin bunched wires beneath the burnished skin, and he knew he could depend on them.

Cummings seemed friendly enough both times McNeely had met him, but there was a deceit about the man that would not let McNeely feel at ease. It was as if he were holding something back. Cummings had talked of trivialities, never about the house or the strangeness of the situation. Such total indifference had to be studied. Any mention of the house or of ghosts that McNeely made was carefully sidestepped, and when McNeely asked Cummings if he'd run into Neville at all, he'd thought for a moment too long before he answered no. Still, he'd been outwardly pleasant, and it was that which irritated McNeely the most. Better outright hostility than a man not to be trusted as either friend or enemy.

McNeely hadn't seen Neville once. It struck him as peculiar, since The Pines wasn't so big that people could avoid each other for days on end—unless, of course, Neville planned it that way, staying in his suite while the others were about, coming out only when they were sleeping, if indeed there was any way he could tell that. Coincidence probably. He'd meet him again sooner or later. Still, it seemed odd.

He pushed open the library door and entered the room. The lights were on, as they were in almost every room, in a futile effort to recreate the total lighting of day. He walked to the bookcase on the far wall, chose a volume by Wodehouse, and turned around. It was then that he saw he was not alone in the room.

At first the phantoms of his mind identified the occupant of the chair as one of the hordes of spirits rumored to haunt The Pines, and he felt in one instant as if his heart had been trapped in a cage of frigid steel. But in the next second he saw that it was only Gabrielle Neville, her head cocked to the side in an attitude of sleep, a book open on her lap. He gave a half-gasp, half-laugh of relief that in the heavy silence was enough to wake her. Her eyelids fluttered, and she gave a little cry of alarm.

"Oh!" she said in embarrassment as she recognized him. "Oh, Mr. McNeely, I'm sorry, you startled me!"

"That makes two of us." McNeely smiled. "I turned

around and saw you and thought . . ." He spread his hands.

"That I was a ghost?" she asked. "Sorry to disappoint you."

"Not at all disappointed. Happy to do without." He sat in a chair near hers.

"How do you like your vacation so far?" she said.

McNeely shrugged. "A bit dull. Thank God for the billiard room. Kelly and I've been keeping it busy. And how are you and Mr. Neville? Are you finding whatever you're looking for?"

She smiled tensely. "People look for different things, Mr. McNeely."

"All right then. You. How are you doing in your *spectral* search?"

"Not very well, I'm afraid. I've heard and seen nothing extraordinary since that first . . . time."

"You were going to say *day*."

"Yes. I was. I hate not knowing *when* things are."

"I'm the same way. It's very disorienting. And how is Mr. Neville?"

She smiled again, but McNeely couldn't read it at all. "He's . . . in his element, I believe. Utterly entranced by the place. Hardly sleeps at all."

"I'd been thinking it odd I hadn't run into one of you before this."

"Oh, I've been spending a lot of time in the suite reading. And I paint, and that's kept me busy."

"Really? Where do you work?"

"In the playroom on the third floor front. It's quite large, and the walls are white, so it's the brightest room in the house."

"Too bad the sun room's not open. Northern exposure, natural light . . . what do you paint?"

"Subject matter?" She laughed. "Landscapes, but that's rather difficult in here. I've been doing still lifes."

"Of what? Fresh fruit? Frozen meat pies? I've noticed fresh cut flowers aren't too plentiful in here."

"Books," she said.

"Pardon?"

"Still lifes of books." She smiled. "I know it must

sound odd, but I love old bound books—the leathers, the binding cloths. It's a real challenge to get the colors right, the way the light shines off that old burnished leather.''

"Like painting saddles, eh?"

"You're mocking me."

"Not at all. Didn't William Harnett paint books? And N. A. Brooks?"

Her eyebrows rose. "Pretty obscure. You know your art."

"A little. What books did you choose for your subject matter?"

"The astronomical notebooks David mentioned to you. The binding is exquisite, a dark blue crushed morocco with a rich chestnut spine. Gold stamping in Latin. And huge. Double quarto size. I put them with a sextant and celestial globe for the grouping."

"What media?"

"Oils. I'm afraid I'm a traditionalist. I'm doing some sketches first to get the lighting."

"I'd love to see them."

"I'd like to show them to you, Mr. McNeely."

"*George*, please. But never fear, I'll still call you Mrs. Neville."

She laughed gaily. "That's not necessary."

"What then? Gaby?"

"Gaby?" she cried. "I've never been called that in my life!"

McNeely laughed. "I'm afraid that must be an American nickname. Gabrielle?"

"Perfect," she said.

"Well, I won't disturb you anymore." McNeely stood up. "Perhaps I'll stop by the playroom sometime to see if you're in, all right?"

"I'll look forward to it, George."

He smiled and left the room, unaware, for all his self-professed knowledge of his fellow man, of the true nature of Gabrielle Neville's feelings toward him.

The soldier, she thought. *This one is the soldier.*

A soldier who knows art, who knows books . . . who knows women as well. She could tell by the eyes. They

were a lover's eyes, a courtier's eyes. Yes, that was it, a
courtier. A noble soldier of the Renaissance with his graying
beard and hair, and his cool cool gray eyes. That straight
sharp nose—Roman of course. And even his mouth. It
would be so grim in its thinness in battle, but soft and
gentle with a woman. A renaissance man.

David had been like that once.

It had all been so easy then. Though they'd both been
twenty years old, they'd really been children. Her father
had told her often that the children of the rich stay children
forever, that it was both their blessing and their curse. And
so she and David had been, even years into their marriage,
the bright shining children of money, untouched by falls of
fortune. Nothing less than the total collapse of the world's
economy could have brought the wolf to their gilded door.
So they had lived in their private world like Gatsby and
Daisy, had they lived happily ever after. *Gatsby* was her
favorite book, except for the ending. "They should've
been together," she'd said to David. "It should have
worked for them," and then she would go back and reread
the book with wary fascination, like a hypochondriac looking for the next symptom that could shorten her life.

The first trial had come when she wanted a baby. After
a year of trying, both had taken tests, the results of which
showed that David had an impossibly low sperm count.
Fertilization *in utero* was attempted, but proved unsuccessful. And then David started having his "problems." It was
only on rare occasions that he was able to produce an
erection, and even then he could not sustain it for more
than a minute or so. Though they still slept together, the
two of them had not made love in over a year, and any
hope Gabrielle had had of bearing David's child was gone.

The difficulties had first appeared a few years before
David's illness had been diagnosed, and the doctors assured them that it was psychological rather than physical,
stemming from David's connection between sperm count
and masculinity. But Gabrielle knew how much deeper it
went. He had told her one night after an unsatisfying
attempt at lovemaking.

"Sometimes," he had said, "I don't feel like a man at
all. But like a boy. A little boy."

That was all. He had gotten up then and left the room. But as she lay there and thought about it, she had realized that his manhood was in question in his own mind because he had never done anything to win it. And at last she knew what curse was upon the children of the rich.

From that night on she had tried to bolster his ego, to praise his slightest accomplishment, but he saw all too easily what she was trying to do, and he resented it. Finally she ceased her efforts and treated him as she had previously.

When, much later, he'd suggested the experiment in The Pines, he had seemed quite honest about his motivations. "Two reasons, Gabrielle," he had said to her. "The first is to find if life can exist after death. The second . . . is to prove something to myself by facing . . . whatever's there."

"Prove what?" she'd asked.

"I have *never*," he had answered sadly, "never in my whole life done a thing that any other man couldn't have done with my background and my money."

"The tennis tournaments," she had offered feebly, "the sailing, the . . ."

He laughed bitterly. "With my teachers, an ape could've done as well."

It was the approach of death, she knew, that had wrought this final change in him. She had hoped that here, in The Pines, he might see that there *was* no conflict in which he was expected to take up arms, that nine out of ten people spend their whole lives without once being called upon to prove themselves. To Gabrielle, it was not a world of high drama, but a world in which people should live as finely as possible and find as much happiness as they could before life ended.

But the instant that voice had come booming out of the silence, as soon as David's eyes had shone with that fanatical light, she knew she had lost him. He would sit in the living room of their suite, staring for hours on end at the logs snapping and flaring in the fireplace. When she asked him if he wanted to join her for a meal, he would decline, saying he wasn't hungry, and when she came back he would be gone. Twice she had gone looking for him, and had found him once in the study, where he brusquely asked what she wanted, and another time she had not been able to find him at all.

She knew that he would die here. He was half dead already.

Dead from the waist down.

She bit her lip at the cruelty of the thought, and looked up in surprise, as if someone else in the room had spoken such vicious slander. But the room was empty.

You bastard.

Where was the voice coming from?

David, you self-righteous, self-pitying bastard . . .

It was *hers*, though she was not speaking. Yet so perfect was the mimicry that she pressed her hands to her mouth to make certain her lips were not open, her tongue was not forming the words that she heard her own voice speak.

Never a thought for me in all your brow-beating.

Never a thought about my needs.

A woman's needs.

Or maybe bastard's the wrong word.

Maybe it's fairy.

Yes, fairy, faggot, gay, cocksucker.

You deserved what I did to you.

I'm glad I slept with Martin! Yes that's right glad and his cock was so hard and it filled me filled me like yours never did never not even when you were Mister Hotshit at the Sorbonne and we used to get it on in that apartment of yours you were at your best then but you could never touch Martin and I'm sorry I killed his baby it was a man's baby and I hope you see it when you die and I hope you look at it and it opens its mouth and laughs at you and says Martin *was my father and Gabrielle my mother and you are* NOTHING *you limp-dick billionaire rotting corpse!*

Then she screamed. Screamed at the horror of the words and the intensity with which she'd felt them, as if her throat and stomach had spewed forth bile that had been festering inside her for years.

Chapter Five

As David Neville stalked the ghosts he thought haunted The Pines, so Seth Cummings stalked David Neville. Maybe Neville *was* insane, as McNeely had thought, but sane or not, to Cummings he exuded power, and Cummings was drawn to power like a moth to a candle. He could *help* Neville; he knew he could. He was bright, aggressive— hell, hadn't he been in trade for years, and in a company second only to Neville's own? He had a lot to offer, that was for damned sure.

All he needed was the opportunity.

All he needed was to find Neville, and the cellar was the only place he hadn't looked.

Since he'd run into him in the kitchen, two sleeps had passed. It had been hard to doze off on that bed where he had seen the man and woman, so he'd slept on the sofa in the suite's living room, and had seen no more manifestations. He hadn't seen Neville either, though he'd looked nearly everywhere. He hadn't really expected to find him in the cellar, so it surprised him when he heard a sound coming from what Neville had called the fire chamber. It was a soft shuffling, and he thought that perhaps Neville was inside checking provisions.

But as he crossed the large central room toward the fire chamber, he noticed that although its door was ajar, there was no light on inside.

The prick. Heard me coming and turned it off. He won't get away that easy.

"Mr. Neville? Hello! You in there?"

The shuffling continued. It was odd. If Neville had wanted to remain unfound, wouldn't he have been quieter? Wouldn't there in fact be no sound at all?

"Mr. Neville?" *Scaring me off?*

Shuffling. So soft in there in the dark.

"Hey? Who's in there?"

Cummings suddenly wished there was more light in the cellar than that of the sixty-watt bulb that glowed thirty feet behind him, throwing his own small shadow partially on the steel door and partially on the dark wedge where the door was open.

My shadow's in there. The thought was absurd and he recognized it as such, but he moved so that his shadow was now totally on the outside wall.

The shuffling grew louder.

"Wickstrom?"

Was the door moving?

"McNeely?"

Moving further open?

"Hey?"

The only sound was the shuffling. And the pounding of his heart.

"Hey . . ."

The door slammed shut with a crash of metal on metal, and Cummings turned and ran, ran across the stone floor, tripping on the step up into the cold cellar, stumbling up the stairs to the kitchen, once more an eight-year-old boy running home through the dark before the things that lived in the shacks caught him and dragged him behind those worn doors and shattered windows to do what those things always do to little boys, and as he burst into the clean bright fluorescent kitchen, it was as if his mother were there smiling, waiting for his return from the night.

He fell into a chair and sat there panting, but then he turned and saw the cellar door still open. He jumped up and pressed it closed, the sound of the clicking latch like a comforting litany.

Even then he didn't feel safe, so he left the kitchen, looking for company. Anyone would do, even Wickstrom. He found the billiard room empty, and moved on to the den. There was no one there either, and the darkly wooded walls gave him no comfort. The study was next, and there at last he found David Neville, sitting and staring mindlessly at a Hudson River landscape hung near the door.

"I was looking for you," Cummings said with relief. He did not choose his words; they simply came.

Neville jerked his eyes away from the painting. "For what?"

"I . . . was in the cellar."

"What the hell . . ."

"I heard something . . . something in the fire chamber."

"What were you doing down there?"

"Looking for you."

"Why, for Christ's sake?"

"I . . . I . . ." He realized he'd been babbling like a frightened child. But he was in too far now. "I wanted to talk to you."

"About what?" It was not a question. It was a snarl.

Cummings started to answer, then laughed and shrugged. "Business."

"Business."

"I think that . . ." This was not *right*, not the way to do it! Yet he could not stop. It had been bottled up too long. "I think I could . . . would be good for you, for your business. I know shipping, I know import-export . . ."

Neville gave an astonished laugh, as if Cummings had just told an outrageously funny and filthy joke in church. Though he smiled broadly, his tone was tight, angry. "You asshole. You're asking me for a job? A *job*?"

"I thought . . ."

"You're getting a million dollars, and you want more? I don't even *hire* people! I don't even hire the people who hire people!" He shook his head in disbelief. "What the fuck do you *want*?"

"I . . ."

"You stay away from me, Cummings." There was no humor at all now, only bile. "You stay out of this study, and if you see me, you walk the other way, or there's no million for you, boy. You're a shit, and I don't like you and I don't like your kind. I know why Stahr fired you and

I know what a mean little bastard you are and that's exactly why—''

"That was a lie!" Cummings exploded. "That was bullshit!"

"I've seen the pictures!" yelled Neville. "And don't ever interrupt me! I said that's exactly why I wanted you here—*because* you're a mean little bastard and—"

"You don't—"

"And because ghosts won't scare you!"

The words rang in the room like the clanging of the cellar door.

"Will they, Cummings?"

Cummings couldn't speak, could only look at Neville's calm eyes that had been so wild only a moment before. Finally the words came. "What do *you* want? What do you really want from me?"

"Not much," Neville said softly. "Just to see you scared shitless. Maybe to even see you cry." He chuckled. "Yes. I want to see you cry, Cummings. How about it?"

Cummings stirred then, clenching his jaw so that the muscles stood out starkly.

"Cry, Cummings. Cry. And I'll give you a letter of reference. Hmm?"

"You're crazy." He could hear his voice trembling and hated himself for it.

"Crazy, huh? Fine. At least I'm not an asshole. Now, get out of this room. You're not to come in here again. That's one of my 'reasonable requests.' Got it?"

It's too late was all that Cummings could think. *I've blown it.* But the *million*—the million would still be his. They'd signed the papers, so Neville could go and . . .

"Fuck you, Neville."

Neville winced, and his smile faded momentarily as if a cloud had passed over a lake at noon.

"Who the fuck do you think you are?" Cummings went on.

"Your employer, for—"

Cummings laughed. "My employer? Sure. But that doesn't keep *you* from being a bastard. And it doesn't mean I have to kiss your ass either. I'll fulfill my part of the bargain. I'll spend the month here with you." Cummings's mind was racing. He knew what he was saying and didn't care. There was no way Neville would ever do a thing for him, and if he had the million, he had nothing to lose. So vengeance sprang up in Cummings's soul as it had done innumerable times in the past. This was a contest he knew he could win. Neville was merely sardonic. Cummings was vicious with the studied venom that only experience can bring.

"Yeah, I'll stay. But I don't like being around you any more than you like me. You stink, Neville. You stink of easy money and never doing a day's work in your life."

Neville whitened, and inside Cummings crowed, *found it!*

"So you play the lord of the manor and get us up here to play your goddamned games with us. Well, *I don't play with kids!* And that's all you are here, brother—a rich kid at summer camp, no better than the rest of us, and when it comes right down to it, a helluva lot poorer, because you don't know how to do *shit!* Your wife wipe your ass for you?"

Neville shot out of his chair, trembling with rage. "Don't you . . ."

". . . dare mention my wife like that," Cummings finished mockingly. "Okay, Ace, I won't. In fact, I won't even talk to you again, how's that?" He started purposefully toward the door, then turned. "As for crying, Mr. Neville, we'll just see who breaks down first before the month is over. And if you care to wager, I've got a million bucks just waiting for a sucker."

He went into the hall, slamming the door behind him. *Bastard!* he thought, not sure whether he meant himself or Neville. He'd been a fool to talk to Neville like that, but he couldn't help it. All his life he'd sucked ass with people just like Neville, wearing that same supercilious look of calculated pomp. *Jesus,* what fun it had been to crack that mask so that the scars showed underneath! Neville had looked guilty, absolutely *guilty.* And angry. There was that too.

But what could Neville do here in The Pines? Not a goddamn thing, that was for sure. But what about later, when they were out? Neville was a rich man with powerful friends, and Cummings knew himself too well—the million wouldn't last forever. Even if it did, if he invested wisely and lived on the interest, he knew he couldn't stay out of the arena. He was a soldier just as much as McNeely was. The competition was his life. To sit on a houseboat in Florida drinking piña coladas all day would kill him as surely as a stress stroke. He'd have to work again, and shipping was all he knew.

Neville could hurt him, hurt him badly.

If Neville survived.

A month was a long time. Things could happen. Things could happen.

The thought of seducing Gabrielle Neville came a short time later. At first it was merely a tickle of thought, as he remembered how long it had been since he'd had a woman. But once the idea had established itself, it would not go away, and he found himself aching for her. He considered masturbation, but something stopped him, and he could not tell whether it was his own pride or the feeling of being watched that had hung over him since seeing the man and woman on his bed.

The more he thought about Neville's wife, the more convinced he became that he could make love to her. He'd never been turned down before, even by the more outwardly virtuous of his associates' wives, although admittedly there were those women to whom he would not make a proposal due to some quality about them that seemed to guarantee frustration.

Or perhaps, he thought, it was the lack of a quality that he sensed in them. There was an aura, faint and indefinable, about those women who responded eagerly. A spoor, was that the word? Whatever it was, Gabrielle Neville had had it. It hung around her like a red shawl.

Like a bitch in heat. He smiled, thinking about when he'd like Neville to find out about it. In one way, it would be nice to withhold the information until the month was up, then spring it as they left. That would certainly be the easiest.

But in another way, wouldn't it be nice if Neville knew *before* they left. Then Cummings could feel his hate and rage at being trapped in a house with the man who'd cuckolded him.

Both had their advantages and disadvantages. He decided to play it as it lays. First things first. He couldn't fuck her if he couldn't find her.

He left his suite and started to look for Gabrielle Neville.

She was in the billiard room.

She was wearing a dark brown bulky sweater in which her trim figure was totally lost, and a pair of camel slacks. She wore no makeup, and she didn't need any. She was alone.

His entrance startled her so that she muffed her shot, but she laughed easily at the rattling balls. "Mr. Cummings," she said, "I'm afraid you caught me at my worst."

He smiled charmingly. "Your form looked good."

She ignored the compliment. "Mr. McNeely and Mr. Wickstrom have been *trying* to teach me eight ball. At their peril, I'm afraid."

"Oh. Are they around?"

"They went up to the lounge for a drink. I decided I needed the practice more."

"I can hardly believe you'd need practice."

Her answering smile was a bit crooked, and he cautioned himself not to move too quickly.

"I mean, surely you've played the game before?"

"No, I haven't. A little billiards years ago," she said, gesturing to the smooth pocketless table across the room, "but David was never interested in pool, so I never was either. But it seems that it's all there is to do around here."

"Well, in that case shall we play a game?"

"Fine. Eight ball is the only one I know so far."

"Eight ball it is, then." Cummings was a fair pool player. He'd had a table ever since he'd had a house with a rec room, and he beat Gabrielle handily in the first game. In the second he helped her more, suggesting the easiest shots, and at one point correcting her stance and grip so that he was able to put his arms around her. When she made no attempt to shrug off his instructive embrace, he grew even more confident. At first he had not been sure that the aura had been there, but now, as they stood pressed together, his fingers intertwined with hers on the end of the cue, he could sense it clearly.

"That's right," he purred into her ear. "That's the way."

"Like this, then?"

"Exactly." He stepped away and let her make the shot. The ball caught the edge of the pocket and swung in with a soft *plunk*.

She laughed. "You're a good teacher, Mr. Cummings."

"Seth. My shot now."

They played a few more games while Cummings let the warmth grow into intimacy, and soon he knew the outlines of her life story. It was only bare bones, but he could see behind the words enough to know that something was missing, that she was desperately unhappy with her life. *She loves her husband,* he thought oddly. But still he knew that she was ready for something more.

After the fifth game, which he only narrowly won, he put his cue into the rack with a mock sigh. "I'm afraid I've had it."

"Oh, come on. Next game I'll beat you."

"I don't doubt it, so call it masculine pride. All I want is a tall cool drink."

"Let's go to the lounge then. George and Kelly are probably still there." She placed her cue beside his in the rack.

"To tell the truth," he said off-handedly, "I've had my heart set on a Gilbey's for the past half hour. There's only Gordon's in the bar, I believe."

"I think you're right. But gallons of it." She laughed.

"I brought a fifth of Gilbey's with me just in case. Can I make you a drink in my suite?" *Come on, baby . . .*

"Oh . . ." The thought bothered her, he could tell. "I don't know, I . . ." *Something quick*.

"I've got ice and tonic. That's one good thing about never knowing whether the sun's over the yardarm or not." He chuckled and crossed to the door. "Join me?"

"Perhaps some other time. I . . . ."

"Have a plane to catch? Come on, I don't bite. At least not on one drink."

She laughed. "All right. I'd love some of your Gilbey's."

In his living room they sat on the couch with their drinks and talked some more. One drink turned into two, then three, and Cummings wondered how long it had been since he'd found her in the billiard room. Two hours? Three? It felt like days.

Finally there was a long lull in the conversation. He swirled the ice around in his glass and watched it as it melted. Then he said very softly, "It's a shame you're here."

"What do you mean?"

"In this house. Shut up like this." He paused. "It's like putting a rose in a dark trunk in the attic."

"Very pretty," she said with just a trace of wryness. "It's not that bad."

"Why did he bring you?"

"He didn't want to at first. I wanted to come."

At last he looked at her, trying to appear confused, strong, and tender all at once. "I'm glad you came," he said. "Otherwise I never would have met you."

She laughed. It was not a polite, flattered, girlish laugh at all, but mocking and superior, a laugh that made Cummings feel like a perfect fool. "Mr. Cummings," she said with a hint of coyness, "I believe you want to take me to bed."

"The thought had"—she said it with him—"crossed my mind." He chuckled, trying to retain as much dignity as possible. "I apologize for being so obvious."

"I'm married, you know," she said, "and you're supposed to be working for me and my husband. I don't think there's anything in our agreement about attempted adultery."

The harsh mockery had softened now into a barbed teasing. Maybe, he thought, maybe there was still a chance. "You can't blame me for trying."

"I suppose not. But it's hard to feel flattered when I have absolutely no competition." She stood up. "Thanks for the drinks and for the compliment, though I don't suppose David would think of it as such."

"You're going?"

"Oh, yes. Now that I know your intentions." The smile vanished. "Don't get me wrong. I'm not cold. I'm not a frigid bitch. But I don't screw on command, and when I do, I do the talking." Her manner was cool, but Cummings noticed the way she clenched her hands, the beads of sweat on her upper lip, the way her voice shook ever so slightly. The toughness was an act.

She was scared. But of what? Of him? Let it go, he thought. Let it go for now. He spread his hands and let a smile's shadow cross his face. "At your service, Mrs. Neville. My door is never locked."

Her face grew flushed, and she turned and walked rather unsteadily out the door.

Cummings sat there, unsure of what had just happened. She'd turned him down, but he knew she hadn't wanted to. It had been the aura he'd sensed on first meeting her that gave him so much certainty. Then why had she walked out? What was she so goddamned scared of?

He reached down and rubbed the erection that pressed against the crotch of his trousers. *Soon. When they want it that bad, it's only a matter of time.* He'd made the offer. She'd come to him sooner or later. He yawned, and stretched almost painfully. Despite the exercising, or perhaps because of it, his muscles were sore. A nap would feel good right now. He tossed off his clothes and showered, keeping an eye on the bedroom through the bathroom door just in case anyone or anything should make a reappearance, but no one did. Then he crawled between the cool sheets of the bed, thinking that he couldn't sleep on the couch all month. No dark images kept him awake, and he fell asleep almost instantly.

He awoke in darkness, and tried to remember if he'd turned out the lamp before slipping into bed. Then a crack of light showed at the other side of the room, and he stiffened, his breath caught in his throat. The door to the living room was slowly being opened, letting a dim distorted triangle of light into the room. It admitted something else too.

She was through the door in a second, so that all he saw was a glimpse of smooth naked skin and dark hair framing a pale face. He started to say "Gabrielle," but her softly whispered *shh* stopped him.

Then she was beside him in the bed, pressing closely

against him so that her body molded itself to his. She was so cold, he nearly gasped with the shock. "Here," he whispered, putting his arms around her. "You're freezing."

She giggled. "I know," she said, "warm me up," and she reached down between his legs and began to pull on him purposefully, like a baker kneading dough.

He moved so that she could handle him more easily, and then kissed her. Her tongue filled his mouth, and he wondered for a moment if this was really happening or if it was a dream. The urgency of her touch convinced him of its reality, and in another moment he was on top of her. She was moist without foreplay and he entered her smoothly, surprised at the rabbitlike quickness of their union. He was usually a slow lover, and enjoyed the hundred touches, licks, and teases of long foreplay, but there was something about Gabrielle Neville, he thought, that made him priapic. As he thrust again and again and felt her answer back with equal force, he was amazed at the transition that seemed to have taken place in her. The aura, he said to himself, the aura never lies.

But suddenly he realized that now, when it should have been at its height, he could not detect it at all.

He froze, although she kept moving beneath him. Then she seemed to notice his lack of activity, and moaned. "What's wrong? Baby? What's wrong? Oh, keep going, keep moving, baby," and her fingers began playing with the space behind his scrotum. He hardened again and started to move.

So what? Aura or not, who cares? He was freaking a little, that was all, thinking things that didn't make any sense. *Aura schmaura. Her whole fucking body's an aura!* And he slammed against her, driving them both to a climax that lasted until he fell into an exhausted sleep.

Cummings didn't remember her leaving, but he was alone in the bed when he awoke. He felt totally rested, and figured he must have been out a good eight or nine hours. He reached over and turned on the bedside light, then flipped back the sheets.

The bed was rumpled as hell, but there were no stiff stains to bear evidence to their lovemaking. It had all, he thought with satisfaction, been tucked neatly away. He wondered if she was on the pill, and hoped that she wasn't, that maybe he'd knocked her up.

Congratulations, Mr. Neville, you're the father of a bouncing baby Cummings.

He ran his finger over her pillow, hoping to pick up a stray hair for remembrance, but there was nothing. In fact, the pillow was fluffed up, so that there was no indentation from where her head had rested. *In case Neville should walk in on me while I'm sleeping, no doubt. Not often you meet a good fuck who's smart too.*

He got dressed. Though he'd thought of washing up, he decided against it. He liked the dried feel of her on his groin. If he ran into Neville, maybe the man would smell his wife's sex exuding from Cummings. That would be nice.

He didn't meet Neville, but he did meet Gabrielle. She was in the kitchen eating an apple and talking with George McNeely.

"Hello, Seth," said McNeely. "Seen any ghosts lately?"

"Please, George," Gabrielle said. "It's nothing to joke about."

McNeely shook his head. "Forgive me, but I think you're wrong. We've *got* to joke about them, like we joke about death. It's the only way we can accept them without descending into pathos." He smiled apologetically and stood up. "Join us for pinochle, Seth? Kelly's looking for the cards and it's a better game four-handed than three."

Cummings considered and nodded. "I need a bite first," he said.

"No rush." McNeely smiled. "We'll be playing in the den."

He walked out, leaving Cummings alone with Gabrielle, who had nearly finished her apple. Cummings sat next to her at the table. "I enjoyed that," he said softly.

She looked at him, not saying anything, a question in her eyes.

"You left abruptly," he went on. "I didn't know you'd gone until I woke up."

"What are you talking about?"

He chuckled. "Like games, don't you?"

She stared at him coldly. "Pinochle," she said. "I like pinochle a lot more than *this* game, Mr. Cummings."

"Seth," he said. "I think we could at least be on a first-name basis again, huh?"

"If you think trying to seduce me makes us intimates . . ."

"*Trying?* Hold on, lady, I just set the stage, you made the entrance." He grinned. "And I'm ready for an encore whenever you are."

She stood up and hurled the apple core into the sink. "They'll be waiting for us," she said, and stormed from the room.

"Jesus," he whispered under his breath, wondering what dumbass two-faced broad he'd found this time. He'd met her type before, the ones who fucked only in bed, who'd cold-shoulder you at a cocktail party even though you'd just humped their brains out the day before. But meet them at the motel that night and they'd be all over you.

Hypocrites. Fucking hypocritical cunts. He sighed and took the milk from the refrigerator. He'd just have to put up with it if he didn't want to go pussyless for a month. She'd come to him when she was hot again, and that couldn't be too long.

And then he'd show her. Then he'd make her pay.

The pinochle session went longer than Cummings liked. He and Wickstrom were partners, and McNeely and Gabrielle beat them at a steady three to one pace, due mostly to Wickstrom's inability to recall the cards played. There was little conversation, as everyone was concentrating on the play, though Cummings noticed McNeely glancing sideways at him on occasion, almost as if he could read Cummings's cards from his expression.

It was after McNeely and Gabrielle won their ninth game that Wickstrom pushed back his chair and sighed heavily. "Wish I had my watch. I feel like we've been going for twenty-four hours."

"Yeah," agreed McNeely, "I believe I've had it myself. All the suits are starting to look alike."

"Think I'll hit the sack for a bit," said Wickstrom.

"This has been fun," Gabrielle said. "Let's do it again sometime."

McNeely laughed. "Sometime is right. How about Thursday evening promptly at eight o'clock?"

"I'll set my watch," Wickstrom said. "G'bye all." He was gone.

"I'm on a slightly different schedule," said Cummings, directing the remark ever so slightly to Gabrielle. "I think I'll have a workout first, then a bit of a catnap. It's been a pleasure getting whipped by you two. Perhaps next time I can get a different partner."

"I'm sure," purred Gabrielle, "that George would be delighted to play with you."

Cummings pushed the anger back. "I was thinking of your husband."

If he had hit home, she didn't show it. "David dislikes cards," she said with a soft smile.

"And company, it appears. Well, I'm off."

He tackled the equipment in the gym as though he meant to destroy it. After what could have been no more than ten minutes, his muscles ached miserably, and he fell exhausted to the exercise mat, thinking what a thoroughly exasperating bitch Gabrielle Neville was.

And how he couldn't wait to see her again.

She woke him with her mouth. It ran over his body like a hot wet animal searching for food, while he jerked awake, not remembering coming back to his bed, not remembering anything after flopping down on the mat and falling asleep.

But he was in bed now, and the woman was with him, warm and naked on top of him. He laughed. "Welcome back. Welcome back, you little bitch."

She gave a grunt of amusement and straddled him, slipping him into her and moving up and down until she was filled with his hardness. He grabbed her breasts and twisted them roughly. "How's that, huh? Little toughie, God, but you love to play, don't you? Bitch . . ."

Half of him wanted to draw her down tenderly, the other half wanted to cuff her across the room. She moaned as he pinched her nipples.

"You like this, huh? You really love it. Does David do it like this?" And he threw her onto her back and entered her again. "I want to see you, Gabrielle, I want to remember you loving this so next time I see you you can't give me your bullshit!"

His hand shot out and turned on the lamp by the bed, and he saw that the woman writhing beneath him was not Gabrielle Neville.

Her hair was dark brown, her eyebrows carefully plucked, and her makeup was heavy with rouge and bright lipstick that smeared across her full mouth like a wound. Her half-opened eyes were brown-irised, and her pink tongue reached upward as if to lick his face like a dog.

"Dream lover," she panted, and her voice was identical to Gabrielle Neville's. She grasped his back, and with long-nailed fingers pulled him down against her.

Horror took him then, and he could only whimper as she slapped her hips against his faster and faster, and he thought that if he came now, he would die. So he struggled to pull himself back, pull out, before the heat mounting in his groin could pour out in a searing flood. But he could not. Her muscles had contracted around him, locking him inside her with a grip of iron.

Panicked, he pushed against the sheets, against her. "Let me go," he whispered, "please let me go." His voice was high, like a child's, but still she clung to him, the kneading pressure of her vagina keeping him hard against his will.

"Let me go!" he cried, striking at her and knowing that what he hit was not, could not be, truly flesh and blood.

The woman only laughed, spitting blood from the cut his heavy ring had made. "Dream lover," she crooned, and moaned again, scratching his buttocks so that he gasped in pain.

Then his hands were on her throat.

He didn't know what he intended to do; there was no thought of murder in his mind, only survival. And as he pressed, striving to bring his hands together, to make the neck nothing but a strand to slide between his palms, a blinding pall of whiteness fell over his consciousness and exploded within him. And he felt release.

And again, impossibly, release.

Then the white fire dimmed, and the room became visible once more.

He was kneeling over the woman. Her face was a nightmare of bulging eyes, purple skin, and lolling tongue. Blood trickled from her mouth and nose. Her neck had been crushed as thoroughly as if in a vise, and her stomach and breasts were splashed with semen.

He realized then who he had seen on the bed that first day.

He threw himself off the woman and scuttled into the bathroom, feeling his stomach start to churn frenziedly. He made it to the toilet just in time, and vomited until there was nothing left. As he stood and turned to reenter the bedroom, he did so with the hope that the bed would be empty, as it had been before.

It wasn't. The woman lay there stiffly, her strangled body a mute accusation. He staggered past her toward the living room, and shivered as her eyes, forced from their sockets like eggs in an egg cup, seemed to follow him. The light was on in the living room, and once inside, he slammed the bedroom door shut so that she would not follow.

Her clothes were draped over the couch. There was a thin purple voile dress with yellow flowers on it, a chemise, short-legged panties they called "step-ins," a brassiere, a garter belt, and a pair of long silk stockings hung over the arm. Her shoes were on the floor, and a straw basket-purse was on the coffee table.

Who was she?

The sight of the empty clothes held more reality for him than the corpse in the bed. These homely souvenirs of a life were no ghosts to vanish in a second. They were real, and he touched them one by one, letting the cotton and silk slip through his stiff fingers.

Who was she?

And then he knew how he could find out. The purse was open.

He picked it up and went through its contents. It was huge, and it seemed as though what was inside had been swept into it from a tabletop in one of the Long Island flea markets that his wife had used to drag him to. There was a Coty lipstick and a bottle of Shalimar, old-fashioned bobby pins and a deco pocket mirror, a real tortoise shell comb and brush, a pair of glasses speckled with small jewels, and a speeding ticket dated July 7, 1925, as crisp and white as on the day it had been written.

When was that? Yesterday?

The coins and bills were all dated before 1926, but the cards and photos were what made Seth Cummings so sure about what had happened. The 1925 New York State driver's license listed a Viola Elizabeth Taggart, born April 30, 1902, brown hair, brown eyes, 5'6", 127 pounds. Cummings found a small black and white photograph beneath the license. It had been taken in front of the main door of The Pines, and showed a fat balding man in his fifties in a brown suit.

The businessman

standing next to the girl in the bedroom,

The mistress

his arm around her and an uncomfortable smile on his face. On his right was a tall stocky man who resembled David Neville,

The grandfather

and on the other side of the girl was a thin ascetic-looking young man holding a book. Unlike the others, who were looking at the camera, his eyes were fixed on the girl's face, a wistful expression on his own.

The poet

His hand shaking, Cummings let the picture drop back into the purse. He felt an uncontrollable urge to run out of the room and keep on running until he found someone alive, alive and real. But he remembered his nakedness, and remembered, too, that all his clothes were in the bedroom. He hesitated, wondering if Viola Elizabeth Taggart would be sitting up, smiling at him with her dead face.

And then he thought, *It doesn't matter. They can do what they want with me—make me see what they want. It doesn't matter.*

He opened the door and went in. The bed was empty.

Of all that had happened, the only sign left was the mark of his semen upon the sheet.

He turned and looked back into the living room. The clothes were gone. The coffee table was bare.

A voice grander than any he had ever heard before spoke within his head.

You have done well.

A peace that he had never known came over him.

My true and faithful servant.

He closed his eyes, letting the voice engulf him.

To you shall be the power and the glory.

To you shall be the power.

The power.

Power.

Chapter Six

David Neville's eyes were hollow, as if he hadn't slept for a long time. Gabrielle sprang to her feet as he entered the living room, watching in concern while he shuffled to the sofa and let himself fall onto it with a low moan. "David?"

His appearance worried her. Could the cancer be progressing into the terminal stages, cutting into him here, where there was no hope of medical help? She touched his forehead. "David, are you all right?"

"It's not working. . . ." There was a haunted look about him.

"Darling, what do you—"

"It's not right!" He looked up at her, and for the first time she noticed how pale he'd grown, how his cheekbones jutted out like they'd never done before. "I haven't *seen* anything," he went on in an impassioned whisper. "Not a thing. I hear them though. It's like they're laughing at me, like they could talk to me anytime but won't.

"What's *wrong* with me, Gabrielle? Why won't they touch me? Why?" She put her arms around him and let him cry, although tears were beyond her now. Though David had told her why they'd come, though she knew what he was looking for, she did not understand him. He had become a stranger to her, made alien by the hand of death.

"I don't know, David. Maybe because . . ." She'd been about to say *because you want them too much*, but instead, far different words came out. "Because you're dying."

His mouth fell open as if he'd been struck.

"They only want the strong," she went on. "What good would *you* be to them? You've got only a few months. What could you *do* for them?"

She could not believe it herself, could not believe that she was being so cruel, was purposely baiting him with what was . . . the truth.

The truth.

And then she knew that someone or something was speaking through her, was taunting David with the horrible fact that he was not wanted by the companions he sought in the house that he owned.

She thought at first that he was going to go into hysterics. He began to breathe more quickly and blood suffused his pale cheeks. But suddenly his eyes lost their desperate glare, and he smiled. It was a strange smile, one that she could not remember having seen on his face in all the years she'd known him. "So." He pulled away from her and stood up. "So that's it then, that's what you think. You think they don't want me because I'm not strong enough. You're wrong. They want me. They do. They know the power I have, the strength. Strength that *you've* never seen, never known about because I never had the chance to show it before. But you'll see it now, Gabrielle. I'll show you."

He grasped her hair and pulled her to him, crushing her mouth against his. Her fear was greater than any passion he'd aroused, and she pushed away, falling back onto the sofa. He was on her in a flash, his hands moving roughly, his breathing stifled and heavy.

"Stop," she said, "David, please don't . . . don't . . ." But he ignored her protests, forcing her sweater up over her breasts, fumbling at the zipper of her slacks.

She surrendered then. She could have fought him off, but if he *could*, she thought, if he could make love to her, then things might be all right, and then she might have her David back again for the short time that remained to them. If he needed to prove himself a man, if this was the only way, she would not stop him. So she continued to struggle only feebly, accepting the near-rape scenario he'd dictated, while he undressed her, and finally mounted her.

It was no use. He was flaccid, and the dramatic struggle only made the result more absurd. He hovered over her, looking down at her tears of hurt and shame, and laughed brokenly. Then the slightly crazy smile vanished, and he stood up, pulling on his pants quickly, as if to hide his weakness. "I'm sorry," he said softly, and there was truth in the words. "I am so sorry, Gabrielle."

He walked out the door into the hall. She rose to follow, then sighed and fell back on the sofa, thinking, *Why? What could I say that would matter?* And even if she could think of the right things to say, she did not think that those words would come out of her mouth.

"So. Any more bad dreams? Fifty-seven . . ."

"Not really."

"What's 'not really' mean? Fifty-nine . . . sixty. That's it."

Kelly Wickstrom sat up on the bench of the Nautilus and groaned dramatically. "Jesus, what a body I'll have when I get out of this place."

"Don't change the subject," McNeely said.

"Aw, shit, nothing to speak of. I had one about snow, I think." He grabbed the chinning bar and pulled himself up.

"Oh? Skiing snow or ghouls of the white waste snow?"

"Just . . . unh . . . snow." He dropped back down. "Don't ask questions while I'm chinning, okay? I lose my count and end up doing extra."

McNeely laughed. "It couldn't hurt. You've still got a little tire there." He pointed to Wickstrom's middle.

"Tire? Bull*shit*."

"Check the mirror."

"Okay. Maybe *bicycle* tire."

"Got to leave those smoked oysters alone, Kelly."

"Hell, I never knew I *liked* smoked oysters before. They really that fattening?"

"Most shellfish are," said McNeely, climbing onto the stationary bike. "Lots of cholesterol. Choke your heart and make you horny."

"I better knock it off then. I don't need that." Wickstrom's expression changed slightly. "Only woman in this place is spoken for. Shame Neville's such a wacko. I wonder how she puts up with him. I mean, she seems so nice, not what you'd expect from someone who's super rich."

"Assholes come in all shapes and colors. So do saints. Not that Gabrielle Neville's a saint, but she's . . . good? Is that the word? She seems like a *good* woman. Kind, intelligent, not obsessed with herself like her husband."

"I noticed that," Wickstrom said. "When we first got here. He was acting like a king and she was showing us where the towels were." He laughed. "You can always trust a woman who shows you where the towels are!" His expression softened. "She's beautiful too."

"That she is."

"I think Cummings has the hots for her."

"I think you're right," agreed McNeely. "He's as smarmy a type as I've ever seen. If he got invited to the White House, he'd probably make a pass at the First Lady." McNeely increased his speed on the bike until his legs were a blur.

"Jesus, George. Your legs'll get so big, you won't be able to get through doors."

McNeely laughed and slowed the machine to a stop. "Don't know about you, but I'm ready for a shower. I don't know why Neville didn't put a sauna in here."

"Yeah." Wickstrom smiled slyly. "Cheap son of a bitch."

The door to the gym opened suddenly, revealing Seth Cummings. He was wearing a pair of trunks and a sleeveless T-shirt that seemed too small for him. There was a hint of a smile on his face as he eyed the two men. "I didn't know there was anyone here," he said. His voice was carefully controlled, the way some men get when they've been drinking, but McNeely smelled no liquor on Cummings's breath.

"We're just leaving," Wickstrom said. "You'll have the place to yourself."

"I just might at that," Cummings said. Then he looked at McNeely as though he shared a great secret with him.

"You're sure I'm not interrupting anything, Geo?" He leered.

He pronounced the name *Gee-oh*, and it shook McNeely, rattled him with the knowledge that Cummings knew more about him than he'd thought, and that there was no way in which Cummings *could* have known.

McNeely was called *Geo* by only one person in the world. It was a lover's term that Jeff used only when he and McNeely were alone. Yet Cummings had just used it as well, and accompanied it with the unspoken yet crystal-line suggestion that something was going on between McNeely and Wickstrom.

McNeely glanced at Wickstrom and saw him glaring at Cummings, a pink flush creeping up his cheeks. McNeely spoke quickly. "Not interrupting a thing, Seth. I hope we didn't sweat things up for you too much."

Cummings merely smiled in a way that made McNeely want to push a fist in his face.

"Come on, Kelly," McNeely said, moving to the door. "Let's grab a beer."

They were halfway down the hall to the lounge before Wickstrom's temper let him speak in a tight voice. "What the hell did he mean, George?"

"About what?"

"That crack about interrupting anything."

"I think he meant to suggest that we were gay."

Wickstrom barked a bitter laugh and shook his head. "That guy is nuts, George. He's stone cold crazy. I bet he's great fun in his gym in the city. Probably thinks that everyone who exercises with a buddy is queer. What's wrong with him?"

"Cabin fever. Or maybe he *wishes* we were all gay so he could get some action."

"Why doesn't he go pound it or something?"

McNeely laughed, then stopped as a strange look came into his eyes.

"What's wrong?" asked Wickstrom at the door to the lounge.

McNeely didn't answer right away. Then he shook his head. "Nothing. Let's have a beer."

But there was something, and McNeely strained to think

just what it was. There had been something very different
about Cummings. He had seemed less furtive and more
confident, but it was not his change in manner that alarmed
McNeely as much as something else. A physical change
perhaps.

Yes. That was it. As he sat back in the easy chair and
let the ale slip down his throat, he pictured Seth Cummings standing there in the gym door looking at him. But
Cummings hadn't been looking up at as steep an angle as
he had before when talking to McNeely.

"Back in a minute," McNeely said, and walked down
the hall to the gym, where Cummings was doing upright
rows with free weights. "Sorry," McNeely said, glancing
about the room. "Thought I left my towel in here. Kelly
must've picked it up. Keep pumping." And he was back
in the hall again, but not before he'd verified what he had
suspected.

Cummings was growing. He'd been about five feet eight
when McNeely had seen him before. But now, in low gym
shoes, he was standing at least five ten. And what's more,
the Adidas T-shirt Cummings was wearing was stretched
across the shoulders and rode a half inch above his waist,
as if it were a size too small.

It made no sense. They couldn't have been there long
enough for Cummings to exercise his muscles out of his
clothes, and even if he had, he couldn't have grown two
inches in height.

In the gym Seth Cummings smiled at the door through
which McNeely had just left. *Geo*. The name had slipped
so easily into his head, along with the thought—*McNeely
is a faggot*. He wasn't sure how he knew, but he knew, as
though McNeely's mind were an open book. Even in the
few seconds when McNeely had returned to the gym (*Looking for a towel? Bullshit!*), Cummings had assessed his
real purpose—to see how Cummings had changed physically.

He looked down at his body. It was true. He *was*
changing. He wasn't sure when he'd first noticed it himself, but it must have been only a short time after the
Master spoke to him in his room.

The Master had promised him strength, and apparently

it meant physical strength as well as the strength of mind
and will he would need to do the Master's bidding.

To do his bidding. Cummings chuckled at the phrase. It
sounded so ancient, so replete with the suggestion of
serfdom. He had never thought of himself as a serf of any
man's. But the Master was different. In a way he was like
Cummings himself, a part of him that he had never known
existed, something inside that sang of strength and glory
and power, of honor and fame and blood.

Blood. Where had that come from? What did blood have
to do with any of it?

Perhaps it had in some way been connected with the
"death" of the girl, the whore he'd thought was Gabrielle.
The Master had been testing him with her, to see if the
strength was in him, the strength to fight back, to kill if
necessary. He didn't completely understand why he had
had to do that, but supposed that the Master had his
reasons. Strange, almost funny, that the girl should be the
one who was killed all those years ago. By the poet,
probably.

What *had* he killed, he wondered. And what had he
made love to? A ghost, but whether a real ghost or a ghost
of his own mind, he couldn't tell. But why had she called
him "dream lover," almost as if the dream were hers?

A knot laced in his stomach as an impossible thought hit
him and he remembered that here there was no such word
as impossible: what if the dream had been *hers,* almost
sixty years ago?

What if he had bridged the gap of years and gone back
to her, rather than she coming to him?

If the poet were innocent?

If *he,* Seth Cummings, had murdered the girl twenty
years before he was even born?

"No . . ." he whispered into the silence of the gym.

But no voice came back either to confirm or deny. The
Master was silent.

The canvas was blank, the bottle of scotch half empty.
She looked at the brush, then at the empty glass by her
side, and picked up the glass. Adding two fingers of

scotch to it, she sat again in the straight-backed wooden chair, and stared at the canvas.

White. Nothing but pure untouched white, all hers to daub on, to turn blue and green and dark brown and whatever else took her fancy. She picked up her sketches and examined them, then looked at the four huge volumes, the compass, and the sextant she'd arranged so artistically so long ago. So long ago that she couldn't remember doing it.

She tossed the sketches on the floor, stood up, and prowled unsteadily about the room. It was larger than any room intended as a nursery had a right to be. Whole families could live in it, she thought in an uncommon moment of humanitarianism that made her feel drunkenly ashamed that such a thought had never occurred to her before. One by one she picked up the toys placed around the room. They gleamed newly after sixty years, as though they'd never been touched.

Perhaps they haven't. How long did the children stay before the boy died? Only a few weeks at most, she thought. Such a waste—all these shelves full of toys— huge wooden trains, shiny tin windups in bright reds and yellows, stuffed bears and elephants waiting half a century for a bedtime hug. She picked up a plushy armful and embraced them, scotch tears in her eyes, ignoring the small delicate clouds of white dust that puffed from them as she squeezed them. Then she set them down carefully, as if they would bruise, and recalled for the first time in years the stuffed animals and dolls that had littered her canopy bed until she'd entered her late teens. But try as she would, she couldn't remember any of their names.

Or had they even had names? Had they just been there in their place as everything else had always been there in its place waiting for her all her life? She tried again, but she couldn't remember their names.

A tin trolley sat on top of a polished shelf, and she picked it up to banish the memory of her girlhood bed. She wound the key in its side and set it down on the hardwood floor. It whirred and rattled madly, then skittered unevenly along, the pressed metal trolleyman jerking the power stick back and forth, rocking on his tin heels. The four wheels were purposely mounted helter-skelter, so that the trolley in motion gave the impression of riding on a notoriously bumpy track, and Gabrielle laughed as it lurched and jolted its way along, the mechanical trolleyman trying frantically to control its unpredictable surges.

And for a moment she forgot, forgot where she was and why she was there, forgot her husband and McNeely and Wickstrom and Cummings and who and what else was there in The Pines, and she laughed and laughed until the tears came and the trolley shivered and slowed and finally stopped, letting her remember again so that the tears of drunken joy turned to sobs of drunken grief that shook her like a giant's fist. *The giant who laughed*, she thought wildly in the second before she heard the voice.

"Things don't run forever."

She swung around toward the door, losing her balance, and would have fallen if McNeely hadn't grabbed her. When she saw it was him, she clutched at him as though she wanted, in a second of madness, to kiss him, to pull him close to her. But when she saw the utter lack of intensity in his eyes, she stepped back, pushing his arms away, and stood there, shivering.

"Machines, I mean," he said, his face solemn. He picked up the now silent trolley and examined it. "Sorry I shook you up. I seem to have gotten into the habit lately." He looked at her, showing concern for the first time. "Are you sick?"

She laughed. "Who isn't?"

"It seems you've been taking some medication for it." He smiled, nodding at the depleted bottle of Glenlivet. "What's wrong, Gabrielle?"

"Nothing." Her voice was choked, on the edge of tears.

"An artist with an empty canvas? That's wrong in itself. Is it David?"

"No."

He watched her for a minute. Liar or not, she met his gaze clearly and directly. "He's very ill, isn't he?"

She was incapable of hiding her surprise; her eyes widened.

"I see I'm right."

"How . . . how did you know?"

"I've been around death all my life, death and the fear of death. That fear's very strong in your husband." McNeely shook his head and sat down in one of the small straight-backed chairs. His large frame made it look lilliputian. "I knew there was something about him that first day. I knew he wasn't here out of curiosity. And once I realized he might be dying, it was easy to figure out why he'd come."

He paused as if to give her time to corroborate his conclusions, but she remained silent.

"To live forever," he said softly. "That's why he came, wasn't it?"

Finally she nodded.

"What did he expect? What in hell did he expect to find here?" McNeely laughed unbelievingly. "A welcoming party of ghosts to escort him painlessly to the other side?"

Gabrielle Neville's cry made her body tremble with its power. "*Yes!* Yes, that's *exactly* what the damned fool hoped he'd find! But since that first day no one, *no one* has seen a fucking thing!" McNeely winced at the word coming from her lips. "I think he's insane," she said, "I honestly do. And I don't think even a week's gone by in this hellhole. What'll he be like when we finally get out?" Her face went rigid, and she whispered, "What will *any* of us be like?"

"All right," McNeely said firmly. "This place is odd, that's certain, and we all heard something that day, be it a ghost or an earth tremor or a cosmic boom. Kelly's had some bad dreams, but that's it. Cummings and I haven't seen a thing out of the ordinary." He didn't mention the change in Cummings's physical appearance, as his goal was to calm Gabrielle, not alarm her. "What about you?" he asked her. "Have you seen anything, heard anything that would lead you to believe there really is something out of the ordinary here?"

"I've been *changing*!" she cried.

"Changing? How?"

"I've been . . . saying things to David, things I never intended to say. Things I didn't even know I was thinking, horrible things. . . ." Her face went blank, invaded by memories, and McNeely walked over to her and took her by the shoulders.

"Listen," he said, "we're in this place with nothing to amuse ourselves but ourselves, and we're five people who, in our own way, have led rich lives. Not all of us in money, but at least in experience. It's only natural that certain barriers should break down, that certain thoughts will come out. Now, if we'd all spend a very uneventful and leisurely month, like characters in a Noel Coward weekend, *that's* what would be odd."

She was looking up at him now, concentrating on what he was saying. Her feeling of helplessness had begun to subside.

He smiled at her gently. "It doesn't matter whether there are ghosts or not. The only thing that matters is how we respond to them. And that's up to each one of us."

She nodded then, and stepped away from him, sitting Indian-style on the floor and cradling her forehead in her hands. "I'm sorry, George. I've had too much to drink."

"There's not much else to do here."

"I shouldn't have told you. About David, I mean."

"You didn't have to. I told you I knew." He sat down beside her. "How long does he have?"

"A few months. No more."

"I'm very sorry."

She tried to smile and failed. "Do you really believe," she said after a pause, "that there's nothing here?"

McNeely considered for a moment, then spoke the truth. "I don't know. I only know that if there's anything here, it hasn't approached me." He rose and looked at the blank canvas, then at the books and astronomical instruments Gabrielle had posed. "How long have you been staring at this? Or," he corrected himself, "how long has it seemed?"

"An eternity," she said. "In the . . . the outside world it's different. There I can sit in front of the canvas for as long as I like. Because I know that in an hour, a day, even a week, I'll be able to begin. But here I don't know *how* long I've thought about it. It's like a plant," she tried to explain. "It needs *time* to grow. How can anything grow without time?" Her voice was pleading, desperate.

"There's still time," McNeely said. "We're just not as

aware of it. The stars are always there, even when the sun's shining.''

"I never realized before how much I always depended on time," she went on, ignoring his remark. "Even though I've never been a slave of the clock—never had to be—I just always counted on day following night following day again. I could tell the time I needed to by the way shadows lengthened through the windows. And now . . ." She gestured about her. "Everything's in shadow. And they never shorten, never lengthen. Everything's always the same.''

Her shoulders slumped. "Please, forgive me. I think I'm very drunk.''

McNeely indicated a small pile of drawing paper. "Are these your sketches?" She nodded dully. "May I?" Receiving no response, he picked them up and carefully thumbed through them. "These are good," he said. "Excellent. Why've you put off oils?"

"Nothing comes. I did all the sketches a short time after we arrived here. They came easily enough. But now . . ." She shrugged. "It's like something's holding me back.''

"Nothing's holding you back but you," said McNeely. "And often that's enough." He looked around the room, hoping to find a topic of interest that would change the subject. He found it in what he took to be a Maxfield Parrish print hanging in one of the darker corners. "Now, there," he said, lightening his tone, "is a Parrish I've never seen before. God, I love his work, especially the thirties landscapes. Do you like him?"

She looked up, her eyes slightly glazed. "Yes, I do. The earlier work.''

McNeely walked into the far corner to see the picture more closely. As he examined it, he frowned. "Have you looked at this?" he said. "Really looked at it?"

"Just from a few feet," she answered. "Why?"

He reached out, gingerly took it from the wall, and carried it over to her. "At first I thought it was a print," he said, "because it was glassed. But look. It's an original oil.''

He was delighted at her response. It was the most

animated she'd been for a long time. "My God, you're right—look at it, it is!"

"They probably had it behind glass because it was up here. Prey to bouncing balls and sticky fingers and all," McNeely conjectured.

"All these years," said Gabrielle, "stored away where no one can see it."

Together they gazed at it for a long time. It depicted a young boy by the mouth of a cave, from which came thin tendrils of fog shaped like wizened hands. The boy's face bore a look of expectation mixed with fear, as if he had known that the fog would be there, but was uncertain of how to deal with it.

"What is it from?" Gabrielle finally asked.

"I'm not sure. The boy's dressed like an Arab, so it could be *Ali Baba*, but I don't recall those ghostly hands in the cave."

"It's like Pandora's Box," she said dreamily, "as if he's opened the door and let out all the evils into the world."

"If that's the case, he doesn't look too upset about it."

"And the colors . . . aren't the colors beautiful. . . ."

Chapter Seven

Seth Cummings laughed. It was a deep laugh that started low in his gut and bubbled up out of him, filling the small gym with its jubilance. He'd been there for hours—he was sure it had been that long—and now, after exercising all that time with no pauses for rest, he lay on the weight bench with only a light patina of sweat coating his frame.

Every plate in the gym was on the bar, five hundred pounds of iron. And Seth Cummings could still laugh as he pressed it at arm's length, holding it over his chest as easily as if it were empty.

Instead of putting it in the rest, he sat up, muscles still tensed, and brought it down to clean position. Then he set it on the floor and touched the muscles of his arms and chest. They felt like steel. There was no give at all when he pressed them. His skin seemed like no more than a thick coat of paint on a tank.

The Master was giving him his strength.

Gabrielle Neville was almost sober. She sat at the kitchen table sipping scalding coffee, breathing heavily, watching George McNeely watching her.

"I never drink that much," she said apologetically.

McNeely smiled, pouring himself another cup. "In that case, your tolerance is doubly remarkable. Half the bottle would have put most longshoremen flat on their backs."

"I behaved like an ass."

"Some good came out of it. We found a hidden Parrish, eh?"

She nodded, smiling. "It's been hiding too long. I think we'll donate it to the Brandywine Museum." Her face grew solemn as she added, "If David agrees." She looked up at McNeely suddenly. "George," she said, "if I wanted out of here—or wanted to get David out before he . . . before something terrible happens, what would you do?"

McNeely took a slow sip of coffee. "Do you mean would I put my key in the lock?" he asked, his hand going involuntarily to his throat, where the cool metal hung.

"Yes. And lose the money." There was life in her eyes again. The dulling liquor had almost vanished.

"I don't know. If I was convinced there was a good reason to, I suppose I would."

"And lose the money?" she repeated insistently.

"I didn't come here for the money," McNeely said calmly. "It would be nice, but I don't need it."

"Why *did* you come?"

He laughed self-disparagingly. "I suppose the same reason your husband did. Curiosity at first, then to see if there was really anything here. If there was—" He stopped.

"If there was what?"

He'd been about to say, "If there was a battle to fight," but he realized how absurd, how little-boy-looking-for-fun it would seem to Gabrielle Neville. So instead, he said, "If there were really ghosts."

"Would you like there to be?"

He thought for a moment before answering. "I think so. I think we'd all like to believe there's something after death. Thomas Hardy said he'd give ten years of his life to see an actual ghost. It would be a small price to pay for a guarantee of immortality." He shook his head and a strange look came into his eyes. "But then sometimes I think that this life should be enough."

"You said before," said Gabrielle, "that you haven't seen anything here so far. But what do you *believe*?"

McNeely stared into his coffee cup as into a black pool, waiting to see what rose from its depths. "I think . . . I *do* believe that something's here. I wouldn't have stayed otherwise. I don't pretend to know what it is. It may be only random energy of some sort, but I believe there is something.''

Gabrielle noticed how far away his eyes seemed.

''It's like when I was alone in the jungle,'' he went on. ''Even on the days when the wind is still, when the birds are all hushed or dead or sleeping, there's still the feeling that something is there, and you turn to see what that movement was in the corner of your eye, and there's nothing. But you know that if you'd been just a little faster, just whipped your head around a flash sooner, you'd have seen what was near you.'' He paused. ''It's like that here, only it's not in the corners of your eyes you sense it, but in the corners of your mind.

''And you think. And you concentrate. But whatever it was that stole into your thoughts is gone, and it's just the shadow you remember, and you're not even sure if you remember that.''

He sighed sadly. It was such an empty, despairing sound that she wanted to hold him. ''I know what you mean,'' she said. ''I felt like that when I talked so horribly to David. There was something else in my mind beside me. Maybe the thoughts *were* mine, the ones that we all store deep down away, the thoughts that we couldn't conceive of having if we heard them aloud. But I *know* it wasn't me that turned them into words. It couldn't have been. There was something else inside me.'' Her mouth twisted with disgust. ''It was like being violated—worse than rape. But I don't know what it was. I don't have the haziest idea. Like you said, just a shadow. And I can't even remember its shape.'' She looked at McNeely, and he could see the strident lines of near panic marring her features. ''What can you do? How can you fight something you can't see or hear?''

How, McNeely? If this were a battle, how? ''You make it show itself. You make it speak.''

''How?''

How, McNeely? How? ''Wait it out. It can only go so far. Just wait it out.''

The door boomed open and Gabrielle Neville screamed.

In the hallway a hulking figure loomed on the border of the light. George McNeely tensed and rose halfway out of his seat, his arms coming up to a defensive position. Then the thing came through the doorway into the light, and McNeely could see that it was Seth Cummings.

But a different Seth Cummings. He was shirtless and the gym shorts he wore were just so much fabric stretched tautly over buttocks and groin, shamelessly outlining his genitals against the light blue material. He stood well over six feet tall in his bare feet, but he looked larger because of his tremendous girth. His chest was huge, his arms massive, each thigh as thick as the trunk of a healthy pine. Yet something was horribly wrong with the whole of Cummings's body. It was as though a champion bodybuilder had been disassembled and rebuilt by a slightly mad committee.

The muscle groups on each side were in shockingly different proportions. The upper left arm was well muscled, but the forearm was so overly developed in contrast that it reminded McNeely of Popeye. The right pectorals were so large that they drooped pendulously, like a breast, the lesser developed deltoids unable to bear their weight, while the left chest and shoulder were formed perfectly. From midthigh down, thick boles of muscles protruded in uneven waves like rampant tumors. It was impossible to tell where the kneecaps were located, lost as they were among the lumps of fertile muscle.

The head was the worst. It was cocked at a fantastic angle, pressing Cummings's right ear against the slab of muscle that coated his shoulder. It was not the weight of the head that had toppled it over as much as the pressure of the left neck muscle, which protruded like the god of all goiters, forcing the head to the right so that the only slightly smaller right neck muscle was squashed and flattened like a fat pink slug.

But the face was smiling. It was almost lost in the ridges of thickened flesh that seemed stuck to the skin like modeling clay, but it was there, and McNeely shivered as the white teeth glittered deep within the cavernous mouth. They seemed to be all that was left of Seth Cummings.

Then, though McNeely would not have believed it possible, the mouth twisted even more, and words came out. They were distorted and muffled, as if Cummings were buried deep inside that mass of flesh and muscle, but they were understandable.

"A little hungry," he said bubblingly. "A growing boy needs his food."

The incongruity of the cliché shocked McNeely into silence. He could only sit and stare uncomprehendingly as Cummings shambled across the room to the refrigerator and pulled open the door with such force that the handle gouged a two-inch trench in the plaster of the wall it hit.

Cummings croaked out a laugh as he examined the damage. "Getting stronger," he said. "Getting so I don't know my own strength, huh?" He looked at Gabrielle. "Huh, Mrs. Neville?" McNeely hadn't been able to take his eyes off Cummings since he'd entered the kitchen, but now he looked at the woman across the table.

She was barely there. She had started in some way to slip into herself, to deny through unconsciousness the impossible creature that shared with her the quaint hominess of the kitchen. Her eyes were partially closed, and her mouth, to McNeely's astonishment, seemed to be almost smiling.

"I'm getting real strong," Cummings said, his white marble eyes set on Gabrielle Neville, "and big. Bigger all over, Mrs. Neville. Maybe soon I'll show you just how big I'm getting. Think you'd like that?"

McNeely started to say Cummings's name, but saliva made it only a wet click in his throat, and he cleared it violently. "Cummings," he said successfully, "Seth. Are you . . ." *What do you say to a monster? What?* "Do you feel . . . all right?"

Cummings laughed again, still keeping his eyes on Gabrielle, as if he had nothing to fear from McNeely. "Feel all right? I feel perfect! I feel big and strong and filled with so much power that you can only *begin* to guess, Geo!" He looked at him then, and McNeely couldn't ever remember seeing such satanic joy in a human face. "I'd tell you more about it," Cummings went on, "but I'm hungry." He turned back to the lost Gabrielle. "Hungry for food now. For other things later." He pulled a cooked five-pound beef roast from the refrigerator and slammed the door shut so that every dish and glass in the room clattered. Then he stalked across the kitchen and stepped into the hall, turning back to look at Gabrielle again.

"Other things later, Mrs. Neville," he gurgled. "Don't worry. I'll find you." And he was gone.

There would be no reason, McNeely thought dully, to shut the door, to try and secure it in any way. He had no doubt that Cummings would simply batter it down. He started to think of what kind of weapon he could bring to bear against Cummings, when he remembered Gabrielle Neville.

She was unmoving, and he thought for a second that she had stopped breathing. Her eyes were fully closed and her expression was blank.

"Gabrielle," he said, taking her hand. At the contact, her eyes leaped open and her nostrils flared with the sharp intake of breath. She twisted in her seat and drew away from him so that her chair rocked precariously before being stopped by the counter.

"I dreamed," she said, a thrill in her voice, "I must have fallen asleep and I dreamed that Seth Cummings had"—she laughed shrilly—"had turned into a *monster*! Can you believe that? He looked ridiculous! Like . . ."

"I saw him too."

She looked at him as if he'd kicked the chair from under her.

"It was no dream. You really saw it, but you couldn't accept it. Cummings *has* changed."

"Then what he said"—she sounded frightened, but strangely excited as well—"about coming back for me? That was real too?"

He nodded, wondering if she was playing a game or if she really thought she had dreamed it all. "All of it. You didn't dream. All of it was real."

"But how? What happened to him?"

"I don't know, but I do know we'd better find your husband and Kelly damned quick." He pulled the key out from under his shirt. "There'll never be a better time to use these than now."

"We're getting out?"

"There are four of us without Cummings, and four is

enough to open this place up. We'll get out, get help for
Cummings. But first we've got to find the others. You go
. . .'' He'd been about to tell her to search for her husband, but the thought of her running into Cummings in the
hall made him change his mind. ''We'll stay together,'' he
said. ''Where do you think Neville might be?''

She shook her head. ''Our suite perhaps. The study. I'm
not sure.''

''All right. Let's start with the study.''

They stepped into the hall and went toward the west
wing. As they moved into the open space where they
would be visible to a watcher in the Great Hall, McNeely
took Gabrielle's hand and walked faster, glancing out of
the corner of his eye at the heavy wooden doors that
masked the locking unit, praying that they'd be able to
activate it while Cummings was holed up in some dark
corner wolfing down his meat.

When they'd passed into the west wing hall, McNeely
spoke in a harsh whisper. ''We'll try every room he might
be in. Let me open the doors.''

''What if—'' She paused.

''What if we find Cummings first? That's why I'm
opening the doors and not you. I'd lock you in a safe if I
could.'' And just for a moment McNeely pictured the steel
doors of the fire chamber.

''What's wrong? What are you thinking?''

He shook the idea from his head like a terrier shaking
off a rat. She'd be safer with him. ''Nothing. Let's try the
study.''

They continued down the hall, McNeely suddenly aware
of the nearly solid silence of the house. Their footsteps,
even on the thick Oriental runner that stretched down the
hall, made a dull padding that he felt could be heard
everywhere. Then Gabrielle tensed, her fingers grasping
his with a strength that surprised him. ''What is it?'' he
whispered.

''Listen.'' Only her eyes moved, darting from floor to
walls to ceiling as if she could see the source of her
phantom noise dancing about like some housebound
will-of-the-wisp.

''What did you hear?'' McNeely asked.

"A shuffling." She answered slowly and carefully, as if fearing that her own words would drown out the stealthy approach of what she had heard.

"We've got to move," McNeely said. "We don't have forever."

But if we meet Cummings, he thought, *then we have forever. And ever and ever.* McNeely had no doubt that Cummings could destroy them if he chose. He had the strength and he had the madness. No man could have remained sane after such a change. He'd looked at McNeely and Gabrielle like a giant cockeyed cat eyeing two fat mice he was saving to play with, a cat that had had a bit too much catnip, a drunken cat.

Drunk with power.

McNeely couldn't guess what had happened to Seth Cummings, except that the house was in some unimaginable way responsible. And there was no way, once the change had begun, that Cummings would ever be what he'd been before. That tremendous muscle growth must even now be pulling Cummings's bones and internal organs into an irreparable new alignment. No doubt about it, Seth Cummings was a dead man.

And so would they all be, unless they could get the hell out of that house and away from what had been Cummings. But the only way to do that, McNeely thought desperately, was to get four keys and four people to turn them. Cummings's own key was out of the question. It was undoubtedly buried somewhere along with its chain in that thick cord of neck muscle.

They were at the door of the den now, and Gabrielle walked by it, wanting to move on to the study to find David Neville, but McNeely stopped, grasping the knob. Gabrielle looked back at him, and the fear in her eyes was just as great as that in his stomach, but he turned the knob, knowing that they had to find Wickstrom as well, and knowing that he could be anyplace.

So could Cummings.

The den was empty, but McNeely wouldn't believe it until he checked the other side of the high-backed leather couch to make certain Kelly Wickstrom wasn't napping there (*or Seth Cummings wasn't crouching in wait*).

They tried the study next, and found it vacant. The library was across the hall, but McNeely paused at its door. He had suddenly thought of a TV game show he'd seen once in a Chicago hotel room, where the contestant picked one of nine numbered squares on a screen. Behind each number was either a word or an amount of money, and you could keep picking until you hit a thousand dollars or got the right combination of words.

Only there was a catch. Behind one of the squares was a cartoon dragon with long teeth and flaming nostrils, and if you picked *that* square . . . well, the game was over. You lost.

Pick the rooms, George, he thought, *but don't pick the room with the dragon.*

Or you're burned.

Kelly Wickstrom was thirsty. He had grown extremely fond of Bass ale in the short time (*Long time? Who cares?*) he was in The Pines and decided that when he got out, he would forsake Pabst, his long-time favorite, and pack Bass away by the case. Maybe he'd even buy the brewery. He tossed the coffee table book on baseball down on the couch, saluted a farewell to Willie Mays, who was smiling at him with "say hey" in his bright eyes, and left his suite.

The hall was empty, as usual, and he walked briskly down it until he reached the stairs, which he took two at a time to the third floor, thinking longingly of the half case he'd stuffed into the lounge refrigerator before his last sleep.

At the door of the lounge he hesitated, though at first he couldn't say why. Then he remembered. The door was closed.

It had always been open before, the lamps always on, pouring a welcoming wedge of light out onto the wall and floor of the hall. *The tavern door is never closed.*

But it was closed now. Wickstrom put his ear to the door and listened. He thought (dreaded) that perhaps Gabrielle and McNeely, or, worse, Gabrielle and *Cummings*, might be in there seeking privacy, might be—may as well say it to himself—*fucking* in there on the couch. She had the hots for George, Wickstrom noticed that easily enough, and it made sense. Her husband was a royal asshole, and George was a helluva good guy. Still, Wickstrom felt, if not jealous, a bit sad at the thought.

He listened more closely and thought he heard a faint sound from within. Should he open the door, see who was there?

He decided it was foolish not to. If anyone was having sex, surely they'd choose one of the bedrooms, which had so far been private and sacrosanct. If either George or Cummings were looking to pull off a quickie with Gabrielle Neville, it would only be natural to seek the privacy of a bedroom, where no one thirsting for a beer would catch them *in flagrante delicto* (*flagrante delectable,* Cohen at the station house had called it).

He opened the door. It was dark inside and he was fumbling for the light switch when he heard the noise. It was a growl, low and throaty. *Polar bear.* The thought came lightning fast, the inner vision followed: a mound of white, pure white, heaving up on its haunches, nearly invisible against a snowy background. The eyes, the tongue, even the claws were white, and he felt as if the dream he'd had had burst out of his head and taken form there in the darkness of the so familiar lounge. For a second he could not move. It was long enough to hear the other sound, a wet, smacking sound, and for a relieved moment he thought his first suspicions had been correct after all, that someone was having wet, sweaty sex on the couch, that what he heard was nothing more frightening than hot sex-slick asses slapping against leather.

"Hey," he said nervously, "sorry . . ."

The sound stopped. The growl returned, a growl with a chuckling laugh in its center. And the wet, rhythmic noise started again. He recognized it now for what it truly was. Chewing.

There is a monster here, Kelly Wickstrom thought dully, taking his hand away from the light switch as slowly as he would from a rattlesnake. He was more careful than he had ever been in his life. He did not want to bump that switch, to turn on those bulbs, to see what thing of madness burrowed there. It was something the house had made, something to frighten him, to drive him crazy if he'd let it.

Well, he would *not* let it. He would leave the room dark, and close the door, and go find someone to talk to.

And he did.

Gabrielle Neville saw him first, gliding down the stairs to the first floor like a wraith. She and McNeely had just finished checking the dining room, and she'd stepped into the hall when she noticed Wickstrom's stealthy form in a pool of shadow on the landing. "George!" she hissed fearfully before she realized that it was Wickstrom. McNeely was with her in an instant, and when he saw Wickstrom, he smiled in relief.

"Kelly," he called softly, beckoning to Wickstrom.

"Jesus, George," said Wickstrom, "there's something in here, something up in the lounge . . ."

"The lounge," McNeely repeated, glancing at Gabrielle. "We've seen it too, Kelly. Listen, take Gabrielle up to my suite. It's got hall doors in both the bedroom and living room. Good place to escape from. Maybe Cummings isn't fast enough to catch us if we've got a jump on him."

"Cummings?" Wickstrom said, shaking his head. "What do you—"

"Gabrielle will tell you about it. I've got to find Neville. Whatever you two do, stick together. I'll be there soon as I can."

Wickstrom and Gabrielle went up the main staircase while McNeely finished searching the first floor. Neville was neither in the pantry nor in the small rooms of the servants' quarters. McNeely went up the east wing stairway then and found the Nevilles' suite empty. There were two things he could do now.

One was to tackle the third floor—the observatory, the playroom which Gabrielle used as a studio, the gym, the three small bedrooms, and the large vacant room in the west wing—the room across from the lounge.

The other was to look in the cellar.

He felt uncomfortable with either, but knew that in order for them to get out of the house, Neville had to be found. He decided on the cellar first. There was only one way down, leaving no escape route, but the cellar was large enough so that if he had to, he might evade Cummings by slipping around him. That misshapen body had been created for strength, not speed.

McNeely padded down the east wing stairs and went into the kitchen. He hadn't noticed it before, but the door to the cellar was slightly ajar.

Could Cummings have come down here, have gone into the cellar while they were searching for Neville? Could he even now be crouching down there in a blot of shadow, or behind the stairs, ready to reach through and grasp McNeely's ankles with those nightmare hands, sending him crashing down the wooden steps to lie half-stunned at the bottom until that great hulking shape poured out into the dim light to do . . .

Whatever he wanted?

Come on! a voice yelled inside him. He'd been in 'Nam, Thailand, in Angola, in half a dozen more shitholes around the world, where every step was a step with death. What made this place so goddamned different?

Because, he told himself as calmly as he could, in 'Nam, in Angola, in Nicaragua he had *known*—known who his enemy was, known where he came from, known his firepower, *known*.

But how on God's green earth could he *know* what Seth Cummings had become or what had made him that way?

He made himself walk down the steps, thinking how good an Ingram .45 would feel right now, its butt cool against his palm, its trigger kissing his finger, its muzzle ready to explode into flame and cut the monster in two. But there was no Ingram, not even a fart-sized .22, though he doubted if a .22 slug would even partially penetrate those sacks of muscle that surrounded the essence of Seth Cummings.

At the bottom of the steps he turned and looked through the sideways gaping teeth of the stair boards. Nothing. No Quasimodo/Jonah in the cellar's belly. He hurried across the cold cellar into the large central area. The light was on, and McNeely wondered why there was nothing more to illuminate so large an area. The cellar seemed empty, but he wanted to check the fire chamber before he went back upstairs. It would be a perfect place for Neville to seek the solitude he seemed to want so desperately.

The door was closed and locked. McNeely ran his hand over the cold steel, looking for a keyhole. Finding none, he knew that Neville had to be inside. "Neville?" he called, knocking on the door, wincing at the loud clanging sound his knuckles made.

There was no answer.

"Neville!" he called again.

Neville's voice came back to him, thin and far away. "Go away. Leave me alone."

McNeely hammered violently on the door. *Fuck the noise. If Neville doesn't come out, we've all had it.*

Suddenly the door swung open, and for an instant, as he looked into the blazing eyes, McNeely thought that Cummings had tricked him, had spoken in Neville's voice, had lured him on to death. But the furious eyes were only Neville's, who shrieked in his rage.

"God *damn* you! I'd almost reached them! They're here—it's the strongest place in the house. They're all down here, and I almost *reached* them, and *you*! You come, ruining my concentration, frightening them—"

"Shut up." McNeely's voice was cold as ice. "Shut up and listen to me. We've got to get out of here. Now."

"Now? You're crazy! I won't leave now, not when I'm so close."

"If we don't leave now, we're all dead. Something's happened to Cummings. He's . . ."

He stopped dead as Neville's eyes widened in fear and wonder at something behind McNeely. He knew what it was even before he turned, and saw the huge twisted body of Seth Cummings in the doorway to the cold cellar.

Its arms and legs were still, but its shoulders vibrated up and down with a life of their own, sympathetically shaking the entire frame. McNeely realized it was laughing.

Then it spoke. "You were never close, Mr. Neville. Never even remotely. Your wife was right. The Master doesn't want *you*. It's *me* he wants. You're dying even now. I'm healthy, and strong. I'm going to live a long long time. But you? And you, McNeely? Oh, no, I'm afraid not."

It moved then, shuffling raggedly across the stone floor. "You have to die, both of you. And Wickstrom too. I'll let the woman live. I need her. For *this* . . ." He thrust a sausage-fingered hand between his legs, ripping away the last vestiges of cloth. "And for when we leave. I'll have all *you* had, Mr. Neville, but I'll use it more wisely than you ever did. I'll use it for *the Master*."

It was about twenty feet away. When it came closer, perhaps ten feet, McNeely intended to charge it and quickly veer to its left and up the stairs.

But then he remembered his job.

It seemed like years ago, but he'd been hired to protect the Nevilles, and right now David Neville was within several yards and several seconds of having his head ripped off. The soldier took over then, with never a thought as to whether or not Neville was *worth* saving. McNeely edged closer to Neville and whispered. "When I say, run up the stairs."

Now stall. Relax him. Off his guard.

"Who is this Master?"

Cummings laughed gutturally. "Me to know, you to never find out." He came closer. It looked to McNeely as though the creature was ready to take them both. The mammoth arms were coming up and out, blocking their way to the stairs. One man, fast and agile, might be able to get past. But two? Never.

McNeely let his voice go softer. "Why kill us, Cummings? What's the point?" His voice cracked on the last word, so that a slight sob echoed and reechoed in the dismal room.

"Look at me!" Cummings boomed out. "The point is power! And I will have it all! Here first, then . . ." He gestured with an arm like a railroad tie, "Out there! Out in the world." His voice dropped to a whistling husky sibilance. "The power to take those like you and crush you like bugs." He looked from McNeely to Neville and back again. Then he split the twisted clay of his face in a parody of a smile.

"Who's first?"

"Please . . ." McNeely choked out. "Please let us live. . . ."

"McNeely!" Cummings crooned in mock surprise. "I never thought you'd beg . . . such a *strong* man, a *soldier*, a man of such . . ."

"Don't kill us." McNeely's head drooped like a whipped dog, but his eyes still watched.

". . . of such *power*! What a liar!" Cummings started to laugh, great dry heaving laughs that shook his body, relaxed the bunched, corded muscles. "What a liar!"

And McNeely moved.

"*Now!*" he shouted to Neville as he feinted right, then twisted left as if to run past Cummings's right side. But instead of dashing past, he threw himself into the air and lashed out with his right leg at the spot where Cummings's right ear pressed against his shoulder.

It was intended as a delaying maneuver. McNeely had hoped at best to stagger the behemoth, throw him off balance, perhaps with luck even to topple his top-heavy body so that there would be time for both him and Neville to get by and up the stairs. So it was a surprise to him when what happened happened.

It began when he was in the air, drawing his leg back to lash out. It was as if time suddenly slowed for him, as if he had all the time he wanted to hang there in the air, measure his goal, take the move only when it felt absolutely, perfectly *right*. When that moment came, he unleashed all the power of his hip and thigh muscles, with the whole weight of his body behind it.

Then suddenly, terrifyingly, there was *more*.

He felt absurdly enough like a flyswatter made of iron. An unknown hand took him and wielded him and thrust him against his enemy so that his foot hit the hollow of Cummings's neck with pile-driver force, ramming the head to the left, compressing the thick neck muscles so quickly and powerfully that they exploded outward through the leathery skin, spraying a wet fog of blood and tissue into the air.

Neville had hesitated when McNeely had attacked. Instead of dashing past Cummings immediately, he had watched as McNeely had made his leap. Only when McNeely's foot smashed against Cummings did Neville start to run, just in time for Cummings to collide with him and bring him solidly up against the rough brick wall. Neville cried out at the pain, and in response Cummings's head swayed up on his ruin of a neck and turned almost completely around until it saw the man crumpled at the base of the wall. McNeely could scarcely believe that something that had taken a blow that had nearly decapitated it was capable of such blinding speed.

Cummings sought to cry out in anger and pain, but there was nothing left to scream with, and the air still in his lungs brought forth only a bloody froth that bubbled from his tattered throat. Then suddenly his arms were around David Neville.

Neville's face became a palette. It went from pink flesh to the white of shock to the gray of understood terror. Then the redness began, all in the time it took McNeely to cross the room. When he arrived at Neville's side, the man's eyes were already beginning to bug from the sockets.

McNeely grasped Cummings's arms, which embraced Neville's trunk just under the heart at the bottom of the rib cage. That some ribs were already broken McNeely knew. He'd heard them snap like dry sticks when Cummings had made his grab. But Neville was still alive, and McNeely intended to die himself to keep him that way. He tried to dig both hands around Cummings's left forearm, but could not find a hold. Cummings's arms seemed one with Neville's midsection, as if whatever warped alchemy that had changed Cummings was now exerting its force upon both attacker and victim, merging the flesh of the two men in a deadly union.

Neville's face was beyond red to purple now, and the whole upper half of his body seemed bloated with the lower organs that Cummings's arms were displacing. McNeely thought involuntarily of a tube of toothpaste squeezed in the middle, then of a balloon twisted tighter and tighter in the center until just a touch light of . . .

Bursting.

A hiss left Cummings's lungs, and a new smile contorted the face on the head that dangled from a few strands of flesh and stringy muscle, and McNeely knew with queasy certainty that if the throat had been whole, he would have heard a laugh.

Bursting . . .

Neville's tongue protruded farther than McNeely had thought possible, and blood began to arc from his nose, stream from his ears.

And still McNeely could not break Cummings's grasp.

McNeely went berserk then. He smashed at Cummings's back with fists clenched together, hammer blows that might have splintered the spine of any other human, but Cummings squeezed on.

McNeely kicked with the sharp edge of his shoe, taking running starts that crunched against Cummings's forearm and elbow like the blade of a pickax, but Cummings squeezed on.

Then McNeely wrapped his arms around Cummings's body and sought to lift him by brute force, to pick up both men if necessary and fling them to the stone floor in the hope of dividing them. But it was like trying to move Pine Mountain itself.

Cummings squeezed on . . . *pressed on.*

Press on! Press on, men!

> *(Colonel Ortega . . . the only English he knew)*

Press on! Press on!

> *(he called, just before the shell hit him full in the chest, turning him into a pink cloud in the jungle)*

Press on!

McNeely screamed and grasped Cummings's head, jerking and wrenching again and again until the few shards of tissue ripped loose and he fell over backward, striking the base of his skull on the stones, as the head rolled into darkness and monstrous arms tightened in a final spasm and the upper half of David Neville's body did what the balloon and the toothpaste tube and everything that can hold no more always has to do.

Part III

Whoever battles with monsters had better see that it does not turn him into a monster. And if you gaze long into an abyss, the abyss will gaze back into you.

—Friedrich Wilhelm Nietzsche,
Beyond Good and Evil

Chapter Eight

George McNeely was swimming.

He knew it was a dream, but that didn't keep him from enjoying it. He needed something like this after what he'd been through. Though he couldn't remember what it was, he did know it had been very unpleasant, it had made him hurt, and it had made him think he might be crazy.

So it was good to swim like this, to float on his back and have the cool water wrap around him and feel the warmth of the sun edge through it to touch his bare skin. He looked across the sparkling ripples at the shore and saw Jeff there, hands on his hips and a smile in place under his thick brown moustache. McNeely waved, but as he did so, he sank beneath the water, feeling no panic, but only a little sadness that he would have to wake up now.

When he did, the pain came back. The back of his head was throbbing, and when he touched it, his fingers came away wet. It was too dark to see if the wetness was blood, but he felt sure it was. For a moment he really didn't know where he was, but slowly that grim knowledge returned.

The Pines.

Oh, yes, The Godforsaken Goddamned Pines. And the fight with that giant from a ten-year-old's nightmare. And Neville being crushed by those immovable arms. He had tried to save him. He had done his duty. But where was Neville now?

McNeely shook his head and blinked his eyes savagely to dispel the blurriness that plagued them, but scent was the next sense to return. The air was sharp with the smell of feces, rank with the sweet scent of blood. He remembered the head tearing loose, the heart pumping furiously, sending the geysers of red spewing aloft as he had sunk into darkness. Now, slowly, his vision cleared, and he saw the huge shape of Cummings's body lying a few yards away.

McNeely staggered to his feet. He was sore, but the head wound seemed to be the only real damage. He walked shakily over to the corpse, not seeing Neville, thinking, hoping that he'd recovered and gone upstairs to get help. Then he saw the thin leg sticking out from beneath the lump of death that was Cummings.

A cry escaped him, a tiny whimper of pain and frustration that seemed an incongruous coda to the titanic struggle that had been waged. He sank to his knees and pushed the great bulk over so that it struck the stone floor with an elephantine, blood-wet slap.

George McNeely had only vomited twice in his life from nonphysiological causes. The first time was at eighteen, five minutes before he was to face his first live fire. The second time was ten minutes later, after he was forced to gut a man from scrotum to heart so the man would not do the same to him. Not once, after that first kill, did his stomach ever turn at the sight of violence again.

But he had never before seen a human being squeezed in two.

He closed his eyes and let the feeling sweep over him, knowing that there was no other way to respond, not for any man who would cling to the semblance of humanity, to the most infinitesimal touch of sensitivity. He emptied his stomach on the stones, then made himself look back, and brought up the little that was left. Afterward, he looked again. And again.

Finally he could look at it without feeling the peristaltic muscles twitch at all, and he knew he could do what had to be done.

His legs stronger now, he walked up the cellar stairs into the cheerily lit kitchen. Opening a drawer by the sink, he removed four damask tablecloths. There was nothing of lesser quality, and he thought it ironically fitting that these should be the shrouds of millionaires. He took them back into the cellar and covered Neville's body with one of them. He found Cummings's head, made himself pick it up, and placed it between the legs of the body. It took the remaining three tablecloths to cover Cummings's hummock of flesh. Then McNeely went upstairs to join Wickstrom and Gabrielle Neville.

He knocked at the door of his suite and called out, "It's me." His voice was choked, husky. His mouth tasted bitter.

The door clicked open. "George," Wickstrom said softly. "Jesus . . ."

Wickstrom was looking at him in horror, and McNeely realized he'd done nothing to hide the effects of the fight. He looked down at himself.

He was bathed in blood, like an uncaring butcher after a long day's work. His shirt was sodden, his arms were coated. He knew that he must smell terrible. "Oh, shit," he said. "Oh, God, I can't . . . I've got to wash."

McNeely turned away, shaking his head, but Wickstrom put his hand on McNeely's shoulder, oblivious to the soft squelching noise the shirt made. "Wait! Are you hurt?"

"No, no, not my blood." McNeely was tired. To find somewhere to sleep again, to sleep and dream about swimming, that would be very nice.

"Whose blood then? What *happened*, for Christ's sake?"

McNeely heard a slight cry and turned. Gabrielle Neville stood inside the doorway, just behind Wickstrom. "George . . ." she said, her face going white.

McNeely nodded at her. "It's over. Cummings is dead." He closed his eyes, squeezing them shut in the pain of failed trust. Then he opened them and looked straight at Gabrielle. "David's dead too. Cummings killed him before I could stop him."

Her pale face grew taut, the muscles contracting the skin over the bone so that she looked as she might when she was seventy. McNeely saw no tears, only that terrible tension of the features. She turned and faded back into the room.

"Look after her," McNeely told Wickstrom. "Don't go

anywhere. Just stay with her until I come back.'' Wickstrom nodded and went to comfort Gabrielle Neville.

McNeely walked down the hall. He decided to use Cummings's bathroom, as he didn't want to have to pass by Gabrielle to get to his own. He didn't want her to see him again with her husband's blood on him. Looking down, he saw the dark trail he was leaving. There would be time to clean it up, he thought. With only three people alive, there would be no leaving. There was all the time in the world to clean up the blood.

In the bathroom he peeled off his clothes and flung them into the shower stall. Then he stepped in and turned on the spray. After several minutes of standing there, letting the almost unbearably hot water rinse off the dried and coated blood, he plucked with his foot at the wet pile of clothes, dragging them beneath the spray. He stamped on them slowly, like a primitive washerwoman pounding rags on stones. The blood passed from the cloth with each step, and pink water swirled and eddied its way down the drain, a tiny whirlpool of shed life.

McNeely closed his eyes and tried to forget the scene in the cellar, but found it impossible. It had been a scene of blood, of violence, of battle, and he had come out unscathed. Such an experience would have normally electrified him, but there was no battle joy, none of the feeling of healthy catharsis that usually resulted.

He had let Neville get himself killed, and that was bad enough. But there was something worse, and that was the extra strength he had felt, the extra time he had had when he'd delivered that near decapitating blow.

That there was such a thing as increased strength under stress he knew. He'd felt it himself—that adrenaline pump, that extra oxygen that made normal muscles strong and strong ones superhuman. The phenomenon had saved his life several times. But this time it had been different. It hadn't been he who kicked Cummings. He simply was not capable of that kind of blow under any circumstances.

Then what was it? He was afraid that it was the same thing that had given Cummings *his* strength.

Am I next? Dear Jesus, am I next?

He struggled to calm himself, to tell himself that Cummings must have wanted it to happen that way. *What did I say to Gabrielle?* he thought. *It's not whether there are ghosts or not, it's how we respond to them that counts.*

How did Cummings respond?

McNeely turned off the shower. There were no towels on Cummings's rack, so he lay down on the bed, letting the air and the spread share the task of drying him. He stared at the ceiling and thought it through.

If McNeely could accept what Cummings had said as at least partially true, and not just insane ravings, Cummings had been approached by something, something he'd called *the Master*. The Master, then, had changed Cummings, had given him power, but in a cruel and ghastly way. Perhaps *the Master* was insane himself, or perhaps Cummings was not capable of controlling the power.

Wait, said a corner of logic in McNeely's brain. What if there were a *natural* explanation, no matter how farfetched? Wouldn't it make more sense to accept that than to imagine a supernatural origin?

Of course it would, if this were a *natural* place on the earth. However, to give logic the benefit of the doubt, he conjectured upon what diseases could have so wrenched Cummings's body. Acromegaly? It was the only disfiguring disease he was familiar with. He'd known a young merc who'd had it—a kid from Michigan who hadn't been able to join the Army because of it. He became a soldier anyway, and died at twenty-two in Africa, sliced in half by machine-gun fire. It gave him a kinder death than the disease would have. McNeely sighed as he remembered the boy, the ugliest human being he'd ever seen—beetling brows, large ridges of pouched flesh that contorted his muscles painfully, puffy sacks around his eyes that still couldn't prevent him from being a crack shot. "Call me Beast," he'd said when he joined them, as a black man might call himself "nigger"—to use it so it lost all power to hurt. He'd talk often about Rondo Hatton, a grade-Z movie actor of the forties who'd had acromegaly, and had made a living grunting and menacing maidens in the dark castles of second-run features. Everybody had their heroes—even the acromegalics.

But the kid had had it for a long time. It had come on

slowly, not in a matter of hours. *Radioactivity then*. Maybe they were on a big lump of uranium, or maybe Grandpa Neville sold part of the mountain back to Teddy Roosevelt, and the government secretly dumped plutonium in a hidden cave far beneath the mountain.

Sure. And maybe Cummings was a changeling. Maybe he'd sold his soul to Satan and this was collection day. Maybe it was just too many vitamins.

Maybe. Maybe. *Shit*.

He wrapped a bedspread around himself toga-style and went down the hall to his suite. The bedroom door in the hall was locked, so he rapped on it and called for Wickstrom, who opened it a few moments later. "I didn't want to disturb her," McNeely explained as he entered the room and took some clothes from the drawers. "How is she?"

"She'll be all right. I gave her a drink."

"Oh, great," McNeely sighed. "That's all we need."

"How are *you*?"

"Bruised. Nothing worse."

"What the hell happened?"

McNeely told him, leaving out only the part about the extra strength in his kick. By the time he was finished, he was fully dressed. "The thing now," he concluded, "is to decide what to do with the bodies. I want to get them somewhere where she won't have to see . . ."

Wickstrom's expression was grim. "That's right. We're trapped here. There's no getting out, is there?"

"No. We've got the keys, but only three people to turn them."

"Maybe we could rig something up," Wickstrom said. "I'll see if I can find any scrap wood."

"In the meantime, we've got to do something with those bodies. I don't know how long we've been here, but you can bet that if we don't get out on our own, there are going to be some pretty bad smells in here before those steel panels open. I don't want Gabrielle to . . . experience that."

Wickstrom bit his lower lip. "What about the fire chamber?" he asked. "It seems pretty tight. We could put them in there."

. McNeely shook his head. "If there *were* a fire, the

place would be uninhabitable, even if we did have time to take out the bodies before we sealed ourselves in. The wine cellar might be our best bet. We can close it off pretty tightly."

"What about the freezer," said Gabrielle Neville.

Both men turned. She was standing in the doorway, the drink Wickstrom had mixed for her nearly empty in her hand. Neither of them knew how long she'd been there, how much she'd heard.

"That's the place to keep meat, isn't it?" The words were bitter, but the voice was feeble, finally breaking over the edge into tears. She dropped the glass and sobbed heavily. Wickstrom was at her side in an instant, holding her and letting her pour out her sorrow and anger on his shoulder.

When the tears were gone, she looked up at McNeely with a determination that pushed out her jaw, narrowed her eyes. "The wine cellar would be best," she said. "Let's put them there."

McNeely shook his head. "You shouldn't see them. It was very ugly."

"He was my husband."

"It made me sick. I had to vomit. And you've no idea of what I've seen in my life."

"He was my husband. I'm going down there with or without you."

As they entered the cellar, McNeely was thankful for the dimness of the light he had cursed such a short time before. Cummings and Neville were no more than pale lumps at the other end of the cellar floor.

"All right?" McNeely asked her. "Have you seen enough?"

"No." She walked over to where Neville lay. There was no possibility of her mistaking the small mountain of Cummings's body for it. Kneeling, she drew back the tablecloth and stared into David Neville's face.

Both Wickstrom and McNeely watched her, the tension in them building as they waited for a scream, for hysterics, for a faint. But Gabrielle Neville only leaned over the dead face and came up again, like a pilgrim drinking from a holy well, and George McNeely knew she had given her husband a parting kiss.

She pulled the tablecloth gently over Neville's face once more, straightened up, and looked at the stunned men. "When you love someone, George, no matter what they do or what happens to them, they're *never* ugly." She looked back down at Neville. "I'll help you carry him into the wine cellar, but you two can handle *that* by yourself." She gestured toward Cummings's corpse, her face twisted with loathing. "I won't touch him."

They carried Neville into the wine cellar, Gabrielle taking his legs, McNeely and Wickstrom holding the upper part of his body together. Then Gabrielle went upstairs to let the men struggle with the body of Cummings. When they had grunted and jerked the dead flesh into the room and closed the door, they went upstairs.

"I could use a drink," said Wickstrom. Not once had he looked under the tablecloths.

McNeely nodded and they went up to the lounge. Gabrielle Neville was nowhere to be seen.

"What did it?" Wickstrom asked, pouring himself a bourbon. His need was greater than ale could supply.

"The house," answered McNeely. "It was the house, or something in the house. It sounds absurd, but it's the only thing possible."

"You think the *house* turned Cummings into a monster?"

"What other explanation is there?"

Wickstrom shrugged helplessly. "But why? What would it want? What purpose could it have? Just to kill us all?"

"Maybe. But I think it's smarter than that. I almost feel as though it wanted to use Cummings in some way, but he got out of control. Like he couldn't handle the power." *And maybe*, McNeely thought, *that's why it helped me kill him.*

In her bedroom Gabrielle Neville lay and played with her thoughts like a child dropping marbles into a tin box.

David was dead.

He had suffered horribly in his dying.

Yet perhaps not so horribly as he would have with the cancer.

Cummings was dead too.

That was good, because she hated him. . .

. . . hated him for being a pig who thought with his crotch, who thought he could have her because he wanted her, hated him because oh goddamn it but it was true she wanted him to take her and fill her up and make her feel again and it had been so long since she'd felt anything from a man and when he came into the kitchen she had been repelled by him, terrified so much that she had withdrawn into herself, but it wasn't really for that alone, was it, Gabrielle, that you had shut the doors of your mind, wasn't it that he *excited* you because he was so big and virile and you could see his cock and you wanted it and if you shut your eyes you could make believe it was David whole and healthy and not David dead in a dirty cellar David was dead

David was dead.

And all the marbles rattled in the tin box and she grasped it with her guilt to stop the racket, and turned and buried her face in the pillow, but her eyes still saw everything. And as she clenched her hands into fists, she felt her wedding ring, and she thought for the first time that she was free.

The marbles rolled slightly, then settled. The box was still.

Trapped in a fortress, she was for the first time in her life free.

Kelly Wickstrom paused before he knocked on the door of the Nevilles' suite. He wished that he had X-ray vision so that he could look in and see if Gabrielle was sleeping. If so, he would have walked away to his own room and tried to lose in sleep the memories of the horror he had just seen. But he kept imagining Gabrielle Neville sitting staring empty-eyed at nothing, Gabrielle Neville eyeing a bottle of sleeping pills with unconcealed desire, Gabrielle Neville lying weeping, uncomforted, alone on her bed.

Gabrielle Neville, alone on her bed.

There was something in that that gave him pause, but he killed the thought before he could follow it to a conclusion. It was not the time. She had been through so much that he could not bring himself to violate her, even in a fantasy. But he could not make himself leave her alone either.

He knocked on the door. There was no answer, so he knocked louder. Finally he heard footsteps crossing the floor, and Gabrielle opened the door.

She was not, as he had expected, prostrate with grief. On the contrary, her face was bright, as if she had scrubbed it to make it shine all the more. She had changed her clothes and now wore close-cut jeans and a yellow top. A bright purple scarf was tied around her neck. She looked young and beautiful and utterly unlike a woman who had been widowed only hours before.

"I'm sorry. I didn't hear you knock at first." She was smiling and her eyes were clear. Wickstrom wondered if this was how the rich mourned their dead, remembering when his mother had died. It had seemed to him at that time that the earth should have stopped in its orbit to weep. She'd been married only a year to Frank, his stepfather, when it had happened, a car wreck that had taken her out quickly and unexpectedly, leaving no time to say good-bye or to love away the bitterness he had felt and revealed on her remarriage. His only consolation had been that she hadn't suffered. Impossible to suffer when your chest is crushed in an instant. Seeing Gabrielle's almost cheerful face, he recalled his own miserable one as he looked into the mirror before the funeral, trying to see if it looked as if he had been crying. Then, at eighteen, it was important to him not to weep no matter how great his grief, important to say farewell like a man.

It was only when he saw Frank alone at the gravesite after everyone else had gone, when he saw Frank's tears running down his cheeks, and his shoulders shaking in great silent heaves for the wife he'd lost, only then did he think that *that* was the way to say good-bye, stunned by the realization that the strange man who'd come to his mother's arms and bed had loved her as much or more than he did himself. He had not gone up to Frank that day, but they had become friends since, and Wickstrom still visited him on holidays.

"Come on in, Kelly. You look lost." Her voice brought

"Sleeping. He was exhausted."

"Oh." She looked down for a moment, then back at Wickstrom. "I wanted to thank him."

"Thank him?"

"For trying to save David. How did it happen? Did he say?"

Wickstrom went through what McNeely had told him, leaving out the more gruesome details. Gabrielle sat stone-faced through it all. When Wickstrom had finished, she smiled grimly.

"I know you may think me callous, Kelly, but I'm almost glad for David's sake that it's over. Did you know that he was dying?"

"George told me."

She nodded. "He was so afraid of the pain. At least he was spared that."

"Yeah." Wickstrom hadn't looked at the body for any period of time. A quick glance and he had turned his head away until the sodden tablecloth had been drawn back over the face. But that glance was enough to tell him that although David Neville's suffering had not been long in duration, it must have been phenomenal in its intensity. Wickstrom thought there was no way in which a man could bear so much pain and retain his sanity.

He must have died mad.

"Tell him," said Gabrielle, "tell George, if you see

Chet Williamson

"George?" she asked.

were a receptionist with an unpleasant visitor. "Where's

She winced, but locked the smile back on as though she

up. Roughly."

that uncaring smile off her face. "Everything's cleaned

her husband still clinging to the cellar ceiling would take

He nodded, wondering if the mention of the pieces of

everything downstairs?"

unsure of what to say next. "Did you . . . take care of

"All things considered, I'm holding up." She shrugged,

She nodded, and her smile lost some of its buoyancy.

"I wanted to check on you, make sure you were . . ."

face of what had . . .

Gabriele ___ door of his room, glaring across ___ dull, bitter malevolence that frightened him.

Stop it, he told himself. *What the hell right have you got to feel this way?* He was not by nature a jealous man. He hadn't known or even suspected his wife was having an affair until she'd come right out and admitted it, so this new feeling surprised him. It must be the house, he thought, and then he actually smiled. If making him jealous was the worst it could do after what it had done to Cummings, he'd consider himself very lucky.

But the thirty-one days weren't up yet, and wouldn't be for a long time.

him back from the graveyard in Brooklyn, and he wondered again how she could seem so unconcerned in the face of what had happened.

"I wanted to check on you, make sure you were okay."

She nodded, and her smile lost some of its buoyancy. "All things considered, I'm holding up." She shrugged, unsure of what to say next. "Did you . . . take care of everything downstairs?"

He nodded, wondering if the mention of the pieces of her husband still clinging to the cellar ceiling would take that uncaring smile off her face. "Everything's cleaned up. Roughly."

She winced, but locked the smile back on as though she were a receptionist with an unpleasant visitor. "Where's George?" she asked.

"Sleeping. He was exhausted."

"Oh." She looked down for a moment, then back at Wickstrom. "I wanted to thank him."

"Thank him?"

"For trying to save David. How did it happen? Did he say?"

Wickstrom went through what McNeely had told him, leaving out the more gruesome details. Gabrielle sat stone-faced through it all. When Wickstrom had finished, she smiled grimly.

"I know you may think me callous, Kelly, but I'm almost glad for David's sake that it's over. Did you know that he was dying?"

"George told me."

She nodded. "He was so afraid of the pain. At least he was spared that."

"Yeah." Wickstrom hadn't looked at the body for any period of time. A quick glance and he had turned his head away until the sodden tablecloth had been drawn back over the face. But that glance was enough to tell him that although David Neville's suffering had not been long in duration, it must have been phenomenal in its intensity. Wickstrom thought there was no way in which a man could bear so much pain and retain his sanity.

He must have died mad.

"Tell him," said Gabrielle, "tell George, if you see

him before I do, that I'd like to talk to him. Will you do that?''

"Sure. I think I'll get some sleep myself.'' He stood up and walked to the door. "Listen,'' he said, turning, ''I know this must be hard on you. If you ever want to talk about it, or anything else, well, just let me know, okay? I mean, I'm a good listener.''

She smiled again. "Thank you. I'll remember that.''

As Wickstrom walked to his suite, he tried to interpret the things she had said (and more important, the things she had *not* said). That she was hiding something he was sure. There was something more than simple gratitude behind her interest in McNeely, but what was it? Did she want a more complete account of her husband's final minutes? If so, he thought she'd be disappointed. If McNeely had been hesitant in describing the details to him, in a way a fellow soldier would be, how much more reluctant would he be to recreate the scene for the widow?

Or was there something else? Why had she changed her clothes, made herself appear so casually attractive? He'd noticed and averted his eyes from the tight wool sweater and the tighter jeans. Christ, he hadn't expected her in long black, but what she had worn seemed just a bit too provocative to be fitting.

Maybe that was the point. Not for him, though. For McNeely. *He'd* been the one she was interested in talking to, not him. Once again he felt that odd inappropriate jealousy wash over him as he wondered precisely how Gabrielle intended to thank McNeely. Then he was at the door of his room, glaring across at McNeely's suite with a dull, bitter malevolence that frightened him.

Stop it, he told himself. *What the hell right have you got to feel this way?* He was not by nature a jealous man. He hadn't known or even suspected his wife was having an affair until she'd come right out and admitted it, so this new feeling surprised him. It must be the house, he thought, and then he actually smiled. If making him jealous was the worst it could do after what it had done to Cummings, he'd consider himself very lucky.

But the thirty-one days weren't up yet, and wouldn't be for a long time.

Chapter Nine

Actually, only twelve days had gone by from the time the five of them had entered the house, and while Kelly Wickstrom was closing the door of his suite, Simon Renault was sitting in his Manhattan office just about to start the second cup of coffee of the three he allowed himself every morning. It was steaming hot, and he bent his head and brought the cup up under his eyes for a moment, letting the steam tease tiny sweat droplets from his eyelids while the damp heat pressed against them like a tender hand.

It didn't work. The headache was still there. He added the cream and stirred the mixture until the coffee turned a light golden brown, then sipped it delicately. Best to make it last. It would be 11:30 before he allowed himself his third cup. He wished he could take it without cream, black, as so many Americans did, but he found it bitter and undrinkable, even the finest blends. So he added his cream and counted his calories, finally emptying the cup in four huge and heavenly swallows before looking at his watch to find that it would be an hour and twenty-five minutes before his next.

As he glanced at the Rolex, he wondered again how the Nevilles were doing. It would be horrible, he thought, to be without time. That would be worse than ghosts. Renault lived by the clock. His days were filled with meetings and luncheons and dinners, appointments and transatlantic calls. He owned three watches in the fear that two could break down at one time, yet the Rolex John Neville had given him on his fortieth birthday had not failed him once in nearly a quarter of a century.

But in The Pines, he mused, there would be no need for a clock. No appointments, no phone, no television (he was most secretly addicted to Johnny Carson and Benny Hill), nothing to distract them from any communication with . . . with what?

Renault did not believe in ghosts, not even after what John Neville had told him had happened on that brief visit back in the forties. Imagination pure and simple, and he felt wise enough to know that even a pragmatist such as himself would not be immune to its powers. Lock *anybody* up with a tale of ghosts for thirty days and they'd obligingly create their own before the month was out. Though he realized that the ghosts had been David's prime motivation for going to the place, he had as much as told him that his quest would be fruitless. But while the old man could have joked and laughed about it with David's father, David was another story. Renault had never been able to establish the easy rapport with the young man that he had had with John Neville. No doubt it was partially a matter of generations, but it stemmed more deeply, Renault thought, from something in David's character that had been lacking in his father, a heavy reliance upon class distinction.

Quite simply put, David Neville was a snobbish little prick, and though Renault had loved the boy and still loved the man, he found it difficult to combine that love with any amount of respect. David had never shown the slightest degree of interest in the business his father and grandfather had built other than to ask Simon offhandedly how it was going every once in a long while. As far as David seemed to be concerned, the business existed only to supply him with the money he required.

John Neville had been disappointed in his son's lack of interest and, once into his final illness, had been very open about it with Simon. He had not died happy, and Simon Renault would always carry a trace of bitterness toward David because of that.

But for all his flaws, Simon did love him, and he hoped that David's deteriorating body would last long enough for him to find one of the two things he was looking for at The Pines. The immortality, or at least the comforting illusion of it.

Renault also hoped that David would *not* achieve the second quest he had set for himself—the quest for revenge.

The plot had frightened Simon at first, indeed even now. He was still against it, thinking it stupid and childish and possibly deadly, but he had been unable to convince David to turn from it. David had explained it to him when he told him of his desire to go to The Pines.

"This ghost-hunting is all well and good," Renault had said, "but you don't really expect to go alone, do you?"

"No, I don't. I want three bodyguards."

"Fine. We have a good many top men who guard our executives abroad. I'll have Mayo select the top three and—"

"No, Simon. I want special bodyguards for this. Three very special men."

Simon shrugged. "Who did you have in mind?"

"Two of the men are known to me. The third is not. Kelly Wickstrom is the first. Do you recall three years ago when my cousin was arrested?"

The older man nodded. He recalled it well. David's younger cousin, Jean, with whose family he stayed when he and Gabrielle visited Paris, had been arrested in Manhattan in front of the Neville office building. He'd refused to pay for the cab ride from Kennedy, an irrational act due to the amount of cocaine he'd been snorting on the trip in. When the arresting officer had checked his bag, he found it to contain eight ounces of the drug. That was when the boy had gone for him. The officer had responded with a fist in the face that had quickly and almost painlessly blinded the boy. David had been furious when he'd heard of it, but John Neville was unsympathetic, firmly believing that Jean had deserved his fate. He did use his influence to insure that his nephew drew only a suspended sentence, but refused to bring any charges against the arresting officer. The family connection was kept quiet so that not even the officer knew the boy was a relative of one of the richest men in the city.

"This Wickstrom was the policeman who blinded Jean.

He's the first. The second is a man named Seth Cummings. He works for Stahr. When Ralph McCormick killed himself because Teresa was fucking around, it was Seth Cummings she was fucking around with. The more you hear about Cummings, the uglier he gets.

"The third is a man whose name I don't know, but I want you to put some of your international connections on it. In Africa in 1974 my Uncle Philippe was connected with some rebels. Not as a mercenary, but as an advisor, to help pull down a corrupt regime. He was killed, murdered by a group of mercenaries hired by the government. They were commandeered by an American known only by the code name Hammer. I want to find out if this Hammer is still alive and where he is now."

"I don't understand," Renault had said, although he was afraid he did. "Even if these men would be willing to go with you, why? What could you want from them?"

"First, revenge."

"You're not suggesting anything violent?"

David hadn't answered at first, had only stared into Renault's eyes as if attempting to gauge how far the man would go to satisfy his employer. "If there is violence," he answered finally, "it won't be me who starts it."

"I can't condone that," Renault said, his voice as cold and firm as he had ever dared make it in front of a Neville. "If you wish to draw these men to that house to attempt to harm them in some way, I—I would have to leave your employ."

"*I* won't harm them, Simon. I promise you that. But these things—these acts against friends and relatives—are things that have gnawed at me over the years. And if I'm to die, I want to settle the scores."

"But how?" Renault asked, exasperated. "What on earth do you intend?"

"I intend to pit myself against them." David had spoken with passion, and there was a fire in his eyes that had not burned there for many years. "Simon, I truly believe that there is something in the house, something preternatural. Since I know I'm going to die, life after death holds no terror for me. On the contrary, it holds only hope. What I want"—and he leaned forward in his chair like a bird of prey—"is to see them break, watch the fear of the unknown cut into them and reduce them to the"—he searched for the word—"to the cowards they really are. Every one of them," he went on in a softer but no less intense voice, "has harmed someone I've loved. My cousin Jean, my uncle, and Ralph—one of the few real friends I've ever had. And each one is such a *man*," he sneered the word. "A soldier, a policeman, a tough businessman. I want to see what men they are when they're locked inside The Pines for a month."

Renault could restrain himself no longer. "David," he said, "I have known you all your life. When your father died, I promised him I would look after you as best I could." He shook his head. "It is my tragedy that I could not keep you from the same fate he met, but at least perhaps I can persuade you to die with your dignity intact." David opened his mouth to speak, but Renault rolled on. "This plan of yours is undeserving of you. If you wish to go to the house to investigate these rumors, then do so. But do not tarnish your final days by toying with petty vengeance. . . ."

"Dignity?" David burst out. "Dignity's exactly what I'm talking about, Simon, dignity and honor. *Justice*, not vengeance. Can't you understand that?"

Renault couldn't, and he told David Neville that, but it had no effect on the dying man, who directed Renault to find the man called Hammer and to then come up with a plan to get the men to the house.

Several phone calls were made, and in a matter of days Simon Renault had a copy of a C.I.A. file on George McNeely. From other sources he learned that McNeely, due to a blunder in which several colleagues were killed, was considered *hors de combat* in the mercenary community. It was a fortuitous occurrence, and Renault was grateful for it.

Wickstrom and Cummings had posed greater problems. At length, Renault had employed the services of a Juan Garcia who, as planned, pulled off a burglary in Kelly Wickstrom's precinct at the precise moment when Wickstrom was walking his beat past the store. Garcia allowed himself to be arrested, then resisted, throwing a punch at

Wickstrom who, true to form, launched a fist at the man's face. Instead of blocking or rolling with it, Garcia threw himself into it, ending up with a classic broken nose and a clear-cut case of police brutality. An attorney was there five minutes after Wickstrom and Garcia arrived at the station, and the case against Wickstrom was smoothly begun. Garcia was now out on bail, many thousand dollars richer, and he would be richer still after his case was brought to trial. He would receive ten thousand dollars for each month of time served. Garcia was hoping for a long sentence.

Discrediting Seth Cummings had not been as formidable a task. A party at Stahr's, a security guard with a small camera, and a set of prints sent anonymously to Vernon Warren, Cummings's chief internal rival, had been enough to do the trick—that, along with Cummings's own weakness for wealthy, powerful, and desirable women. Cummings was unemployed within the week.

"They are yours," Renault had told David Neville after the three had accepted the first part of the offer. "I have no doubt that these three will choose to remain in The Pines for the million. However, at this time *I* have certain requirements."

"You, Simon? And what makes you think I'll go along with them?"

"If you don't," Renault replied calmly, "I'll inform the three gentlemen involved that you intend their deaths. You may then fire me, or sue me for slander, or even"—here he smiled wryly—"hire me as your *fourth* bodyguard, but your plan will have been ruined nonetheless."

"Someday, Simon," said David coldly, "you'll push me too far and I'll forget that you used to tell me bedtime stories. But what are these demands of yours?"

"They're simple. No weapons inside the house. No firearms, no knives, swords, or spears hung as decorations on the walls. No poisons or materials that could be used as such. That's all."

"What about no rope—I might garrote them. What about no forks—I might go for their jugulars. What about no socks—I might fill one with stones and cosh them. Oh, Simon, you've left me a veritable array of death." David laughed chillingly. "You still think I intend to kill them then?"

"I don't know, but I won't take the chance. I've done enough simply by arranging it so that they have to take your offer. I won't be party to any deaths as well."

"I'm going to tell you something, Simon, and I'll tell you only once. I will not cause these men's deaths. I swear it. I'll do nothing to prevent harm from coming to them, but I won't be the cause of it myself." He was silent for a moment, staring into Renault's eyes. "Do you believe me?"

Renault thought, then nodded his head. "But no weapons," he repeated.

"No weapons," David Neville agreed.

Now, as Renault sat there trying not to think of his next cup of coffee, he almost wished he had not made that demand, that David and Gabrielle had had perhaps a small handgun to protect themselves if things got touchy. He did not feel that either Wickstrom, McNeely, or Cummings were dangerous men, despite their reputations or lines of work. But in such a situation, and with a woman as desirable as Gabrielle . . . he shrugged and whispered a silent prayer that at least she was all right.

He'd thought David had been a fool to allow her to join him, even though he'd told Renault that he was powerless to stop her once she had her mind made up. Renault thought the truth was somewhat different. He believed that David intended to die in The Pines, and could not conceive of leaving this life without Gabrielle at his side. For this reason, and in respect of their love, Renault had made only feeble protests to Gabrielle, who had dismissed them with a seemingly unconcerned lightness.

"He's my husband, Simon, and I intend to be with him. The Pines holds no fear for me, and it means so much to David. It's the only hope he has left."

David had cautioned Renault not to tell Gabrielle the truth behind the choice of their three "bodyguards," so a story was concocted regarding David's desire to see how different men from different yet ruthlessly similar professions would function under conditions of unseen stress. She had thought the explanation odd, but so much that

David had done in the past few months had been strange
that she accepted it without question.

Renault wished again that David had permitted him to
wire the house for sound, but he had been adamant. "This
is me and the house, Simon—and me against them. There'll
be no last-minute rescues. I want to be on my own in
there. And what's more, I don't want anything to destroy
our chances of finding what I want to find there."

"You mean ghosts."

"Yes. I mean ghosts."

Well, thought Simon, they'd all be damned lucky if they
didn't all end up as ghosts before the month was out. He
couldn't check up on them personally, so he did the next
best thing. He picked up the phone and dialed John Sterne.

Sterne was watching television when the phone rang,
and the shrillness of the sound in the small room made him
jump. He grabbed it before the second ring. "Sterne."

"This is Renault."

"Simon. What's up?"

"I just called to . . . to see how things are going."

Sterne sighed. "Quietly, Simon. You know I'll call you
as soon as"—he corrected himself—"*if* anything happens."

"Yes, I know. I suppose I'm just worried."

"Well, don't be. Everything's quiet as . . . as can be
up here." *Quiet as death? That's what I was going to say.*

"How are *you* getting along, John? And Monckton?"

"Just fine." Monckton and John Sterne, Renault's righthand man, were stationed in the caretaker's cabin at the
bottom of Pine Mountain, waiting for the month to end, or
for something else to happen. "We've gone on a twelve-
hour shift. Monckton's a nighthawk, so I'm dawn till dusk,
and he takes the dark."

"May I speak to him? Is he sleeping?"

"He's . . . he can't come to the phone right now. Shall
he call you?"

There was a slight pause. "No, never mind. I'll try not
to bother you again."

"No bother, Simon. We're concerned too. But like I
said, it's been quiet."

"All right. Try not to get too bored. Good-bye, John."

" 'Bye, Simon.'' Sterne hung up and breathed a heavy sigh of relief. Thank God Renault hadn't asked *where* Monckton was. Orders had been for both of them to remain in the cabin for the entire thirty-one days so that they could respond quickly to any emergency call from the house, and Neville/Renault orders were not to be taken lightly, even though they may have been given that way.

But Monckton was not at the cabin. He was at the house.

It had started only a few days after the five were shut in. When Monckton got off his shift at dawn, he would go outside and stand at the bottom of the road, looking up toward where it became lost in the labyrinth of trees that cupped the first turn. He'd watch for a few minutes, as if expecting to see something coming from around that curve, down from the top of the mountain. Then he'd go into the cabin and sleep, or eat a light meal and watch early morning television. He had a drafting table there, but so far he hadn't been able to make himself sit down and work on any of the upcoming projects he had.

Two days ago he'd driven up the mountain for the first time since he'd come down with Renault. There'd been no preamble to the act, only that restless unease that had possessed him since their vigil had begun.

"We were told to stay here," Sterne had reminded him, but Monckton had only shook his head.

"I know that," he answered, "but I've got to go up there, got to check it out."

"Check it out? What do you expect to find? The place is tightly sealed, Monckton. They could all be screaming and shooting guns off inside and you'd never know it."

"I guess you're right," Monckton grudgingly acknowledged. "*Maybe* you're right. But I think I'll know if everything's okay. Besides, what's the difference if I'm there or here when the alarm goes? It's not like I drove down into town."

"What if Renault calls?"

"You can handle him. Tell him I'm sleeping or on the john or something. Don't worry about it. It's no big deal."

No big deal my ass, Sterne thought. He had considered

calling Renault and reporting Monckton's insubordination, then thought better of it. If the alarm *did* go off, Monckton would be that much closer to doing something about it. The two .38 revolvers and the .12 gauge in the Jeep would insure that he could handle whatever problem came up. Sterne had felt a sudden queasiness in his stomach at the thought of Monckton driving away, leaving him alone with the silence of the forest and that squat black phone connected to The Pines. But Monckton would not leave; he was fairly confident of that. The man seemed enthralled by the house a mile above, and their conversations had usually drifted back to David Neville's grand experiment. Sterne suspected that Monckton knew more about the house than he let on, but Sterne had never tried to push him into any revelation. Instead, it was Monckton who kept pressing the subject.

"Is it possible, do you think?" he'd ask Sterne over and over again. "Even if *you* haven't, has there been anyone in your family who's claimed to see a ghost or anything like it?"

Sterne could only sigh and say no. He, like his entire family, was a realist with no time for haunts. This month was to him simply an inconvenience that lengthened his term of apprenticeship to Simon Renault, delaying Sterne's ultimate goal of taking over the old man's position when death or old age retired him. At least this time of deadly dull service above and beyond should put a feather in his cap, if Monckton's short drives were not discovered.

He felt guilty about covering for Monckton on the phone with Simon. He should have reported it and covered his *own* ass instead of setting himself up to be caught in a lie. But it seemed so harmless, and how would Renault ever find out? Besides, Monckton was just curious. Sterne had asked him when he'd come back from his first visit what he'd done, and Monckton had simply shrugged. "Nothing," he'd said. "What *could* I do? I just walked around the house and listened at the doors."

"Hear anything?" Sterne had inquired with sarcasm.

"Nothing. It was like a tomb. Not a sound. Absolutely nothing."

But the next day he'd gone back. And now today. "Why?" Sterne had asked as Monckton plucked the Jeep keys from the peg on the wall. "You expect to hear something or what?"

"No, I don't expect to hear anything. At least not with my ears." He opened the door. "I'll be back soon."

But this morning, the third day of his vigil, Whitey Monckton *did* hear something. He'd followed the same procedure as on the first two days, parking the Jeep by the garage, and walking around the house, working from the back patio around to the west wing and on from there. He was, as he'd told Sterne, not listening with his ears alone. He let all his senses open, not knowing how the entity he thought of as The Pines might choose to approach him.

In the few days he'd spent with Sterne in the two-room cabin near the mountain's base, he'd come to conclusions that had changed the way he looked at the world. Between what he had seen and what he had heard in The Pines, he had become a firm believer in the existence of life after death. Monckton had *seen* things, and he was not one to doubt the evidence of his own senses. At first he had tried, like Scrooge, to blame the manifestations on "an undigested bit of beef, a fragment of an underdone potato." But Monckton had a cast-iron stomach and a constitution to match. He had seen, he had heard, and therefore whatever it was was real. And though he had experienced nothing since coming down from the mountaintop, still he was haunted by the house. Its mystery crept into his thoughts and dreams until he could think of nothing else.

So now he stood, head poised, at the west wing door, not listening as much as sensing. He stood there for nearly ten minutes, then turned and walked toward the front of the house, his shoes crunching the dry brown and rust leaves that carpeted the lawn and walkway. Even though no trees stood within the triangles the wings of the house formed, they'd blown over in profusion from the treeline until they were piled knee-deep against the western side of the south wing that housed the Great Hall.

Wind from the west, Monckton obxered, and shivered

Wind from the west, Monckton observed, and shivered as a chilly gust tore through his light jacket and swirled dead bits about his ankles. He stopped at the huge front door. The leaves skittering dryly across the jagged flagstones drowned out all other sounds, but as he stood waiting, the wind receded until the rat-scrabbling of the leaves had stopped and Monckton found himself in a total silence, like the eye of a psychic storm.

And then he heard it, high up in the air. At first he thought it might be the air circulation system in the attic, but remembered that it could barely be heard in the house, let alone outside. But the sound had the suggestion of machinery in it, of some great engine that was cranking into life after a sleep of decades, of millions upon millions of cogs and gears and wheels that had never before worked in unison now all at once coming together in some disharmonious hymn of power. And as he listened, each fragment of sound seemed a voice that whispered in rhythm, an insignificant voice that, when combined with uncounted others, formed a strength, a single note like the hiss of a billion leaves scratching stone. The sound grew louder and louder, becoming from its myriad parts one giant engine that throbbed with a universal heartbeat, roared like all the seas and skies of earth roaring in one storm, one cataclysmic symphony composed to split the planet's crust and litter the cosmos with its leavings.

Under the sunny October sky, Whitey Monckton pressed his palms over his ears only to learn that the song he was hearing was not heard with his ears, but with his skin, heart, brain, soul, with every part of him, and he listened for a long time, until it died away to a low dull pulse and the wind returned once more, lifting the leaves and making them dance to its own comparatively uninspired tune.

Chapter Ten

George McNeely awoke to a face hanging over his bed.

At first he thought it was Kelly Wickstrom, peering in to make certain he was all right, but immediately realized his error.

The eyes were slanted like an Oriental's, and narrowed dangerously. The teeth were bared, their whiteness almost startling. The long black hair hung in matted clumps made damp by something red. It was an instantaneous picture, since the face vanished in less than a second after McNeely's eyes opened; but it hung there a moment longer, implanted on his pupils.

Dream, he told himself, and no wonder. It was surprising that he hadn't awoke to an entire platoon of gooks staring through the bars of the Vietnamese rat cage. Or worse yet, he might have seen David Neville's face—if you could call it that—floating luminously over his head.

He sat up in the bed and stretched, luxuriating in the feel of his stiff muscles drawing to their greatest length. Then he pulled on a pair of slacks and a jersey and walked into his living room. He was not alone. Gabrielle Neville was sitting in an easy chair, a book in her long-fingered hands. She smiled at him.

He nodded. "How long have you been here?" he asked as he sat on the sofa.

She shrugged. It was answer enough. "I wanted to be here when you woke up, to thank you. For trying to save David."

"It's what I was supposed to do. I'm only sorry I wasn't better at it."

"You tried."

"Not hard enough."

"It wasn't your fault. It was fated to happen."

"Fated? You believe that?"

She frowned. "I believe that once David decided to come here, it was inevitable that he would die here."

"What about the rest of us? Are we *fated* to have something similar happen to us too?"

"I don't know. Some things just seem to happen."

"Jesus, *that's* profound." He hated himself for saying it, but she irritated him, played on his nerve ends like a five-year-old on a violin. All he'd wanted was to relax for a few hours, to read, have a bite to eat, and then start to figure out how to escape from this tomb. But instead, he had to talk karma with the widow of the man he'd let die. Though he felt he'd slept for hours, he was unaccountably weary.

"I'm sorry if it sounds simplistic," she said, unoffended. "But things happen. When they do, they do, and we're fools to be concerned about them afterward, because we could not ever have done anything differently, because it *happened*."

"No second chances, huh?"

"No, no second chances at all. Just . . . similarities in the future."

He sighed and lay back on the sofa, throwing his bare feet up on the back. "And I suppose you've never wanted something to happen again, so you could do something differently?"

"I have, but I know when I do that the feeling is pointless. So I try not to think like that."

"No recriminations."

"No recriminations."

"You're one tough broad, Gabrielle." He threw his forearm over his face and closed his eyes. "I've thought most rich women were stupid and happy and pampered."

"Most rich women aren't married to a man like David."

"Neither are you anymore." It was a thought that slipped

out, a cruel, involuntary lunge that had taken voice, and he
kept his eyes closed so that he couldn't see her face.

"That's true," she said finally. "But you must remember that I've been expecting to be a widow for some time
now, so the shock isn't as great as it might be." She paused.
"Besides, it hadn't been much of a marriage lately anyway."

Now he looked at her, his eyes narrowing. "Isn't that a
bit callous?"

Her face was set. "No, it's not. It's the truth. He'd
changed so much through his illness. Not physically, but
his mind. He was always self-centered, but in a charming
sort of way. He could laugh at himself and his own
pretentions so that, although they were still there, they
weren't nearly as offensive as they might be otherwise.
But once he got cancer, he changed. He lost that sense of
humor, which was what kept him from being a prig." She
paused. "He changed in other ways, too . . . toward me."

She looked at McNeely as if expecting him to say
something to make it easier for her, but he remained silent.

"We hadn't made love for over a year," she said
harshly, as if throwing down a challenge. McNeely looked
away from her. "We couldn't," she went on. "He was
impotent. But I still loved him."

"Why are you telling me this?" McNeely asked, watching the ceiling.

She stood and walked over to where he lay on the sofa.
"I just want you to . . . I want *someone* to know and
understand how I feel, what I've gone through." There
was no mistaking the pleading in her voice.

"Why not Kelly? He's got a sympathetic ear."

"I want *you* to know, George." She reached down and
put her hand on his forehead, pushing his black and silver
curls back to reveal a smooth and unscarred brow.

McNeely didn't recoil from her touch; he merely closed
his eyes and smiled thinly. "I see," he said. "I think I
see. But to post with such dexterity . . ."

". . . to incestuous sheets," she finished for him. "I
know the quote, and it's not accurate. Not incestuous, not
at all. And as for dexterity, I'm not newly widowed.
David's been dead for a long time."

"And you've already grieved, is that it?"

She nodded. "A long time ago." She knelt down to kiss him and he let her. Her mouth fit smoothly over his, and their lips parted shyly so that their tongues barely touched. Then she drew back a few inches and looked into his eyes.

"Will you make love to me, George? Now? Right now?" She asked the question as if fearing both possible answers. In response, he cupped her face in his hands and pulled her gently to him for another kiss, deeper, more intense.

They walked together to the bedroom, where they undressed each other tenderly and made love on the rumpled bed. There was kindness in their lovemaking, each surrendering completely to the other so that nothing should be taken by force. It was long and warm and beautiful, and they came together in the kind of eternal moment she had always dreamed of and had too infrequently experienced. Then she fell asleep, her arms around McNeely's waist, her head nestled in the hollow between his arm and chest.

But George McNeely did not sleep. He had been full of sleep only an hour before. Now his eyes were wide open, staring at the shadowy walls of the room, down at the naked woman pressed against him, down at his own body, shining with the thin sweat of passion.

He had made love to her.

The knowledge was blinding, staggering. She had come to him with caresses and desires and he had responded to them and gloried in them, filled with the need for her. He had loved her like a man loves a woman, and his body had satisfied her with its hardness, his touches with their softness.

And she had satisfied him. The things he had felt were unparalleled in his experience, even in the best times with Jeff, his own Jeff, whom he tried now to conjure up in a sense memory, to recall *his* touch, his tenderness.

The memory came, and left him unmoved. He could recall the acts, the words, but none of the passion, none of the love was remembered. He forgot it like a surgery patient eventually forgets his pain. McNeely frowned and swallowed to drive the lump from his throat, but it would not leave. He had a sense of something, a teasing notion in the back of his mind that whispered to him that this was what he'd really wanted all his life—this *woman* in his arms to love and to hold. It had seemed so natural to him, so overwhelmingly right, as if this were the way it had always been meant to be. In contrast, the mind pictures of himself with Jeff seemed awkward, desperate, almost ugly. They seemed unnatural.

Unnatural.

That was not the worst he had been called. Faggot, cocksucker, he knew the pantheon of epithets well, although few people had wielded them within his hearing. Those who had, he had ignored, or simply stared at without expression until, discomfited, they moved grumbling back to their bedroll, or out of the bar. He had never fought for his sexuality, never struck a man for telling the truth as he saw it. He liked to think of it as dignity, but at times he feared it was guilt, the same guilt that had tortured him in high school, that had knotted his stomach as he lay in his bed in the big house he lived in with his parents in Larchmont; the guilt that made him call Tommy Reynolds a fairy when the other guys did, and that made him hate himself for doing it when all the time he knew he was the real fairy—Quarterback and Student Council Vice-President George McNeely the Fairy.

It was that same guilt that had made him enlist after he was graduated from high school. He'd gone to his father's office one morning in mid-June, had sat across the desk from him like some nervous client, and told him that he had decided not to take prelaw at Temple in the fall, but to join the Marines instead. When his father asked why, he told him it was because he was homosexual and thought the service could help him, make a man out of him. Then his father began to cry. McNeely had never seen this before, and it frightened him. He told his father that he would talk to him about it later at home. That evening his father would not look at him, and said in a chilly tone that if he wanted to enlist, it might be the best thing. His mother remained stonily silent, her thin lips pressed together so tightly that she could have dried rose petals between them. He had never been close to either of them, and in the three weeks before he went to boot camp, only the absolutely necessary words were exchanged. He boarded the bus with great relief.

The guilt had lingered, but slowly faded out of sight like a scab that leaves only a pale white scar. He soon found others with his preferences, and learned that guilt did not have to be the screaming monkey on the back of a homosexual. His liaisons were very infrequent and securely discreet, and when on occasion a perceptive and vocal comrade would make a suggestion that McNeely might have less than totally masculine leanings, he would find McNeely thoroughly imperturbable on the subject, and, receiving no satisfactory bites from his baiting, would reel in his line and shut up. McNeely was so popular among his fellow Marines that nine out of ten of them didn't give a damn if he fucked donkeys. Even in combat, when tensions were strung as tight as Cong wire traps, McNeely's sexuality was not a point of conflict. He had learned to live with it until he had ceased to think of it as a flaw. It was natural, for him at least. Natural.

Until that limey in Africa. He'd been a Colonel Blimp type—early fifties, overweight, large gray moustache, bald head that shone like crystal. McNeely couldn't imagine why Briggs had hired him until he saw him shoot. McNeely had seen good marksmen before, but the limey was something special, putting every round of an automatic clip into a body target at fifty yards. When McNeely went to talk with him after their first round of practice fire, the limey had politely but firmly told him that he didn't wish to fraternize with McNeely, that his reputation had preceded him, and that, although he would fight with him and die for him if necessary, he would not be his friend "because I find what you do unnatural." Then he turned and walked away as casually as if he'd told McNeely the time.

Unnatural. The word had shaken him as no gutter slur ever had, and the next day he killed a rebel whom he could as easily have taken prisoner. The power of the word had done that to him. And now it returned in the context of his relationship with the person he loved. Compared to him and Gabrielle, his couplings with Jeff *were* unnatural. It seemed to him as if he saw and understood for the first time, as if his homosexuality *had* been as perverse as his parents had thought.

So it seemed. So it seemed.

He reached down and passed his fingers over the woman's bare shoulders, across her collarbone, and down to cup her breast. His caresses made the nipple harden, and he felt himself swell once more, felt the need for her rise in him until he had kissed her awake and they made love again, no less intently at having lost the novelty of newness. Afterward Gabrielle turned onto her stomach and looked at McNeely through dream-thick eyes.

"What can I say now that wouldn't sound like a cliché?" she asked.

"Not that," he replied.

She laughed deep in her throat. It was a sound of pure pleasure, joy, contentment. She shook her head in disbelief. "Wonderful," she whispered, "perfect. Do you think that making love is better under stress?"

He smiled. "I don't know," he said, then added, "I've never been under stress."

She laughed again and he laughed with her while she kissed his chest and he mock-combed her short hair with his fingers. Her smile shrank, and when she looked at him again, some of the joy had left her violet eyes. "What happens now?"

He kept smiling for her. "You mean now or later?"

"Both."

He slid down farther in the bed so that he was looking at the ceiling. "We stay here. You paint. I read. I shoot pool with you and Kelly. We play cards. And when the end of October comes, we leave."

"Do we sleep together too?"

"I think so. If you want to."

"I do." She turned on her back and they both watched the ceiling. "And when we leave . . . then what?"

He lay silently for a moment. "I don't know. That depends on a lot."

"Like what?"

"Like if we still like sleeping together."

"And if we still like each other," she added.

"Yes."

"And if we're still alive."

"Nice," he said with enough irony to hide the chill he felt. "Beautiful thought."

"It's a possibility, don't you think?"

"That we'll *all* be dead before Halloween? Sure, it's possible. But I don't think it'll happen."

"Why not?" she asked. "Tell me why not. Reassure me."

She wanted him to think she was joking, but he could tell how serious she was. He gave a serious answer. "Cummings and David *asked* for what they got, Cummings more so. He was after power and he got it. Your husband wanted to see if there was really something here, and he found out there was. All *we* want—you, me, and Kelly—is to just get through the rest of the month. At this point I'm not after a damn thing but freedom."

" 'At this point,' you said. Were you after something before?"

He thought for a while before answering. "Yeah, I was. I wanted to see if there was something here myself. And now that I know there is, that's enough. I just want out."

"Do you think there's any way to get out before the thirty-first?"

"We can try. But I wonder if Kelly will want to."

"What do you mean?" she said, leaning on her elbow. "Why wouldn't he?"

He shrugged. "Maybe the money. It's still a million dollars."

"No," she said. "You've earned it, both of you. David's dead. I run things now. The money's yours, stay or go."

"That's generous of you," he said with a chuckle.

"I didn't mean . . ."

"I know what you meant." He sat up. "Look, I'm hungry. Why don't we get dressed and cook something. I'll get Kelly and we'll see if there's some way we *can* get out of here. If not, well, we'll be damned good cardplayers by the time the month is up."

Kelly Wickstrom was sleeping when George McNeely knocked on his door. The noise from the other room woke him and he opened his eyes to find a white face hovering above his own, staring down at him with a sort of mindless, detached interest, like a man in an asylum watching an ant crawl across a wall.

Wickstrom started, his eyes opened wide, and the face disappeared, shut off like a suddenly extinguished light. Wickstrom relaxed and rubbed the dust of sleep from his eyes. *Dreams*, he thought. *Goddamned place is full of nightmares*. He didn't think it odd that he couldn't remember what the dream had been about. He was thankful he couldn't.

There was another knock at the door. He slipped on his old terry-cloth bathrobe and went into the living room, but paused when his hand touched the knob. He had locked the door before he lay down, and wondered now if he should open it so freely to whatever might be on the other side.

But then he heard McNeely's voice call his name, and he flung it wide. The moment he saw McNeely's face he knew that something had happened. It was alive and open, quite unlike the friendly but guarded countenance McNeely'd worn before. Only now did Wickstrom think that there was a possibility of going behind the mask and *knowing* George McNeely. *Something* had happened—it was either Gabrielle Neville or the house, and for the first time Wickstrom hoped that McNeely *was* sleeping with Gabrielle. The alternative was unthinkable.

McNeely looked at Wickstrom and gave a small laugh. "Good God, what's wrong with me?"

"Huh?"

"The way you're looking at me. Like I was . . . a ghost." The last word sounded choked, as if McNeely wished he weren't going to say it just as it left his mouth.

Wickstrom realized that his own mouth was open, and that he was staring goggle-eyed at McNeely. "I'm sorry," he said. "I was sleeping. I guess I'm just not awake yet."

"Sorry for waking you. But since you're up, would you want to come down to the kitchen? Gabrielle and I were talking about what our plans should be and we need you in on it."

It's Gabrielle. Thank God it's Gabrielle. The way McNeely said "our plans" had given it away. It sounded too much like a fiancé planning a future to be coincidental.

"*We need you in on it*"—almost as if Wickstrom were an afterthought. A third wheel.

"Let me get dressed," Wickstrom said, and walked back into the bedroom. When he returned, McNeely was relaxing on the sofa, whistling softly. On the way to the kitchen he told Wickstrom of Garielle Neville's decision to let them retain the money no matter what happened from that point on.

"She figures we earned it," McNeely said.

Sure. Anyway, you earned it, stud. But Wickstrom's thought lacked vitality and conviction. It was as though the jealousy he had felt before at mere suspicion had been feigned, and he could only see it now that certainty was here. Even when he entered the kitchen and saw the cat-and-cream look on Gabrielle's face, there was no flare of anger, only a natural wish that he had gotten there first. But he hadn't, and he felt strangely at peace nonetheless.

McNeely made corned beef sandwiches and tomato soup, and they sat and ate, and drank orange juice, and tried to think of possible avenues of escape. "What about the ventilation system?" Wickstrom suggested.

McNeely shook his head. "The ducts are too small."

"You sure?"

"I checked the day we got here." McNeely swallowed the last of his sandwich. "I don't think we can force the plates either. If we had a crowbar, maybe, but there's nothing like that here. No tools at all."

"What about the bedframes," said Wickstrom. "Could we tear any of them apart for metal?"

"They're all wooden," Gabrielle reminded him. "But how about the refrigerator, or the other appliances? There's metal there."

McNeely frowned. "Nothing big enough or strong enough. We're talking about heavy steel plates here. And the real bitch is that they're in four-inch-deep slots. Like I said, I'm not even sure a crowbar would work."

"Then the hell with the windows and doors." Wickstrom turned his chair around and straddled it. "What about the walls—or the roof? Is there a cellar entrance we don't know about? And how about the doors to the sun room?"

"Forget those doors," said Gabrielle. "They have the

same steel plating as the rest. The walls are thick, though it might be worth a try. As for the roof, I don't even know where the attic entrance is.''

''If there is one,'' Wickstrom asserted, ''we can find it and go from there.''

''Walls or roof, we've got to have something to pry or dig with.'' McNeely stood and leaned against the sink. ''So what can we use?''

The three of them frowned and thought for a long moment. Then Gabrielle's eyes brightened. ''The telescope,'' she said with a thrill in her voice. ''The telescope in the observatory. It's got brass fittings, and the mount is either iron or steel. We could break it apart!''

The two men caught her excitement, and Wickstrom jumped up. ''Let's see.'' They took the stairs two at a time and practically ran into the high-domed room. The light revealed the huge scope, its lens still fixed on the metallic dome overhead.

''Jesus!'' shouted Wickstrom. ''The dome!'' he turned to the others. ''We can get out through the dome! The mechanism's locked, but we can bust it easy enough. With some of these fittings—''

''No, Kelly,'' Gabrielle said. ''It won't work. The dome is locked, but even if we get it open, there's a steel plate over it on the outside.''

''Shit,'' Wickstrom snarled. ''Didn't miss a fucking trick around here.''

''At least the telescope looks promising,'' said McNeely. ''Some of the parts of the mount could be used as pry irons if we can shape them a little, though it seems a shame to break this apart.'' He gazed admiringly at the eight-inch reflector, still gleaming brightly and untarnished after seventy years.

''I'd vandalize the Louvre to get us out of here,'' Gabrielle said. ''Let's take what we need.''

The three of them worked the scope loose from its mounting, then attempted to lower it gently to the floor. As Wickstrom looked up its tall smooth length, his arms wrapped around it like a Scot about to toss the Caber, it suddenly reminded him of something, something that meant escape quite apart from the iron fittings that had held the shaft in place. And as it came to him, his grip relaxed slightly, so that the poorly distributed weight settled precisely where Gabrielle was supporting the scope. It tipped too far, and despite McNeely and Wickstrom's frantic grab, the top end came crashing down on the hard wooden floor, splintering the objective lens into hundreds of tiny shards.

"Oh, Jesus," Gabrielle moaned. "Oh, *shit!*"

"What happened to vandalizing the Louvre?" asked McNeely. "Don't take it so hard. At least the fittings are free."

"It wasn't your fault, Gabrielle," Wickstrom said. "I lost my grip. I just had a thought and there it went."

"A thought?" McNeely's face went serious, concerned. It seemed as if sudden thoughts in this house were mostly a danger.

"The long tube," Wickstrom went on. "It reminded me of the chimney."

"The chimney?"

He turned to Gabrielle. "Yes. The chimney wasn't shut off—we've built fires in it. Is there anything over the top?"

"I—I don't know. But, Kelly, it's three stories high and only a bit over a foot in diameter. Besides, it's copper. Nothing to grab hold of. It'd be like climbing up a soda straw."

"There's got to be a way," Wickstrom said. "I'll bet anything there's no plate over the top. Neville never would have imagined anyone trying to go out that way."

"He imagined everything else," Gabrielle said, almost defensively. "Windows, doors, dome . . . what makes you think he'd miss the chimney?"

"It's just too unbelieveable that we'd try to escape that way. You're the only one small enough to fit up there, and you were in *his* camp, not ours."

"Wait a minute, Kelly." McNeely frowned. "You want Gabrielle to try and get up that chimney?"

"*We* can't," said Wickstrom.

"There's no way. How could she climb it? There's not enough room to maneuver even if there *was* something to hold on to. Christ, even if we had *pitons*, she couldn't hammer them in. Besides, what if she gets to the top and finds out it's hooked up to the ventilation system?''

Wickstrom shook his head. ''I know,'' he said dejectedly. ''I know you're right, but what else can we do?''

''We can try the walls,'' said McNeely. ''We can try the plates, we can try to find the attic. We'll get through somehow.''

''And if we don't,'' Gabrielle said, smiling grimly, ''I'll try the chimney. Santa Claus in reverse.''

They started in the study, but behind the boards the walls were brick, the mortar tough. Their makeshift prybars bent when they exerted any great pressure on them, and when Wickstrom and McNeely jabbed at the brick point-first, their only reward was a series of small gouges as inconsequential as a pockmark on the face of a titan.

''We'll never get through this way,'' said Wickstrom, throwing down the metal bar. ''Brick,'' he said, shaking his head. ''The outside of the house is *stone*, not brick!''

''Two walls,'' said McNeely glumly. ''An outer one of stone, an inner one of brick. What the hell did they build this place for? For the ages?''

Gabrielle leaned on her prybar like a cane. ''That's what the Nevilles built everything for. I wonder if it's brick all around.''

''Almost certain,'' McNeely said. ''If there'd been later additions, maybe not, but this place was built all at once.''

''What about the cellar?'' Wickstrom asked.

''That's brick-walled too.''

''But maybe there's no stone wall behind it. If we could get through the bricks . . .''

''We'd find twelve feet of earth in our way and not a shovel to be had.'' McNeely sighed. ''It doesn't look too good.''

''Let's try the plates,'' Gabrielle suggested. ''Maybe we can force them.''

They discovered quickly that the plates were tight against the slots that housed them, so snug that none of their crude implements could even be inserted in the space, let alone any pressure be put on it to dislocate the steel.

The third floor was next. They stayed together, going from room to room, looking for a trapdoor that would lead them to the attic. Finally, in one of the small bedrooms in the east wing near the gym, they found it, a wooden trap with a huge new lock and hasp. Wickstrom dragged a chair under it, worked Gabrielle's thinner prybar inside the hasp, and wrenched down.

The third time, he succeeded, yanking the hardware out of the wood so that screws fell like metallic rain. Wickstrom laughed in triumph as he pressed upward, but his face fell at the sound of wood against metal.

"Fucker!" he yelled, pounding on the trap with his fists. "That's *metal*! There's a goddamn metal *door* up there!"

"Get down, Kelly." McNeely's voice was calm.

"Why? What . . ."

"Just give me the chair."

Wickstrom clambered down dejectedly and watched as McNeely moved the chair two yards away from the trap-door, stepped up onto it, and drove his heavy bar straight up into the ceiling. Painted plaster spattered down as he thrust again and again. In between the thrusts he spoke.

"He can't . . . have covered . . . the whole roof . . . with steel . . . A ceiling's . . . just plaster and wood . . . We'll get through."

He broke through then, and the sudden move threw him off balance so that he tumbled off the chair, the bar crashing down dangerously beside him, narrowly missing his neck. He leaped up, grabbed the bar, and climbed onto the chair once more. "That did it," he snarled. "Now, you bastard . . ." He thrust the bar up again and twisted it back and forth to widen the small hole he had made. Then he screamed.

The scent of ozone bit through the air like summer lightning as McNeely let go of the bar and flung himself backward. He would have fallen again if Wickstrom hadn't caught him by the arm.

"Jesus!" McNeely howled. "My hands!" He held them up so that Wickstrom and Gabrielle could see. The palms were fiercely reddened where he had grasped the bar, and small white blisters were starting to form.

"A generator?" Wickstrom asked. "Could you have hit the generator?"

McNeely shook his head, gritting his teeth at the searing pain. "I've been shocked before. This wasn't electric. With that power it would have traveled through my whole body. No, this was like . . . like the bar just turned to fire in my hands. One second it was cold, and the next—pow."

Wickstrom knelt beside the bar and gingerly put out a hand. "Don't!" McNeely and Gabrielle cried at once, but by that time Wickstrom's fingers had contacted the metal.

"Cool," he said softly. "It's perfectly cool." He held it out to the others, who touched it delicately. There was no indication that the metal had ever been warm. "Let me try," Wickstrom said, righting the overturned chair.

"No!" McNeely said, starting to put a hand on Wickstrom's arm before he remembered his burned palms and stopped. "Look at me! You want this too?" he added, holding out the reddened hands for Wickstrom to see.

"You said yourself it wasn't a shock," Wickstrom replied. "And the bar is *cold*, George. Maybe"—he gestured loosely at McNeely's upturned hands—"maybe you did that to yourself."

"To myself!"

"Yes! Psycho . . ."—he searched for the word—". . . somatic."

"Why? Why would I want to get burned?"

"I don't know, George . . . I . . ." He was out of words. Instead, he got up onto the chair and pressed the bar through the hole, which McNeely had widened to six inches across. Wickstrom rotated the bar slowly, making ever wider circles, as if to feel the presence of any malignant stoppage above. "I don't feel anything," he said. "No heat, nothing up there—just the edges of the hole. I'll try and make it wider."

Wickstrom jerked the bar back and forth like a bellringer ringing the changes. Plaster began to flutter down again, and then Wickstrom's eyes went wide, and he stared at the bar in horror, his mouth dropping open.

"Kelly?" said Gabrielle, her voice trembling. "What's wrong?"

A small whimper escaped from Wickstrom's throat as he stared at his hands grasping the bar. They saw the muscles of his arm flex, as if trying to release it, but the fingers would not respond. McNeely reached up, grabbed the end of the bar, and found to his relief that it was still of normal temperature. He pulled down on it until the top of the bar was once again in view, and tried to yank it from Wickstrom's grip.

Wickstrom yelped in agony, and McNeely saw that although the bar had come partially loose from the younger man's grasp, a raw flap of the skin of Wickstrom's hand coated that part of the metal where the contact had been broken.

"Don't pull!" Wickstrom moaned. "Cold! It's cold!"

"Water!" barked McNeely, realizing that Wickstrom's own frozen flesh bound him to the iron. "Cold water!"

A bathroom was only two doors away, and Gabrielle dashed out of the room and down the hall.

"I can't let go," Wickstrom grated. "I'm stuck fast to it."

"It's okay, just relax," said McNeely. "The water'll free you. Like getting your tongue stuck to the pump in the winter, huh?"

"We didn't have a fucking pump in Brooklyn," Wickstrom answered gruffly.

"Well, we didn't have one in Larchmont either."

"Then how the hell do you know so much about it?"

"I used to watch *Lassie* on TV." They both laughed.

"Holy shit," Wickstrom grunted. "What the fuck are we laughing for? I'm stuck to this bar, you've got your hands burned, and we can't get out of this shithole for love or money—so what the fuck are we laughing for?"

"Maybe we're just sick of crying." The smile vanished from McNeely's face. "But you're right. There's nothing funny about it, Kelly. First hot, then cold . . . there's something in here that doesn't want us to leave. Not yet. I think that if instead of stone and brick those outside walls were paper, it'd still find a way to keep us from tearing them."

Gabrielle returned with a basin of cold water. "Just pour it over his hands," said McNeely. "That's right, slowly. How's it feel, Kelly?"

"I . . . I'm not sure, I . . ." The bar slipped from between his hands and thudded to the floor. McNeely knelt and touched it.

"It's not even cold," he said. "Just about room temperature."

"Room temperature didn't do this," Wickstrom said, showing the square inch of seeping redness at the heel of his left hand.

"The same thing as when *you* had the bar, George," said Gabrielle. "You were the only one who could feel the change in it, the only one it harmed."

"We're stuck, chillun," Wickstrom said with a laugh. "We ain't gettin' out of here nohow noway. The bastard's got us where it wants us now. Christ, if it's up there"—he pointed toward the attic above—"then it's all around."

"Let's go down to the kitchen," said Gabrielle, despair in her voice. "There's ointment in the first aid kit for your burns, George, and we can bandage your hand, Kelly." She looked up at the gaping hole in the ceiling. "And afterward we can cover that up."

If either of the men thought such a gesture would be foolish, they didn't say so.

Chapter Eleven

"We've got to make plans now," McNeely said after Gabrielle had treated and bandaged their wounds. They were sitting around the huge fireplace in the Great Hall. Every light in the room was on, and Kelly was tossing one last log onto the fire they'd built. They'd talked briefly during the wound dressing about the chimney escape and had decided, after what had happened on the third floor, not to attempt it. Even if there were a way to get up and into the attic, what was to guarantee that the copper would not become instantaneously hot enough to fry the climber? So they had built a fire, Gabrielle had made cocoa, and the three of them sat closely together, watching the flames dance on the broad stone stage of the fireplace.

"Well, we'd planned to escape," Wickstrom said dryly. "If our other plans work as well, we'll all be dead by sunrise. Whenever it is."

Gabrielle ignored the jibe. "What kind of plans, George?"

"We're here for a reason," McNeely said, concentrating on each word. "Here because it *wants* us here, because it can't let us go, because it *needs* us somehow."

"You don't *know* that," Wickstrom grunted.

"If you can come up with something better, let me know," said McNeely without anger. "Now, it got hold of Cummings when he was *alone*. And it'll probably try to do the same to us. So I think we ought to try to spend as much time together as we can . . . short of sleep time and personal needs of course."

"Sure we shouldn't have a permanent buddy system, George?" asked Wickstrom. "It might try to get us in the john, y'know."

"That might be truer than you think. It could approach us anywhere. And even being together is no guarantee as far as I'm concerned. I don't *think* we'll be approached when we're together, but I don't know either."

Gabrielle opened her mouth to speak, then took a sip of cocoa instead.

"What is it?" McNeely asked.

"I was just wondering, how strong can this thing really be? I mean, could it destroy us all if it wanted to?"

McNeely shook his head. "Not physically, I'm betting. But what it can do to our minds is another story. I don't know why, but I keep thinking that *will* has an awful lot to do with it. If we refuse to have anything to do with these things, then maybe there isn't that much that they can do to harm us."

"That's a lot of guessing and not much knowing," Wickstrom said with a trace of petulance. "Let's face it, George, Gabrielle, we don't really know shit about what's here. Hell, maybe it could turn us all into jelly in the next second for all we know. Maybe . . ."

"No," said Gabrielle. "It couldn't do that."

"Why the hell not?"

"If it could, it wouldn't be playing cat and mouse with us. It would simply *make* us do what it wanted."

"Oh, come on! How do you know it's even sane enough to know the difference between cat and mouse and bash 'em on the head? I mean, I can't make any sense at *all* of what's been happening here, and you two are already writing a book!"

"Look," said McNeely, holding up his hands, "we probably don't have enough input to make any real sense of what's been happening, so we can only theorize, Kelly. But we've got to start somewhere."

"Why? What's so fucking important that we know? I don't think we *can* know. Why don't we just stick together as much as we can, and try to get through the next week or so without going crazy? I don't know about you, but I just want to forget all this stuff and concentrate on other things,

like how I'm gonna spend my money when I get out—
think pleasant thoughts, y'know? What my mother used to
tell me when I'd have a nightmare, and Christ knows this's
been a nightmare all right. So if you think we oughta stick
together, George, well fuckin'-A with me. I *hate* being in
this place alone.'' He stopped talking at last. His face had
gotten red, and his frantic gestures had worked the adhe-
sive tape loose from the gauze that covered his ripped
hand. "Okay," he said, "okay, that's enough of a speech.
I'll do whatever you two want to do as long as it keeps us
safe and sane. All right?"

McNeely nodded. "We'll set up a schedule. We'll eat
together, be together as much as possible when we're
awake." He looked at Gabrielle, a question in his eyes.
She read it immediately and nodded. "Kelly, there's another thing. A complication you should know about."

Wickstrom smiled tensely. "I think I know already.
You two . . . you two are more than, uh, just friends,
right?"

McNeely was surprised, and tried in vain to hide it.
"Yes. Yes, that's true. But how did you . . ."

Wickstrom chuckled and relaxed a bit. "You hide most
things real well, George, but that one was obvious." He
glanced at Gabrielle and was amazed to find a splash of
pink on the sophisticated cheeks. "It doesn't matter, okay?
I don't need to know any more than I already know."

"It must look awful," Gabrielle said. "So soon after
David."

"You don't owe me any explanation. And you don't
owe your husband an apology. It's just the way things
are."

And the three of them sat there with their separate
thoughts, Wickstrom's about another wife who'd been
unfaithful, Gabrielle's about another lover with whom she'd
cheated a *living* husband, and McNeely's about an unfa-
miliar weakness that at last let his features betray his
thoughts.

They spent as much time together as was realistically
possible. McNeely and Gabrielle, except for bathroom
privacies, were never apart, and Wickstrom was with them

except when they all slept. Gabrielle had moved into the Whitetail Suite with McNeely, so the three of them all occupied the west wing only. They ate together, played games together, read books together—McNeely was reading aloud *The Brothers Karamazov*, which neither Wickstrom nor Gabrielle had read—and when one was tired, the others usually were as well. If Wickstrom awoke first, he would rap softly on the door of McNeely and Gabrielle's suite. If there was no answer, he would return to his own rooms and read, and within a short time they would knock on *his* door. Then they would have breakfast together.

Wickstrom had been concerned that he would be approached the first time he was alone again in his rooms, but nothing happened. He had slept soundly and dreamlessly, or at least he had thought until he opened his eyes from sleep and saw another face gazing down into his.

It was not the same face that he had seen before at that time in that position. This one was a pale face with straw-colored hair and sky-blue eyes, a young face with features so fair that it was all the more shocking to see the unmistakable stamp of madness on them.

But it vanished as quickly and completely as the other had, leaving him with a pounding heart and the thought that it must be only the least unforgotten fragment of a dream. And since it was a dream, he saw no point in telling the others.

Just as the others saw no point in telling him or each other about the faces *they* saw on awakening.

Several sleeps later the three of them sat in the white playroom on the third floor. Breakfast was far enough removed so that they no longer felt full, but recent enough so that there was no hunger in any of them for the next meal. Like savages, they lived by their stomachs. McNeely was in the middle of one of a row of Edgar Wallace thrillers he'd discovered in the library, and Wickstrom was doing a crossword puzzle, working his way through a paperback book full of them, throwing away each page as he completed it. Though McNeely's attention was held fast by Wallace's prose, Wickstrom glanced up from his puzzle frequently to check Gabrielle's progress with her still life.

She'd resumed her drawing six sleeps previously, had

finished her preliminary sketches, and was now putting the finishing touches on the large blue bound volumes she'd positioned on the table. Wickstrom had marveled at her ability to turn pigment into the reproduction of realism that was forming on the canvas, and now, as she brought more and more tone and shading to what had been only bare outlines, he was finding it impossible to deal with his puzzle at all.

Finally the last bit of color left her brush to settle on the canvas, and there were the books, burnished leather gleaming in the light, every pore of the binding pulsing with energy as though it were once more the living skin of the beast it had clothed.

"My God," he said in awe. "Gabrielle, that is incredible."

McNeely glanced up from his book. His eyes widened as he saw the painting, and then narrowed in intense scrutiny. "It's clearer than a photograph," he said. "It makes the superrealists look like Monet. And yet," he went on, rising and crossing to the easel, "there's more to it than that. It looks *more* than real."

Gabrielle smiled, embarrassed by the praise. "It *is* good. It's far better than anything I've ever done." She wondered if it might be because there was no more David to make her work seem so unimportant. "But it's not finished, you know. I've still got to paint the instruments."

McNeely stepped next to the table. "May I take the books? Are you finished with them?" She nodded, reminding him not to disturb the sextant, and he picked the volumes up, bringing them back behind the easel and holding the reality up to the image. "I hate to gush," he said, "but this knocks me out."

Wickstrom looked at the comparison and shook his head in wonder. "A good thing you paint still lifes, Gabrielle. If you painted anything alive, it'd probably step down off the canvas."

"Don't say that, Kelly," McNeely joked. "In this place it probably *would*."

Wickstrom and Gabrielle laughed. They were all finally able to joke again, even about the house and their being trapped within it. It was the timelessness that had made it so easy. When it seemed as though things had happened either a moment or a year before, it was easier and less painful to imagine the latter. " 'We have always lived in the castle,' " McNeely had quoted once when they'd been discussing the phenomenon, and although neither Gabrielle nor Wickstrom seemed to recognize the allusion, they understood it well enough.

"I'm thirsty," Wickstrom said, turning toward the door. "Anybody want anything?"

"We'll go with you," said McNeely, setting the books on the small table by his chair. Gabrielle put down her palette.

"Look, isn't this a little silly?" Wickstrom objected mildly. "I mean, it's been quite a while now since . . . the trouble, and nothing's happened. Hell, I sleep alone—if the creepy-crawlies wanted to get me, they'd get me then, right?"

"I guess, Kelly. It's just that I don't think we ought to take *any* chances."

"George, my chances of being grabbed while walking down the hall to the lounge for a glass of water are pretty small, wouldn't you agree?"

"Sorry, Kelly. I guess I've seen too many horror movies. The monster hardly ever comes out unless the victim's alone, you know?" McNeely waved a hand. "Oh, go ahead. Just yell if you need help."

"My feets are very capable of doing they stuff, thank you," Wickstrom joked as he stepped into the hall.

As soon as the door closed behind him, he wished he'd listened to McNeely. He couldn't ever remember feeling so alone. It was worse, far worse, than being in his bedroom with George and Gabrielle across the hall. Since there were two of them, they'd always seen him to his rooms first, then gone into theirs. And, too, the rooms were *his*—he felt safe in them. Nothing had ever happened there, nothing except seeing the nightmare faces that he felt sure were his own creations.

But now he felt naked, exposed, like an ant fallen onto a spider's web in which all the strands but one were sticky, and if he could scuttle quickly and silently across that single strand and back again, everything would be fine.

But if he made a noise, or stepped too hard, or went too slowly, the spider would hurtle down, his massive bulk knocking him against one of the sticky strands, where his struggles to get free would only entangle him further. And the spider would laugh a deep roaring laugh before it began at last to feed.

Go on, dummy! he told himself. What was it, eighty feet? Twenty to the Great Hall, another forty across the balcony, and a final twenty to the door of the lounge. That was all. Eighty feet.

And back again.

And inside the lounge, where he'd heard Seth Cummings shambling in the darkness. And back again.

Had heard was right. Seth Cummings was dead as dead could be. He wasn't going to be there waiting for someone to push the door wide and turn on the lights and see . . .

Seth Cummings standing by the bar with his head stuck on one of the spigots . . .

Shit. Just do it. Just walk. If it's gonna get me, it's gonna get me one way or another. Walk.

Wickstrom walked to the lounge. He didn't look to the side; he didn't look in back of him. He stared straight ahead and walked down the hall. He didn't look over the balcony rail when he passed it because he knew that if he did, he'd see all those people down below looking up at him, those people just like Seth Cummings, and there would be dozens of them, maybe even hundreds standing down there looking up at Kelly Wickstrom, not saying anything, not having to, because he knew what they wanted, what they wanted to do to him. Or maybe they'd all be dancing down there around the big fireplace with a chimney that didn't go out into the clean air but recirculated its smoky essence so that the air got harder and harder to breathe. Dead air. Dead like everything and everybody else in here but the three of them, and he would *not* look down over that railing.

He was past it now, he was by the stairs, and he had only another twenty feet to go. But the feet stretched to yards and the yards became *back*yards with a psychic fence between each to climb over. He climbed and walked as though through the thick jelly of dreams. The stairway on his right was hunched in shadow, the steps like slanted fingers ready to reach up and smash the ant that scurried forever across the dry strand of Oriental runner. The vacant rooms just past the stairs (*past the stairs, yes, I am moving*) were suddenly filled with terrors that the closed fists of the doors threatened to release and scatter like a boy scatters the lightning bugs he's captured on a windless summer night. They would dart about the hapless ant, blinding him with their fiery white phosphorescence so that he stepped off the single strand of safety, so that one leg touched that wet stickiness that held him tight, and without wanting to, he twitched and pulled at the strand.

And woke the spider.

The lounge door stood open before him, and the light glowed inside. He walked through the doorway into the warmth of the room, and felt as though the trek there had taken hours, but now he was back to normal again, crossing the floor to the bar and pouring three fingers of bourbon as he muttered, "Fuck the water."

The liquor burned its way into his stomach and he sighed in relief and delight at feeling a sensation other than fear. What the hell had come over him? There was no point to his terror, none at all. He had seen and heard nothing, all the imagined horrors being exactly that— imagined. "Get ahold of yourself, man," he quoted in an old school tone of voice. But instead of amusing himself, the words chilled him as he wondered who else might be hearing them. He propped himself on a barstool and looked around the room. It was closetless, and there were no other cubbyholes behind or inside of which anything large enough to be harmful could hide. But still . . .

"Hello," he said, not at all tentatively, but forcefully, as if he expected to be answered. "Hello, hello, hello. Nice to be here." He swallowed heavily, antithetical to his manner. "I'm starving for conversation," he went on. "Isn't anybody going to talk to me?"

He paused then, listening, watching, eyes roving recklessly over the room, fearing to stop at one place for too long.

"Well, all right then." As he heard his words, he knew his voice was wrong. Nonchalance should not tremble;

sarcasm should not shake. "I hate to drink alone, but you've had your chance." He finished the drink and put the glass into the small sink, running water into it, then turning it upside down. He opened his mouth to say more, but thought better of it, and made himself walk out into the hall. He stood there, his eyes on the closed door of the vacant room directly across from the lounge. The decision made, he crossed to it and turned the knob.

But doubt beat him down as he prepared to push, and he could only stand statuelike, hand on doorknob, frozen in a scene he'd played in a dozen busts in a dozen dingy apartment halls. And what good would it do to shout "hold it, police" to a room empty of all but phantoms? He didn't even have a backup.

So he let go of the knob and turned away, the door unopened. At the balcony he stopped and listened. The only sound was the infrequent dull pop of the few logs left from their last fire, engaged in a slow destruction in which no visible flames chewed and bit at the fuel. Instead, they turned slowly, invisibly, to ash, the combustion working its way into the core of the log inch by inch, so slowly as to be unnoticeable to a watcher. But in the silence of The Pines he could hear it three floors below, could hear the cancer of oxidation turning the hard wood from brown to charred black to the gray powder that dropped off speck by speck. Then he looked down.

The space below was empty. There were no grinning specters, no malformed monsters, no quasi-Quasimodos beckoning to him to join their throng. Except for the few pieces of furniture that dotted it, the Great Hall was bare. He smiled as manfully as he could, then walked the rest of the way to the playroom.

As he entered, Gabrielle looked up from her canvas and smiled. "That was fast."

"Fast?"

"You've barely been gone," she said. "I didn't even have time to worry about you."

"No worry," Wickstrom answered, confused at the dichotomy of their individual perceptions of time. "Didn't see a thing." He sat and picked up his puzzle book. McNeely had only glanced up when he'd entered, and seemed enthralled in the blue quarto volume he held in his lap. "What're the books, George?" Wickstrom asked.

"Oh," McNeely answered, distracted, "the ones Gabrielle was painting."

"I *know* that," he said. "I mean what's *in* them?"

McNeely looked up in slight exasperation. "Astronomical notebooks. These are the ones old Robert D'Neuville kept the summers he spent here." He looked back at the pages. "I wish to hell that dome were open. We might see quite a show."

"A show?"

"It's strange," McNeely said almost to himself. "D'Neuville had literally hundreds of meteors recorded—"

"Oh, yeah? Like meteor showers?"

"So it seems, but meteor showers are generally predictable. He seems to have seen them nearly all the time. In the summer the Perseids are prominent, but there's no sign of them here."

Generally meteors would have bored Wickstrom, as did anything of a scientific nature, but in the captivity of The Pines, the mention of them stirred his interest. "What kind of meteors? I mean, I don't even know what they are, really."

"I'm no astronomer," said McNeely, "but I think they're outer space debris, pieces of comets' tails that are caught by the earth's gravitational pull. When they enter our atmosphere, they ignite. Most of them burn up before they hit the surface. But if these *were* meteors, they sure as hell behaved oddly. Listen to this." He read:

June 12th. Started to observe at 8:45 P.M. While searching for Mercury low in the east, I became aware of a pinpoint of light moving into my field. I followed it and traced its journey from above the eastern horizon, where I first saw it, *upward* approximately seven degrees. There it seemed to stop and increase in brightness to roughly −3.00 magnitude, at which point it seemed to break apart into a cloudy luminescence. I have seen nothing like this before. I was so amazed that I went and told Smith, who has a bit of a layman's interest in astronomy. He suggested that it might be a phenomenon similar to an aurora, but I doubt it. It did not appear auroral in nature, more meteoric actually, only what kind of meteor sails upward from the horizon?

McNeely looked up from the book. ''That was only the first of them. When he started observing again, he saw them everywhere. Listen to this observation a few days later.''

June 19th. I have struggled to imagine what these bits of light might be, but I can come up with nothing. Smith, at my invitation, has been observing also, and is astonished by the things. They come approximately once every three or four minutes—that is, at any certain point in the sky five degrees across. They never rise higher than twenty degrees from the horizon, at which point they brighten and seemingly disintegrate.

June 20th. It is extraordinary. Smith and I walked out to the overlook at 10:30 this evening. There was no moon, and the stars glittered like jewels. The meteors came in profusion, and I can see there is a pattern now. From the northern horizon, and also from the west and east, come the lights. They are very dim at first as they come into view, like far-away rockets being shot off from over the edge of the world. Then as they rise in the sky, they grow in luminescence until they approach the brightness of fireflies, at which point they burst apart like fireworks, scattering their faint light over a huge area of the sky. They arrive incessantly, and at times many come at once. We saw dozens in the short time we observed. The sight is unparalleled in my experience. Although this is totally illogical and must be nothing but a twist of our perceptive sense, I could swear that Pine Mountain is the *target* of these lights. Other meteors I have observed elsewhere (if meteors these are) have crossed only a small portion of the overturned bowl of the night sky. But Smith and I,

as observers, seem to be at the focal point of these
phenomena. No matter at what point on the horizon
they originate, they seem to come straight toward us.
I shall make it a point to ask Wilkes at Yerkes about
this.

"Holy shit," muttered Wickstrom.

McNeely nodded. "Curiouser and curiouser."

"Did he keep seeing them?" Gabrielle asked, mixing
the colors on her palette.

"Don't know. I haven't gotten that far." He thumbed
through the rest of the volume and then picked up the
others. "A lot of gaps," he said. "Every two pages is a
day, every volume a year. Only a few weeks filled in
every year."

"He spent only a few weeks here every year after his
son died," Gabrielle reminded him. "I suppose the books
stayed here exclusively."

"I suppose." McNeely glanced at the spines. "The first
is 1919. That's the summer his son died. Then 1920,
1921, and 1922. By '22 there are only a few days worth of
notes. Suppose he lost interest?"

"He had new toys to amuse himself, probably," said
Gabrielle.

"Oh, you idle rich."

"Terrible, aren't we?"

"What do the final volumes say about these . . . these
lights?" Wickstrom asked.

"Let me look." McNeely started thumbing, stopping
three quarters of the way through a volume. "In 1920
D'Neuville had up this Wilkes he mentioned. Looks like
Wilkes didn't know what the hell the lights were either.
Listen to this. 'Wilkes feels the phenomenon may be
terrestrial in origin rather than from outside our atmosphere, possibly of the nature of St. Elmo's fire.' Nice try,
Wilkes, but no cigar. What's he say in '21? 'The lights are
here again this year, as frequent and as bright as ever.
Neither Wilkes nor the colleagues he's told of the phenomenon have any solid idea as to what causes it. I fear it may
remain unfathomable. A party from Princeton has requested
a visit to observe, but I am not sure I shall grant their

wish. I am beginning to think that there is more to this than science can fathom.' ''

"What the hell did he mean by that?" Wickstrom mused.

"Maybe he was getting the first tinglings himself of what this place was really like. The more we learn about The Pines, the weirder it gets."

"Does it say," Gabrielle asked, "if he ever found out what the things were?"

McNeely scanned through the rest of the 1921 volume and then turned to 1922. After a short time he spoke. "No. He says he was still seeing them, and that's all. Nothing about the boys from Princeton either." He let the last volume fall shut and piled it on top of the other three. "Quite a waste of journals. He could have put all that he wrote in a thirty-page looseleaf."

"Don't worry. He could afford it," said Gabrielle. "I wonder what those things were."

"Or maybe *are*," McNeely said.

She looked up from the canvas. "You don't mean they still might be there?"

McNeely shrugged. "Possible. Did you notice anything strange in the sky the night before we were locked in?"

"No. Nothing unusual." She thought for a moment. "But the trees are much higher now. Far higher than they were in the twenties, most certainly."

"Then even if they'd been here," said McNeely, "you wouldn't have seen them. According to D'Neuville, they never got that high."

"We'll look when we get out," Gabrielle said thoughtfully.

"You can look," said Wickstrom, "but I'll be long gone. I don't intend to wait for night." He smiled bitterly. "I'm tired of night. Besides," he added, "I already know what those lights were."

Gabrielle and McNeely stared at him. "What?" McNeely said. "And how would you know?"

"You can make theories, *I* can make theories." He settled back in his chair and laughed softly. "They're ghosts."

"Ghosts?"

"Sure, what else? Ghosts from north, east, west, probably from the south too. Eskimo ghosts, white ghosts, nigger ghosts, gook ghosts, ghosts from all over the world. Sure, that's it! I finally figured it out! The Pines is a big convention hotel for ghosts!'' He laughed.

Gabrielle and McNeely laughed too, if a trifle uncomfortably.

''I think I'm kidding,'' Wickstrom said with a twisted smile. ''I *think* I'm kidding, but I don't know. Maybe I'm serious. Think about it,'' he said, his eyes suddenly far away. ''People dying, dying all the time all over the world—how many hundreds, thousands a day. And when they die, maybe something leaves their body—spirit, soul, whatever. Where does it go? Heaven? Hell?'' His words had grown so soft, the others had to strain to hear, even in the tomblike silence. ''Pine Mountain?''

Gabrielle took a step toward him. ''Kelly, I . . .''

He went on, not hearing her. ''What if—what if Pine Mountain was like the North Pole? What if it was a big magnet, but instead of drawing compass needles, it drew ghosts?''

The three of them sat there in the room, and in their minds they were the three loneliest people on earth. But they were not the most alone. Wickstrom's words had turned a playroom on the third floor of a large, lonely house into the focal point of attention of an endless line of watchers, watchers who stretched back through the centuries, back to when man first walked the hills and deserts of earth. They thought of the faces then, the faces that had loomed over them as they woke, faces they had believed were no more or less than nightmares—black faces, Oriental faces, white faces, faces that could have lived today and faces so primitive they were nearly bestial. Faces that could have spanned the cavalcade of man's life.

''It's impossible,'' whispered McNeely.

Wickstrom barked a dry laugh. ''Yeah,'' he said. ''Just like what happened to Cummings was impossible.''

''The mountain *drew* them,'' said Gabrielle, ''like a giant lodestone. Is that what you mean, Kelly?''

Wickstrom shook his head back and forth, back and forth, not in answer to Gabrielle's question, but to clear his mind, to drive out all the ideas and theories and questions that were pushing down on his brain with unrelieved pressure. "I don't. No," he said finally. "I don't know *what* I mean. That's a . . . . a crazy suggestion. Real Looney Tunes."

"I just can't see it," said McNeely. "I mean, all these things that have been happening here—there's got to be some kind of explanation, some kind of *logic* behind them, even if it *is* a supernatural logic. But why here? If anywhere, why here?"

"Why the North Pole?" asked Wickstrom.

"The North Pole is in line with the earth's axis," McNeely answered.

"My ass! Not *magnetic* north!"

"Birds don't come here," said Gabrielle, "nor animals. The Indians stayed away. It's as if they all knew."

"Something that folks more civilized forgot," Wickstrom finished.

"No," said McNeely firmly, "it's too much."

Wickstrom flushed a deep red. "Goddamnit, just because it's not *your* idea!"

"Bullshit! It's not that!"

"All right!" yelled Gabrielle, the shrillness of her voice cowing the men. "You both know the only way we're going to get out of here is to stay together—and that means our minds as well as physically. It *wants* us to fight. Whatever it is, I'm sure it wants *that*."

"I'm sorry," Wickstrom said, and his face looked like he meant it. "I lost my temper."

McNeely pushed his fingers through his thick hair. "Yeah. Me too."

"Um . . . you're probably right, George. There's nothing to it, just a wacky idea. I'm grabbing at straws."

McNeely smiled. "I thought you were the one who said before that it didn't matter."

"Did I say that?" Wickstrom answered, returning the smile. "What I say and what I think are different. I just hate to talk about it because it makes me *think* about it. Look," he said, rising, "let's forget about this shit for a while. I think the best way to combat spookhouse fever—which is The Pines' form of cabin fever—is to play a hot game of Monopoly. Have I got any suckers?"

The others forced smiles, but didn't speak.

"Come on, folks," said Wickstrom with a weak chuckle, "don't make me play with myself. Boardwalk's pretty lonely without friends."

Gabrielle set down her palette and untied her apron. "My painting will keep." She ruffled McNeely's hair. "And you can find out who killed Colonel Appleyard later."

"His name's not Appleyard, and I already know," said McNeely.

"Well, if you know, what do you read it for?"

"For the excitement."

"For the excitement?" boomed Wickstrom. "Jesus!"

They laughed their way into the hall, and they kept laughing through the Monopoly game. Despite the unease that Wickstrom's suggestion had caused, the simple act of his going down the hall for a drink without incident was more influential. It seemed that much time had gone by without any strange occurrences, and after the next sleep, all of them awoke without seeing any disembodied heads over their beds. They began to feel more confident, and two sleeps later George McNeely awoke before Gabrielle and went down to the kitchen alone to eat a piece of toast. He didn't wake her to join him or to tell her where he was going.

It was just what The Pines had been waiting for.

Chapter Twelve

The caretaker's workroom was thick with dust. It had not been opened when the recent renovations were made, nor at any time during the previous fifty years. It was merely an annex behind and attached to the six-car garage. Its door was secured by a rusted lock that Whitey Monckton's booted foot easily snapped from the brittle wood. The light did not work, so he depended on the morning sunlight that was reflected into the room. It took his eyes a moment to adjust to the dimness, but when his pupils had expanded fully, he found the light sufficient.

The room was larger than he had thought, roughly twenty by thirty, and seemed as temporary as The Pines itself was permanent. The floor was dirt, and he could see patches of light against the east wall where rain and wind had dug their way inside over the years. A workbench and three long tables occupied the room, and rusty tools hung from brown ten-penny nails driven into the opposite wall. A small wooden box of magazines with titles like *All-Story* and *Adventure* sat beside one of the tables, and Monckton picked up a few. They fell apart in his hands in large damp flakes, sending up a stale musty odor. He grimaced, and wiped the clinging gray dust from his fingers.

Dust was over everything; it was not a dry dust that could be blown away, but a thick dust that hugged whatever it coated like a sickly mildew. Monckton fancied he could almost see it growing its way over his boottops. Absurd, but it made him keep moving, walking across the

rough earth floor. As he looked at the filthy array of tools
lying haphazardly on the table and hanging from the nails,
as if their owner had had little affection for his charges, he
catalogued them mentally.

Hammer . . . chisel . . . saw . . . crowbar . . . He
could scarcely believe that these things were still here,
waiting for his practiced hand. Glancing at his watch, he
wondered if he would have any time to begin, or if he
should get back to the cabin a mile below. Monckton had
been driving up every morning for days now, staying
longer on every visit, with Sterne getting more and more
pissed each time.

"What in hell are you doing?" he'd cried the morning
after Renault had called. "Good Christ, I covered for you
once, but that doesn't mean I can keep doing it! What if
Renault calls again?"

Monckton had calmed him and told him that Renault
would *not* call again, and that he'd probably felt dumb
calling the *first* time. Fortunately, he'd been more right
than he thought. Renault hadn't called since, but that did
nothing to ease Sterne's paranoia.

"Look," he'd said after Monckton had returned from
his second visit, "what if Simon *had* called? He didn't,
but what if he had? What am I supposed to say if he really
wants to talk to you?"

"He won't."

"Goddamnit! Monckton, why the fuck do you wanta go
up there anyway?"

"I'm psychic." It was out of his mouth before he'd
even thought of it, but when he heard himself say it, he
knew it was the truth. He didn't know if it would be the
truth back in New York, or in Frisco, or in Glamis Castle,
or in any other place on earth, but here in Pine Mountain,
Pennsylvania, he was without a doubt mother-fucking sure-
as-shit *psychic*. Whatever the hell that meant.

But what it meant to him was that something was up
there in that house on the mountaintop, something big and
powerful, something that had already done *something* (he
didn't know what) to *someone* (he didn't know who), and
that something worse was going to happen if they didn't

get their asses out or somebody else didn't get their ass *in*, and he was afraid that he was elected.

One catch though: there *was* no way in. To release the steel plates would take two of them. The plan was that if there were an unforeseen emergency, and the fail-safe system in The Pines failed to open the plates, he and Sterne were each supposed to turn a key in an override system in the cabin, which would allow the occupants to escape. But Monckton knew that short of that unimaginable emergency, there was no way Sterne would agree to free those inside. Such an act would be against Renault/Neville's (he'd started to think of the two men as a single unit) express orders, and Sterne would be horrified at the thought. *God keep me from ever kissing ass that deep,* Monckton thought. He could smell the fear on Sterne—not any kind of sensible fear, but the fear of displeasing his superiors.

Monckton never thought of himself as having any superiors—just people he worked for for a while. If they didn't like him, or vice versa, there was always another client looking for his kind of thinking. But Sterne was a sycophant who would most likely smother a baby if Renault had told him to, the kind of man who was more afraid of a disapproving frown from Renault than of all the horrors The Pines might hold. He was the right man for *this* job, that was sure. Monckton wasn't and knew it. He used his own judgment too much and valued it too highly, though not to the extreme of refusing to listen to the advice of those who knew more than he did about a certain subject.

But on the subject of The Pines he felt he knew as much as anyone, except perhaps for the five who'd gone in there on the first of October.

He started to look about the room again. There was at least one more thing he would need, and finally, on the floor against the far wall beneath a rotting tarpaulin, he found it—an extension ladder. It was crusted with mold, but Monckton knew that once he cleaned it up, it would be serviceable. The rungs were still tightly secured to the uprights and the extension hooks seemed in good shape. He guessed that extended it would be forty feet high, not long enough to reach the roof from the ground, but enough to reach the second floor balconies of either suite in the rear of the house.

Monckton glanced at his watch in the half darkness of the shed and cursed. He'd already been gone nearly an hour, longer than ever before. Sterne would . . .

Fuck Sterne, he thought grimly as he disentangled the tattered tarp from the ladder and dragged it out into the sunlight. He grabbed handfuls of leaves and began to scrub the rungs with them, trying to wipe off the dust and mold. But the leaves merely splintered and stuck to the old damp wood, and after some experimentation, he found that the high grass at the edge of the yard made a sturdier abrasive. In fifteen minutes the rungs were clean and dry enough so that he felt fairly sure his boots would not slip on them.

He dragged the ladder over beneath the balcony of the Eagle Suite, and set its base firmly on the ground, tamping the uprights a half inch into the damp earth. Then he raised the extension until it locked in the highest position, and leaned it against the wrought iron of the balcony above. He shook it a few times, but it seemed fully as sturdy as he had thought. But before he began to climb, he listened.

He had no illusions that whatever lived in The Pines would welcome an intruder, and he had no wish to climb partway up the ladder only to be hurled down again. So he listened for the roar of power, the dynamo of life he had heard on his first visit but had not heard since.

It was nearly silent. The only sound beside the wind in the needles and the dead and dying leaves was a low hum, like a generator, far above his head. But he knew it was no generator. It was the aural embodiment of the thing he had heard before, only now it was low, so very low that he could barely hear it at all, like the muffled snore of a hibernating bear in a dark cave.

He started up the ladder, pausing every few rungs to touch and to listen, but nothing out of the ordinary occurred. The dull humming was still there, and he wondered if it wasn't indeed the ventilating system in the attic, soundproofed or not. At last he swung his leg over the railing and stood on the balcony. Walking over to the French doors of the Eagle Suite, he pressed his ear against the steel plate that covered them. He'd expected to hear nothing, and was not disappointed. Even the hum was gone, drowned out by the wind that had continually been growing stronger all that morning.

Monckton pulled the ladder up onto the balcony and leaned it against the top eave of the house. With its base wedged against the balcony, its top just touched the overhang of the roof, and Monckton swallowed heavily as he looked up the ladder's length. There was little room for error. If the ladder should sag while he climbed it, he might lose those extra few inches, sending the top thudding against the side of the house. He wondered if he could hold on, or if the shock would jar him loose, throwing him thirty feet to the tile floor of the balcony. But then he realized that the caretaker had had to get to the roof somehow, and this was the only ladder available, so odds were it was the one he had used, and in just this way. There was, he remembered, no trapdoor from the attic to the roof.

Just the same, he decided to climb up without the added weight of the tools. If the climb were uneventful, he could always get them later. He stepped up onto the balcony railing, took a deep breath, and started to climb.

There was a bad moment halfway up, when he felt the ladder sway slightly and dip, as though its rigidity were failing and it was slowly becoming elastic. He froze at first, then looked up in panic at the roof edge to see scarcely an inch overlap of the top of the ladder where there had been two inches before. It *was* sagging, and as he stared, the ladder seemed to shrink even further. He sobbed, and jerked with his hands on the uprights in an attempt to straighten the wood, to pull the ladder back from its fatal sag. Everything he knew about physics told him that it should not work, that in fact it should put *more* stress on the weakest point in the ladder, but to his astonishment, it *did* work. Though the two-inch safety margin did not fully return, he lost no more space at the top, and soon had his arms over the roof edge and was pulling himself up onto the black slate.

The roof had absorbed enough of the morning sun to bear a slight warmth, and he lay on his back for a while until he felt it permeate his light jacket and shirt. His exertion had warmed him before, but now he could sense the first true chill of winter in the whirling winds that raced over the unprotected roof, and the warm slate felt good.

After a bit he sat up and looked around. The roof was on a level with the surrounding treetops, and he could see the horizon far away to every side, though the trees prevented him from seeing the closer topography. Through the shaking uppermost branches to the north, he could glimpse the small town of Wilmer twenty miles distant, though it appeared to be no more than a patch of grayish-white in a sea of dark reds, flat greens, and muddy browns.

A short walk over the roof verified what he had already guessed—there was no method of entering the house from the roof. No readily accessible method, at any rate. He knelt down and tried to fit his fingers beneath one of the black slates. It was easier than he had thought. The slate seemed to crumble in his grasp, and, pulling it away, he saw the dark wood beneath. One-by-eights, he thought. As solidly as the place was built, two-by-eights wouldn't have surprised him. A keyhole saw would be ideal, but he didn't have one. He'd have to gouge his way through.

Sitting down once more, he looked out at the horizon and wondered if he really was crazy to be trying to get inside a house from which any sane man would be fleeing in terror. He didn't owe anything to the people inside— why not leave them alone with whatever they'd gone in there to meet?

But he couldn't do that. He was the only one in the world who could save them, assuming there were any left to save. The thought that he might get inside and find them safe and well and angry at being disturbed did not even occur to him. That they wanted out was certain. That they were not able to get out was even more certain. And perhaps he could free them.

Yet underlying his mission of mercy was another urge that he himself could not fully understand. Curiosity was too mild a term for it, obsession too strong. One is neither curious nor obsessed when the telephone rings or the doorbell chimes; one simply picks up the receiver or opens the door. Monckton was in his own mind merely opening the door, responding to the knock, so that getting the people out was secondary to his own goal of getting in. He didn't think about it much, because there was so little to actually *think* about. It lay beyond that, in the misty realm of feeling.

A dull roar rumbled in his ears, and he thought at first it was the house awakening, but instead it was a plane, so high that he could barely make out its shape. He looked at his watch once more and frowned. There would be no time to try to get in today. He was surprised that Sterne was not already firing one of their rifles into the air to beckon him back down to the cabin. Perhaps tonight, when Sterne was sleeping soundly, he would come back up with a rope and flashlight and probably a pistol, and try to get in through the roof with the crowbar and hammer and chisel in the bright moonlight.

He looked toward the south and smiled. The moon would be high and just past full by the time Sterne slept. It would be just like daylight. He had always liked the night, bright moonlit nights in particular. It made the whole world magical with mingled planes of light and jet black pockets of shadow that no other light, bright or dim, could duplicate. It would be that way tonight, he thought. The only clouds were low on the eastern horizon—rain clouds perhaps, but too far away to worry about.

He stood up and walked over to the ladder, then reached down and drew it up until it was almost perpendicular to the ground. It gave him an extra foot of space at the top, but if it would tip outward once, it would be gone. He toyed with it so that the $=$ se touched the iron balcony once more, leaving only a bare two inches sticking past the edge of the roof. Inside his head he said a prayer, and swung his legs over the side onto the rungs.

God was not listening. But something else was.

A third of the way down, the ladder shivered, a slight tremulous shudder that Monckton would have failed to notice had he been a bit less tensely suggestible. But as it was, he froze in place, muscles locked, breathing halted, cursing his own heartbeat as it pounded in his ears. It happened again, stronger now, as if a fist had struck the uprights at the base, and slowly the ladder began to bend

in the center. He sucked in the chill air as he saw the top
shrink from the roof edge until his margin of safety was
only an inch, then a half inch, then . . .

His stomach dropped away as he saw the ladder top
shoot toward the wall of the house. At first he could not
understand that he was moving with it, so he was unprepared for the force with which it struck the wall, the wood
ratcheting madly in his ears as it scraped against the stone.
He lurched sideways, hanging on with a death grip to the
rungs, throwing away the tenuous hold the ladder had
maintained against the house. It was falling, tipping to the
side like a child's pile of blocks stacked too high.

The horror of his choice came upon him immediately.
To hang on would mean being thrown over the side of the
balcony, being smashed on the walkway below, and possibly crushed by the ladder as well. To let go would mean
falling onto the rough tiles of the second floor balcony,
letting the ladder slide over the edge and farther down.
Logic screamed to let go and take the nearer fall, while
raw survival told him to hold on to whatever he had, even
though it might take him down to death. But it was the
other voice, the voice that was not his own that told him to
hold on to the plunging ladder, that forced his decision.

It wants me to fall! Fall all the way!

With an outburst of air he unclenched his fingers from
around the wood and tried to will his body back within the
borders of the balcony railing. He was only partially
successful.

The ladder struck the iron rail at the same time Monckton
did, and was bucked off and down to clatter heavily
against the walk below. Monckton was luckier. His legs
struck the rail, his body inside its relatively safe confines.
Both legs broke, cracking like dry sticks, the bone of the
left jabbing out redly through his brown wool pants and
the skin beneath. He hit the balcony floor with his left
shoulder, shattering the joint and snapping both clavicle
and scapula. Four ribs cracked. His hip was dislocated.
Since most of the weight was taken by the shoulder, his
head only bounced lightly on the tile with the sharp deft
sound of a cue ball breaking the rack. It caused a mild
concussion, but not enough for him to lose consciousness.

It would have been better if he had, for what followed was far worse.

The faces were back, the faces that he had seen in the observatory. Corll, Hitler, Fish—they were all there, bathed in such a pure whiteness that he felt dizzy looking at them. He struggled to close his eyes against the light, but was powerless to. There were more now, savage faces, fiendish and brutal, that seemed to go on forever, like in hotels where there was a mirror on the door and a mirror on the wall and he could see himself, a million naked Moncktons going into the mirror forever and ever, and they would never stop coming, never stop looking at him and *wanting* him to *be* with them, to be *one of them*, and the faces looked and *knew* him, and two faces came out of the mass and four eyes looked into his, and through the pain and the blood and the tears of fear he knew them for who they were, knew them even though neither one looked like a real face at all.

David Neville and Seth Cummings.

Monckton screamed. It was a scream so intense, so piercing, that it brought him the peace of unconsciousness while it filled his throat with blood. It was a scream so great that it carried down Pine Mountain, unchallenged by sound of bird or insect, so powerful that inside the caretaker's cabin a mile away, Sterne heard its dim echo through the window he had cracked open to relieve the stuffiness the wood stove had caused. He heard, and stiffened, and rose, looking fearfully toward the door and more fearfully toward the black telephone that sat by the overstuffed couch. He sighed and cursed and left the cabin, pausing only long enough to grab a thick down-filled parka from the coat tree by the door.

Then he started running, running through the bristling brown and gold leaves and dead needles that layered the dirt road up Pine Mountain.

Chapter Thirteen

The marmalade was good. Fresh fruit was long gone, but the marmalade was sugared lightly enough that McNeely could taste the tartness of the oranges on his tongue. He popped the last morsel into his mouth and put another slice of wheat bread into the toaster, pressing the lever down with a sharp click. He smiled slightly and dipped a finger into the jar, then transferred the sweet orange stickiness to his mouth. His mother would have killed him if he'd ever done that at the dining room table in Larchmont. In fact, he would never have done it had there been another person in the room. But Gabrielle was still sleeping upstairs, and so probably was Wickstrom. And no one else was there.

No one else was there.

He was beginning to believe that. For what must have been days, none of them had experienced anything abnormal. It was like what he had thought it would be at the beginning of the month. Waiting. Playing games, reading, and waiting for the month to end and the steel plates to shoot up, letting five people leave, three of them a million dollars richer.

Those five people were only three now, but those three *would* leave. He had told Gabrielle that after they had made love, just before this past sleep.

"I think we're free of them now," he'd said. "We'll walk out of here together."

"I keep wondering," she had said, snuggling closer against him, "what if we couldn't get out. What if they

191

forgot us or left us here on purpose or the plates didn't open when they were supposed to?''

"That won't happen.''

"What if it does? What if it *did*, George? We don't know. What if we've already been here a month? What if it's November now? We could never tell.''

"I could tell.''

"You couldn't.''

"I've got a great internal timer. Actually it's now 9:37, the evening of October twenty-fourth.''

"Oh, bullshit.'' She'd laughed. "Be serious.''

"All right. We *will* get out of here. The plates will open when they're supposed to, and if they don't Monckton and Sterne will have the Marines up here to cut their way in with lasers. We'll get out.'' He had kissed her then on both eyes, and reached across her to turn out the light.

He'd been on the edge of sleep when he'd heard her speak. "I love you, George.'' It had been the first time she'd said it. She let her hand trail down his body. "I love you, my poor George. So many scars.''

He'd smiled in the darkness. "Do you love my scars too?''

"I love you all. All of you.''

"Do you know that I love you too?''

"I'd hoped so.''

"If you had to give up your whole fortune to be with me, would you?''

"Why? Do I have to?''

"You answer first.''

"I *don't* have to give it up. That's the wonderful thing, isn't it? We can live happily ever after after all.''

He'd thought of Jeff then. "Did you know,'' he'd said, "that I had . . . have a roommate?''

She'd been silent for a moment, and he'd noticed an almost imperceptible stiffening. "David mentioned that.''

Just say it. Get it out and it can never hurt you again.
"Did he add that my roommate and I were lovers?''

"No. Not in so many words. But I assumed as much. Most men over thirty as well off as you don't take room-mates out of financial necessity.''

"That's true.''

"Are you bisexual?"

"No. I . . . was gay."

"Then why—"

"I don't know," he'd interrupted, and turned to face her in the blackness. "I don't know. All I know is that I love you. Anything I felt before, did before . . . it's like some faraway dream."

At first a chill had gone through him when he'd felt her body shake. He'd thought that it might be laughter. But another second and her arms were around him, her face pressed closely to his so that he felt her tears against his cheek, and he was crying, too, and when the tears were gone and the promises made, they had slept.

The snap of the toaster startled him, and he brought his thoughts back to the present long enough to spread butter and marmalade on the toast. As he sat nibbling at it, he wondered what had happened to him that had made him feel this way about Gabrielle. Then he smiled. Maybe Gabrielle had happened to him. Maybe it was that simple.

No.

The word echoed in his mind with perfect clarity, as though his brainpan were an open pool and someone had dropped a diamond into it. It was not his word, not his thought. It was alien, and it had entered his consciousness not through his ears, but through his mind alone.

I was a fool to come down here alone, he thought.

No.

It came again, with a distinctness that made his heart leap. Then, in a tone of unsurpassed calmness, he heard—*Do not be afraid. Whatever you see or hear, do not be afraid.*

Light began to glow in front of him, near the refrigerator. It was a white light of the purity of a nun's surplice, and a strange peace came upon him at the sight of it. There was a moment in which he began to tense as the face started to form, and he thought it might be one of the faces he had seen on awakening from sleep.

But as it took form and he could glimpse the lineaments of it as through a mesh, he could see that there was nothing of the bestial in it. It was as pure as the whiteness that surrounded it. The skin was fair and unmarked, the brow high and crowned by what seemed a skullcap of white silk. The mouth was straight, the lips thin, the nose long and well-shaped. But it was the eyes that held him. They were the young-old eyes of the very wise. A god would have eyes like that.

Do not be afraid.

"No," McNeely whispered. "No, I won't."

He heard no more for a moment. The face merely watched his own. It was as if it were reading his thoughts, probing into his brain with a million tiny waves of power. He could swear that the inside of his head was buzzing.

I am touching you.

"Yes. Yes, I can feel it."

I must know what you are thinking if I am to help you.

"Help me?"

As I have already helped you.

"As you've . . ."

With the woman.

The peace fled. The chill came into McNeely's heart. The face trembled slightly, as if it sensed the sudden change.

It was what you wished. We knew it was.

McNeely started to shake, first his fingers, then his whole body. The face began to lose its tranquillity.

Do not be afraid. Why are you doing this? We cannot feel why.

McNeely jerked his head away and looked down, but still the white light streamed peripherally into his vision. He pressed his eyes shut, and the image of the face, now puzzled, was impressed upon the inside of his lids. "No," he said, his voice breaking, "no."

It was what you wanted. The voice seemed petulant now.

"No, you're lying."

We changed you, gave you what you asked for. Angry at its own lack of understanding.

"Please . . ."

Asked for way in the back of your mind, far, far back.

"Get out," he moaned.

It was what you wanted.

He screamed, each word a hammer. "*Get out of my head!*"

The light dimmed and vanished, the voice fading with
it.

It was what you wanted. . . .

He ran out the kitchen door, sobbing with pain and
rage, ran up the stairway to find Gabrielle, a robe thrown
about her, just coming out the door to the suite. He
clutched her and buried his face in her neck, not noticing
through his teary eyes how white and drawn her face had
grown at the sight of him. He pressed against her, his
hands passing over her back, down to her buttocks, his
lips against the coolness of her neck, searching for the
heat that he knew, he *knew* was there, listening, feeling for
the response in his body and mind that would tell him it
was not true, it was *she* who had made him what he
wished to be, and what he wished with all his will to
remain.

He listened. He felt. He could not find it.

She was next to him when he awoke. For a moment he
hoped that it might have all been a dream—the kitchen,
the face, the realization that nothing had truly changed.
But then he remembered what had happened afterward in
the hallway, how Wickstrom's alarmed face had peered
out of his door, of holding Gabrielle tighter and tighter
until she moaned with pain, of Wickstrom pulling him
away from her, of lying on the hall floor while Gabrielle
cradled his head and Wickstrom poured a shot of whiskey
that burned his throat, then Gabrielle and Wickstrom carrying him like a drunken man into the bedroom, and sleep
coming again, deep, welcoming sleep that allowed him to
forget, to pretend in darkness that what he had heard and
felt and known were lies.

Now, as the memory came back to him on awakening,
he wished that he had remained asleep, or that time had
stopped when he and Gabrielle were making love, or that
he had died then. Anything but awakening to see the
woman that he had loved looking down at him, and being
unable to *feel* anything for her that touched the physical.
He wanted her with every thought, every desire he held,
but knew that it would be useless. Nevertheless, he held

his arms out to her and she entered them, leaving her chair to lie beside him.

"What happened? What happened to you?" Her voice was soft, soothing, but edged with fear.

He shook his head. He could never tell her, could not let her know that he was as he had been before. "I—it was nothing, really. I suppose I . . . had a dream."

"A dream?"

"I went downstairs for a bite. And then . . ." His mind was juggling lies, looking for the right one to pull from the air. "Then I went into the library. I was still tired, and I sat in the big chair and fell asleep. I dreamed . . ." He could not condemn the house to her. The dream could not be about the house. *He must not slur the house*.

He needed the house.

It was a barely formed thought, a thin green stalk just beginning to push aside the soil of consciousness. He could not then have even admitted it to himself, let alone the woman, but it was there, and his subconscious made straight the way before it. *He needed the house*.

"I dreamed of when I was a little boy," he said, and she believed him. "There was"—his words stumbled, lying came hard to him—"a cellar in my grandfather's house. I thought there were men down there. And I dreamed my cousin locked me down there, and the men started to come out of the shadows toward me. Then I . . . I woke up and didn't know where I was, and I ran out of the room and up the stairs and you were there," he finished feebly.

"This house," she grated, "this damned house."

"It wasn't the house!" he said. "No, it wasn't the house. It was *me*, that's all!" She looked at him oddly, and he laughed in discomfort. "Just me. And a silly nightmare."

She touched his face. "You shouldn't have gone off by yourself."

He laughed again, hollowly. "That had nothing to do with it. It's something that I've carried for years, a stupid fear. And it just picked now to come out, that's all." He smiled at her and kept smiling until she smiled too. "Where's Kelly?"

She cocked her head to indicate the adjoining living room. "He wanted to stay close until you came out of it."

"Ah!" he nodded. "Good. That was good." He looked down, then back up at her still concerned face. "I'm sorry about this. I feel like an ass."

"Don't be sorry. Let's get dressed and start the day."

He watched her as she took off her robe and thin nightgown, watched as the soft lamplight shone on her naked body, let his gaze trail down her swanlike neck, over her small breasts with the large roseate nipples, across the flatness of her stomach onto the smooth rondure of her hips, the sloping cleft of her mons. But his were the eyes not of a lover, but of a clinician, examining for the sake of reaction, checking the stimuli to see if a response was caused.

There was no reaction until she turned her back to him and he saw her lower back and buttocks in the half-darkness, small and compact like the tight body of a young man. It made him think of Jeff, and he felt a warm stirring. He sighed painfully and closed his eyes to drive out the vision.

"What is it?" Gabrielle asked.

"Nothing. Headache."

"Shall we go out?" she asked him.

"You go."

"I won't leave you alone again."

"Just for a minute. You're right in the next room."

"Why?"

"I just want to be alone for a minute, that's all. I just want to . . . to think the dream out." She didn't move. "Please. I love you."

She looked at him with sad eyes. "Just for a minute then." Leaning over to where he sat on the bed, she kissed his cheek. "I don't want to lose you." Then she was gone.

His gut twisted. Did he so much want to be straight? All the time he had thought he had come to terms with himself, did he really want, in the true heart of him, to be *straight*, to love women and not men? He remembered himself with Jeff, and with the other men before Jeff, drew up the sense memories as vividly as he could, playing them across the screen of his mind like the X-rated gay films he had gone to once and never again because there was no love in them. *Gay people should not be romantic*, he thought, and there, he surmised, lay his flaw. Even though nearly everyone who'd ever known him had thought of him as a hard-headed pragmatist, he *was* a romantic, and had looked for years until he'd found Jeff, who was just as romantic as he.

But now, as the moving bodies writhed in his mind's eye, although he felt aroused, there was nothing of love in the acts, no tenderness. If there had been once, he was now incapable of seeing it. Coupling bodies, sweaty release, the ease of climax, relaxation of tumescence, all, all, all senses were remembered, deeply felt, even treasured.

But where was love?

And now he knew. All these years he'd blamed *guilt* for his life, but he knew that guilt was innocent.

It was romance that had made him join the Marines, that had made him become a mercenary, the last dog soldier in these days of push-button wars.

It was romance that had drawn him to Jeff and kept him there for years.

It was romance that had led him to The Pines, that had pushed him into the arms of Gabrielle Neville and had pushed the love of her into his heart to stay even after the house had withdrawn what it had given him.

And it was romance that would lead him to ask the house for it back again.

He did not plan to do it, not consciously, but that he would was as certain as the fall of leaves from the trees outside.

The three of them spent the waking time much as they'd spent every other—they ate breakfast, played some pinochle, then went up to the third floor playroom, where Gabrielle painted and the two men read. Wickstrom was working his way through *Moby Dick* ("I like it when something happens, but that's not very often," he'd told McNeely), and McNeely resumed his Edgar Wallace. Though he had only thirty pages of the book to finish, he took forever to reach the last page. The words were little more than black bugs on which he placed his eyes while he kept thinking about other things. And the longer he thought, *the stronger the question grew, until he could ask it to himself consciously.*

How could anything that could bring me so much good be truly evil?

After all, what had the house done? It had changed Seth Cummings into a beast, but was that the house's fault? Wasn't it more likely, as he'd suggested to Gabrielle, that the evil had been in Cummings and not the house, that what it had offered him in innocence—even perhaps for *good*—he had turned to evil because of his own lust for power? And if that were true, what else had the house done?

It had given him the strength to kill Cummings, but that had protected them all, had saved the lives of Gabrielle and Wickstrom and himself. There were the dreams and the faces, but those could have been born of their own fears. In fact, that was a much more rational explanation than any malicious intent on the part of whatever lived here in the house. Perhaps all one really had to do to contact it was to reach out a hand. Or a mind.

They'd been so careful, the three of them, to avoid being alone, to avoid any possibility of the house contacting them. Why? he thought almost joyfully. To approach it with good intentions, *honorable* intentions, might bring out the good in it. And if he sensed anything else, he could always pull back, seek the others. He had pulled back before, when he had met it in the kitchen, and it had left him when he'd wanted it to. What's more, it hadn't seemed angry, had it? Only confused. "It was what you wanted" —that was all it had said. And perhaps because of his own fright, it had grown confused enough to think it had erred, and, so thinking, had made him the way he'd been before. If that were the case, all he had to do was to ask to be changed back again.

Simple.

And then he remembered from somewhere an old saying that came unbidden to his mind—he who sups with the devil had best use a long spoon. He laughed it away, closed the unfinished book, and waited for their appointed night to come.

It did, after a session in the exercise room, another meal, and more reading aloud from Dostoevsky. When they finally went to their bedrooms, he had had his excuse planned. As they lay together and her kisses grew more demanding, he sighed.

"I'm sorry, love, but I'm just exhausted. That damned thing earlier got to me, I'm afraid." He shook his head, then touched her face tenderly. "Let's sleep a bit. Then, who knows?" He kissed her with as much passion as he could muster, heard her whispered "all right," and moved up against her when she turned her back to him so that they lay like spoons in a silverware drawer. His groin pressed her buttocks, but neither of them moved in a way that would lead to more.

He kept his eyes open, listening in the dark for the sounds of her sleep.

Chapter Fourteen

Sterne was out of shape. If he hadn't known it before, he knew it by the time he reached the house. It was slightly less than a mile from the cabin, but it was uphill all the way and took him over ten minutes. Once he got in sight of the huge stone building, he tried to call Monckton's name, but all that emerged from his aching throat was a dry croak. He stumbled on, falling once and bruising his knee against some loose stones. When he saw that the doors and windows were secure, he breathed a sigh of relief and relaxed, bending his body in the middle to try to comfort the side stitches that seemed to be eating their way through him. Straightening up, he called Monckton's name loudly, but received no reply. He began to walk around the house, his eyes sweeping the high grass of the lawn, searching for a larger mound amid the clumps of wind-twisted grass and leaves. The chill air stung his over-worked lungs and he paused, resting again until his breathing came more slowly. Then he moved on around the west wing toward the back of the house.

He noticed the ladder immediately. It was lying half on the walk, half on the lawn, like some toy flung away by a giant. Then he looked up and saw the arm dangling over the edge of the balcony.

"Oh, Christ!" he muttered. "Oh, you asshole . . ." Tears of frustrated rage welled up in his eyes. He ran to the ladder, picking it up and propping it against the wall, then climbed up it as quickly as he could.

He found a shattered Monckton lying on the tiles, legs impossibly awry, blood coming from one of them. There were also slow trickles of blood from both nostrils. Sterne gingerly picked up a wrist and felt for a pulse. It was there, faint but steady. The idea struck Sterne of running to the front door of The Pines and banging on it for help, but behind the door, he remembered, was a steel plate. And even if he could have gotten in, there would have been no way to get help from Wilmer—there was no phone.

Down the mountain, he thought wildly. *I'll get him down the mountain and then Renault will never know he was here. He could have fallen off the cabin roof, out of a tree. . . .* He wondered if he could get Monckton down the ladder, then put his hands beneath Monckton's armpits and exerted slight pressure.

There was a dull pop and a feel of something *giving* beneath his hands, and he quickly let the body slump back to the balcony floor. He swallowed painfully and looked around in panic, but there was no one to help him. The perspiration was soaking through his underclothes, and he wrenched off the down-filled jacket, tossing it on the tiles. Manhandling Monckton down the mountain could very well kill him, of that much he was certain. Even if he survived, how could he explain away the injuries—and would Monckton even back him up when he regained consciousness?

If he regained consciousness.

Sterne licked his lips nervously as he wondered whether or not the plan would work.

Simon, Monckton's gone . . .

I don't know. The noise of the Jeep woke me, but by the time I looked out he was gone.

He'd been acting strangely, Simon. Saying funny things about the house. I'm not sure, but I think he might have been planning to leave for a while.

I can handle it by myself until you send someone up. No problem.

Renault couldn't have Monckton searched for—it was Monckton's Jeep. The worst that had been done was breach of contract. And once the month was up, nine days from now, they would find Monckton, and it would be a shame.

It would work. It would clear Sterne, it would shut Monckton's mouth, no one would ever know that Sterne had let Monckton go up to the house.

Sterne decided to let the man die.

"I warned you," he said, kneeling down as though Monckton could hear him. "It's not like I didn't warn you. You'd probably be dead before help could get here anyway."

At that moment Monckton's eyes jerked open spasmodically. They were tired, pained, but clear, and they recognized Sterne. Some blood had dried on Monckton's lips, and the chill wind had chapped them further, so that when he opened them, they made a sound like softly ripping parchment.

"Ster . . ." He struggled to speak, but stopped, a cough shuddering through his body. It started his nose bleeding again, but he seemed unaware of it. "Sterne," he got out breathily. "Dead . . . dead."

Sterne could barely hear the words over the rush of wind. "What? Dead? Someone's dead?"

Monckton nodded, grimacing at the pressure his muscles placed on his shattered shoulder.

"Who? *Who's* dead?"

"Cum-mings." He said the name in two distinct syllables, as if to make sure Sterne would understand.

"Cummings? Seth Cummings?"

It was less painful to speak than to nod. "Yeah. 'N Neville."

Sterne's eyes widened. "Neville? David Neville?"

"Yeah."

Sterne grabbed Monckton's head between his hands, ignoring the man's sharp cry of pain. "How do you know? How do you know that?"

"I—I saw. Saw them . . ."

"Shit!" Sterne spat out, letting go of Monckton and leaping to his feet in one motion. Neville dead? But how? If Monckton had been responsible . . . Sterne knelt again and looked into Monckton's eyes. "You *saw*," he said with a sneer. "How could you see? This place is shut tight!"

Monckton started to shake his head; instead, croaked out, "No . . ."

"What do you *mean* no?" Sterne wanted to grab Monckton, wanted to take him and shake him like a rat, but if he did he knew he might lose him as a source of information completely. Then he remembered—he hadn't seen the windows and doors on the east wing of the house. It might be possible that one of them had been forced, that Monckton had gotten in that way.

Then why had he been apparently trying to get to the roof?

Sterne shook his head savagely. Not a thing made sense, not a damned thing. But if there *were* an entrance open, if Monckton had somehow breached the defenses, and if as a result David Neville were truly dead—well, then the shit wouldn't just hit the fan, it would mean a manure truck into the windmill.

He turned and threw his leg over the railing. "Wait," Monckton groaned, "help . . . help me . . ."

"Help yourself," Sterne shot back, and started down the ladder.

It was a combination of things that made him fall, none of them preternatural in origin. The first was the fifth rung from the top that had split when the ladder had taken its two-story drop; the second was the smooth-soled shoes Sterne was wearing; the third was the haste with which he came down the ladder; and the fourth was his overall physical condition that left him unable to retain his hold when the rung snapped in two beneath his foot. The foot went through the gap, he fell backward, and rocketed headfirst down the incline, his shoes tapping a tattoo all the way down like a stick on a picket fence. He hit the bricks with the crown of his head.

On the balcony above, Whitey Monckton heard the sound of the rung breaking, and actually saw Sterne's fingers open from around the higher rung like a time-lapse flower and disappear. He wondered only for a second if Sterne was dead, only until he saw Sterne's face appear in a blaze of white, confused, frightened, and annoyed all at once before it faded into the blueness of the sky.

Monckton lay there for another hour, too tired to move, and watched overhead as the few clouds he'd noticed earlier gathered and multiplied, turning the sky to a pale gray, then to a dark slate color. When the rain began, he was able to pull himself the few feet in against the house. He did not mind the rain. The coldness of it took his mind ever so slightly off his pain, and, too, it washed away the blood. It seemed to hurt less if there was no blood. He closed his eyes and wondered how long he would have to wait.

Simon Renault looked at the receiver and frowned. He'd be damned if he'd call again. Sterne had treated him like a worrisome old woman the first time. Besides, there was no need. If something happened, Renault was sure that Sterne would call him immediately. He was insufferable at times, but efficient. And Monckton, too, seemed like a man who was always in control of himself and his surroundings. *Come now, Simon,* he told himself. *Trust them. After all, having them there is the next best thing to being there yourself.*

He made himself smile, then took another sip of coffee.

Chapter Fifteen

At long last her breathing grew easy, her muscles relaxed. It was as if she had been trying to stay awake. Several times he'd heard her breathe in sharply, catching herself asleep. He was certain that if he'd been able to see her eyes, they would have been open, staring at the darkness like a lioness protecting her sleeping mate. After he thought she was asleep, he counted very slowly to five hundred, then undraped his arm from around her. When there was no response, he inched over to the edge of the bed and got up, feeling about in the dark until he located his pants and shirt.

He'd turned the lights off in the living room before they'd gone to bed so as not to wake Gabrielle when the door opened. He eased it shut now, waiting for a moment after the soft click of the latch before he fumbled for the lamp. The light was reassuring, and he crossed the room purposefully and stepped into the hall.

He wondered where he should go. The kitchen? That was where he had seen the unearthly, strangely beautiful face before. But it seemed so pedestrian, so *unromantic* somehow (God, there it was again!). He decided to go there nonetheless, and walked slowly down the central staircase. His emotions were ones that he remembered from long years ago—a mixture of excitement and youthful terror. It was walking up to Judy Marlowe's door the night of the junior prom, walking into the Marine induction center for his physical, climbing the stairs to a one-room apartment with the first man he had ever picked up: exquisite foreboding, breathless anticipation.

He entered the kitchen and sat at the table as he had before, wondering how one *opened* oneself to the scrutiny of whatever he had seen and talked with before, and finally deciding on relaxed concentration. He closed his eyes and did the breathing that a TM freak in Angola had taught him. After a bit he opened them again and looked around. There was nothing.

He decided to try speech instead. "Are you there?" he whispered. "Is anyone there? . . . Hello? . . ."

There was no answer. *Line busy?* Then he remembered what Neville had said when he'd found him in the cellar: *It's stronger here.*

The cellar then. It was not better or worse than any other room in the house, despite what had happened there. Perhaps Neville was right. Perhaps the thing was stronger the closer to the earth it was.

It's like a lodestone, Gabrielle had said, and McNeely paused at the idea. A lodestone buried beneath the earth of Pine Mountain, drawing to it and holding fast . . . secrets. He opened the cellar door and started to walk down the steps.

The odor hit him instantly, and he frowned. So the wine cellar hadn't been as airtight as they'd hoped, he thought grimly. He breathed through his mouth and prayed they'd never have to come down here to stay. Even though the smell was vile, he felt far better than on his last visit, when Seth Cummings was prowling the house like some blood-mad animal. But Cummings was gone now, safe and dead behind those oak doors, with only a dark stain to mark his passing.

McNeely stood in the center of the stone floor and looked around him. He started to say "hello" again, but stopped. It would not need his voice to tell it he was there. He remembered that Neville had been inside the fire chamber, so he walked over and opened the ponderous steel door.

The room's smell was flat and lifeless, though there was little trace of dampness as there was in the rest of the cellar. The few pieces of furniture sat expectantly empty, but the shelves were well stocked with provisions, and the fluorescent fixtures overhead cast a more intense light than the sickly bulb that so incompetently lit the rest of the level. The odor from the wine cellar had barely permeated the air of the shelter, and McNeely unconsciously pulled the door closed behind him to further escape the smell. With the door closed, the room was so quiet, he heard his own heartbeat, and fancied he could hear the blood rushing through his veins and arteries. The rest of the house had been quiet, but quiet like a coffin in a crypt. Now the coffin was in a crypt that lay hundreds of miles beneath the surface of the earth. It made a huge difference, if not in the silence itself, then in his perception of the silence. It was a thick cotton snake that stretched through his brain from ear to ear.

And it was because the silence was so great that the voice came as such a surprise. It seemed to fill the small room at first, unaware of its own strength, lifting his unprepared body and shaking it with sound before it could properly gauge how much power it would truly need. In fact, its first words were unintelligible to McNeely precisely because of the force with which they were delivered. After the first shock came a panicked certainty that Wickstrom and Gabrielle two floors above would hear, *must* hear the voice. But a second of consideration was enough to tell him that the voice had been inside his head, had been meant for his *inner* ear alone.

The psychic rumbling receded like an ocean wave, and the words became intelligible.

You have returned.

There was glee in the tone, and McNeely thought of himself as the Prodigal Son come home to his family's good graces.

We thought you were frightened, but you have sought us out. There was a pause. *You have sought us out of your own free will?*

McNeely nodded. "Yes," he said, surprised at how his voice caught in his throat. He cleared it and repeated, "Yes."

That is good. We can help you. McNeely heard a vast outpouring of winds, a titanic sigh. *We tried before. A puzzle*. The last two words were given no inflection, so that McNeely could not form a context. He thought perhaps that the thing was puzzled by his previous reaction when it had told him what it had done for him.

"I *was* frightened," he said, "frightened when you first made yourself known to me. I didn't know that I could be so . . ." He searched for the word, and heard the voice speak it in his mind just as it was about to leave his lips.

Manipulated. (Had it read his mind?) *It was not manipulation. It was only making you as you most deeply wished to be. It is good for one to be as one wishes*.

It was a soothing voice, a soft, deep, mellifluous baritone that touched his mind with cool word-fingers. The inflections were like music, like the voice of Dylan Thomas reading *Fern Hill*, but with such a quality that one would have thought the throat that formed the words was made of velvet.

Do you know now what you wish to be?

"I wish (*'Oh Jeff I did love you'*) I wish to love a woman as I've loved men."

You are certain? It was what you wanted before, yet . . .

"*Yes*. I'm certain."

Then it is yours.

"Always?"

For the rest of your life.

McNeely shuddered when it said that, even though there was no trace of malice in the tone. Almost immediately he felt something change within him. It was not a great change; no epiphany that showed him whirling clouds and suns that blazoned "heterosexual" across the sky in letters of fire. Rather, it was a subtle reorganization, a *shifting* of things inside him, lasting only a second. But afterward he knew he could love Gabrielle the way he had loved her before. A thrill went through him as he thought of her body opened beneath him.

She is beautiful.

McNeely drew up with a start as he realized that *it* had seen precisely what *he* had. "You read my mind?" he asked in a tense voice.

We see thoughts.

"Always?"

Chet Williamson

When we wish.

The face began to form then, the same gentle, peaceful, godlike face that he had seen in the kitchen. It was smiling benignly. "I can see you now," McNeely said.

We did not wish to frighten you again, it said by way of explanation.

"I'm not frightened," he said, thinking as he did so that it already knew that. "Thank you. Thank you for doing . . . whatever you did."

You are welcome.

"Is there—" He paused, thinking that he could not ask it after all. It seemed too Mephistophelean.

You wish to know if there is anything you can do for us in return.

He swallowed, then nodded.

Perhaps there is something. In the future.

Jesus, he thought. Why did it suddenly sound like Marlon Brando in *The Godfather*? And with a strange glee he realized that even if it was reading his mind, it could not grasp the allusion. Perhaps that was the way to keep thoughts private—think in symbols: contemporary archetypes.

"Who are you?" he asked.

Friends.

"Are you ghosts?"

It did not answer. *We can do much for you.*

"But what are you?"

We can give you power.

"You gave Seth Cummings power," he said, surprised at his own boldness.

The thing was silent for a while, its face expressionless. *We erred with Seth Cummings.*

He laughed shortly. "*Erred?* Damn right, you erred!" He slapped his mouth shut then as the thought hit him that he should not antagonize this thing, that whatever it was, it had proven itself powerful beyond his comprehension.

Seth Cummings was weak. He had no strength of will. No image of himself as anything great. He thought only in terms of what we could do for him. He could not hope to cope with the power we gave him. He abused it for his own petty urges.

"And what about me? When I killed Cummings with that kick? Did you give me the power to do that?"

We did. Else he would have killed you all.

"He *did* kill Neville."

He was inessential.

A chill went through McNeely. It was as if he had been waiting for it to say something like that, to expose, if not its evil, its godlike insensitivity to human affairs. "Inessential to whom?" he asked, sounding braver than he felt.

To anyone. Surely he was inessential to his wife. She desired you. And if a man is inessential to those closest to him, does it not follow that he will be inessential to others as well?

"I asked you before. Who are you?"

Why do you wish to know?

"To . . . to call you by name, maybe. Do you have a name?"

We have many names. Millions of names.

(We. Millions of names. What the hell *was* this?) "Are there millions of you, then?" he asked.

The face moved up and down. Nodding. *Yes. All in one.*

"You mean you're composed of many . . . intelligences?"

Oh yes. There was pride in the tone. *Many.*

He made a connection, hazarded a guess. "The lights in the sky . . . the lights at night . . . are they from you?"

They are to *us. New ones. New ones coming all the time.*

"Then Gabrielle was right. This place *is* a lodestone. Drawing what? Souls?"

Souls. What are souls? Some things survive, others do not. What needs to survive survives. What is content to sleep sleeps.

"But you're *not* content to sleep?"

No.

"Why not?"

There are things to be done.

McNeely felt suddenly weary, drained of vitality. Yet he did not feel he should sit down in front of the thing that confronted him. "Now, let me . . . let me clarify this if I can. Do you mean to say that you—and by you I mean all the . . . the *people* that create you—that you are all dead?"

We are. We were.

"And that those of you who have survived come here?"

Yes.

"You come here of your own free will?"

We are drawn here.

The lodestone again, McNeely thought. "Can you leave?"

The thing started to say something. McNeely could hear the vibrations in his head preliminary to a "word"—but nothing happened. Then came a long sigh and a single word accompanied by an almost pleading look from the pale eyes.

Perhaps.

McNeely swallowed, but his throat still held a shapeless lump dead center. "I can help you," he said softly.

You can.

"You want to leave?"

We do.

"Why?"

There are things to be done.

"You said that before!" McNeely was starting to lose control now, starting to break. "What kind of things?"

Things not for your knowing.

"If I'm going to help you, don't you think I'd better decide that?"

You are growing frightened. Think of what we have said and done. Think of what we can give you still. It smiled benignly. *We will speak again.*

The face faded. In less than three seconds it had vanished. McNeely listened, but the voice was gone.

"Are you there?"

There was only silence. He sighed, turned, and left the room.

As he crossed the stone floor to the staircase, there was a faint sound on the edge of hearing that he could have sworn came from the wine cellar. *Rats,* he thought, and frowned at the picture of what they might be doing to the two bodies behind the door.

But then he remembered there were no rats in The Pines, no animal life at all, and paused mid-stride, looking with narrowed eyes toward the door. If not rats, then what?

Don't be a fool. They're dead, both of them.

Still, he did not step nearer to the door. He only listened, and heard nothing more. *Isn't it enough?* he asked himself. *Isn't what you've already seen here enough? Must you reanimate corpses too?*

He laughed at himself, a small warm laugh that drove some of the chill from the damp cellar as he started to climb the steps, started to go back upstairs to Gabrielle, carrying his newfound sexuality like a trophy.

The cellar light went out, the kitchen door closed, and in the darkness from behind the wooden door came the sound once again, a light pattering of fingers on stone beneath a stained tablecloth. Unheard by living ears, the fingers continued their spastic chattering, then fell silent all at once, as if a larger, stronger hand had come down atop them.

She was sleeping when he climbed into the bed, and the close warmth of her aroused him. He moved her into a moaning wakefulness with his hands and they made love, she leisurely, contentedly, he assuredly and forcefully, driving her climax before him like a dog drives a sheep. They came together and drifted back into sleep. Later he had a dream that his semen had turned to blood, and he awoke in a damp sweat, confused and alarmed at first by the wet stickiness on his thighs. Then he remembered his first nocturnal emission. He had been eleven, and had awakened in a sleeping bag next to his father's. They were camping with the Scouts and were sharing a pup tent. McNeely had awakened as the spasm passed, to find his pajamas and sleeping bag sopping wet. His cry of fear woke his father, and he'd whispered, "Blood, blood, Dad, I'm cut, oh, I'm cut!" and his father had grabbed a flashlight and opened the sleeping bag.

In the light that reflected off the mud-brown canvas walls, he'd seen his father's expression turn from one of alarm to a puckered look of disgust. "Oh, Christ," he'd said. "Go clean yourself up." The boy had gone down to the creek and washed, confused and scared. When he'd returned to the tent, his father was feigning sleep, his back to McNeely. The sleeping bag was stiffening where his father had wiped most of the fluid away with a handkerchief. He said nothing to McNeely about it that night, the next day, or ever again. For weeks the boy thought he'd been bleeding white blood and was going to die, until a friend a year older told him what it really was.

And now so many years later he lay in another bed, feeling the stiffness like starchy paste against his legs, like the blood he'd spilled and had had spilled on too many humid battlegrounds, and thought of his father and the Boy Scouts and the damp sleeping bag for the first time in twenty years, and wondered why, why did the memory come back *now*?

When he awoke again, Gabrielle was looking down into his face, her breasts nudging his forearm.

"You were shivering," she said. "I thought it was another bad dream."

He smiled. "If it was, I don't remember it." He touched her breasts and joyed in the turgid response he felt. "Sorry I woke you up earlier."

"I'm not," she said, and kissed him. "I *am* anxious for a shower though. We smell like a whorehouse."

"When did you ever smell a whorehouse?"

"Hmm. How do you think I got rich?"

He laughed and smacked her lightly on the bottom as she stood up.

"Come on," she said, "I'm starved."

"Insatiable, aren't you?" he growled as she giggled her way to the bathroom. He sat up and stretched. Good God, but he felt good. Whole again. Though he couldn't see outside, he was certain the sun was shining, the sky was the blue of lovers' eyes, birds were singing.

Birds. No, there would be no birds, would there? There were no birds at The Pines, no rats either.

So what had scuttled on the floor behind the oaken . . .

Stop it. That was not a worry now. He had no worries, only happiness. He was with Gabrielle again, really *with* her, and that was all that mattered. He heard the water in the shower blast into life, and thought how good it would feel to join her under the spray. It . . . *they* had done it, had restored to him what he had hungered for. But through the joy, the thought kept beating like a tinny drum high up in an attic room—*what will I have to do for them?*

No such thing as a free lunch—there was nothing new in that. Deals, everybody made deals. The heroine of *Rumpelstiltskin* made a deal—her firstborn for the ability to spin straw into gold. Only she had welshed and gotten away with it. He wondered if he could be so lucky. And even so, could there be that much harm in helping them leave?

But he would play it safe, find out *why* they wanted out, and what those "things to be done" really were. They couldn't buy him with power. The only bargaining point they had was something they'd already given him, something they wouldn't take back. So what did he have to lose?

He began to smile again as he walked toward the bathroom.

Chapter Sixteen

It was dark on the balcony. Whitey Monckton eased his arm up and looked at the glowing LED crystals. 3:24, 10-25. He had trouble deciding what the numbers meant, and then it came to him. Six days. Six days and nights until something inside that house went click and doors and windows would open and people would come. He tried to remember how long he had been up here. Two days maybe? Three at most. The pains in his body had receded to little more than dull aches that never slept. Now the real pain was in his stomach, a sharpness as though the steel ball of a mace were rolling around inside, sending its spikes into every area of his midsection. His thirst had been quenched by the rainwater that had gathered in depressions where the tiles were chipped and broken, but the hunger was growing worse. From time to time he eyed the ladder with longing, but knew he could never use his shattered legs and shoulder to take him down it. And if he could, what then? Drive the Jeep with his teeth? Crawl the mile to the cabin by dragging himself on one arm? *Forget it, I probably couldn't even clear the railing.*

His strength had returned slowly after the accident. He had slept in spite of the pain and was surprised on awaking to find that he was still alive. Surprised and disappointed. At first he did not see how he could stay alive until someone came to help, but the bleeding had stopped and he was not coughing or passing blood. He urinated and defecated where he lay, pulling his pants down one-handed when the urge took him. After a while he would drag himself farther along the wall.

He could not hear any trace of the thing that lived there, that had toppled him from the ladder. Strangely enough, he held no malice toward it for that. If a bear you're hunting attacks you, do you hate the bear for it? No, he'd gone to The Pines intending to fight, and had been beaten. The thing would leave him alone now, and turn its attention back to those inside, those who still survived. That he hadn't been able to help them made him sad, particularly when he thought of Gabrielle Neville. But McNeely and Wickstrom were strong men. Perhaps they could still come out alive.

He wondered then if *he* would, and shivered with the cold, praying for the dawn to come soon.

Chapter Seventeen

"I'm sick of Dostoevsky," McNeely growled, tossing down the book. Wickstrom and Gabrielle looked up in surprise. "I'm sorry," he went on, "it's just so damned . . . *oppressive* all of a sudden."

Wickstrom shrugged. "Okay with me. I don't think I've been getting it anyway. Besides, we're not even a third of the way through. No way we'd finish it before we leave, right?"

Gabrielle touched her tongue thoughtfully to the end of her brush. "Are you feeling all right, George? You look a bit pale."

He shook his head testily. "I'm fine. Just . . . I don't know what it is. I suppose I'm eager to leave."

"Nothing new there." Wickstrom smiled. "I've been eager to do that ever since we came here." He nodded toward Gabrielle. "Maybe you oughta take up painting, George. Get your mind off things."

McNeely glanced up quickly at Wickstrom, but the man's face was innocent. *No way he would know,* McNeely thought. *No way he could possibly know. But what did he mean, get your mind off things? What things?*

It was unlike McNeely to feel paranoia, and he struggled to hurl it from him. He stood up and crossed to Gabrielle's easel. Her painting was nearly completed, as perfect as any work he'd ever seen. The detail was superb, the texture exquisite, and the use of light rivaled the Flemish masters. "If I could paint like this," he said, "I *would* take it up."

"Have you ever tried?" Gabrielle asked. He shook his head no. "Here," she said, handing him a charcoal pencil and a sketch pad. "Try a drawing of Kelly."

He laughed and held the materials out to her. "No use," he said. "I nearly flunked art in high school."

"Aw, come on," said Wickstrom. "It's easy. Two circles for eyes, one for the nose, a line for the mouth. I won't move."

"Oh, hell, all right." He felt a little irritated at their prodding, but decided that it might take his mind off thoughts of the entity, thoughts that had been plaguing him despite his facile rationalizations. So he sat and started to sketch, and before too long he realized that what was taking form beneath his fingers was not the bunch of crude blocky lines he had expected, but a carefully rendered, technically flawless drawing of Kelly Wickstrom's head. His hand moved like quicksilver, shading, rubbing, finding just the right thickness of line; his head twitched from pad to subject, his eyes unmistakably sending the messages to those clever darting fingers to put the face on paper.

And George McNeely knew he was doing none of it himself. He sat amazed, watching his fingers move, pulled by phantom muscles, ghostly will, though it was still *his* hand, *his* muscles that performed the actual motion. It was as though *he knew*, knew all that Dürer and Rembrandt and Goya had known (*especially Goya, oh yes!*), and now he was finished, the hand was his again, and he looked down at the drawing he had not made.

"My God," Gabrielle said softly.

"What?" Wickstrom hopped to his feet. "Done already?" He whistled when he saw the sketch. "I thought you said you flunked art."

"I, uh . . . I used to do *some* sketching like this," he lied. "That's all. I guess you never lose your talent completely, huh?"

Gabrielle stared at him, her forehead etched with disbelief. "What's wrong?" he asked her.

"Nothing. I just . . . find out more about you all the time."

Their eyes held until he tore his away. "I'm tired," he said. "Think I'll stretch out for a while." He crossed the room and lay down on the overstuffed sofa, pillowing his head on his forearm and facing the high back, but though his eyes were closed, he did not sleep. His head was too full of questions. He was certain that their strange talents were the gift of the thing. But what reason could there be for this new gift?

To show you.

McNeely stood in the cellar, watching the face. Upstairs, Wickstrom and Gabrielle lay sleeping. "Show us what?"

What we are capable of granting. Delicacy, beauty, art. There is that in us too. Not merely the brute force you saw in Cummings.

"What's the point?"

The point is that we can do many things for you. And for the woman.

"But what do you want?"

We will tell you.

"Will you tell me the truth?"

The eyes of the face changed slightly, a wry cynicism invading them. *It will do no harm. You would know eventually if you wished.* It paused. *But are you sure you wish to know?*

"I'm sure."

We want to be away from here. We have been here for a long time.

"How long?"

Longer than you or any man could conceive. Beyond the memory of the race. There are those of us who wielded sticks and rocks to slay our enemies, who lived in holes in the rock and dressed in stinking skins. There are those who banded together for strength, and fashioned spears from sharp stones to pierce the hearts of those who stood against us. We are very old.

McNeely felt as he had when Wickstrom had brought forth his theory about the lights in the sky, a theory that

McNeely now knew to be at least partially correct. It was as if a great cosmic gulf opened beneath his feet, and looking down into it, he could see all the times of man, back to when man was barely man at all, a splay-footed savage pounding at his prey with hammy fists, and beyond that, deep in the abyss, blackness unbroken by the twinkling of stars.

But we have the new in us as well. New ones all the time. We are not entirely primitive. We have great wisdom.

"But not enough," stammered McNeely, forcing his mind back from the chasm over which it tottered, "to free yourselves."

We know how to be free. But it is— It paused, as if deciding whether or not to reveal a secret. *—difficult.*

McNeely didn't want to talk about their escape yet. He had to find out more about the creature, what it was, what it wanted. He reversed, trying to think clearly yet obtusely enough so that the thing could not easily read his thoughts. "You said *new* ones. Even now?"

Even as we talk. We are always growing stronger.

"These are *people*? People who are dying?"

Who are dead. What needs to survive comes here, joins us.

"I still don't understand. *What* needs to survive?"

A part of certain men. Like Neville.

"Neville?" The thought dazed McNeely. "David Neville? David Neville is . . . part of you?"

Part of him is part of us. The part that needed to survive.

"What part is that?"

The face smiled. *The part that hates you. That hates Wickstrom. That hates his wife. That wants to kill you all.*

McNeely could feel the muscles in his legs quiver in fear. In another few seconds he knew they would be too rubbery to hold him. He looked away from the face that held him enthralled, concentrated his gaze on the small shelf of canned goods against the fire chamber's walls until he felt the blood coming back to his face and the dizziness desert him. He thought it through, quickly and chaotically, using the canned goods as camouflage so the

thing should not know, made the visions and thoughts
dance and leap in his head so that they should be secret

the thing that survives

                                   Elberta peaches
evil   16 oz. net weight
                                        hate
      corned beef hash   all the *hate* survives
                              Ingredients: Beef, potatoes,
                    hate
is made of   beef stock, onions
                    Ingredients:
water, salt

                         hate evil
                              all the evil since time
      in saucepan, stir occasionally till
since time began

                                   Hell.
                  till boiling

                                   This place is
            over medium heat

                                   This thing is
      to full boil

                                        Hell.

McNeely bit down on the inside of his cheek, hoping
the pain would diffuse his thoughts, confuse his own mind
so that the thing would stay confused as well. ''The part that
survives,'' he said in a weary voice, ''is the part that seeks
revenge?''
What survives is what is strongest.
''But you said that the part that *hates* survived Neville.''
That was the strongest.
''Is that what always survives?''
Not always.
''What else then? Love?''
The face smiled twistedly at him, as at a foolish child.
Love does not survive. Not here.
''Then what else? What else besides hate?''
*Sometimes it is only need. There is no hate involved.
But the need is strong. As strong as hate.*

"The need for what?"

For blood. For pain. Often there is no hate in these things.

Oh, God, McNeely thought, *oh God this thing is Hell Mary had a little lamb little lamb little lamb this is pure evil pure evil all the Mary had a little lamb its fleece all the evil that's ever been on earth was white as snow talk to it talk to it*

"How can there be no hate?" he asked. "How can that be?"

There was no hate in DeRais. No hate in Fish. No hate in Kürten. There was only need. Yet they are here.

DeRais? Fish? Kürten? The names, unread and unheard of for years, came back to McNeely. DeRais, the notorious child-killer who would coo to and cuddle young boys a second before he'd slash their throats; Albert Fish, the quiet old man who strangled little Grace Budd and then ate parts of her; Peter Kürten, the Düsseldorf killer who slew for joy alone—all psychopathic, all hideously insane, all *evil* in its purest form.

"They are here?" McNeely asked, his mind growing numb with its overload of horror.

Yes. We are here.

It was then that McNeely realized fully and for the first time to whom and what he was speaking. This face, this voice inside his head, *was* DeRais and Fish and Kürten. It was Attila and Hitler and Caligula and Jack the Ripper and all the evil that had lived on after a million million deaths, all here in one collective consciousness, one supremely godlike face that McNeely knew could not be its real face.

Surely you can understand need.

He looked up at it, and it seemed the face had changed, grown harder. "Me?"

The need for blood. For killing.

"You mean . . my being a soldier?"

It smiled. *There is more than that. More than simply a job. You like killing.*

McNeely shook his head.

It is a need in you. War. Battle. Death.

"No! It *was*. But no more."

You think now that you fuck women that need is gone.

McNeely felt the muscles of his jaw grow rigid.

It is not gone.

"Stop it, damn you! Stop toying with me!"

We enjoy toying with you. And with the others.

"What do you . . ."

When you first came. The voices. The visions. The dreams. The woman speaking what she truly felt to her husband.

"You did all that?"

We did.

"Why?"

To explore you. To see what you feared, thought. What you desired.

George McNeely felt utterly naked, like a victim in the shower in one of those mindless slasher movies, eyes blinded by soap, with the black shadow looming larger through the opacity of the plastic curtain. But instead of seeing only his body, the grinning slasher saw through to his soul, seeing and relishing every goddamned thing he'd ever wanted to hide, laughing out loud at every secret he'd ever had. The thought was unbearable. He pushed it away by going back to something the voice had said earlier.

"You said that . . . Neville hates us . . . Gabrielle and Kelly and me. Why did he . . . *does* he hate us so much?" *So much that that hate still survives,* he thought, but did not voice it.

He hated you from the start. That was why he brought you here.

"Why he . . ."

You had done something to a relative in a battle. Wickstrom harmed a cousin. Cummings destroyed a friend. Neville hates you for that. He wants to destroy you.

"That was why he chose us?"

He wanted to set his courage against yours.

"But why Gabrielle?"

His hate for her has come since he has been with us. Since you have fucked her.

McNeely grimaced at the word. "How do you . . ."

Know all this? You forget. He is not only with us. He is us.

"That means that"—McNeely's face grew stern—"that *you* want to destroy us too."

No. Far from it. We need you.

"Oh, yes! To help you escape!"

Yes.

"Do you honestly think that . . ." McNeely stiffened, his head suddenly pinioned in an attitude of listening.

What is wrong?

"I thought I heard . . ." The creak of a door, slow and subtle, as though Wickstrom or Gabrielle had sneaked quietly down the steps, and even now stood on the other side of the slightly ajar fire chamber door, through which a weak slice of light shone sickly from the main part of the cellar.

What?

How can it not know? thought McNeely. *I'm sure I heard . . .*

Then the door slashed fully open and nightmare burst in.

At first McNeely thought he had simply gone mad, that nothing that looked like that would be capable of locomotion in the real world. But The Pines was not the real world, and the remnant of humanity before him was most definitely moving, cannoning toward him with a force that smashed him to the hard concrete floor before he could raise an arm to defend himself. He struggled to make himself fight back, to grasp the arms and fists that were pummeling his face and head with hammerlike strength, to twist and roll and throw off the fetid half-decayed lich that straddled him like some frenzied lover. But fear had crushed his heart with a grip of ice, and horror had thrown his stomach into rebellion so that his nose and mouth filled in seconds with his own vomit until his breath was gone and his strength was stolen, leaving him as malleable as a half-dead puppy, his lungs clenched with a grasp past breaking, as had been the lungs of David Neville, who now ceased his blows and grabbed McNeely's thick neck like a drowning sailor grabs a hawser.

The eyes that Seth Cummings had squeezed from their sockets had shriveled into little more than parched yellow grapes, but there was enough left to burn with a hatred that stunned McNeely even more than the physical attack. The lolling tongue, now black with old blood, had fallen away in places like a rotting sponge that dripped venom onto McNeely's lips. Still horribly distorted from Cummings's fatal embrace, the upper chest and shoulders seemed huge, a grotesque balloon filled with noxious gases in the shape of muscles monstrously rigid, decaying muscles with strength enough to drive their force down the yellow-white arms into the stinking wrists and fingers that embraced the neck of George McNeely, stopping the blood, stopping the air so that McNeely choked on the contents of his stomach that his own muscles kept sending up to his throat in involuntary mindless frenzy.

The raisin eyes grew brighter and brighter, burrowing like rats through McNeely's own eyes, deep, deep into his brain, a burning brightness that suddenly faded, dimmed, and was extinguished completely, plunging George McNeely into the deepest blackness he had ever known.

He regained consciousness slowly and painfully. The first thing of which he was aware was the hot stinging ache in his throat, as though fire had seared it and it now lay caked in salt. He actually thought that he was dead, and found himself hoping that he would not be in The Pines for all eternity, but would be in that place where love survives.

George

Soft voice. *Gabrielle? Has she joined me? Are we together?*

He coughed, bringing up a gobbet of half-digested food that had lodged in his trachea. The taste of it told him he was not dead. Other sensations followed: the tingling of his face where Neville's fists had scored the flesh, the pounding roar at the back of his head where he'd struck the floor, that dank, rich odor that cut like a razor through the scent of the vomit drying in his nostrils, and finally the dead weight that pressed down upon his tortured chest. When he was conscious enough to recognize it for what it was, he struggled to push it off, but his strength was not yet sufficient. He let his head fall back and took deep racking breaths. The second attempt was successful. Neville's body did not so much roll off him as *slide* off. McNeely turned his head away and shut his eyes.

George . . .

The voice was weak but insistent. When he looked, the face was there. But now it seemed less distinct, as though it were peering through seawater.

"You . . ." He coughed, spat on the floor.

George . . .

"You did *that*," he snarled.

We were not responsible.

"Bullshit! Who was?"

We saved you. Neville would have killed you. But we brought him back.

McNeely frowned and tried to think. What *had* stopped Neville after he'd blacked out?

We did.

"Get out of my mind!"

You're upset. . . .

"Hah!" It was too much. He started to laugh. For as bizarre and grotesque as this was, some cynical corner of his mind still saw humor in it. "Hah! I'm upset? Fucking right on! Oh, *Jesus*! Oh . . ." He leaned against the wall and laughed until he started coughing again and the tears ran. The spasm shook him and he pressed his palms against the wall until he felt in control. Then he looked at the face again. It was so goddamned expressionless. "All right," he said, a bitter smile wrenching the corners of his mouth upward. "Now you just tell me what"—his hands fluttered wildly in the air—"*that*"—they gestured, shaking, to Neville's decaying corpse—"was all about? *Accident? Quality control fuck-up?*"

An accident. He broke away from us.

"*Neville* did?"

He and others.

McNeely's jaw dropped open. "Others?"

There are those of us, as in any group, who lack a sense of organization. Neville is one of these. There are others. They are easily swayed. Neville, being dead such a short time, retains much power.

"What do you mean, power?"

Life force. Will. That which survives. They went with him. Broke away from us.

"You mean that what attacked me wasn't just Neville? That it was dozens of others as well?"

It paused a second too long. *Perhaps.*

McNeely's eyes widened. "Dozens, hell. *Thousands.* Maybe *millions,* isn't that right?"

The voice said nothing. The eyes stared blankly ahead.

"It went *crazy,*" McNeely went on, not knowing whether what he said was truth or lies, but filled with the sense of *knowing.* "It went mad with the urge to kill that Neville brought to it, and it went with Neville into his body to kill me. And then Kelly and even Gabrielle. And *you* stopped it—or you stopped *yourselves,* that part of yourselves that's mad."

It is . . . something like that.

"Holy Christ, what are you?" He looked at the face, wondering how he had ever seen godhood in it, how he had ever asked it for what it had given him.

What do we seem?

"All the evil in the world," McNeely said with quiet awe. "And all the madness."

You knew that. You knew from the beginning.

Its voice was calm, and in its words and the truth of them there was, to McNeely, the greatest horror of all.

"I'm going upstairs," he said. "I'm going upstairs and going to sleep." He tried to make his mind a blank, and turned and walked zombielike out of the room. He knew he should have moved the body back into the wine cellar, but he could not bear to, not now. He was stuffed too full of horror to face any more. *Bed,* he thought, emblazoning the concept in the front of his brain. *Soft, soft bed. Warm and safe. Sleep.*

He approached self-hypnosis. Every emotion within him wanted him to scream, to cry out *No!,* to deny the thing that smiled in his face, to attack it even though he would only be thrashing the stinking air of the fire chamber. But he could not bring himself to assault so much power, so much evil. Not now, when he knew so little.

And yet so much.

Time was what he needed. He would have to stall it, keep it thinking *he* was thinking, considering. For as long as it knew there was a possibility of his accepting it, it might not attempt to force him. Evil was like a cancer cell. It grew in its own, metastasizing over and over again until the organism was riddled with the disease. So it must have happened with Cummings, and so the thing would think it would happen with him. But it would not. He would not let it.

Or had it already?

No! Safe warm bed, soft sleep, sleep . . .

He struggled to suppress the thought that had so viciously sprung to the forefront of his consciousness, trying to force it down to a nearly visceral level, where he could deal with it unheard by the thing that peered into him. *Dismiss it,* he thought, *hide it, banish it,* and he wondered whether he wanted to hide it from the entity or from himself.

He succeeded in keeping his thoughts blank until he reached Cummings's old suite, where he showered off the blood and the stench that had resulted from the attack in the cellar. Then he padded down the hall and into the suite he shared with Gabrielle, slipping into the bed where she still slept peacefully. As he lay there, staring into the darkness, he knew that he *must* think, consciously and logically, of what had happened and had yet to happen. Then, perhaps, when he formed the outlines of a plan, he could smother it under duplicitous thoughts, could learn how by then.

Gabrielle's body was warm, almost feverishly so, and he pressed his own body into her, stealing her warmth to soothe his own chilled flesh. What he had seen and heard in the cellar was nearly incomprehensible, but it was true. He had experienced enough firsthand to be sure of that.

Slowly his memory brought forth all the strange, formerly inexplicable events that had occurred since they had come to The Pines. There was that first booming laugh as the doors and windows had slammed shut—what else but a laugh of triumph? Perhaps not from the total entity, but only from that part of it that embodied—what was it the voice had called it?—*need.* The madmen. Yet they were all mad. The sane madmen and the mad madmen. McNeely shivered on the verge of laughter again at the absurdity of the thought.

Then there was the sound of the wind in the trees outside, a sound that Neville had sworn was not possible. *We enjoy toying with you.* Oh, they had done that royally. The sounds, its preying on Wickstrom's fears by visiting him with nightmares of agoraphobia, the way it had baited Neville, first with the most deeply suppressed thoughts of the wife who had loved him, and then with the voices Neville had claimed to hear, voices just beyond intelligibility.

And Cummings. What in that name of all that's holy could it have done for Cummings? What did it grant him, or what did *he* do that opened himself to it? Was it for power alone? Maybe. Cummings was a fool, McNeely'd seen that quickly. So why had it chosen Cummings to approach first? Another proof of its fallibility? And where was it now? *What was its position?*

There was the key. How stupid of him not to have thought of it before. Warfare. Treat it like a tactical exercise. Where is the enemy? What are its strengths? What are its weaknesses? Know these things and you can defeat it.

But can you ever *defeat* evil? he thought sadly. Can you ever hope to do anything but wrestle it to a draw until you meet it again on some other battlefield in some other war? He could not destroy it. How do you destroy a thing that's already dead, that lives forever? A draw would be the best he could hope for. But he would try.

He'd always slept well before a battle, and now was no exception. He dreamed himself back into green jungles with overhanging vines, lianas trailing tendrils down like cool streamers. There were others with him, standing under the huge trees, leaning against their thick boles, but he could not see their faces. They were all in shadow, shaded either by the trees or by the long bills of their fatigue caps. Somehow it didn't matter that he didn't know their identities. He was merely content to be there with them.

Then suddenly in the dream a shell burst overhead, bathing them and the jungle in the glow of white phosphorus. But instead of momentarily blinding him and fading away until the outlines of sight returned, the stark whiteness remained, allowing him to see fully illuminated the faces of the men with whom he served.

They had no faces. They were blank white masks like the surfaces of eggs, but eggs stunningly white, and one by one they changed their form, becoming thick stalks of white, their uniforms now lit a lime green, now vanishing completely. The stalks broadened, thickened into slabs of purest ivory, until the men around him had become a wall on all sides. He looked up, but the whiteness of the sky had joined seamlessly with the white slabs. He looked down, but the spongy jungle floor had become as hard and white as the walls that now seemed slowly, slowly, to contract toward him. The air had grown thick and viscous, more like a stringy liquid than a gas, and as he struggled to breathe, he thought in a dull, druglike horror, *I am in an egg. I am trapped in an egg.* And the whiteness all around him continued to draw nearer, making the egg-white air even more dense, so that his lungs were clogged like a drowning man's. He threw up his arms in agony, but they struck the top of the hard whiteness, which pressed down on him until he was forced to crouch, and finally to wrap his arms around his knees, tuck his head between his shoulders, and assume the fetal position. The white shell still shrank, and his claustrophobia shrieked out its agony, a hundred, a thousand times worse than the Vietnamese rat cage that had nearly driven him mad.

Now the shell had reached the point where it could no longer maintain its egglike shape without crushing the body of that which it held. So it adapted itself to the fetal shape McNeely had been forced into, pouring itself like white liquid steel along the contours of his body, rolling around knees and elbows, sliding over taut scalp, rippling around buttocks and back until he was encased head to foot in an impenetrable carapace of soul-blinding whiteness, screaming his madness through shock-thickened lungs forever and ever and ever. . . .

"George!"

A hairline crack in the shell.

"George! Wake up! George!"

Greater cracks now, a piece of whiteness falling away, comforting darkness beyond.

"*Please* wake up! George!" Then louder. "Kelly!"

All around him now the shell was cracking, falling

outward. There! A foot was free! A hand! He could move
his elbow again! The darkness, sweet soothing darkness,
was returning.

"Kelly! Oh, George, wake up!"

He could breathe again. *Air*, not the thick life-soup
inside the egg. Eyes opened to dim light. Gabrielle's face,
formed and featured, hung above him like a friendly moon.
She gasped in surprise as she saw his opened eyes, as
though she had never thought she'd see them again.

"Oh my God, are you . . . all right?"

He moved his head back and forth slowly, half-expecting
his neck to be broken from the nyctalopic ordeal. "I . . .
yes . . . a dream . . ."

"God *damn* dreams!" she cried. "God . . ." A banging on the door interrupted her.

"Hey! Gabrielle!" Wickstrom's voice.

"Come in!" she barked, still full of fury at what had
happened to George. The bedroom door opened and
Wickstrom stuck his head through. "It's all right, Kelly.
I'm sorry." The apology softened her tone. "George had a
nightmare. I couldn't wake him up."

Wickstrom was too open, McNeely thought, to keep the
suspicion out of his eyes. "You okay now?"

"Yeah, yeah. . . ." He nodded, smiling wanly to reassure them.

"Was it the house?" Wickstrom asked point-blank.

Everything's the house! McNeely thought, but instead,
he laughed. "No. You know I'm claustrophobic. I just
dreamed about it, that's all. I've had nightmares like it
before. No big deal."

"I couldn't wake you," Gabrielle said.

"Sure you could. I'm awake." He spread his hands to
indicate the obvious.

"I mean, it was like you didn't *want* to be awakened,"
she tried to explain. "As if it were horrible, but still you
didn't want to wake up."

"That's ridiculous. Why would I want to *stay* in a
nightmare?"

She shook her head, looking at him with pleading eyes.
"I don't know."

A long moment passed while they looked at each other.

Finally McNeely turned to Wickstrom. "Thanks, Kelly. Sorry we woke you for nothing."

"S'okay. Sleep well," he said, and disappeared.

McNeely looked back at Gabrielle. She was still staring at him with a deep frown. "Are you sure you're all right?"

"Jesus," he said, "you've been asking me that for ages. What makes you think there's something wrong? A few stupid nightmares?"

"Maybe."

"There is nothing wrong with me," he said solemnly, his hand going out to touch her cheek. "Nothing. Believe me." He pulled her to him and kissed her, but she turned her head away after a moment. "What's wrong?" he asked.

"Nothing. I just don't . . . want to right now."

A dull anger ran through him. He hadn't intended the kiss to lead to sex, but now that it was denied him, an unidentifiable perverseness gored his newly found sexuality. "Sorry," he said coldly. "You call the shots."

"I didn't mean it like that."

"Oh? How then?" He felt his need for her growing, but whether born of tension, desire, or rejection, he could not say.

She shook her head. "I just want to sleep."

"Fine." He lay back, turning away from her and closing his eyes. He heard her turn out the light, and felt her lie down, not touching his body with any part of hers. For several minutes they lay there, and finally he felt her move until she was beside him, her hand on his shoulder.

"George," she said, "I'm sorry. I'm just scared."

He turned and embraced her. "Don't be. It's all right." He kissed her deeply then, and though she did not resist, neither did she fully respond. But he kept on, his hands moving over her, and soon they were naked, she guiding him half-heartedly into her.

Something came over him then, a sudden anger that he knew to be irrational even as he manifested it. He began to drive into her, not with burning speed, but with a slow cruel force, until she moaned, not from pleasure, but from pain. But instead of stopping, or changing position to relieve the pressure that was hurting her, he continued to push down on and into her.

"Please . . ." she grunted, trying to shift his weight. "It's *hurting* . . ."

He thrust into her sharply once more, making her gasp, then moved down lower on her body, relieving the tension of aching tissues he'd purposely caused. "I'm sorry," he whispered, and part of him was, but inside him another voice cried, *Your fault, not mine. Because of you, because of you.*

All because of you.

A moment later he came without pleasure, and from there they moved into separate, dreamless sleep. Sometime later the sound of her moving about in the bathroom woke him, and he looked at the towel they had kept by the bed to put under her after sex. His semen had drained out from her while they'd slept, along with something reddish, and now lay on the towel like a thick mixture of eggwhite and blood.

He shivered, folded the towel over, and tossed it on the floor.

Chapter Eighteen

Monckton pulled Sterne's down-filled jacket up over his head. Just for a moment, he thought. Just long enough to breathe warm air again, to melt the ice that his own breath had formed on his moustache. It had grown colder since his accident, much colder. He guessed that it was below freezing, though he couldn't be certain. He tried to remember if breath would freeze above freezing. Freeze above freezing? No, that was just stupid. It *must* be freezing then.

He took some more deep breaths and joyed in the ecstatic warmth his lungs created within the nylon cave. Freeze above freezing. Was his mind going? He felt so stupid, as if the things he remembered, things he *knew*, were all slipping away from him. *Is this what dying of exposure is like?* he thought with a fleeting smile, and wished again that he *had* died when he'd fallen, landed smack-dab on his white bushy head like that bastard Sterne must have. Died right off and not had to worry about starving and freezing to death.

At the thought of freezing, his leg tingled again, and he shivered. With a sigh he pulled the down coat off his head and spread it once more over his legs and hips. All he had were a pair of denims, and they had ripped open during the fall. *Thank God for Sterne,* he thought with irony. *If he hadn't taken his jacket off, my legs'd be icicles by now. Small favors.*

He glanced at his watch again and immediately wished

he hadn't. 1:47, 10-26. And in New York people would be walking down Fifth bundled against the winds pushing up the stony canyons. The late lunchers would be scurrying out onto the sidewalks to get back for their two o'clock meetings, the shoppers at Bloomie's would be hunched over like stylish gnomes clutching their knapsacks. And in his own warm office Trish would be making the afternoon pot of coffee. Hot, rich coffee, the steam rising like a cloud of benediction . . .

What time now? 1:48. Good. That fantasy had killed a whole minute. *Call, damn it! Renault, you fat pompous old prick, pick up the phone and call! You know you'll have to sooner or later!* Monckton growled deep in his throat. It was that damnable certain *hope* that kept him going. Because Renault *would* call. He'd be coming on the thirty-first when the house opened, and Monckton was sure he would call to tell them (them! One dead, one dying) when he'd be arriving. And when he called and no one answered, then . . .

Then rescue.

And if he didn't call until the thirtieth? Four days from now?

Monckton started to cry in frustration at the thought, but quickly made himself stop. He couldn't afford to waste the moisture, not knowing when and if it would rain again. He wiggled his toes and was relieved to feel them respond. The socks were thick, the boots heavy. But at this point the loss of a few toes would be a small price to pay if he could get out alive.

A sharp gust of wind caught a corner of Sterne's jacket and flipped it back, exposing Monckton's thinly covered legs to the cold. As he patted it back into place, tucking the edges beneath the muscle of his shattered leg, he felt a strange rigidity to the material that should not have been there. Was there something in the pockets he'd missed when he'd gone through them earlier? Something to eat? His stomach crawled in anticipation as he yanked the jacket off his legs and burrowed into the pockets.

The left one was still empty, but in the right pocket he found, snagged under an overlapping seam, two wooden matches.

"Barnburners," he whispered, using his childhood name for the big white phosphorus matches that needed no special striking surface. There'd been a box of them next to the stove in the cabin. No doubt Sterne, who smoked cigarettes, had pocketed a handful before going out to chop wood one afternoon.

At first disappointment flooded through him at finding something so inedible, but a second's thought told him that these could be a hundred times more valuable than a fragment of Hershey bar or a lint-covered cough drop. These could bring him warmth and even (he hardly dared think it) act as a signal. Wilmer was north of here, and he was on the northern side of the house. If someone noticed smoke . . .

He shook his head. Twenty miles away—who'd notice smoke from a small fire twenty miles away, even assuming the absence of autumn haze?

Flame then, he answered himself. If the flame were high at night, maybe then . . .

But it would have to be a high flame to clear the tops of the trees, higher than he could ever hope for. He looked around the wide balcony to see what fuel the matches could ignite. There were dead leaves in abundance, not only those he had blanketed himself with to keep out the cold, but more that the wind had trapped in the area between wall and side railing. They were still damp from the rain, but the sun was bright in spite of the chilling air. If it could dry *most* of the icy moisture out of them, leaving just enough to make them smoke . . .

Monckton gritted his teeth and began to drag himself over to the mound of leaves against the wall. It took him several minutes, and when he got there, he began to methodically take the pile apart, spreading the ice-crisp leaves in layers on the dark sun-warmed tiles of the balcony floor, cursing bitterly when a gust of wind would undo his handiwork.

Chapter Nineteen

Wickstrom cooked breakfast. "Something special this morning," he said, grinning as he put the plates on the kitchen table.

"This *morning*?" queried Gabrielle, a slight frown on her face.

"Sure. It's when we get up and have breakfast, so what else should we call it?" Both Gabrielle and McNeely could easily see that Wickstrom's enthusiasm was feigned, no doubt in response to the distance he'd felt between the two of them. They'd dressed in silence when they'd gotten up, and hadn't spoken to each other since. McNeely had wanted to apologize, but something in Gabrielle's manner made it impossible for him. So now they sat not looking at each other while Wickstrom set down on the table with a great flourish a large plate piled high with fried chicken and biscuits.

"A good old southern breakfast," Wickstrom babbled, "just like my mama used to make. She was from South Carolina originally." There was no response from the others. "Well," Wickstrom said, picking up a drumstick, "help yourself. There's plenty of it."

Gabrielle took a small breast while McNeely chose a thigh. Wickstrom continued to make small talk to which they responded, but no more than was necessary. It was during his second cup of coffee that McNeely began to notice the smell. He tensed so that his cup rattled against the saucer, making the others look up. He smiled crookedly and dabbed at the spilled drops with his napkin, wondering if the others had sensed the sour odor that was emanating from behind the cellar door.

"Well," he said with unfelt joy, "anybody ready for some cards in the den?"

"I'd like to finish my coffee first," said Gabrielle dryly.

"Yeah, what's the rush?" Wickstrom smiled. "You have an appointment?"

McNeely gave a hollow chuckle, and sipped his coffee. Minutes passed and the smell grew stronger, yet the others made no mention, so that he wondered if he was imagining it or if the entity was keeping it from the others. But finally Gabrielle looked up, her frown deepening.

"What *is* that smell?" she asked.

Your husband. Did you forget already? McNeely thought wildly. "Some food that's turned, probably. The refrigerator won't keep things fresh forever."

"Well, good God," she said, standing and going to the refrigerator, "why don't we throw it out then?" She opened the door, but no odor escaped, only cold fresh air. The pallor that leaped into her cheeks told McNeely that she'd suddenly realized the source of the smell. In her white face and suddenly trembling hands he could see all the memories come rushing back, and then he was beside her, his arm around her supportively, closing the thick white door.

"I'll take care of it," he said softly. "You and Kelly go get the cards ready. Take your coffee along. I'll clean up here. Clean up everything."

She turned blindly, then paused, looking at McNeely with new conviction. "I can help," she said.

"No!" he barked. "I'll take care of it." He tried not to let his panic show. There was no way he could explain the presence of Neville's body in the fire chamber without revealing a good portion of the truth to them, a truth he was not yet ready to share. "Really," he said in a gentler tone, "go ahead. I'll join you in a minute."

Wickstrom stood and shook his head. "I don't think any of us should be alone."

"I'll be safe," McNeely said firmly.

"I'm thinking about the safety of all of us," Wickstrom replied.

"Nothing's happened," McNeely lied, "and nothing's going to. I mean it."

Wickstrom hesitated for a moment, then gave a sharp, quick nod of acquiescence. Why, McNeely wondered, had he given up so easily? Perhaps he thought that McNeely's self-perceived guilt could be purged by tidying up the remains of the man he let die. Or perhaps at heart he just didn't want to go into that cellar again. Whatever the reason, Wickstrom picked up his coffee mug and smiled at Gabrielle. "Let's shuffle the deck and wait for George, okay?" He looked back at McNeely, his smile stiffening. "Don't be too long." He left the kitchen, Gabrielle following him unwillingly.

McNeely waited until their footsteps faded into silence, then opened the cellar door. He winced at the pungency of the odor and started down the steps, closing the door tightly behind him, wondering if the thing would confront him, fearing that it would. He steeled himself against both the odor and the sight of what was on the fire chamber floor, and walked in.

The lights were still on, as he had left them. David Neville was still lying on the cement, cold, unmoving, ripe with decay. McNeely looked away from the corpse, upward to where he had last seen the pale, wraithlike face hanging in the air. But there was nothing, only an empty room and silence.

He waited for only a moment longer, then knelt beside the corpse, searching for an untainted place to grab it. His fingers closed around a soggy clump of wool sweater, and he dragged Neville out of the room, across the wide floor of the cellar, and into the wine cellar, leaving a red-brown trail as he went. He repositioned the tablecloth over the twisted form, looked uncomfortably at the huge covered bulk of Cummings's corpse, whose decomposition had stained the tablecloths in a dozen places, then he left the wine cellar, closing the door behind him.

Again he stood in the dimly lit main cellar; again he listened for the light, easy voice, looked for the classically featured glowing face. But still there was nothing. He was unable to sense its presence in the slightest.

Where was it? It seemed illogical that it would not

confront him here, particularly since he was alone. Was it gone? And if so, where? Why? Could it be resting, completely unaware that McNeely was in the cellar alone? *Think*. Could that be one of its weaknesses? That it did indeed need to rest?

The thoughts bombarded his mind, and he boldly sought to deal with them, to put them into a recognizable context. The thing was force, a combination of forces, millions of them, and it could manifest itself *physically*, even enough to cause a dead body to rise and walk again. So obviously it expended power. And if power were expended, would it not have to be built up again, like a battery recharging?

Perhaps individually these *souls, revenants, thoughts*, call them what he would, were infinitely weak, in most cases totally unnoticeable. It would only be when they coalesced, joined those millions upon millions of bits of power together, that they became something to be reckoned with, to be feared.

But power fades and weakens with use. McNeely remembered how pale and weary the face had appeared after his confrontation with Neville's corpse, as though something had been drained from it. Could it still be somewhere sleeping, letting its power build up again for its next meeting with him?

If so, there's weakness number one. It can't be everywhere at once, or in one place all the time. Yes, it was a weakness, but a weakness that suggested a disquieting question: how would he know when it *was* with him? He felt like a suspect behind a one-way mirror. Were they watching him now, silent and unseen behind that one-sided piece of psychic glass, or was the room next-dimension empty, or occupied only by a dozing sergeant?

He made himself relax again, tried to let his mind open. If it was there, he would *know* it. Wouldn't he?

His thoughts were his own, he felt oddly certain of it. And he used the assumed liberty to try to think of what his next plan of action would be. If it confronted him again with new and more detailed demands, he might be able to stall it, to fake cooperation by actually *thinking* himself into the role, at least enough to fool them. *But*, asked a bitter voice inside him, *to fool them for how long?* Just

then he would have given his left arm for his wristwatch—
hell, just for today's paper. How long did they have left? A
day? A week? *We've lived here forever already.*

And what if he didn't do anything? What if he stayed
out of the cellar, made himself forget about the entity?

(Fat chance!)

All right, then, what if he just ignored it, even if it
spoke to him?

Ignore it, George, and it'll go away.

That's what he'd done to the ones who'd called him a
fag, and it'd worked then. They'd tired of their game.

But these things weren't raw recruits or green mercs,
were they? He shook his head in frustration and made his
decision. *Stay away from them. If they try to speak to you,
ignore them. Stay with Kelly and Gabrielle. And love her,
damn it. Don't hurt her.*

He turned and walked up the creaking stairs, afraid to
look behind him, afraid not to, for fear that he would miss
the pale face forming, or the quietly walking corpse dog-
ging his steps. But he reached the kitchen safely and
pushed the cellar door closed, wishing that there were a
sturdy lock on it for all the good it might do.

As he walked down the hall toward the den, he found
himself more at ease. The mere knowledge that they were
not there in the cellar waiting to confront him had done
wonders for him. He'd never backed down from a fight,
and now that he felt he could indeed fight this entity, that it
was capable of being defeated, that it had strengths and
weaknesses as did enemies of flesh and blood, he felt
much more secure. Besides, the time when the house
would open could not be far away.

He entered the den with a reassuring smile. Gabrielle
was pale, and Wickstrom looked uncomfortable. But
McNeely disarmed them both after a few minutes, and in a
light moment took Gabrielle's hand under the table. He
squeezed it gently and hoped she could read the apology.
She did, and smiled back openly and forgivingly.

The remainder of the "morning" went well. After cards,
they'd gone up to the nursery *cum* studio, and Gabrielle
had painted while Wickstrom and McNeely worked together on a few puzzles. Gabrielle was disappointed with

the work she was doing, but she seemed glad to see the two men enjoying themselves, laughing and teasing each other over the solutions.

McNeely was the first to suggest lunch. "Is it my turn to make it?" asked Gabrielle, putting down her brush.

"Let's see, I made breakfast," mused Wickstrom. "George, you made dinner last night."

"Are you sure?" Gabrielle said.

Wickstrom nodded. "I'm sure. We had steak."

"You must be right then. That's all George knows how to make."

McNeely chuckled self-deprecatingly. "So I'm not Escoffier. Nevertheless, you're elected for lunch, my dear."

"Don't 'my dear' me." She pouted archly, then grinned. "Grilled cheese and bacon sandwiches, snapper soup, white wine, eh?"

"Sounds good."

"*Très élégant.*" McNeely laughed. "Say, why don't we build a fire in the fireplace? We haven't done that for ages." It would be something different, McNeely thought. Besides, he felt he could use the cheerfulness of a bright and snapping blaze. And, too, he was enough aware of his fears that he was able to draw a conscious parallel to the caveman trying to keep the dark beasts away from his home with the light that burned.

"I'd like that," Gabrielle concurred. "It does seem a little chilly today. I hope there's nothing wrong with the heating system."

"I doubt it," said Wickstrom. "Probably it just got a lot colder pretty fast outside and we haven't had a chance to catch up." Wickstrom looked at McNeely and frowned slightly. "Shall I help Gabrielle with the lunch, George?"

McNeely read his concern. He didn't want to leave Gabrielle alone in the kitchen, and yet he felt uncomfortable leaving McNeely alone as well. McNeely waved a hand casually. "Help Gabrielle. I'll be fine. You can open the wine."

"Hah!" laughed Gabrielle. "He's a fiasco with a corkscrew. That Bordeaux had more floating cork than after a shipwreck."

"Okay then, I'll stir the soup!"

They walked down the main stairs together and into the Great Hall. The wood was stacked neatly, and McNeely started to arrange kindling while the others watched, obviously hesitant to leave. "Go on," he said. "By the time you get back, this place will be warm as toast. Besides, I'm only twenty, thirty feet away, so you can yell if you need a sommelier."

Gabrielle and Wickstrom disappeared into the kitchen, and McNeely continued to pile the kindling, stacking it Indian-style. He'd generally been the firemaker of his squad, gathering just the right woods, knowing what was best for tinder, what to add to make the flames grow safely after the tinder caught, how to place the larger logs just so as to get the optimum amount of heat from the minimum amount of fuel. He grinned as he remembered the faces of the green ones who'd been ordered to help him gather firewood on the savannahs or places where scrub was all that kept it from being desert. "Jesus," they'd moaned, trudging behind him picking up sticks, "a fire in this heat—bloody fucking brilliant." They'd been glad for it, though, after the sun had set and the cold crept in. Then they'd huddle toward the fire like the cold little animals they were. Like the cavemen.

God, but he wished he were there now, under a clean black night sky aflame with stars, with maybe just a crescent of moon low on the horizon like a scythe ready to reap those stars with its greater light. Cool outside air, breathed by trees and grasses, would pour into his lungs, and the earth would be comfortably firm beneath his bedroll, the rich earth-smell sharp in his nose. His mind would be racing with the seed of his senses, and his thoughts would be on the next day, a day filled with enemies, perhaps, but enemies one could see and touch and kill if necessary under the wide and arching canopy of sky that had looked down on all soldiers and all wars since time began.

And how many of those soldiers are here now, he thought. What energies could be left of those men who fought under Alexander, marched with Caesar, raged at the pass of Thermopylae? He'd met his share of evil men in battle. Perhaps one in ten had that combination of qualities that marked him as a killer, one who relishes not the act of war, the excitement of battle, so much as the joy of taking human life. If that was not evil, surely nothing was, for it was that that had sparked the imaginations of DeRais, of Albert Fish, of those monsters the thing had freely admitted as being part of it.

And what of himself, he thought uneasily as he finished laying the last stick and took the box of matches from the low table on which they sat. What did *he* draw from war? There was excitement, yes, but in killing? True, he'd been ready to do solo work, but his targets (he would not think of them as victims) would have been somehow deserving of their fate. They would not have been gas station attendants whose wives wanted them done away with so that they could marry the neighbor they'd been fucking; these would have been generals, politicians, despots who had climbed to the top over the bodies of those weaker than themselves. Their deaths would have been *good* for their countries. In the eyes of the people, their killer would be a hero.

Hero. McNeely bit his lower lip and pondered the word. Wasn't that really what he'd always wanted to be? Wasn't that the one thing that would make everything else all right? Nobody gave a damn if Alexander the Great liked boys or if Patton got his rocks off by slapping people around. They transcended that by being heroes. And so had he, at least among the people he fought with. At least with most of them.

But why did he have to go on being a hero? Relief surged through him at the thought. He hadn't needed the money, but he'd been ready to go out and look down a gun barrel and kill someone who wasn't firing back. That was the one thing he'd never done, never had to do. And now he never would. Gabrielle had changed all that. *He* had changed all that.

The Pines had changed all that.

It was a disquieting truth, and to drive it into shadow, he struck a match and held it to the crumpled paper beneath the thinner twigs.

In a moment the fire was snapping and barking, growing larger while the sweet-spicy scent of wood smoke teased his senses. The larger branches were catching now, the air pushing the flames upward toward the skillfully balanced thicker pieces until a bright orange pyre glowed and chattered. Knots coughed and twigs laughed merrily; wooden pockets split and spat, showering sparks harmlessly on the stones that encircled the fireplace. Within a minute he was luxuriating in the warmth of it, stretching his muscles and thinking about how good Gabrielle's soup was going to taste.

Then the room shifted.

At first he thought it had been a trick of the light, that the flames had rattled his optic nerve so as to give the illusion that the walls had moved slightly. But as he looked more intently he became convinced that it was not an optical trick. The room *had* shifted, moved, *hiccuped* its giant stones inward. Again it occurred, and this time he heard the scrape of stone on stone above and below as the walls contracted, making the huge room hundreds of square inches smaller. He stood now, his heart tripping over its own beats, sweat that was not the result of the fire's heat starting to bead on his face. His stomach tingled.

Overhead something cracked. He looked up quickly and saw a section of beam disengage itself from a longer one and come hurtling downward to land thirty feet away. The ceiling seemed lower than it had been.

Again the walls moved spasmodically, jerkily, inward, like vast legless men dragging their misshapen trunks along the ground with sinewy arms, lurching drunkenly toward their goal. The ceiling grunted again and more debris fell, spattering about him like deadly rain. The actions of walls and ceiling increased in tempo and ferocity, shards of stone and splinters of wood snapping like dry twigs.

At first he had been too startled to run, then too fascinated. But he moved toward the northern end of the Great Hall now, with its twin escape routes of west and east wings. His mind screamed at him to run, but his legs only labored slowly, as if through a sea of thick jelly. His stomach knotted as he saw that the north wall had hopped, like some monstrous toad, so far toward him that only a foot of space remained through which he could gain access to the wings. Another lurch of the walls, and that space had disappeared. He looked above, wondering if he could climb up the wall and over the second story balcony; but the rough dark surface of the ceiling had already descended to the bottom of the third floor level and would cover the second long before he could find a route to it.

A tortured scream of metal filled the hall, and a glance directly above told him the chimney had surrendered to the unimaginable force that was compressing the room. It had bent until it could withstand the pressure no longer, and now tore itself in two, dumping hundreds of pounds of metal down onto the fire, scattering blazing logs and branches like sparks in a wind. McNeely gasped as a flaming oak limb batted him on the side of the head. He could hear his hair sizzle as he muscled it away.

The walls were hopping faster, sending physical shudders through McNeely's body with every lurch. The ceiling had lowered itself to less than twenty feet above him, covering the second floor balcony. The width of the room was down to only ten feet, and its length was now a good deal less than thirty. The space actually seemed smaller because of the great bulk of the fireplace as well as the heavy pieces of refectory furniture that were all drawing madly together.

McNeely looked about in panic. Through the red-orange haze that clouded his vision, he recognized the dark thick velvet curtains at the south end of the hall, curtains growing ever nearer as the wall continued its clumsy but inexorable progress. They were, he remembered, the curtains to the small entryway with cloakrooms on either side. Perhaps, once behind them, he could nest there or in a cloakroom while the walls finally met, like a small fly escaped through a broken strand of the swatter.

He ran toward the curtain, a victorious joy surging through him at the thought of escape, a joy that turned to despair as he threw back the thick draperies to find the massive solidity of a steel plate pressed flush against them.

Reason left him then, and he screamed in fear, turning and pressing his back against the plate. The walls lurched again and threw him forward onto the stone floor. He scuttled toward the hall's center, fearful that the next motion of the wall could pin his legs between wall and floor, crushing them like grain on a millstone.

The planes of the room moved faster now, covering nearly a foot with each stony spasm. McNeely drew his knees inward as the room's width narrowed to seven feet, then six, then five, the length shrinking to fifteen, ten, eight . . .

Where has the furniture gone? he thought madly. *Where's the fireplace? The fire?* All sucked up at the juncture of floor and walls?

Another lurch, walls closer still, and before his prone body could be pinned, McNeely leaped to his feet, striking his head on the ceiling only five feet from the floor.

"Jesus!" he screamed, and the word reechoed deafeningly in the tiny space as the once Great Hall contracted again so that both side walls pressed against his shoulders and the ceiling struck the back of his bowed head with stunning force. He turned his shoulders diagonally so that the next spasm would not crush him, and the house moved again, pinning him snugly in a box of stone that would in no way conform to the shape of trunk and limbs as had the egg of his dream.

Every cell in him shrieked, every orifice opened in terror. Every fear he had ever known, every pain, every agony, seemed as nothing in comparison to the purity of the torture he now experienced. This, for George McNeely, was Hell.

And the house moved for the final time.

Death, he thought, was pleasant. There did not seem to be any constriction, any closing of his physical boundaries, at least nothing that could be felt. It was deliciously warm as well, and though he could not see, he could hear a comforting sound, like a low fire snapping and curling.

A fire.

He opened his eyes.

He was standing straight and unbowed four feet away from the round fireplace in the Great Hall of The Pines. The ceiling and walls were all in their usual places. There was not a trace of debris on the broad swath of the floor.

It never happened. It never happened, none of it. "Oh my God," he whispered to the crackling fire. "Am I going mad?"

Not yet.

He stiffened, nostrils flaring like a hound on the scent, his eyes stabbing into the dark corners of the hall. *That voice* had not been madness; he had heard it as clearly as he had heard the harsh whispers of the fire, as surely as he had heard that same voice speak to him before in the bowels of the house. And he knew what had made him see the walls close in and brought him to an agony he had not believed possible.

He turned and walked quickly out of the Great Hall and into the kitchen. The steamy smell of soup permeated the room. Both Wickstrom and Gabrielle looked at him as he entered, and from the way their faces suddenly became drawn with concern, he knew that what he had experienced was clearly limned on his own features.

"What happened?" Wickstrom asked with the certainty that something had.

McNeely smiled. It was a smile that made Gabrielle draw slightly away from him. "It's this place," he said. "You were right, Kelly. It's not good to be alone in here."

"What happened?" Wickstrom repeated.

McNeely shook his head. "They . . . it touched me. Touched my mind. Made me think things . . ."

"Oh, George . . ."

He looked at Gabrielle. "It didn't . . . *hurt* me."

"What things?" Wickstrom pressed. "Made you think what?"

"I thought . . . I thought the walls were closing in on me."

"Your claustrophobia," Gabrielle said.

McNeely nodded.

"You're sure it wasn't just . . . in your mind?"

"It was in my mind, but I didn't put it there."

They were silent for a moment, then Gabrielle asked, "What do we do?"

McNeely shrugged. "What *can* we do? Wait, that's all."

"*Shit!*" roared Wickstrom, slamming a hammy fist on the table with a force that made the dishes jump, spilling soup over the sides of the bowls. "What the hell is it gonna do? It hasn't said boo to Gabrielle or me! It's just been fucking with *you*, George . . . oh, shit,'' he moaned, slumping into a chair. "What does it want?"

"It wants *you*, George," said Gabrielle, her voice tight with tension. "Just like it wanted Cummings."

He shook his head. "No . . . no, I don't . . ."

"I'm not letting you out of my sight, not for a minute." Her eyes were blazing, reminding McNeely once more of the lioness. But now, instead of vigilance, they burned with the fury of an animal whose mate is captured by natives. He felt that at any moment she would perform the equivalent of leaping the kraal wall and scattering the little black men in a bloody froth. But even a lioness would be helpless here.

"All right." He nodded. "You stay with me. Safety in numbers." He smiled.

"How long can it be," Wickstrom said softly, "till we're out of here?" No one answered. "*Too* long," he said, sadness in his eyes.

They ate lunch half-heartedly around the fire. McNeely had only a few spoonfuls of soup and a little wine. He kept glancing around the room involuntarily, almost expecting the walls to move again. The others noticed his preoccupation but didn't mention it. As he picked at his food, his mind was set on one thing alone. He would have to talk with them again, have to do something to prevent a recurrence of what they had done to him after he'd built the fire. For he knew beyond doubt that if it happened again, he would come out of it either dead or totally insane. He could not remember the pain, but he could remember the fear, and though he hated to admit it, the fear was far greater than his ability to conquer it. It had been so great that it had made him go to Gabrielle and Wickstrom and tell, if not all, at least too much. What more could it make him do? He felt as if he would do anything, say anything to escape a next time, and he ached with the need to go and confront the entity and beg, if need be, to be spared a similar experience. Where would it happen the next time, he wondered. In bed with Gabrielle? Would his mind feel the walls pressing them together, merging flesh to flesh until the two of them were nothing but an unrecognizable mass of blood and tissue? A spoonful of soup caught in his throat, and he coughed it away, grabbing a napkin and gesturing to the others to sit as they rose to aid him.

After lunch they shot some pool, then changed into gym clothes for a brief workout. Gabrielle's protectiveness was in evidence, and McNeely realized with a dull shock that her attitude toward him was much the same as she had had toward Neville when they'd first come to the house—as though she expected his imminent death, feeling furious at her inability to prevent it. The sensation only heightened his unease, and he longed for their self-proclaimed night, when he could steal away to confront the source of his terror.

"Night" came slowly, but finally he and Gabrielle were in bed. Neither had the slightest interest in lovemaking, but she stayed pressed against him, her arm thrown across his chest as an unmistakable token of ownership that annoyed even as it comforted him. It seemed to take hours before she drifted off to sleep.

The face was waiting for him in the fire chamber, smiling and glowing as brightly as a small sun. If it had been weakened before, it had since recovered its robust strength. It was, he thought, positively rosy.

It is good to see you.

"What do you know of good?"

It looked humorously petulant, as if appreciating the play on words. *Much.*

"And of evil?"

All.

"Did you do that to me today?"

In the Great Hall.

"Yes."

It was not a great hall by the time we were done. It was rather small.

"You bastards," McNeely snarled. Although he sensed that abject servitude would be the course to take, his anger was too strong to check.

It was a lesson. Simply a lesson. It was unfortunate that we had to resort to it, but you seem to require ever more direct proofs of our power. The smile broadened. *We do not like to be ignored.*

McNeely's jaw trembled. "Don't . . . you won't do it again."

We hope it will not be necessary. You would be of no use to us dead or insane. The pale eyebrows rose, as if in sudden memory. *By the way, David Neville wants you to know how much he enjoyed your cowardice in the Great Hall.*

"Neville . . ."

His delight was so great, he nearly broke away from us again. He would have finished you if he had. Perhaps next time he shall determine your discipline.

"All right! You want to scare me, I'm scared! I almost lost my mind up there. And maybe next time I will!" His voice softened dangerously. "Now what do you want? I mean, what *exactly* do you want me to do?"

We wish escape.

"How? *How* can you escape?"

You will take us out.

"Me?"

Within you. Of your own free will.

"My own *free will*? That's absurd! You do things to me like what you did up there—you *force* me into helping you—and you call that my own free will?"

You feel coerced?

"Yes!"

There is no coercion. The choice is yours.

"Choice? *What* choice?"

To help us or die. Everyone has a choice. So do not say you have no choice.

McNeely stared at the face, his words lost. The face looked back, watching him with seemingly slight interest. McNeely wondered if those strange eyes actually saw as humans see. "If I help you," he said finally, "will you let us go, let us leave here?"

When we are satisfied that you are in earnest.

"What do you . . ."

You could attempt to lie to us. You could dissemble.

"I have to be your man then?" He smiled bitterly.

You have been ours since you first sought us for what we gave you. We require obedience, not ownership. That we have already.

"You . . . you're a *liar*."

That and many other things. Believe what you will. Will you aid us?

"How could I . . . take you out?"

Let us come into you. Do not frown so. There will be no pain.

"And once out, once away from here, then what?"

Not what you expect. You see yourself loosing a plague on mankind, like Pandora and her box. But the box was opened years ago.

"What do you mean?"

We will leave here, you, Gabrielle Neville, Kelly Wickstrom, and us. You will marry Gabrielle Neville in a few months.

"I . . ."

You do . . . love her, and she loves you. You will marry. Her wealth will disguise your past. And then one day we will no longer be with you. No trace will remain.

McNeely shook his head in confusion and licked his dry lips. "What if . . . if I wouldn't marry Gabrielle?"

You must. The answer was terse, commanding.

"You'll have to tell me why."

Why would you not want to marry her? She is beautiful and intelligent. She has control of the Neville businesses and will exercise that control far more wisely than her husband did. She will have much power.

"I don't *care* about power!" McNeely cried, and the thing in his mind started to respond automatically, stopping before the words actually registered in the network of McNeely's senses. But he knew what they would be all the same:

We do.

And something unexpected to both McNeely and the collective beast with whom he conferred leaped between the single consciousness and the mass mind, and the man saw it all, saw it as it had been so carefully planned. He saw himself at Gabrielle's side, both of them in evening dress, Gabrielle's hand being kissed by an older man who looked tantalizingly familiar, then the man's hand grasping his own, and himself responding with a firm shake of that hand, and of something passing between them like a nearly undetectable electric shock, just enough to make both of them flinch ever so slightly, and himself suddenly feeling more buoyant, as though a weight of which he had not been consciously aware had nevertheless been lifted from him, and the older man turning back into the elegant crowd, a hint of newly found cruelty twisting his lip, a touch of evil in the eyes, a bit of madness in the mind that would the next day, next week, next month, sit in judgment on the fate of the world, a fevered, almost lustful trembling in the hands in which rested the nuclear trigger.

Things to be done.

"You want to destroy . . . *everything* . . . kill *everyone*."

The thin nostrils flared, and a light leaped into the placid eyes. *No. That is not true.*

"You called yourself a liar! Why would you tell the truth now?"

It is not true.

"It *is* true! You're after the . . . the end of *everything*." It was as though McNeely heard someone other than himself shouting at the thing. "*No!* Not me! I won't do a thing to help you. You hear me, you . . . *pricks*? You want to kill me, kill me! You want to scare me till I go crazy, go ahead!" He crossed the few feet toward the wall until the face was only inches from his own. "Kill me, bastards— that's what you want, well, go ahead, I'm waiting—kill me!"

He spat savagely into the pale face, and saw the spittle disappear, as if the white skin had abruptly parted to allow it to enter, then sealed itself up in an instant. At the same time, the face started to fade, vanishing in the space of two heartbeats, leaving McNeely alone in the fire chamber.

"Bastards!" he yelled, swinging around to put his back to the wall. "You *scum!* Where are you! Come on, then, who's the coward now?" His fingers flexed, eager to tear into anything in his path. "Neville!" he cried, venom in his tone. "Where are *you*, Neville? Frightened? Shivering in some corner?" McNeely stormed out of the fire chamber, crossed the cement floor, and ripped open the door of the wine cellar, oblivious of the stench that pushed out in a wave. "Are you there?" His foot swung back and arced into the smaller body beneath the cloth with a damp thud.

The sense of something yielding beneath his blows mad-
dened him, and he kicked again and again at the covered
corpse. "Wake up! Wake up! Let him come out, damn
you! He wants me, let him come out and play!"

More kicks as a rotting arm was forced from beneath the
cloth, fingers bent and clawed like twigs dripping with
dark rain.

"Come on! Where's your guts? Hah! Your *guts*!" he
cried as his foot tore into wet softness.

Now the cloth was off the head, and the face gazed up
from the floor, devoid of expression, vacant of life or of
the half-life that had once possessed it. To McNeely, the
sight was more horrifying than if it had been leering at
him, clacking bared teeth and lifting ruined arms. But its
face was merely dead, so that he knew he had been kicking
a corpse.

He stepped back, looking down at his feet as if they had
suddenly swollen with leprosy, then back at the unmoving
face peering out from beneath the stained cloth. "You—
every one of you," McNeely said, "when you're ready,
you can come for me. And you can kill me if you can, but
I swear that I'll make you hurt." He walked to the heavy
door and turned. "Damn you.

"*God* damn you."

A short time later Kelly Wickstrom was awakened from
his sleep by a slight pressure on his bladder. *Shit,* he
thought. *I knew I shouldn't've had that last bottle.* He
made his way into the bathroom, tugged down his boxer
shorts, and sat slumped on the toilet, eyes half-closed.
When he finished, he stood, pulled up his shorts and
walked into what he thought would be his bedroom.

His bedroom was no longer there.

Instead, freezing cold surrounded him, and a blaze of
white light seared his eyes with its brilliance. A shrieking
wind buffeted him, making him stagger backward so that he
twisted around to support himself against the bathroom
door. But the bathroom door was gone, and he toppled on
his side onto a smooth sheet of white ice that clamped his
skin with cold. He scrambled once more to his feet and
looked around in desperation. There was nothing but a

field of unbroken whiteness on all sides as far as he could
see, with no dividing line where the horizon met the sky.
It was as though the land and sky went on forever.

He closed his eyes to escape the sickness that was
overwhelming him, only to discover that his eyelids had
become transparent. Clapping his palms over his eyes, he
found he could see through *them* as well. There would be
no escape through blindness.

The sensation went beyond nausea or dizziness. It was a
feeling that made his whole body want to scream, that
gave him the desire to pummel himself into unconsciousness. Had he had a pistol, he might have shot himself. As
it was, he could only stand and look at the vastness before
him, knowing that in no way could there ever be more
space.

Then the unseen planes of land and sky started to curve
away from him. It was something felt rather than seen, as
the ice beneath his freezing feet curled down on all sides
and the illusion of flatness faded until he felt as though he
were perched on the top of an enormous ball whose sides
swooped down and out from his position until he was
standing in pure space.

He looked overhead, but the sky, too, had curved up
and away so that he could no longer detect it, and while the
rest of his mind shrank into itself in fear, the part that still
retained logical thought told him that he was lost in infinity,
never to return, that he was forever a denizen of the void,
a dweller in limitless space, endless emptiness.

And his heart panicked, tripped, slowed then raced until, with a wiser knowledge all its own, it refused to grant
the shrieking brain enough blood to continue the fantasy
that had invaded it between the bedroom and the bath.
Blessed darkness flooded Kelly Wickstrom's mind, and he
fell roughly to the floor.

Then there was dimness, a strange sound, and a voice.
The sensation of being turned and held, and finally the
ceiling of his bedroom, the walls, the furniture, the sacred
solidity of matter. George talking to him.

". . . walking by, and I heard you fall. Jesus, your
head . . ."

Wickstrom touched the back of his head and winced as his hand contacted the lump. His fingers came away red.

"Don't move. Gabrielle! *Gabrielle!*"

Gabrielle stood framed by the doorway, light coming through her gown. She looked so *solid* . . . the floor felt so good beneath him.

"Get the first aid kit. Quick!" McNeely was holding something like a handkerchief at Wickstrom's head now, and he wondered how badly he was bleeding. "What happened, Kelly? What happened?"

Wickstrom told him about the ice field, about the space curving and flowing away until he was all alone in *nothing*. By the time he finished, he was crying softly while McNeely held him, and through his tears Wickstrom heard McNeely whisper, "Oh no, oh no, oh please God no, not them," and then gasp in horror, "Gabrielle!"

The scream came a second after the name had left McNeely's lips. How could he have been so stupid, so mindless as to send her alone down there, he thought, springing to his feet and racing into the hall. He'd been so concerned with Wickstrom, the idea hadn't crossed his mind that they'd want *her* as well. He practically fell down the stairs in his haste to reach the kitchen, dashed down the hall, and threw himself against the kitchen door.

He smelled it before he saw it. They were on the floor on the other side of the large table, Gabrielle on her back, her shredded nightgown pushed up to her chest, her eyes staring ceilingward, the blankness of madness in them. Her legs were spread shockingly wide, and between them, hips moving in quick sharp thrusts, was David Neville.

McNeely stood stunned as the movement stopped, and the shattered head turned to look over its shoulder. The torn lips split wider in a grin that was more glee than death rictus, and the remnant of a right eye gave a very definite, conspiratorial wink. Then the corpse collapsed like an empty sack, sinking onto the unmoving body of Gabrielle Neville.

Sobbing, McNeely ran to her, praying that she was still alive, clenching with frenzied fingers at the thing on top of her, moving it off her frighteningly still body. He searched for a pulse and found it, slow but steady. Then he held her, rocking her gently, and smoothed the gown back down over her bare stomach and hips. Aside from the wet leavings of Neville's corpse, he could see no blood on the floor between her legs, and he wondered if Neville had really raped her. *Jesus, how? There's not enough blood left in him!*

And dead men didn't walk either. McNeely looked at the corpse lying on its side and noticed with relief that its clothing was still on, that no dead shriveled thing protruded from the front of the pants. At least, he thought, she had not been penetrated.

But what of her mind? It would have been better for the thing actually to couple with her and leave her mind untouched than to have her remain in this comatose state. "Gabrielle," he called softly. "Oh, Gabrielle, please, please hear me. Come back. . . ."

"Christ." Wickstrom stood in the doorway, a hand still pressed to his bleeding head. "What happened?" His voice was dazed, and McNeely feared his sanity was on the line. "What's happening to us?"

If he could get Wickstrom to help, get him *doing something*, perhaps he'd come to himself. And there was something that McNeely had to do too. "Kelly," he said, "take care of Gabrielle. Just hold her. I've got to . . . I'm going to take this out of here so she won't see it."

"Did it . . . come up . . . on its *own*?" Wickstrom asked in childlike awe.

"Yes," he said coldly. "On its own. *Take* her." Wickstrom knelt obediently and cradled Gabrielle in his arms. "And don't follow me," McNeely ordered. He dragged the corpse through the open cellar door and pushed it ruthlessly down the stairs, following its flopping descent. One foot awkwardly on the bottom step, the other limbs beneath its torso, it looked like nothing human as he reached down again and hauled it for a third time into the corruption-rich air of the wine cellar. Then he slammed the door shut and ran across to the entrance of the fire chamber.

"*Where are you!*" he hissed.

There was no face present, but the voice was there. It seemed thin, airy. *Here.*

McNeely entered the room and closed the door behind him so that Wickstrom would not hear in the kitchen. "Leave them *alone.*"

When it answered, it sounded almost weaker, as if compelled to retreat by his ferocity. *Then serve us.*

"*Fuck!*" McNeely spat out. "You did that? With Kelly?" *Yes.*

"And with Gabrielle . . ." His voice broke. "Did Neville *get away* from you again?"

He did not get away. We turned him loose.

"Oh you . . ."

Her mind is not gone. Nor Wickstrom's. Not yet. There was a small appreciative chuckle. *Neville fucked her well. It was the first in a long time for him.*

"He *didn't!*" McNeely snarled. "Didn't rape her . . . I saw."

You saw what eyes can see.

"You bastard! *Where are you?*"

Everywhere.

"I can't see you."

We wish to be unseen.

McNeely could only stand, breathing heavily, wishing for something to kill.

Will you serve us now?

"*Serve* you?"

What happened to Wickstrom and the woman was nothing to what we can do. Do you think she would like to see the child she had aborted? Have it speak to her and call her Mama? Would she like to see you with Jeff? Or with that Senegalese boy, the one whose buttocks were so tight . . .

"*Stop* it!"

How old was he? Thirteen? Twelve? Younger? But you were high on kif, not really responsible.

"Shut up, God *damn* you!"

Would she like to hear how he whimpered, how he cried? Would she like to feel what he felt at your hands?

"Shut up, shut up, shut up . . ."

Then serve us.

"*No!* Go ahead and tell Gabrielle. Show her whatever you want. You want to kill the world, and if I serve you, you'll do it, so why should I care? Either way we die, all of us. Why should I care?"

It's a dying world, dying for decades. We only wish to speed the process.

"Why?"

To pay our debts! There was a pause, then a low laugh, as if it were amused at McNeely's childishness. *The earth is dying every day, from a hundred different diseases. Would you have it die slowly, from a multitude of cancers? Or would it not be more noble, more heroic, for it to hold a gun to its head and pull the trigger? Do you not value heroism?*

"It's our choice, not yours," McNeely replied, his voice firm. "It's for the living to decide, not dead things. Besides, there's still *hope*. We've not given up yet."

There is no hope. That we lie, you know. The Father of Lies. But this much is true: Earth is dying, and there is no hope. So the choice is yours. Serve us and die with the cataclysm. Or die now.

McNeely opened his lips to speak, and there was fire in his eyes.

Before you speak, think well, the voice interrupted. *If you choose to die now, you will stay here.*

"Stay here . . ."

With us.

"Am I . . . so evil then?" The fire dimmed to a spark.

Every man has evil within, but often the good overbalances it. It is different here. We are too strong for you to escape. Too strong for anyone who dies here to escape. You will be with us, part of us, for eternity.

Eternity. The word echoed inside McNeely's head. He had known this place was Hell, but he had not known he would be one of the damned. He struggled to find a mental path out of the dark wood, but could only spy a barely comforting rationalization. "If I served you," he said calmly, "I'd be yours anyway. Either way . . . I'm damned."

A murmuring noise came back to him, as if the thing

had not considered that point of view. Then came the words that pinned McNeely to the wall:

But she is not.

"She . . ."

Your death means hers. She will be with us. It would be interesting to have a guest with so much goodness in her. Mr. Fish would be delighted. And M. de Sade. And her husband. Especially her husband. He will make her realize how long eternity is. And she will learn that among us there are enough different . . . needs to fill eternity quite easily.

"I . . ."

You wish to speak?

"I will . . ."

Take your time. We have all there is

"I will serve you."

Part IV

I myself am hell;
nobody's here—
                    —Robert Lowell, "Skunk Hour"

Chapter Twenty

Monckton was of two minds about the rain. In one way he had been glad for it; the water in the depressions had evaporated sometime before, and his throat had been parched. The rain also meant that the temperature had risen to above freezing again, and that was something for which to be thankful. However, the rain had also dampened the leaves once more. It had been only a brief shower, but enough to turn them from their crisp dryness back to the consistency of damp newspaper.

And now the rain was over, the sun was out, and he was scattering the leaves over the surface of the balcony once again. He had gained a drink, something to fill his raging stomach, but he had lost more time, and time was the commodity he could least afford to squander.

Several hours later the leaves were dry again. Not perfectly, though—he made sure that there was enough moisture left so that they would smolder and smoke as well as flame up, if indeed he could get them to burn at all. The sun seemed to take forever to set. He'd decided upon dusk as the best time to start his fire. That way it might be dark enough for the flames to be noticed by some distant observer, yet light enough that the smoke could be seen if the flames proved deficient. In preparation, he dragged the leaves in small piles over to the balcony railing, thinking to use the wrought iron as a hearth against which to build his fire. But the wind proved treacherous, gusting in all directions so that first handfuls, then armloads of his precious fuel were lifted over and through the decorative ironwork. Monckton cursed weakly as he tried to save the leaves from the wind, and painfully hauled them back, pile by pile, to the protection of the house wall.

When he had finished, the pile was smaller by a third, but there was still enough, he hoped, to make an observable conflagration. He looked at the sky. It was clear, tinted by the reddish-gray of mid-dusk. He took one of the two matches from the pocket of the parka and wiped it carefully on the sleeve to remove any moisture that might be clinging to it. Then he took out a nearly shredded Kleenex from his pants pocket and rolled it into a ball, tucking it beneath the leaves so that a small strip of paper protruded. He waited until the breeze died down, whispered a prayer, and struck the match on the rough mortar between two of the tiles.

It blazed into flame with a noisy rush, and he cupped his hand around it, lowering it to the tattered Kleenex, lowering it too fast. Had he moved slowly, the matchstick might have remained afire, but the quick motion weakened it, making it an easy victim for the breath of wind that seemed to come from nowhere, and suddenly Monckton was holding no more than a thinly smoking slice of wood.

At first he could not believe it, but when the truth came to him, he dropped the match with trembling fingers and fumbled in the pocket until he found the other one. This he drew out and dried quickly, putting his finger behind the phosphorous head to strike it on the mortar. Then he looked at it hard, and thought, *What if it dies too? What if this one dies too?*

He continued to look at the match as the sky became darker, until it was so dark he could not see the match at all.

it wasn't sure, if it does, then I'd have killed it, destroyed it by taking it out, but to take it out I have to kill Kelly, and can I kill Kelly to kill the thing? Or would it not die at all but get stronger away from here?—did it make me think it doubts to trick me oh Jesus oh Jesus a maze a fucking labyrinth and if I don't kill him they kill him anyway and Gabrielle with them forever and ever and ever and ever and ever and ever and ever

You must kill him. You can see that.

McNeely nodded. *Of my own free will.*

Of course.

Then the voice was gone, and McNeely felt suddenly free. He looked up and saw the others. Gabrielle was sitting on one side of the small table, Wickstrom on the other. They were casually studying a chess board that lay between them, its surface covered by gold and silver chess men. How long, he wondered, had they been playing? They'd just finished setting the pieces when the voice had spoken to him. And now Gabrielle lifted her hand and moved a piece. He tilted his head and saw the move.

Pawn to K4. A response to Wickstrom's first move. It had been only seconds. McNeely's carnival of thoughts, his maniacal discussion with the entity inside him, had taken only seconds, and he realized that time would not save him. Or Wickstrom.

Then Wickstrom gasped, a sharp inhalation that brought his knees up toward his stomach, striking the underside of the table and throwing the chessmen right and left.

"Kelly!" Gabrielle cried, leaping to her feet.

McNeely ran to Wickstrom's side. The younger man's eyes were rolling up so that only the whites and the bottoms of the irises showed. His lips were flecked with foam, and a slight trembling shook his entire frame.

"What's wrong with him?" asked Gabrielle desperately.

"I don't . . ." The body slumped in the chair, as if whatever had been animating it had fled. Wickstrom's eyes opened, and he looked up foolishly at the other two.

"What happened?" he asked.

"What happened?" Gabrielle repeated. "You . . . you went *out.*"

became? Could the psychic pinhead hold an *infinity* of devils?

You will wait with us. As will she.

No! No! And what if he *did* take it out, what then? Would it prove as strong as it had thought? Or would it find itself weak, shrunken, powerless as a vampire in sunlight? The psychic lodestone that was Pine Mountain kept it here, but what if it had *sustained* it as well? What if, on taking it out, he would destroy it? It had never *been* outside, never been set free before.

How do you know? his mind shrieked at it.

There was a silence. And out of it came a sigh that was edged with the slightest note of doubt. No words answered to confirm or deny.

Then very softly the voice spoke. *Kill Kelly Wickstrom.*

Listen! McNeely thought savagely, grasping at straws. *It isn't right! It isn't logical!*

How do you mean?

McNeely made his thoughts become slow and methodical, as if explaining to a small child. *You are in me. You wish to be in someone else, someone I can reach only through my contact with Gabrielle. Now. My contact depends upon her marrying me. If I kill Wickstrom, that marriage is over before it begins. Don't you see? She'd never marry a murderer!*

We have thought of that. You will kill Kelly Wickstrom in self-defense.

Self . . .

You will be a hero. You will kill a madman. And only you and we will know that it is murder.

McNeely's mind raced as he tried to sort through the possibilities, knowing that it was listening but unable to stop. *Don't want to kill him, don't want to, but he'd die anyway, they'd kill us all, all three of us here forever with them, in agony forever, and Gabrielle what they'd do to Gabrielle, and they'd get out anyway, nothing could stop them, they'd get out, and then if they survived or died either way it would be a waste of our lives, of Gabrielle's I mean. Don't want to kill him, but if I do, then we can leave, Gabrielle and I, and it would get out anyway, and maybe it dies if it goes out, maybe it does. It didn't know,* he thought consciously, *then there's a way to defeat them.*

No way, the voice replied, and McNeely's stomach twisted. *You will leave the house first, or no one will leave. Condemn yourself, and you condemn her. Banish treachery from your mind.*

I can't, he thought involuntarily.

It is easy to obey. Your problem is that you do not want to. The voice paused, then went on while McNeely tried to cleanse his mind of thought. *We attempted to teach you, but it seems that you require us to give you a test.*

A . . . test.

It will not be difficult. But you must prove to us that you will obey.

What? What do you want me to do?

Kill Kelly Wickstrom.

The knot in McNeely's abdomen tightened and expanded quickly, over and over again, an inner fist flexing. *Kill Kelly Wickstrom,* he thought, *Kill Kelly Wickstrom,* and in one moment of disorientation he could not tell the thought-tones of the alien voice from his own.

Kill Kelly Wickstrom. It was the other voice now, low and insistent.

I won't . . . No . . . I won't . . .

You must. Otherwise we will not trust you. Otherwise we will destroy you. All.

I cannot deal with this! McNeely thought with full knowledge that the thing heard all. *No one should have to deal with this!* And he wondered feverishly what he could say, what arguments he could make against them. *If you destroy us all, then all your plans are dead as well. There'll be no one to take you out! You'll have . . . you'll have waited all these years, these centuries, for nothing.*

We can wait again. And while we wait we will grow stronger. Still more will join us. We can wait.

And McNeely saw the dead souls hovering over Pine Mountain like a thick cloud of darkness, a tornado whose whirling edges expanded ever outward. How far could it go until it touched weak humanity again? Or would it be doomed to remain here no matter how great its numbers

Chapter Twenty-three

Do you want to die so soon?

McNeely shivered. It had been hours since he had heard the voice, hours of white-knuckled fear, with thoughts of escape and betrayal rising involuntarily, only to be pushed down into a morass of trivia. He could not think of it, he told himself over and over again, and cursed himself for *telling* himself. And the more he tried not to think of it, the more he *did* think of it, until he knew the message must be written in fire for the entity to see. He repeated nursery rhymes to himself, he did the multiplication tables, he tried to list the titles of series books he'd read when he was a boy, but through it all, through Mary, Mary, quite contrary, and eight times eight is sixty-four, and *Tarzan and the Lion Man* and *While the Clock Ticked* and a hundred others, came the inner scream, *How can I stop them!*

And now he knew the screams had been heard.

We asked if you wished to die.

No.

You will if you try to betray us. You cannot, you know.

What do you expect of me! His thought burst like a flare. *You know I don't want to help you!*

You took us of your own free will.

Free will, he thought bitterly.

You must obey. You will not be harmed if you obey. But your treachery makes us uneasy.

McNeely could not help himself. *If they're uneasy,*

naked waist. He had had to throw away her nightgown.
"Don't be stupid," he said. "You can hardly stand."

"Help me into the shower. Then we'll get something
together. Just don't leave me now."

Once inside the bathroom, McNeely stripped and got
into the shower stall with her. He was glad he had; she
almost toppled over twice. But soon he had scrubbed her
clean, and she smiled for the first time as she blinked
water from her eyes and pushed back her close-cropped
hair.

"A bath now," she said. "I just want to sit and soak."

He filled the tub and got her into it, then dried himself
and dressed, leaving the bathroom door open so she could
see him in the next room. Her reaction to what had happened
surprised him. He didn't know what he had expected—
hysteria, trembling fear that would refuse to go away—but
whatever it was, she hadn't evinced it. For all the shelter-
ing he knew that her money had provided, she was a tough
woman nonetheless, and he smiled at her as she looked at
him from the tub.

In a few minutes she was out and dressed in clean
clothes, her hair still damp from the shower. "Are you
sure you want to go into the kitchen?" he asked her.

She shrugged. "It's just a room," she said, but he could
sense the hesitation. "You . . . you took it away?"

He nodded. "Yes. There's nothing there now. And
there won't be anything either."

Gabrielle moved into his arms and pressed her cheek
against his chest. "I want to believe that," she said. "I
really want to."

"Believe it." Together they walked out of the bedroom.
Wickstrom was dozing on the sofa, the bandage new and
white around his head like a surgeon's cap. "Don't wake
him," McNeely whispered. "Sleep's the best thing."

"But to leave him alone . . ."

"Believe me. Nothing will hurt him now."

When they entered the kitchen, she drew back, but only
for a second. She opened a beer and sat drinking it at the
table while McNeely heated the soup and threw a frozen
steak into the microwave. He began to talk to her about
things on the outside, where she spent her summers, whether

Stowe was the best skiing in the East, who had the finest veal Orloff in San Francisco, and he was pleased to see that her glances toward the floor at the far end of the table had lessened until now she was looking only at him and the food in front of her.

Then there was a pause in the conversation, and he knew that he had to put into words what had been bothering him. "I'm sorry," he said, "about the other night." She looked up curiously. "Making love. I don't know what happened to me."

"This place. The strain. It's all right."

"I'm not . . . a cruel person."

"I know that."

"It won't happen again."

"Once we're away from here . . ." She left it unfinished, and he nodded. "Let's go into the den," she said.

They walked arm in arm down the hall. The den felt comforting, its dark woods enfolding them like birds in a nest. McNeely felt no trace of the claustrophobia that had tormented him. He built a fire, and soon they sat together on the sofa, watching the bright flames prance behind the screen. McNeely knew it was the time.

"When we leave," he said, his mouth close to her ear, the clean, sweet soap-smell of her pleasantly strong, "will you stay with me?"

"I want to," she answered after a pause.

He swallowed, hoping that she wouldn't hear the clicking in his throat. "What would you say if I asked you to marry me?"

He hated himself for saying it, not because he did not want to, for he did, but because he was required to.

"I think I'd say yes." She turned to him, and he kissed her lightly, with lips closed. It was a young lover's kiss, chaste, and somewhere in the middle of it he forgot about The Pines and the horrors and the things whose rule he must obey, and he was glad that the woman he loved loved him, loved him enough to marry him, and they *would* live happily ever after despite it all. He would find a way.

They sat there for a long time, saying nothing, watching the fire, happy in their closeness. After a while the flames burned low and blue. McNeely took his arm from around

Gabrielle and started to get up. "Let me," she said, moving to the fireplace and setting another log on the grate, positioning it with the poker.

McNeely watched her, smiling.

Nicely done.

His smile vanished, and ice ran down his backbone. It had been the voice, but speaking to him here? With someone else present? Even if Gabrielle couldn't hear, how could he be expected to answer?

Think. We will hear you.

He opened his mouth to reply, then snapped it shut again. She was still busy with the fire. He concentrated: *Can you hear this?*

Yes.

But how?

We were not in you before.

In me! McNeely thought in panic.

Do not worry.

What's happening to me? What are you doing?

Just then Gabrielle set down the poker and rejoined him, putting an arm around his waist. He smiled crookedly and she lifted an eyebrow. "Anything wrong?"

"Uh . . . the soup? Stomach's a little funny."

"Oh, thanks a lot. You'd better get used to my cooking."

He heard himself chuckle. "Firing your cooks?"

"I always used to cook. I like to."

"Ah." He nodded, drawing her head down so that it rested on his shoulder and she could not see his face. He tried to keep his mind clear until he felt certain she would not continue the conversation. Then he thought: *Why are you in me?*

We must be in you when we leave.

Are we leaving then?

Soon. We are coming into you slowly, little by little.

Why not all at once? When we leave?

We entered Cummings all at once. It was too fast.

Why didn't you enter me before?

For a moment there was no response. *It had to be of your own free will. Otherwise we could not leave with you.*

What if I change my mind when I leave?

We will already be in you. And we will punish you if you

do such a thing. And her. A soft breath hissed dreamily in McNeely's mind. *She is so warm. Soft.*

McNeely almost withdrew his arm from around her. *Will you be coming into me from now on? From now until we leave?*

Coming into you. It is a suggestive phrase. Coming into you, slowly. Little by little. There was a time when you'd have liked that.

You go to Hell!

We are Hell.

There was no more. McNeely thought consciously, but his thoughts brought no response. And he was *afraid* to think, afraid to plan against them, for now they were in his own headquarters, spies behind every panel, listening to . . . what? How deeply could they probe? Could he mix his thoughts as he had done before? Confuse the inner listeners by scrambling the message? And even if he could, could he then uncode it enough for it to make sense to his own waking self?

He felt like a blind madman in a maze with no exit. And the woman he embraced wondered at the unexpected stiffening of the arms that held her, almost as if the man were afraid to move, to breathe, even to think.

Chapter Twenty-two

By the third ring Simon Renault started to wonder. By the fourth he began to worry. By the sixth small droplets of perspiration dappled his florid complexion. He let it ring five more times before he hung up.

Stop worrying, he told himself. *Don't be an old woman. There's certainly a logical reason. Both outside perhaps.*

But his specific orders had been to have a man in the cabin at all times. He was not sure of Monckton, but he knew Sterne would never disobey his orders. Unless . . .

Unless something more important countermanded them. *The alarm.*

He dialed the number again. This time he let it ring only six times before slamming down the receiver. He sat for a minute trying to think, then picked up the receiver and jabbed a button on his console.

"Yessir?" Harrison's voice, thin and reedy, responded.

"Something's wrong at The Pines," he barked. "There's no answer on the phone."

"Yessir?"

"Can you hear me?"

"Y-yes. Yes sir."

"Good God! Just shut up then! Call the police at Wilmer. Tell them to get a car up to the cabin right away. And get a Learjet ready for takeoff. I want to leave as quickly as possible."

"Yessir."

Renault slammed down the phone. "Good God . . ."

He threw a few things in the overnight bag he kept at the ready, cursing the luck that made him rush. It was the twenty-eighth of October, and he'd hoped to fly up on the thirtieth, spend the night in Wilmer, and drive to The Pines the following day to be there when the house opened; he'd been calling the cabin to let Sterne know of his arrival. And now this. Scenarios ran through his mind. Fire? Madness? Murder? He hadn't believed anything would happen, but now he was horribly unsure.

He closed his bag, snapped the latches. Then he grabbed the phone again. "Harrison? The plane?"

"The plane will leave in a half hour, Mr. Renault." The voice shook. "Can you be on the heliport roof in five minutes?"

"Of *course* I can! What about the police?"

"I was just about to call them when you—"

"Do it then!" he yelled, hanging up. He threw his topcoat over his shoulder, grabbed his bag, and rolled his prodigious bulk out of his office past a quivering Harrison, who was frenziedly searching for the correct area code.

Sterne had better either be up at the house or dead, Renault thought grimly. *Otherwise he's fired*.

She nodded. "And then a bath." She seemed to remember then. "Kelly! How is he?"

"Dented but alive. He's sleeping in the next room."

"What happened, George?"

"It . . . they . . ." *How much should he tell?* "It got to Kelly first, and then I think it wanted to get you alone."

"It, *it*? What is *it*?"

He held his palms out to slow her down, calm her. "The house. It, uh, *occupied* David's body. . . ."

"It wasn't David then?"

"No."

She looked past him at the opposite wall. "I didn't even recognize him at first. The cellar door opened and there it was and I screamed. When I saw it was David, I just blacked out. I mean, I knew what was happening, but it was like it was happening to someone else. I remember you coming into the room and thinking that it would be all right now, because you were there. Oh, George!"

She broke then; huge, wrenching sobs burst out of her, and they held each other for a long time before her crying stopped. All the while he whispered, "It's over, it's over."

When she lay back on the bed, she looked at him like a scared and angry little girl. "How do you know? How do you know it's over?"

"I know. Believe me. They've got what they wanted. They won't bother you again."

"I don't believe you."

"Do you believe that I love you?"

She paused. "Yes."

"Then believe me when I say it's over."

The doubt was still there, but she nodded her head tersely.

"You need something to eat. I'll heat up some soup."

"No!" she cried. "Don't leave me."

"It's all right now."

"Wait, please. I'll go with you." She threw back the covers and lowered her feet over the side of the bed. Immediately a wave of dizziness swept over her.

"You should stay in bed."

"I won't." With some difficulty she stood up.

McNeely was at her side, putting an arm around her

The reply had left McNeely silent and stunned with the implied worth of the woman he loved, and he felt more than ever that he had to free her from this house. "Why are you so sure," he'd asked after a moment's thought, "that you have anything to offer the ones that I'll meet— the presidents, the politicians?"

The voice had laughed. *They will absorb us like a sponge does water! They have prayed for such as we can give them.*

The answer made McNeely's stomach turn, and he promised himself in the most private sector of his mind that he would not allow the cataclysmic contact to occur. There had to be a way out, even if it meant his own death. If he could maneuver it somehow so that Wickstrom and Gabrielle left the house first, then he would remain, remain in The Pines with *them*, and they could do with him whatever they wished. He felt at times as though he were past saving, but he would not allow them to take Gabrielle. He would not.

The movement of her fingers broke his reverie, and he glanced up to see her eyelids flicker like leaves in a gentle wind. Then the eyes were open, and she was looking back at him with a strange mixture of relief, love, and horror. She whispered his name softly and he tightened his grip on her hand and nodded reassuringly, tears hot in the corners of his eyes.

"Just rest," he said, his voice nearly choked with the joy of her coming back to him. "Rest for a while."

She shook her head in refusal and spoke, the whisper louder. "Was it David?"

He nodded. "His body. Something else inside," he lied.

She shut her eyes, but opened them almost immediately, and cleared her throat. "Where is he? Now?"

"It's gone from him. It won't be back again. I promise."

She looked down at the soft curves her body made under the covers. "I feel like I'll never be clean again. I can . . ." Her voice choked, but she spoke over it. "I can smell it."

"I washed you up before I put you to bed. A shower's what you need."

"This ever happen before, Kelly?" McNeely heard himself ask. "Aside from your dreams in this house?"

"No, never." Wickstrom shook his head. "Those other times . . . here . . . I remembered. *This* time it was just like . . . like nothing."

"It was the house," said Gabrielle. She looked at McNeely, suppressed fury broadening her features. "You were wrong, George. It's still here."

"No," said McNeely. "It's not."

"It didn't feel like the other times," said Wickstrom. "I gotta lie down." They helped him to his bedroom. As soon as he closed his eyes, he was asleep.

"The truth, George," Gabrielle said accusingly when they were alone in the hall. "Tell me the truth."

"I couldn't with him there," McNeely replied, thinking how easy it had become to lie when so much was at stake. "I did tell you the truth about its not being the house." She frowned, but he went on. "It's Kelly. Kelly himself."

"What do you mean? Are you saying he's going crazy?"

"It's a wonder we all haven't," McNeely answered, his face lined with concern. "I've seen this before. Once in South America. We were pinned down by a group of rebels for days. No food or water at all. The one who went first was the one we'd least expected, the vet of a hundred battles." McNeely was amazed at how effortlessly the lies flowed, as though he were speaking long-memorized lines in a play. "He'd lose consciousness just like Kelly did, eyes rolling, foaming at the mouth. Then he'd come out of it okay. Until the last time."

Gabrielle looked oddly at him. He could not tell whether she believed him or not. "What happened," she asked, "the last time?"

"He went mad," McNeely answered quietly. "Took his rifle and opened fire on his own squad. Killed one man and wounded another before we finally brought him down."

Gabrielle's face was expressionless. "And you think that's what's happening to Kelly."

McNeely nodded. "Yes. I do."

"And how long did it take for this man you were with to get violent?"

"A matter of hours."

"*If* it happens to Kelly, how can you be sure that he'd respond violently?"

"Would you expect anything else from this place?"

"But what could he do? We have no weapons."

"Madness brings out amazing strength. He wouldn't need any weapons."

She shook her head, and though her jaw was firm, tears were pooling in her eyes. "I can't believe it. Not Kelly."

"I know you like him. I like him too. But he could be dangerous to us."

She laughed in bitter disbelief. "So what do you want to do? Kill him?"

"If I have to, I will."

She looked at McNeely as if he were a stranger. "If he goes mad, it's because he's *sick*. You can't kill a man for being *sick*!"

"I'll do anything I have to to protect you!" The words were spoken by McNeely alone, from the heart, and Gabrielle quailed at the quiet ferocity of them. For a moment he wondered if he had gone too far, overplayed his hand, wondered if the truth had shaken her more than the lies. So he made himself relax, and let the cunningly easy manner of the thing inside him take control once more. "We'll just watch him closely," he said. "If there's anything really wrong, we'll be able to tell."

She nodded in agreement, but her eyes were frightened, and he felt as though he had to get away from her accusing stare, had to speak to the entity to find out what had happened, where they were headed, what to do next. He felt drawn in half, as though he were two different people over neither of whom he had complete control.

"I'm tired," he said. "I think I'll take a nap." He walked down the hall and into their suite, listening to her footsteps slowly following him. Turning at the bedroom door, he watched her sit on the sofa and stare at her hands on her lap. When he realized she was not going to join him, he closed the door and lay down on the bed.

What happens now? he thought.

You'll kill Kelly Wickstrom.

She didn't believe me.

We planted the seed. It will grow.

McNeely asked no more questions, and the voice within him was silent. He felt like a machine whose battery had run down and was being recharged. And when the power had been restored, what then?

Then he would kill a man.

He must have slept, for the voice seemed to pull him out of a strange dream of odd, twisted faces in a red haze.

She is with him!

"With . . . who?" He spoke aloud, forgetting.

With Wickstrom! In his room!

McNeely sat up. He swayed slightly, still half-asleep, then ran into the living room. Gabrielle was not there.

Go into the hall.

He opened the door slowly and stepped through. There was no longer any question of whether or not to obey. He had come so far that he had to go on, not even wondering if he was truly possessed. It was not as though it commanded and he obeyed; instead, its mind was his. He was the thing's hands and body, moving when it chose. He knew he should be terrified by the concept, but he felt strangely emotionless, unwilling to rebel.

The door of Wickstrom's suite was slightly ajar, and he listened to the conversation within.

". . . like somebody clobbered me over the head and I stepped out for a minute. Like it wasn't really *me*."

"Do you think it was your mind or not?" Gabrielle's voice, pressing.

"It wasn't. I swear it wasn't. And still it wasn't like the other times."

"George thinks you're . . . you might be dangerous."

"Dangerous? Oh, Christ."

Come away! the voice hissed.

McNeely stepped back from the door and reentered his suite. He lay down once more on the bed.

You must do it now. Before it is too late.

Too late?

You fool! She's warning him!

McNeely smiled, pleased at the irritation in its voice. *I told you she didn't believe me. It was you in Wickstrom then, wasn't it?*

There was no reply.

I felt something leave me just before he went out.

They're plotting against you, the voice snarled. *Not against us.*

You're changing the subject.

We'll change your life to death in another second. Have you forgotten what happens if . . .

McNeely interrupted verbally. "I've forgotten everything." His voice was far away, as though he were forgetting even how to speak.

Do not forget her. The voice was softer now, oddly matching McNeely's tranced, puzzled mood. *His death means her life. She will believe you.*

"What do *I* believe?" he whispered into the dim light.

You believe in her.

It's no use, McNeely thought to himself. *It doesn't matter now.* Then, aloud, he said, "I'll need your strength."

You shall have it.

Chapter Twenty-four

Renault, holding a small microphone, sat in the co-pilot's seat. The copilot sat behind him, gritting his teeth in response to the racket Renault was making.

"Of *course* no one was at the cabin! No one answered my calls! What about the main house? . . . What do you mean your men didn't check? For God's sake, that's what I wanted checked! What did Harrison tell you? . . . *Harrison!* The man from my office who called you? . . . That goddamned *idiot*! Now listen, sheriff . . . all right then, *chief*! Get some men up to The Pines right away. And an ambulance as well. I don't care, knock it down! *Damn* the gate! And one more thing. Can you have a car waiting at the airport? I'll want to go right up to the mountain. I'll cover any expenses and more . . . I assure you it is *vitally* important. . . . All right, fine. Yes, thank you." He flicked a switch and sat back in the seat. "*Damn* it." He turned to the pilot. "How long now?"

"Almost there, sir."

"Hmph." Renault noticed something in the dark sky ahead, and leaned forward, adjusting his glasses. "What's that below?"

"Snow, sir."

Chapter Twenty-five

How shall I kill him?
With your hands.
He's strong.
You will be stronger.
Where?
The cellar. You will ask for his help in the cellar.
And then?
He will go mad and try to kill you. You will act in
self-defense.
What if Gabrielle comes with us?
She will not.
I do not want this.
Yes. You want it.
When?
When she returns. Pretend to wake as she comes in.
I don't know what to say, what to do.
Leave that to us. Save yourself for killing.

For the first time McNeely noticed that the voice shook.
Not from weakness, not from any lack of power . . . but
from excitement.

He tried very hard not to think about it.

Chapter Twenty-six

It was the snow that finally forced Monckton to light the second match. He had planned to every minute, but every minute fear stopped him. If the air was still, it was only because a fresh breeze was about to spring up. Besides, it was too dark now, wasn't it? Who would see the smoke in the night? And when dawn came, and both the smoke and the flame might be seen, well, no one would be up at that hour, no, and the wind was too brisk anyway. Only one match now, only one match.

So he sat on the balcony all day and watched the sun pass overhead, the precious match tucked down deep in an inner pocket, scurrying about on his elbows and stomach to keep the leaves from blowing away. *Dusk,* he thought. At dusk he would try again, and he let dusk fill his stomach and warm his limbs.

It was growing colder again, and by mid-afternoon dark clouds covered the sun. *It's going to do something,* he thought. *No rain, oh please no, not rain.* But then he realized that it was too cold for rain. Snow then, and he knew he could not survive a night of snow. He would simply go to sleep and never wake up. The snow would shroud him, and Renault would find him there, a frozen white mound in the sunlight. Unless he used the match.

He waited until dusk. Just as he slipped the match out of his pocket, the snow began. They were small wet flakes, and he gasped as he heard them slowly spatter his leaves with moisture. He breathed into his fists to warm and dry the match, fluffed up the remaining bit of tissue under the leaves, and scraped the matchhead along the mortar.

As it ignited, he cupped it in his trembling hands to keep it from the wind and snow, but suddenly the snow was gone, and he looked up in amazement. The wind had shifted so that it was coming from the south, and the snowflakes were drifting past him and his tinder, leaving a four-foot-wide space in the shelter of the house wall.

"Oh God, oh God, thank you God, thank you," he croaked as he slowly and carefully lowered the small flame to the fuel. The tattered Kleenex caught instantly, its white edges curling, then changing into bright orange flame. The nearby leaves smoked for a moment, then they, too, ignited, and Monckton thought he had never had as exquisite a sensation as the warmth that suddenly touched his face. He actually smiled.

But he realized that just sitting and watching the fire could prove disastrous. He had to tend it, to feed it methodically so that it would become what he wanted it to be. He rearranged the dead leaves around the small blaze so that the fire would spread outward, catching all the fuel so that one large flame would result. "Here y'go," he muttered, patting the pile into place like a child building a snow fort. "Here now, eat it all . . . eat it and grow big and strong."

The wind was still coming from the south, the snow falling heavily now, but neither on Monckton nor on his fire, which burned brilliantly, sending up a flame nearly six feet high, not enough to clear the tops of the trees that surrounded the house, but perhaps sufficient to make a visible glow to a distant observer in the dying light of dusk. Though the heat was intoxicating, Monckton was forced to move back from the fire along the stone wall. As he did so, he laughed to himself until he began to cough. Even if no one saw the fire, he thought it was worth it for the warmth alone. Now death would not seem so cold.

Then the wind shifted. It was only for a moment, but long enough for a ribbon of wind, like an invisible hand, to lift a smoldering clump of leaves the size of a cabbage away from the mother pile, and to hurl it upward on a geyser of cold air until it was stopped by the roof eave

some forty feet above, wedged between the wood of the
roof and the stone of the wall.

A small shower of sparks cascaded down, all dying
before they reached the balcony floor, but the clump remained solidly in place, glowing redly far out of Monckton's
reach. Then the wind, as if finished with what it had been
sent to do, turned northward once more.

Monckton's fire burned brightly, sending flame up to
brush against the gray stones, throwing white smoke high
above the treetops. The aroma was so sweetly pungent that
Monckton could sense it even through his cold-clogged
sinuses. But in a minute a new speck of light caught his
eye, and he looked upward. There, a yellow flame danced
mindlessly, up there under the roof, up there at the only
place on the building where there was exposed wood,
since the doors and windows had been sealed. Way up
under there where no wind would reach to blow out the
flames, where they could sit and dine leisurely on the old
dry wood, and perhaps work their way from one piece to
the next until they were inside where *he* had tried to go
and failed.

The flames grew as he watched, spreading along the
eaves with their red, then blue, then orange-yellow palette
until it seemed to Monckton that a Milky Way of fire lay
in a broad band across the black sky.

And then the meteors came. Tiny bits of burning wood
detached themselves from the whole and began to rain
down on Monckton and his smaller fire below, and he
thought for the first time, brushing off the glowing shards
that blackened his jacket, *The roof's on fire. The whole
roof is on fire.*

The burning debris fell faster now, and he brushed it
away frantically, thanking God that he had gloves on. But
the gloves, he thought suddenly, wouldn't keep off the
roof when it fell.

A falling slate cracked on the floor beside him, throwing
sharp splinters toward his face, one of which neatly
sliced his cheek. Then another fell a few feet away, and
another. The roof was going. He had to get off the balcony.

The ladder was still there. He knew that he would fall,

at least part of the way. But he had fallen before and he was alive.

Slowly, painfully, he dragged himself across the snowy stones while bullets of smoldering wood and hot slate dropped all around him.

Chapter Twenty-seven

A gun went off in McNeely's head, and his lips split in a smile as he vividly pictured Gabrielle at the other end, her face sick with pain, her fingers clenched at her stomach. *I think I would like that*, he thought.

The voice within him was quiet for a moment, as if stunned by the unexpected violence of McNeely's fantasy. Then it spoke. *You must not harm her.*

She was plotting against me. With Wickstrom.

Yes, she was warning him . . .

Does she love him then? Does she love him too?

She won't love him when he's dead.

Or when she's *dead*, he thought brutally, picturing Gabrielle's neck in his hands, her eyes bulging, her tongue protruding.

No! the voice cried. *Nooo . . .* And it trembled as McNeely intensified the image, adding more and more detail to the mental picture until he could see the blue veins pressing against the mantle of flesh on his dream-wrists, see his hands dig so deeply into Gabrielle's neck that the fingertips disappeared completely. *You love her! Do not harm her!*

Yes, McNeely answered, letting the vision fade. *Yes, I suppose I do. This is all for her, isn't it? Nothing for George . . . That bitch! Warn him!*

You must relax. You must not be angry toward her. It is only he who— It paused. *She is coming! Remember. The cellar.*

Stay with me!

We will! The voice quivered and faded as though down a long hall.

The bedroom door opened, and Gabrielle entered. "I thought you were sleeping," she said guardedly.

"I just woke up." *Want me to go back to sleep, cunt?* he thought, *so you can fuck Wickstrom?* "I've been thinking," he said, "that I ought to talk to Kelly."

"Why?"

"To try and get a feel for where his head's at. I'm worried about him."

"He's all right."

What do you *know, bitch?* he thought, and the first words of it, "What do . . ." came out unexpectedly, toned with venom that made the woman draw back a step. Then McNeely felt something stop his tongue before the rest of the thought became audible. "I want to talk to him, Gabrielle."

"I'll . . . go with you."

The hell you will! "I want to talk to him alone."

"I don't think you should."

"It's better that way. If he should lose control, he could hurt you. I don't want you hurt."

"Kelly won't hurt me."

Why? You suck his cock? And he saw himself slamming her aside with a forearm so that she struck the wall with a hollow thud that he could hear. "I can't take that chance. I love you."

"I'm going along."

"You'll stay here!" Her jaw muscles tensed; then her whole body grew rigid as she looked at him, eyes blazing. "I don't want to have to tie you down or knock you out (*smash your head open, you . . .*), but I know how to and I will if you make me. For your own good. Now, sit down on the bed."

She hesitated, then sat.

"And stay there—*please*—until I come back." Then he smiled. "Trust me. I love you. And I'm not going to hurt Kelly."

Gabrielle looked away from him in disgust. He watched

her unmoving form for a few seconds, then turned and left the bedroom, closing the door behind him.

Stay with me, he thought. *I don't know what's happening to me. I'm so angry with her.*

Relax. Relax. Let us handle it.

I keep wanting to hurt her . . . to kill her . . .

You love her. It will be over soon. You will both be out, be free. Together.

Yes. Free.

McNeely stepped into the hall and stood listening to hear if Gabrielle would follow, but she did not. Then he crossed to the door of Wickstrom's suite.

Enter. We will gave you the words.

He pushed the door open and dashed into the suite, running through the living room and into the bedroom. "Kelly," he called, but not loudly enough for Gabrielle to hear him across the hall, "wake up! I need your help!"

Wickstrom had not been sleeping. He was on his feet in an instant.

"It's Gabrielle," said McNeely, giving Wickstrom no time for questions. "She's gone to the cellar! Come quick! I'm afraid for her!" And he ran from the room.

Wickstrom hesitated only a moment, then followed. McNeely paused at the top of the stairs long enough to see Wickstrom step into the hall, then started down them two at a time. "George, wait!" Wickstrom called, and McNeely hoped that Gabrielle had heard.

Come on down too, bitch—I'll show you both . . . he thought, swinging around the landing and down the remaining stairs, slowing down by the impotent fail-safe system at the north end of the Great Hall until he heard Wickstrom's footsteps start to clatter down the stairs. "Hurry, Kelly!" he called, and ran on into the kitchen and down the cellar steps. He no longer noticed the sharp scent of decay.

He stopped on the last step and listened again, listened to the kitchen door bang open and Wickstrom's heavy footfalls. On then out of the cold cellar and across the stone floor and into the fire chamber, with one more desperate "Hurry! Oh, God!" thrown in for good measure. And at last he was there where the killing would be, and he turned for the final time and waited.

He heard Wickstrom's weight make the rough boards shiver, and counted the steps as the big man hurtled down them onetwothreefourfivesix . . .

"No!"

Gabrielle's voice. The footsteps stopped.

"No, Kelly! Don't go down! He wants to kill you!"

Then the sound of Wickstrom's foot on a step again, and another, and another, only now the steps were receding from McNeely, going back up to where Gabrielle had called her warning. *Warning! Warned him! Shall I go after them now? Kill them . . . him.*

You will kill him. You love her. Don't harm her!

Shall I go after him? Kill him in front of her . . .

Yes. We will find a way to . . . The voice stopped, and McNeely staggered in response to the sudden discovery that rocked the intelligence sharing his mind. *No. We will stay here. They will come to us.* It laughed, low and mocking. *Listen,* it hissed.

He did, and it was as if he heard with ears made huge and sensitive. There were the sounds of footsteps racing madly, and panting breaths. And then he heard voices.

—Hurry!

—I could stop him, tie him up . . .

—You couldn't! He's insane, the house has got him, oh! . . .

The sound of bone hitting wood.

—We'll hide, try to hide and . . .

—We can't, we'll have to face him, try to . . . what's that?

A sound like cellophane being mangled, a crackling, crisp, dry sound. The sound of

—Fire!

The voice laughed again. *They will come to us! And you will kill him. We will find the way to make her believe.*

Yes. I'll kill him in front of her. Kill 'im. Kill 'em. He heard the voices above as clearly as if he stood beside them.

—Could we fight it? Put it out?

—Gone too far. That whole wing on the third floor must be blazing.

—We can't get out!

McNeely heard them start to cough. *It won't be long,* said the voice. *They will come to us soon.*

—We'll have to go back . . .

There!

—Back down to the fire chamber. It's our only chance.

—No! There's got to be a way . . .

—There isn't! The walls are stone, but the guts of this house are wood. There's not a fucking place we can escape this fire except *down there*!

—But what about *George*?

Oh that bitch! That traitor!

She does not understand. We will make her understand. She will love you still—you will marry her.

I will, I will. Yes, make her understand. By Hell, I'll make her understand!

The cold, hard smile of a skull crossed his face as he strode purposefully out of the fire chamber and across the dimly lit cellar.

Where are you going?

Up.

No. Wait. They will come down.

I want to see him when I kill him. I want to see him die.

But

I want to kill him in the light.

McNeely paused at the bottom of the stairs, looking up at the yellow rectangle the open kitchen door made, smelling the smoke above.

Yes. Do it there. If you like. Then bring her down. Save her. We will make her see.

He went up the steps three at a time, fluidly and without effort, as though his legs belonged to someone else far stronger than he. At the same time as he swung through the kitchen door, the door to the hall opened, and he saw framed there Wickstrom and Gabrielle, their pale, frightened faces lit starkly by the bright light in the kitchen. McNeely stepped toward them, the hate he felt for them advancing before him like a palpable force. He saw them tremble, and he smiled.

Wickstrom spoke quickly. "The house is on fire, George. We've got to go down." The big man's muscles tensed as though he were ready to spring backward, but he did not move, nor did Gabrielle, who stood at his side. McNeely stopped barely a foot away from them, looked into

Wickstrom's face, and shook his head. "No, Kelly," he said. "Not you. Gabrielle, but not you." He thrust out a hand and grasped Gabrielle by the wrist, wrenching her away from Wickstrom's side and flinging her toward the cellar door. She gasped in pain and surprise.

Hurt, bitch? he thought. *It'll hurt worse before I'm done.*

Then McNeely turned his back on Wickstrom and started toward the door and Gabrielle. "Wait a minute!" Wickstrom growled, closing the distance between them. McNeely felt the hand on his shoulder and whirled around. Wickstrom's arm shot up defensively, but McNeely did not strike. Wickstrom was shaking with rage. "What the hell's wrong with you?"

"Not with me, Kelly," McNeely replied with the calmness of the killer who has the only gun. "With *you.* You're crazy. It's been building since the first day you came here. If I let you down there, you'd kill us both (*Kill them both,* McNeely thought). I'm afraid of you, afraid for Gabrielle. Try to get past me and I'll kill you, I swear it. You can take your chances."

"Let him in!" McNeely's legs suddenly shot out from under him, and he fell heavily on top of Gabrielle, who had tackled him clumsily from behind. The air went out of her for a second, but she was able to cry out to Wickstrom. "Run! Past him!"

By the time McNeely was on his feet, Wickstrom was in the doorway extending a hand to Gabrielle, who scuttled crablike across the floor to reach it. McNeely did not have to run. He moved toward the door, thinking how much he would like to kick her in the stomach, picturing her rising from the floor with the force of his heavy foot.

But instead, he grasped her ankle with a steely grip, pulling her away from Wickstrom, and sliding her across the smooth kitchen floor as easily as if she were a child. When he released her, she continued to slide helplessly, like a cat with all its claws out, until she came up against the door to the hall.

Wickstrom left the safety of the cellar doorway to help her, but McNeely whirled, grabbing the man at his neck and groin so that Wickstrom went white, all his strength vanished. McNeely breathed hotly into his face.

"I've got to *kill* you, Kelly. I've got to *kill* you now."

He hurled Wickstrom across the room. Wickstrom's arms flailed, and his fingers caught the edge of a huge wooden cupboard, pulling it over. Cans rattled and jars shattered on the smooth floor, spreading their contents like gouts of blood from a wounded beast. Wickstrom struggled among the broken shelves, shards of glass slicing him as he tried to right himself. Gabrielle knelt near him, her chest rising and falling in fury mixed with terror.

McNeely grinned at them both, his breath hissing raggedly between his clenched teeth. He raised a fist and smashed it into the wall, shattering the plaster. He could feel the blood start to ooze from the knife edge of his hand. *Blood,* he thought. *And now, their blood.*

"Leave him *alone!*" Gabrielle sobbed.

You bitch, how I hate you, you

Kill him. Kill Kelly Wickstrom. The voice was shaking, barely in control.

McNeely took a step across the slippery floor, his shoes crunching the tiny daggers of glass. "I warned you, Kelly, but you wouldn't listen. Now I've got to kill you."

The more Wickstrom tried to rise, the more he floundered, like a swimmer in a dream. He began to whimper.

Gabrielle was on her feet now, shoulders hunched, neck stiffened. With a scream of rage that smothered her fear, she leaped at McNeely, punching his face and neck with heavy blows. He blocked them, sending sharp slaps to her face until her head rocked with the impact, but still she fought on.

And McNeely made the hate within him rise like a red tide, made the thoughts shriek in their power—

I hate you, you cunt, you bitch, hate you, you stupid whore, want to kill you kill you kill you—

—While the voice of the thing inside him cried out as though it were wounded—

No! You love her, love her, love . . .

The voice shook, rocked, trembled, seemed to bubble insanely as if somehow *shifting* from speaker to speaker, and suddenly the voice was gone, and a *new* voice filled McNeely's head, filled the room itself, so that the battling woman and the man struggling to his feet heard it as well, and shivered at the rawness of it.

"HATE her! HATE her! Kill them! Kill them both!"

The beasts had escaped. The savage elements of the entity, held so long at bay, had been prodded and tormented by McNeely's thoughts of violence until they had overwhelmed the part of themselves that had made them captive. The *needs* were free. The hunger, so long checked, had to be fed.

It was just what McNeely had wanted.

What he had thought, he had thought deliberately, and the eyes inside him had seen it as one more violent fantasy; but they had not seen the final act, because McNeely had kept it hidden even from himself. It did not require conscious thought, for he *knew* what it would be. Self-destruction, and with his own death perhaps the death of what dwelled within him as well. *Perhaps*. It had been the only chance for Gabrielle.

But now there was another.

And while the graveled voice of the pit gibbered and cackled and squalled in its triumph, he allowed himself one more conscious thought, a thought he had never had before and would never have again.

Oh God, forgive me.

"Kill them both! Now!" The voice echoed like thunder, and Wickstrom and Gabrielle groaned in agony, their hands trying to shut out the sound that penetrated their very souls. *"HATE! KILL THEM!"*

McNeely held out his arms in front of him. "Then give me your power!" he cried aloud.

"Yes!"

His arms began to tingle, his chest started to swell. He could feel his body begin to grow outward as the force rushed into him.

"All your power!" he shrieked. *"Fill me! All of your power. All!"*

"Yes! ALL! ALL!"

Cloth ripped, and pain shot through him as his body expanded, as the power of a million millions entered him, as all the strengths of the evil of eternity made his flesh their home.

And, astonishingly, as they possessed his body fully, his *mind* felt suddenly *free*, as if the entity, in forgetting its apocalyptic plan, had forgotten the human keystone of that plan as well. The thing was beyond rational plots, beyond reason itself. Only madness remained, and ruled.

As through a reddened glass, McNeely saw Wickstrom and Gabrielle standing together, staring at him, their eyes wide, and it seemed that they were smaller than before, until he realized that it was he who had grown. He straightened, and felt his hair, now thinned into sparse patches by the expansion of his skull, brush roughly against the ceiling. The thing within him shrieked in triumph and rage and hatred, as he thrust his massive arms above his head, his fists piercing the wood and plaster ceiling like buckets of nails through glass, then descending to splinter the kitchen table, from which a leg shot off, catching the cowering Wickstrom and Gabrielle chest-high.

The pain awakened them from the trance in which McNeely's transformation had bound them, and they turned and pushed through the doorway into the hall, the door swinging closed behind them.

"*Run!*" McNeely half-laughed, half-bellowed, kicking the rubble of the table ceiling-high as he crossed the kitchen on huge-thewed legs. "*You can't escape!*"

NO! echoed the overpowering voice of hell. *Can't escape!*

He didn't try to go through the suddenly tiny door. Instead, he battered his forearms against the top of the frame so that the wall splintered and fell, and he pushed the flimsy door aside like a curtain.

The heat hit him in a wave. He looked down the hall of the east wing and saw only a rolling mass of smoke, with fingers of yellow flame barely discernible at the end, faraway candles in a foggy night. A glance to his right told him the west wing was, if not as thickly dark, at least as deadly.

The Great Hall then. There was nowhere else they could go.

He howled with laughter, hearing it re-echo innumerable times from the throats of those within him. Then, his craggy head now scraping the higher ceiling of the east wing hall, he slouched around the corner and found at last that he could stand erect, there in the towering expanse of the Great Hall. The beams high above were hidden in clouds of drifting gray smoke, but all else was clear, and McNeely saw plainly the man and woman standing at the southern end, standing because they could run no farther, because there was no place left to which to run. They stood at the entrance to the small space between the cloak rooms, directly in the center of the hall. They stood as if waiting for death. They stood

"*Trapped!*" screamed George McNeely.

"*TRAPPED!*" screamed the millions so loudly that the stones shook, the smoke far above billowed and rolled.

Then George McNeely, and the millions, and The Pines itself gave one last, deafening, inarticulate cry, and George McNeely began to run. Straight down the center of the Great Hall he ran, gaining speed with each step of his ponderous legs, arms up, elbows out, fists together, his forearms an impassable bar, the whole of his body an engine to crush flesh and shatter bone. And as he ran, he remembered his dream, and again the Great Hall shrank, growing smaller and smaller to crush him once more, but this time it was not the Great Hall shrinking, but he who was growing, growing with every step, and he would *not* be crushed this time, *no,* this time he would grow out and out and *break* the shell of stone, *break* the shell.

And be born.

The man and the woman stood before his onslaught, their eyes filled with the knowledge of death, and now they fell to their knees, awaiting the final blow, the last murderous step of the behemoth. But the step never came.

In that last breath of a moment, with the speed of a thought, the will of George McNeely drove those impossible legs down and up and over the prey, and flung the iron torso, the metal arms, directly at the top of the steel plate that made the house a prison.

The steel did not shatter. But the mortar that held it did.

The plate shivered and bent, and the first rocks began to fall. The keystones gone, their mortar crumbled, the southern wall trembled, sighed, and collapsed, its fragments raining down, burying the titanic and unmoving form of George McNeely beneath the cold gray stones of The Pines.

Part V

And there, there overhead, there, there, hung
   over
Those thousands of white faces, those dazed
   eyes . . .
There in the sudden blackness the black
   pall
Of nothing, nothing, nothing—nothing at
   all.

                 —Archibald MacLeish,
                   "The End of the World"

Chapter Twenty-eight

The snow was falling so heavily that Renault did not see the flames that roofed The Pines until the rental car came out of the thick trees and into the open area around the house. He did not curse nor cry out. He only held his breath for a moment as he felt his heart race even faster than before. When he saw the police car, its headlights on but the flashers off, he released his breath in the minor relief that he had not been the first to arrive, and told his driver to pull up behind the other car.

Renault lumbered out of the passenger side like a bear from a too small cave. Before he took a half dozen steps through the snow, a stocky, bearded man in a uniform was next to him, coat unbuttoned, apparently oblivious to the elements. He carried a huge flashlight in his right hand. "Mr. Renault? I'm Chief Lowry."

"What in the name of God is *happening* here?" Renault demanded. "Where are the *people*? This . . . this *fire*! What is being *done*?"

"Fire department's on its way. Hell, I didn't know this was happening till I *got* here."

"But the *people*? The *Nevilles*?"

"Just found two people. One of them's dead, the other damn near."

"*Where?*"

"Around the back." Lowry turned, and Renault followed him around the west wing. "Didn't want to move the one guy till the ambulance got here," the chief puffed as

303

they trotted, their path illuminated by the ribbons of flame that waved above. "But we had to a little, just to get him away from the house. Not much heat, but pieces keep blowing down off the roof. All these stone walls, it's like a big goddamned chimney. There they are."

Two forms lay side by side, another uniformed man, clean-shaven, squatting next to them. Renault stopped, panting with the exertion, and looked down at the still, battered face. "Monckton," he breathed, then turned toward the other. "Uncover his face," he told the squatting man. Despite the discoloration, Renault recognized the dead man instantly. "*Sterne*. But the *Nevilles*!" he roared, his strength returned. "And the others! Where *are* they?"

"Where *were* they? Inside?"

"*Yes.*"

"Then they're still there. Danny and me tried to get in, but this place is like a *fort*."

Renault thought frantically. "My God, the *keys*. We can open it from the cabin! Quickly! Search them!" He knelt painfully by Monckton. "There will be two large keys, they each should have one. . . ." His mind whirled as he went through Monckton's clothing, trying to be gentle but swift, scarcely noticing the blood or the strange angles at which the man's limbs lay. The roof of the Great Hall had not yet been afire, he was sure of that. They *may* have gotten to the fire chamber in time, but he was not as confident of Monckton's handiwork as David had been. Suppose that something had gone wrong, the same way something had most certainly gone wrong with the escape system. *Fail-safe,* Renault thought in disgust as he turned the last pocket inside out. Stupid word. *Nothing* was fail-safe, nothing foolproof. "*Nothing,*" he spat.

"No key on this one either," Lowry said, pulling a canvas poncho back over Sterne's face.

"They must still be down in the cabin. Come, quickly." Renault straightened with a creaking of joints, and walked as fast as he could around the west wing toward his car. "Why isn't the ambulance here?" he snapped at the police chief.

"Just radioed them fifteen minutes ago, right after we got here. Be another fifteen, twenty minutes. Maybe a half hour in this stuff," Lowry said, gesturing at the snow falling around them.

"*What?* I told you to send an ambulance *immediately*."

"Look, Mr. Renault, I'm *sorry,* but how the hell was I supposed to know we'd find these guys up here? And how the hell did *you* know?"

"I knew," Renault said grimly as they came around to the front of the house. "I *also* know that unless we get those people inside *out,* they may well die."

"Well, do we have to go down to the cabin? Maybe we could just back the cruiser into that front door, knock it down that way, and . . ."

"My God, man, there's a steel plate a half inch thick on the other side of that door. Nothing short of a tank could hope to . . ."

Both men froze as the sound reached their ears. Though a scream of steel and stone, it was strangely human as well, as if a multitude had sung of its own destruction in one mighty yet dying voice. In the same moment, the wall of the Great Hall burst outward, spewing chunks of stone and shards of wood into the snowy night. Lowry and Renault fell to the cold white earth, turning their faces toward the forest, as if not seeing the flying missiles could save them from being struck.

The forest suddenly brightened, and when the two men looked toward the house again, it was as if The Pines had grown dozens of fiery eyes. The doors and windows were once more exposed to the world, the steel plates drawn away from them with the squeal of heat-tortured metal. Windows shattered, and wooden doors and windowframes burst into flames as the cold wind swept through the rooms and halls, urging on the fire to even greater heights of destruction.

Renault gaped at the sight. The inside of the house looked like a blast furnace, except for the great dark breach in the wall of the Great Hall, in which he could see, through the settling cloud of dust, a thicker cloud of black smoke, and the first traces of flame at the hall's far end. The stones had stopped falling. Or at least he thought they had. But it seemed, as he squinted into the darkness, wiping the snow roughly from his glasses and thrusting them onto his face, that some of the stones still moved, rising over the others. "*Look!*" he cried to Lowry. "The *light! Hurry!*"

Lowry, on his knees now, flicked the switch of the flashlight he had gripped like a weapon through the havoc, and turned it on The Pines, so that it shone directly on Gabrielle Neville and Kelly Wickstrom, who screamed shrilly, threw up his arms, and tumbled over the stones into the snow.

Renault moved faster than he had in years, scrambling over the snow, up onto the cyclopean blocks, his footing solid as that of a man half his years. He grasped Gabrielle in his great arms. Confused, disoriented, she tried to push away, her eyes wild. "Gabrielle," he said soothingly. "It is I, it is Simon. Come, come . . ." She gave herself over to him then, her strength gone, and he half-led, half-carried her down over the stones, then to the warmth of the rental car, to which Lowry and the driver had already taken the limping, shivering Wickstrom.

"Simon . . . Simon . . . Simon . . ." she repeated like a litany as he maneuvered her gently into the backseat next to Wickstrom, who dripped blood from a dozen cuts and held his left knee tightly, his face pale with pain.

"I got stuff in the cruiser," Lowry said, shoving the temperature control to maximum heat and turning on the fan. "Patch you up a little. Ambulance'll be here any minute. Ma'am? You okay?"

Gabrielle began, very softly, to laugh. It increased in volume and intensity until Renault sat next to her and put his arms around her and she began to cry instead. "She is all right," Renault told Lowry. "Go. Get what you need for Mr. Wickstrom."

Lowry went to the cruiser. Renault's driver leaned against the car, watching the snow fall and the house burn. The softly roaring fan filled the car with heat, and Gabrielle began to breathe quietly. Wickstrom's eyes were tightly closed. His knuckles were white.

"Gabrielle," Renault said. He could not keep from asking. "David?"

She shook her head. "All the others," she whispered. "All dead."

"The fire?"

"No, not the fire." She pressed her eyes shut. "Leave it alone, Simon. Take out the bodies, and leave it alone."

"All right." He nodded. "Rest now."

The ambulance arrived a short time later. Monckton, still unconscious, was lifted on first, followed by Wickstrom and Gabrielle. The body of Sterne would follow later.

On the way down the mountain Gabrielle became aware at one point of flashing red lights that were not the ambulance's, and a roaring engine that grew louder and then faded into silence. "What was that?" she asked the attendant.

"Fire engine and the tanker," he told her. "Probably called for a cinder truck. They can't get up the mountain. Too icy."

"Good," she said. "Good. Let it burn."

The attendant checked Monckton's vital signs once more, then sat in the front. Wickstrom turned his head and looked at Gabrielle. "I'm sorry I screamed," he said. "I saw . . . the light, so white and big, and I thought it was one of the faces . . . that it was starting all over again."

"No," Gabrielle said softly. "It's over now."

They rode for a while longer. "Did you see his face?" Wickstrom finally asked, gazing up at the whiteness of the ceiling. "Not when he was after us, but when he did it, when he . . . *freed* us. It was like, like he'd *won*, like he'd planned it that way all along, like . . . whatever it was, he beat it."

It was a long time before Gabrielle replied. "I'd like to believe that," she said. And later still, she whispered to herself, "I think I will."

Epilogue

> Of human blood and stone
> We build; and in a thousand years will
>   come
> Beyond the hills . . .
>   —Conrad Aiken, "The Road"

Nearly a year later Whitey Monckton rounded a sharp corner on a battered side road, and saw once more the caretaker's cabin near the foot of Pine Mountain. Smoke was drifting placidly from the chimney, and an addition had been put on the building, doubling its original size. He pulled his car up in front of the freshly painted wooden porch, and got out. The door of the house opened and a tall lanky man in his mid-fifties appeared, a cigarette in one hand. "Yeah?" the man said, neither friendly nor rude.

"My name's Monckton. I worked here last year."

Recognition shone on the tall man's face, and he smiled. "Sure, Mr. Monckton. I remember you now. You look a lot different. Lost weight?"

Monckton nodded. "Been spending most of my time in hospitals. Got out last week."

"Yeah, I remember they thought you were a goner. Any bones in your body that *didn't* break?"

"Not many." Monckton smiled. "They patched me up pretty well though."

"What can I do for you?"

Monckton hesitated, and the tall man pursed his lips. "I'd like to go up the mountain," Monckton said. "I'd like to see the place one more time."

The man shook his head. "Nothing to see. Just walls is all that's left."

"Well, I'd like to see them anyway."

"I got orders not to let anybody up there. Besides, the gate's welded shut. Nobody can drive up there now."

"I'd walk. It's not far."

"I'm sorry, Mr. Monckton."

Monckton reached into his pocket, took out five new hundred dollar bills, and extended them to the man. "I've got no camera, nothing. You can frisk me before I go up and when I come down."

The man snorted. "Nothing to steal up there." He looked at the money for a while, then pocketed it. "You stay quiet, *I* stay quiet."

"It's a deal." He looked at the road leading upward.

"Go ahead," said the man. "I won't stop you."

Monckton stepped around the gate and started walking up the road. At first he stopped and listened every few yards, but he heard and felt nothing strange, although there were still no sounds of insects or birds in the brush and trees. Halfway up he stopped, a small pain in his side. A half-mile walk up a steep grade was more exercise than he'd had in ages, but he knew he could make it to the top and down again. He had to. He had to find out the answer to what he'd been thinking of for a year, a year of lying in hospital beds staring at those white casts above and beside him like ghosts of limbs, a year of stretching and compressing muscles and bones to try to get them to work, if not like before, at least enough to propel him like a living man again, a year of wondering where *it* was, what had become of it.

And now, as he climbed the road one final time under the gray canopy of snow-sky, he hoped again that it *would* be here, confined here on this mountain forever, away from curious and weak men. His side aching, he toiled up the hill, the cold air stinging his nostrils, burning his lungs.

At last he cleared the final curve and saw what was left of The Pines. It sat brooding like some ancient abbey in its clearing, beginning to be overgrown with brush. The walls had not fallen. They stood as solidly as they had for seventy years, no longer gray, but charred black by the fire's breath. He walked across the thick weeds and dead leaves that covered the lawn, walked up until he was within the shadow of the blackened walls, until he could see through the breach into the Great Hall, the huge copper shaft of the chimney lying amid the rubble like the fallen trumpet of a god. Only then did he stop and listen.

There was nothing. Not a whisper of force, not a purr of energy entered his open mind.

Where are you then? he thought. Only two people had left the house—Gabrielle Neville and Wickstrom. They had both visited him at Mt. Sinai, and he had sensed nothing from either of them, only perhaps a newly found joy in life and a tremendous sense of relief to have escaped from what had touched them all so strongly at The Pines. Wickstrom had bought a restaurant in Queens, and seemed to be enjoying the venture. Gabrielle Neville had seemed happy as well, but there was a sense of sadness about her, too, even though she had been a good many months pregnant at the time of her visit. It was akin, he thought, to the sadness of the Madonna, bearing the child she would live to lose.

But perhaps the sadness was normal at that. It would be difficult to bear a child alone. He had read two months ago in the *Times* that it was a boy, David George Neville.

He had wondered then, only for a moment, who the father really was. He wondered again, and an infinitely remote possibility made the wind far colder as he gazed at the suddenly empty shell of the house.

I hope he was born in innocence, he thought. *I hope we all are.*

Or did innocence have to be earned, searched for over the years in the dark forest of the soul? Conceived in sin, do we buy innocence with our own blood? Or with something even more precious?

And those who had died in the shadow of The Pines— what price had they paid?

The trees whispered above Monckton's head, and any answer they could give they kept to themselves. He looked up at them, then beyond to where the clouds were darkening. If he walked quickly, he might reach the bottom of the hill before the snow began.